All That
Is Hidden

All That Is Hidden

Rhys Bowen
&
Clare Broyles

MINOTAUR BOOKS
NEW YORK

First published in the United States by Minotaur Books, an imprint of St. Martin's Publishing Group

ALL THAT IS HIDDEN. Copyright © 2023 by Janet Quin-Harkin (writing as Rhys Bowen) and Clare Broyles. All rights reserved. Printed in the United States of America. For information, address St. Martin's Publishing Group, 120 Broadway, New York, NY 10271.

www.minotaurbooks.com

Library of Congress Cataloging-in-Publication Data

Names: Bowen, Rhys, author. | Boyles, Clare, author.
Title: All that is hidden / Rhys Bowen & Clare Boyles.
Description: First Edition. | New York : Minotaur Books, 2023. |
    Series: Molly Murphy mysteries; 19
Identifiers: LCCN 2022038699 | ISBN 9781250808097 (hardcover) |
    ISBN 9781250808103 (ebook)
Subjects: LCGFT: Novels.
Classification: LCC PR6052.O848 A45 2023 | DDC 823/.914—dc23/eng/20220829
LC record available at https://lccn.loc.gov/2022038699

Our books may be purchased in bulk for promotional, educational, or business use. Please contact your local bookseller or the Macmillan Corporate and Premium Sales Department at 1-800-221-7945, extension 5442, or by email at MacmillanSpecialMarkets@macmillan.com.

First Edition: 2023

10 9 8 7 6 5 4 3 2 1

We dedicate this book to our recent graduates: Anne, Lizzie, TJ, and Mary Clare. May they all go on to do great things (and to enjoy reading good books)!

All That
Is Hidden

❧ Prologue ❧

New York, Summer 1907

I would never have paid attention to the small news article in the *Times* if Daniel hadn't pointed it out to me. "I wonder if my letter to my mother has been lost?" he asked without much concern. "Listen to this." And he read the item out loud.

The paper didn't seem to know exactly how it had happened. The passenger train heading out of New York City and into Westchester County brought the mail just like every other day of the year. Just like every day the postman, having sorted the letters in the mail car, bundled them up into the heavy postal bag and lobbed it out onto the platform at Mount Vernon to be collected.

But something must have been different that Friday night. Perhaps the train was running slightly late, or the postman had not quite finished sorting as they pulled into the station and rushed to get the postal bag off the train. However it came about, one strap of the bag caught below the wheel of the train. As it pulled out in a cloud of steam it dragged the bag about a mile down the track until it broke and letters exploded out. The rain of correspondence floating down over the tracks contained the everyday doings of mothers

1

and daughters, fathers and sons; deals to be made or broken; everyday joys and disappointments.

When the broken bag was discovered the next day, a hunt was on to find the missing letters and restore them to their owners. Some were lost forever or rendered illegible by the mud and mist of the night they spent outside, most were found and sent on battered and dirty as they might have been. And one found its way into the hands of the wrong person.

I couldn't have guessed all of this as Daniel read the story in the *Times*, but it did catch my fancy. I amused myself by thinking of the letters floating about in gusts of wind. Since I didn't know a soul in Mount Vernon, I thought it could have nothing to do with me. But I was wrong. Dead wrong.

✖ One ✖

New York, Sunday, October 6, 1907

So, what is this big surprise?" I asked as I pinned my hat onto my head, checking that it was straight in the entryway mirror.

"Ask me no questions, I'll tell you no lies." Daniel wrapped his arms around me from behind and gave the back of my neck a little kiss.

"Well, it can't be a romantic surprise or we wouldn't be bringing Liam," I mused. "And we are walking so it can't be too far away. Unless we were walking to a train station?" I shook my head. "But we haven't any baggage."

"Molly Sullivan, this is not a case and you are not detecting." Daniel gave me a mock reproving look. "You will find out soon enough." He pushed the pram out of the front door while I lifted Liam, carried him out, and set him in the pram.

"You are getting too heavy to be carried, little man," I said, rubbing the small of my back as I straightened up.

It was a gorgeous day, one of those clear October afternoons with bright sunshine and a cool, clean breeze. We had made it to church that morning, an occurrence that had become rare since

Daniel's mother had left, and I felt clean and bright inside as well. Our ward, Bridie, was with our neighbors, getting help with her algebra homework. I had told her we wouldn't be gone long.

Daniel pushed the pram and I followed in silence as we turned south onto Sixth Avenue. All he had told me was to put on my coat and hat and bring Liam. He had a surprise for me. I tried to judge from the set of his shoulders as he strode ahead whether it was a nice surprise or a nasty one. To tell the truth he did look a bit tense. We crossed the street and walked into the shade of the big trees in Washington Square. The fall colors glowed brightly on the trees, contrasting with a deep blue sky above. The perfect day for a family stroll, I thought. I found myself enjoying the quiet rhythm of our footsteps crunching on the gravel until Daniel slowed to walk beside me. He put a hand on my arm and cleared his throat.

Saints preserve us, he is nervous, I thought. My stomach felt a jolt of fear. Daniel was normally quite direct and forthright. It wasn't like him to make a song and dance about something.

"Where are we going, then?" I asked, keeping my voice light and cheerful.

"We're not going anywhere just yet. I thought it might be best to walk and have a little talk first." His hand squeezed mine reassuringly. "Molly, I want you to trust me." He was not looking at me but straight ahead as we walked. "There are some things I need to do to take care of this family and I hope you will trust I know what I am doing."

"If this is about a helper to look after Liam I'm sure I can sort that out. Your mother has sent me some recommendations of agencies I can try." Daniel's mother had lived with us during the last winter while she recovered from a bout of influenza but was now safely back at her house in Westchester County. I was sure she had been writing to Daniel telling him how unsuitable it was for a police captain's wife to be doing all of her own cooking, cleaning, and child minding. I didn't mind the work, though. I preferred to keep busy and active and spend time with my son.

But Mother Sullivan had plans for Daniel to advance. He had been the youngest-ever police captain in the New York Police Department and his mother was hoping for a career in politics for him. I was fine with him and with our life just as it was. We lived in a sweet little house on Patchin Place that I had purchased myself when I ran my own detective agency. Although I had given up being a detective when I married Daniel I had found myself doing the odd spot of sleuthing since, and between ourselves I did sometimes help him with his cases. That was why I was not opposed to Mrs. Sullivan's plan to have a girl live in and help with Liam. It had been useful, I reflected, to have Mother Sullivan around to watch Liam if I wanted to go out and investigate.

"No, that's not it exactly, although it will change our domestic situation." He cleared his throat while I looked at him expectantly. "It's actually very good news. I've been asked to run for sheriff and I'm going to do it."

"Sheriff? Of what? Of where?" My mind immediately went to the Wild West. Men galloping on horses and firing guns.

"The County of New York. It includes the five boroughs," he said. "It's an important position."

"Asked, by whom?" Questions swirled in my head. A ball came whizzing over our heads followed by a group of laughing college students from the university on the other side of the square.

"Ball. I want da ball." Liam stood up quickly in the pram. I rushed to grab him before he managed to climb out and lifted him down beside me.

"Take Mama's hand, darling." I walked with him in silence for a moment and then turned to Daniel. "It's an elected position? And someone has asked you to run?"

"Actually, I'm on the Tammany ticket. They will be announcing it tomorrow at Tammany Hall."

"Tomorrow?" I stopped and looked at him in astonishment. Liam tugged at my hand.

"Mama. Ball! Liam wants to play." I held on firmly while I tried to compose my racing thoughts.

"But you hate Tammany and all those bribes and kickbacks. Why on earth would you run on their ticket? And who is the sheriff of New York when he's at home anyway?"

Daniel gave the pram a big push and replied without looking at me, "There are a few things I can't explain, Molly. That's why I need you to trust me. The sheriff is a bit like the police commissioner, only his mandate is broader. He runs the prison system and the courts, not the police department. You know how much that needs reforming. The Tammany man who was supposed to run has gotten himself involved in a scandal and has left the city for a while until it blows over. I'm sure you will read about it in that Hearst rag in the next few days. They asked me to step in as a last-minute replacement."

"But why would you want to? Surely you love being a police captain, especially since you've been in charge of homicide. It's a prestigious job, Daniel."

Daniel continued pushing the pram, still staring straight ahead. "It's my chance to do some good, Molly. If I get in as sheriff I can do away with some of the corruption. You remember what it was like when I was in prison myself. I nearly died in that hellhole. I can really do some good."

"But with Tammany Hall? Daniel, they will never let you go your own way. You know that. You'll owe them for your position and they will make you pay them back."

"I'm sorry, Molly. It's settled." Daniel's voice was now firm. "I have said yes and I expect you to support me. There are some things you don't understand."

"Because I'm a woman?" My temper flared. I should mention that red hair and a quick temper are my two leading characteristics.

"Because there are things you don't know and I can't tell you." He turned back toward the arch. "There's more to this surprise. Follow me."

"Jesus, Mary, and Joseph! My heart can't take any more." Daniel put a protesting Liam back in his pram and lengthened his stride so much I had to hurry to keep up. We swept through the Marble Arch at the entrance to the park and then up Fifth Avenue. I wondered where we were heading. To Tammany Hall? "Daniel, slow down, where are we going?"

"You'll see." He looked back at me, gave me an encouraging smile, then strode ahead. A good surprise this time, then. On the other side of Ninth Street Daniel stopped at an impressive flight of marble steps with a wrought-iron railing leading up to a white door framed with a decorated arch.

"Let's pay a call, shall we?" Daniel lifted Liam out of the pram and into my arms then climbed the steps and rang the bell.

"Wait, Daniel," I called after him. "Who are we visiting? You should have warned me. I'm not suitably dressed. A stroll, you said."

Daniel looked back and smiled. "You look fine," he said. "Don't worry."

I came up the steps beside him and stood rather nervously on the stoop. Really, I like a surprise, but this was going too far. Was sheriff that high a position that Daniel would now know people who lived in Fifth Avenue houses like this? Had we been invited to tea and here was I in my usual two-piece costume and not a tea dress? It had probably never occurred to Daniel that women like to know in advance what to wear for every occasion. Honestly, men can be infuriating. But it was too late to turn back now.

The door was answered by a maid who didn't show any surprise at seeing us. "You must be Captain and Mrs. Sullivan," she said, giving us a shy smile as she dropped a curtsey. "You are expected, please come in. I'm Mary." We walked into the front hall and Daniel took off his hat and hung it on the hat stand, then helped me off with my cloak and hung it up as well. The marble floor echoed as I set Liam down and he stomped his foot experimentally then headed toward the staircase in front of us.

"Shh. Liam, come here." I grabbed him hurriedly and lifted him up again. The maid waited and then indicated we should follow her through a curtained doorway. "The parlor is through here, sir."

I walked in with a bright smile on my face expecting to be introduced to the man or lady of the house, but the parlor was empty. A fire burned in the marble fireplace. A table in the center of the room under the electric chandelier held a priceless-looking vase, and ornate shelves across from me were full of decorative plates, cups, and figurines. I instinctively clutched Liam a little tighter, making sure his hands were safely out of the way, and decided that putting him down here was not a good idea.

"The family drawing room is back here, sir." She led us through another doorway and into a comfortable-looking drawing room. The room was crowded with delicate embroidered sofas and chairs and carved mahogany tables in many sizes. There was a beautiful Persian rug on the floor and a large tapestry on the far wall. But still no people. My mind spun. Had Daniel brought me to a murder scene? Hardly an outing to which you bring your son. Were the owners of the house very shy?

"The dining room is at the back of the house and bedrooms are upstairs, sir, if you will follow me." Mary continued after a pause as we looked around the empty drawing room. The bedrooms?

"Daniel." I turned to him in exasperation. "Why are we seeing the bedrooms? Is the owner an invalid?"

"No," he replied, already heading toward the stairs.

"Daniel!" I called after him. "What is going on? Whose house is this?"

He turned to me with a big smile. "Yours." He put his arms around both Liam and me. "Ours. Welcome to your new home, Mrs. Sullivan!"

✤ Two ✤

Sunday, October 6

For perhaps the first time in my life I was speechless. So many things came into my mind at once that I couldn't utter a single word. Was this a joke? Would Daniel really move us across town without my opinion? What about my house in Patchin Place? How on earth could we afford a house like this, let alone a maid who seemed to have expected us? That last thought made me remember that the maid was hovering a few steps up the staircase, waiting for an answer, and I broke away from Daniel's hug. "Let's talk about this later, Daniel," I said, smiling through gritted teeth.

"Thank you, Mary. We would appreciate seeing the bedrooms," Daniel said hurriedly. He knew my temper and that I was inclined to speak my mind in any situation. The girl led the way up the stairs. Liam insisted on being put down and climbing each stair himself, holding on to Daniel's hand. Mary waited patiently at the top of the stairs. If my head had not been spinning I might have enjoyed the fact that I was going to see the upstairs of a Fifth Avenue house. I had often wondered about their layout with the front door not in the center but at the right-hand edge of the house. Now I could see that the stairs

9

went up two stories along the right side. At the top of the first set of stairs was a landing.

"There is a main bedroom here." Mary indicated the room on her left. A young girl in a maid's uniform was standing in front of the door clearly waiting to greet us. "This is Aileen," Mary introduced her. Aileen bobbed a curtsey. She looked to be no more than sixteen. Her unruly light brown hair was spilling out of her maid's cap. She had blue eyes and red cheeks full of freckles. Her eyes lit up when she saw Liam.

"Who's this little man, then?" She crouched down to his eye level. "I'll bet that you want to see the nursery. There is a horse and everything." She had a soft country lilt that took me instantly back to my childhood in County Mayo.

I expected Liam to shrink back against me, but instead he perked up. "Horsey?"

"Is it all right if I take him, miss?" She looked uncertain. "I mean Mrs.?" She made it a question.

"Mrs. Sullivan," I offered.

"See the horsey?" Liam piped up.

"Yes, all right, my boy, go and see the horsey." Daniel patted him on the back and he put his little hand in Aileen's outstretched one. They started up the stairs to the third floor.

Mary looked after Aileen, rather disapprovingly I thought. She showed us around the bedroom, decorated in the frilly Victorian style. There was a lace doily on every surface and the bed was covered with embroidered cushions. There were two dressing rooms, one very masculine-looking with dark wood surfaces and the other just as frilly as the bedroom with a rather sweet embroidered daybed and an enormous mirror. Bridie will love this, I thought, then immediately reproved myself. As soon as we left this house I would have plenty to say about whether we would be moving here or not! Until then, I decided I would play along with the pretense that we were moving here. The rest of the level had two more bedrooms, a spacious bathroom with a large claw-footed tub, and a lavatory. A thought struck me.

"Daniel, those bedrooms have no fireplaces. Aren't they bitterly cold in winter?"

Mary answered before he could. "The whole house is on steam heat, Mrs. Sullivan. Did you see the radiators? The rooms are so warm the family has to open the windows sometimes. Even the lavatory!" She looked at Daniel and looked away with a blush as if embarrassed she had mentioned the lavatory in front of him.

The second staircase led up to the maids' rooms and the nursery. We could hear thumping as we walked down the hall to the nursery and as we opened the door we saw Liam in full gallop on the most enormous rocking horse. It had soft velveteen hair, a braided mane, button eyes, and a bright blue leather saddle and bridle. I could imagine that any child would fall instantly in love with it.

"Giddyup!" Liam was shouting as Aileen stood beside him, arms outstretched in case he fell. The rest of the nursery was like a picture in a book. It had a sweet little child's bed with a lace coverlet, low shelves full of books, wooden blocks and toys, and a tiny desk and chair.

"That's enough now, Mr. Liam," Aileen said, and helped Liam off the horse. To my surprise he put up no fuss at all but just stood by her side holding her hand.

"Mrs. Sullivan, I would be happy to watch little Liam whenever you might need it," Aileen spoke up. "I can still do my work," she said quickly as if we had raised an objection. "Lord knows I've watched my own brothers and sisters and kept house for my da at the same time. Not a house as grand as this," she hastened to add, as if I would be offended by the comparison. "But I do miss the little ones."

I wasn't sure what to say. I could hardly say, "I will not be coming to live here after Captain Sullivan and I have had a talk and I have no idea why we are here or who is going to pay your salary." So I said, "That sounds lovely, let me talk to Captain Sullivan about it and I will let you know."

Mary led us back downstairs. "When will you be moving in, Captain Sullivan? So I can let Cook know," she asked as we came down into the front hall.

"This Thursday. We will be sending our things over on Wednesday evening," Daniel said without looking at me. "Luncheon will be our first meal. Is the cook here?"

"No, sir." Mary shook her head. "A new cook has been hired. I'll write and let her know when you are coming."

"Where is the kitchen?" I realized I had not seen a kitchen in our tour.

"Downstairs, ma'am," Mary replied. "There is a staircase in the butler's pantry just off the dining room, and one from the tradesman's entrance at the front of the house." I realized that I had seen a staircase going down to the left of the impressive front stairs and those must have been the windows of the kitchen that were below street level.

And why on earth would we need a cook, I wanted to demand of Daniel, when you seem perfectly happy with my cooking? But I decided to hold all of my questions until we were alone.

Long ago I had been educated at a rather grand mansion, the local girl who was allowed to learn alongside the young ladies of the family because the mistress took a fancy to me. So I was not unused to seeing maids, butlers, and footmen in a big house. But I never expected to be the mistress of one, even one that was quite modest compared to an Irish manor house. I never expected to have two maids handing Daniel his hat, helping me on with my cloak, and bundling Liam up in his coat before putting him into Daniel's arms. They both stood and watched as we went down the steps.

Outside the front door Daniel turned back. "Until Thursday, then, Mary."

"Very good, sir," she replied. "You'll find everything in order, and if you care to send over your trunks of clothing before then, we'll have them all pressed and properly hung for you."

The front door closed. Daniel retrieved the pram from inside the railings and deposited the now complaining Liam into it. "More horsey!" he yelled, kicking out as Daniel strapped him in.

"You'll be getting plenty of horsey soon enough, my boy," Daniel said.

We walked up Fifth Avenue in silence until we were out of sight of the house. Then I exploded. "Daniel Sullivan, by all the saints and the Blessed Mother, have you lost your mind?" Several well-dressed ladies turned to look in our direction and I lowered my voice.

A hurt expression crossed his face. "You don't like your surprise?"

"You knew perfectly well how I would react to you choosing to move us to a new house without consulting me." I had so many objections I wasn't sure where to start. "Patchin Place!" I began. "Do you expect me to give up my own dear little house?"

"Do I expect *us* to give up *our* pokey little house to move into a brownstone on Fifth Avenue? Is that seriously a question you are asking me?" Daniel put the emphasis on *us* and *our*. His eyebrows rose. He had a point. I loved my house and the fact that I could run across the street to my neighbors and best friends Sid and Gus at any time, but perhaps any reasonable wife would think that moving to Fifth Avenue was a dream come true.

"Besides," he continued. "We don't have to give up Patchin Place. We are just going to live in the brownstone for a while. Perhaps the next six months, perhaps longer."

I tried a different tack. "But, Daniel, how on earth can we afford it? Unless you're going to start taking bribes left, right, and center like half the New York police do."

People were definitely staring now. Daniel looked around embarrassed. "Molly, for heaven's sake lower your voice," he said. His tone said that he believed I was the one being unreasonable. This infuriated me.

"I will not! Not until you explain to me how we can possibly afford a house on Fifth Avenue on a police captain's salary."

"I'll explain it all, just please lower your voice." He grabbed the handles of the pram roughly and turned quickly as we crossed at Tenth Street. Liam started to cry.

"Now look what you've done," I began angrily, feeling like crying myself. An automobile passed behind us and I hurried up onto the curb behind them. Daniel stopped, lifted Liam out of the pram, and let him cry on his shoulder. The sight of the two of them couldn't help but soften my anger a bit. Daniel is a good man, I told myself. At least give him a chance to explain. "Let's get Liam home. He's tired of sitting still," I said in as calm a voice as I could muster. We walked in silence for a few minutes, but I felt too impatient to continue another step without hearing more. "Now, can you please explain what is going on?"

"Molly, I have never pretended that I didn't want something better for our family." Daniel appeared to be choosing his words carefully. "I have an opportunity here. And it has come through the police commissioner so I can have my job back if it doesn't work out." I started to interrupt, but he stopped me with a look and went on. "Okay, you need some political background. You know that Hearst's Independence Party has been taking votes away from Tammany and they are fighting to keep control over the police and the docks." I nodded. I had been reading about that in the papers.

"Big Bill, he's the man who pulls the strings at Tammany Hall right now, needs a Tammany candidate to run for county sheriff. If the Hearst man gets in he will be able to make things very difficult for Tammany. But the chosen candidate, as I told you, got himself involved in a scandal and has had to leave town to ride it out. Big Bill—well, that's what everyone calls him, his real name is William McCormick—wants someone who can bring the police on board, so he asked the police commissioner to suggest someone and he came to me." He paused, inviting me to ask a question.

14

"How could the salary be enough for us to afford a house like that? Even if the salary is enormous, how could we pay for it before you are elected?" I matched Daniel's calm tone.

"The house belongs to Big Bill. He lends it to any candidates he wants to promote. I gather that he even pays the staff. He has offered it to us for six months and said that if I win we can talk about prices then."

"I don't understand how it helps Mr. McCormick if you are the sheriff. How does he benefit?"

"He has been an alderman and he plans to run for mayor. The Independence and Republican Parties are threatening to join forces against him. If they get the sheriff's office they will find all sorts of ways to keep Tammany voters away from the ballot box."

"But, Daniel." My voice began to rise again. "This is how Tammany works, you know that. Someone does you a favor and then you owe them a favor. Someone with a salary of a thousand dollars a year ends up with twenty thousand dollars in the bank. What if they ask you to stuff ballot boxes or keep opposition voters away? You've always fought against that type of corruption. We don't need to get ahead that way. We're doing just fine."

"I do understand how it works and I do not intend to take any kickbacks. This house belongs to Mr. McCormick and he pays the staff. I've checked into it and it is all legal." He looked uncomfortable. "As I've mentioned, there are a few things I can't tell you, but trust me, I am on the right side here."

"Well, don't forget how quickly the police department turned against you once before when they thought you had taken bribes," I said angrily. "I was the only one who stood by you then." We stopped walking and stood looking at each other, both remembering that horrible time when Daniel was in jail and we had no idea how to prove him innocent. The Sixth Avenue el thundered by.

"I will never forget, Molly." Daniel lowered his voice. It seemed suddenly very quiet after the passage of the el. We waited to cross

Sixth Avenue. "I will always take care of you. I want to weed out corruption at Tammany Hall. This is my way of doing it. Will you trust me?"

Did I trust Daniel? I suppose it all came down to that. After all, he wasn't asking me to live in a tenement or go out to the Wild West. He was asking me to live in a fancy house on Fifth Avenue and have all the help I needed. My gut was telling me that he was being naïve; that he was playing with fire and going to be burned. But he had stood by me through my many harebrained schemes. I would have to stand by him in this one, even if it all went wrong.

"So, shall I put on my red, white, and blue sash and come to your political meeting tomorrow?" My smile told Daniel that the fight was over, for now. "I will trust you. But if you find you are in over your head, remember that I don't need to be some highfalutin sheriff's wife to be happy."

"That's good, because I haven't got the job yet." Daniel settled a now calm Liam back into the pram. "And no, a political meeting is not a place for a woman. But thank you for offering."

The sidewalk became crowded as we neared the Jefferson Market. We walked in companionable silence, but my mind was racing. I was determined to pump Sid and Gus for information just as soon as we got home. Daniel might trust this Bill McCormick, but I was going to check him out for myself.

By the time we turned into Patchin Place Liam had fallen asleep in his pram, his thumb in his mouth, his little tearstained face now looking quite angelic. I stood still for a moment, taking in the scene before me. I had never seen my quiet little backwater looking more inviting or attractive. It is really not much more than an alleyway—a small cobbled street of ten houses on either side—simple brick homes fronting the cobbles. But today the red-brown of the brick glowed in the late afternoon sunlight. A pot of yellow chrysanthemums stood beside a front door. It looked peaceful and safe and quite perfect. I felt a lump rise in my throat.

We said no more about it that night. Every time I thought of another question to ask, I decided not to spoil the quiet calm of a Sunday evening. My last Sunday evening in my little house, I thought with a pang. I didn't even tell Bridie as we sat together at the supper table. She had had enough upheaval in her life and I decided to wait until my head stopped spinning to tell her.

❧ Three ❧

Daniel left the house right after breakfast. "I'm meeting with the police commissioner, and then I'll be at Tammany for the meeting," Daniel said. He gave me a tentative peck on the cheek, still wary that I might turn on him. He had every right to feel that way. I was still trying to process what he had told me, trying to reconcile his current plans and ambitions with the man I had known and loved for six years now. A decent man. A man who could not be intimidated or corrupted by politics or power.

"Will you be wanting your dinner, or will your Tammany bigwigs be wining and dining you at Delmonico's?" I asked with heavy sarcasm. I saw him wince a little.

"I'm afraid I will be out this evening—not at Delmonico's, mind you—but the reception at Mr. McCormick's will include food, so you don't need to save any for me."

"If we're to have a cook it may be your last chance for decent food," I shot after him as the door closed. My first thought after Daniel departed was to run over to Sid and Gus's house as soon as Bridie had left for school. I hoped to glean information from them on Big Bill and Tammany Hall.

But just as I was getting Liam ready I remembered they had told me they would be out this morning. I would have to wait until the afternoon when they normally were home to make coffee for Bridie and ask about her day. She had started at a fine new academy for young ladies in September, thanks to the generosity of Sid and Gus, so she had taken to stopping off first at their house to report on what she had learned that day. So I spent the day impatiently cleaning, beating the rugs and scrubbing the floors. I am afraid that the work made me more and more angry instead of calming me down. As soon as I saw they were home I took Liam's hand, hurried across the street, and rapped on the front door.

Sid opened it, today wearing an open-necked man's shirt, bloomers, and a bright purple scarf tied around her black bobbed hair.

"Molly!" she exclaimed. "Come have some coffee with us. Bridie was just telling us about her day. Are you feeling all right? You look quite flushed."

"I've been beating the rugs and thinking about beating my husband," I said, taking off my cape and hanging it on the pegs in the front hall.

"That doesn't sound good. What on earth's happened?" Sid asked.

"My head is about to explode," I replied. "Daniel has just sprung the biggest surprise of my life on me."

She went ahead to the kitchen. "Come and have a cup of coffee and tell us all about it."

I followed her, stepping into the big airy kitchen, which now smelled enticingly of coffee as well as the herbs of something cooking in a big pot on the stove. Something exotic and scented—maybe Moroccan, as that was their latest fad. My neighbors, whose real names were Augusta and Elena, flung themselves wholeheartedly into new ventures and experiments with cooking, only to tire of them after a few weeks. Luckily they had not yet turned their sitting room into a Bedouin tent.

Gus and Bridie were sitting at the scrubbed pine table. They looked up expectantly as we came in.

"Here she is, Bridie," Sid said. "With some big news to give us, eh, Molly?"

"Big news? You're pregnant again?" Gus asked as I gave Bridie a hug.

"I wish that were true," I said. "I'd be beaming ear to ear, instead of having steam come out from both ears."

"Not a good surprise, then," Gus said as Sid poured me a cup of coffee from the pot on the stove and then pushed a plate of ginger-bread in my direction. "Drink that. You'll feel better. Coffee cures all ills."

"Perhaps she needs some brandy in it, by the look of her," Gus said.

I shook my head. "No alcohol, thank you. It would only get me more riled up than I am and poor Daniel might be torn limb from limb."

Sid shot Gus a worried look. "What has Daniel done to deserve such wrath?"

"You'll never believe," I said. "I can hardly believe it myself."

"Molly, don't keep us in suspense a moment longer," Sid said. She pulled up a stool beside me. "Now, take a deep breath and tell us calmly in what way Daniel has upset you."

I tried to comply. "He's just sprung on me that we're moving," I said. "Moving away from Patchin Place."

Gus gave me a sympathetic smile. "Well, I suppose it was bound to happen eventually. I know that President Roosevelt himself wanted him in Washington, and Daniel was considering applying for chief of police in White Plains. He's ambitious with good reason, Molly."

"We're moving? No!" Bridie exclaimed, her face a picture of hor-ror. "Moving away from here? No. We can't."

"Luckily we're not moving as far away as either of those places," I said. "We're moving to a brownstone on Fifth Avenue."

"Mercy me!" Gus said. "He must have come into money."

"I wish it were that simple," I replied. "It seems he has a rich benefactor who has offered us the house, since its previous owner had to get out of town in a hurry due to a bit of scandal."

"And why would a rich benefactor offer Daniel a house?" Gus asked.

"The plan is that Daniel will run for sheriff of New York County on the Tammany ticket."

"Sheriff? What sort of a position is that?" Sid raised her eyebrows. "Will he be catching wild train robbers or subduing the poor peasants of Nottingham do you think?"

"That is pretty much what I said," I agreed. "I had never heard of a sheriff in New York."

"Well, you could knock me down with a feather," Gus exclaimed, shaking her head as she said it. "I always thought Daniel stayed well clear of Tammany—actually that he despised them."

"So did I," I said. "That's why the whole thing makes no sense to me. I'm beginning to think Daniel has taken leave of his senses. It's so unlike him to spring this house move on me or to go for a new job without asking my opinion. I'm beginning to feel that I don't matter at all. That I have no say in my future."

"Well, that is the way with most wives," Sid said, giving Gus a knowing look. "In the state of New York a wife legally has no say in the running of her life, as you very well know. You're a possession of your husband. He can legally beat you, sell any property you brought to the marriage, and shove you in an insane asylum if he chooses to do so. And if you choose to leave him you have no claim on the children. Which is one of the reasons that Gus and I are working so fervently with the suffrage movement. Nothing will change until women can vote."

"But Daniel's never been like that before," I said. "He's always acted as if he valued my opinion. He's always . . ." I couldn't go on. I felt myself choking on the words and gave a great hiccupping sob. "I'm sorry," I said, putting my hand to my mouth in embarrassment.

Sid immediately put an arm around me. "It's all right, Molly

21

dear. You go ahead and cry if you want to. A good cry is sometimes needed."

"But I hate anyone to see me cry," I said between sobs. "I almost never . . ."

Then I stopped talking to look for my handkerchief. I held it to my mouth while I tried to control my sobs. The others waited in silence, the two women looking at me with sympathy, Bridie with horror, having never seen me like this. I made a supreme effort to collect myself and wiped my eyes. "I really am sorry," I repeated. "It's just that I was so shocked to find out . . ."

"Of course you were," Gus said. "But think of it this way, Molly. It's not the ends of the earth or Timbuktu. You can come round here for a chat any time you feel like it. We can pay you a visit on Fifth Avenue—wearing our best clothes, of course."

"That's another thing, clothes," I said as the thought struck me. "How am I supposed to appear at Daniel's fundraisers and political rallies dressed in what I have? I never had many clothes to start with and I've had my wardrobe destroyed twice."

"You're more than welcome to raid our closets," Gus said. "And we know a delightful little Jewish dressmaker who can whip you up a wardrobe in no time at all."

"But new clothes cost money," I said.

"Molly, if Daniel is making you move to a new house to take up a new lifestyle the least he can do is to wheedle money for clothes out of his Tammany benefactors." Sid shook her head so that the purple scarf danced. "But what I want to know is why Daniel of all people? Surely there are candidates who would bend more easily to their bidding?"

"That's what I thought," I said. "Daniel said they asked the police commissioner for suggestions and his name came up. He sees it as a noble challenge, I gather. That he will be in charge of jails and docks and he can reform things."

"When in reality what Tammany will want is to cement their own hold over the longshoremen and the jails and hope he'll be their willing puppet," Sid said, looking at Gus for confirmation. "But why this sudden interest? What has happened to galvanize them?"

"You know what, don't you," Gus said. "William Randolph Hearst."

"That's what Daniel said," I agreed, "but I don't understand."

"He's very ambitious. He has announced his intention to run for mayor. He is accumulating powerful backers and he aims to destroy Tammany. It's the kind of challenge they haven't faced in years."

"But the mayor's election is not for more than a year," Sid said.

"No, but they want to make sure of the slate of lesser officers in this year's election," I said. "Sheriff is one of them. And one of the Tammany bosses, a man called Big Bill McCormick, is running for mayor. He's behind all this."

"Oh, we've read plenty about Big Bill in the *Times*, haven't we, Sid?" Gus said. "Fingers in lots of pies. He owns ships, doesn't he? Or is it docks?"

"Both," Sid said. "A ferry service here and bigger vessels too, I think. And he's somehow involved in warehouses and docks. He was cited in that case when the thugs broke up a strike at the Chelsea Piers."

"So of course Hearst would want to run against him," Gus said. "He represents everything Hearst despises."

"Don't tell me Hearst is above corruption." Sid gave an exasperated chuckle.

"Not exactly. But he has a personal vendetta in this, doesn't he? Remember what Frederica Walker told us at that suffrage meeting? About her brother?"

What now? I thought. This was becoming more complicated by the minute.

"That's right." Sid nodded, making the scarf flutter out again. "Her brother is a journalist who works for the Hearst newspaper—or rather he *was* a journalist. He was investigating something to do with docks and longshoremen and he disappeared. Never been found. His body is probably feeding the fishes."

"Don't," I said. "This is all too horrible. What has Daniel got himself mixed up in?"

"One has to assume that Daniel knows what he's doing and has enough friends in high places to keep him safe," Gus said. "Besides, he'll be under the protection of Big Bill, won't he?"

But I didn't find it very reassuring. We would be living in the house of a man who broke the law with impunity, and Daniel would be beholden to him. I didn't want to talk about it any more until I could confront Daniel again. Instead I turned to Bridie. "I'm sorry, we've been neglecting you and I haven't even asked how your day at school was. Are the girls starting to accept you a little more now?"

Bridie's new school catered to daughters of the elite and I worried it might make Bridie feel out of place or show her a glimpse of a future she could never have. But my neighbors had set their hearts on sending Bridie to Vassar, their alma mater, and they wanted to prepare her for it. Hence the Briarwood School for Young Ladies, run by another Vassar graduate and her sister. There Bridie would learn Latin and French as well as mathematics beyond the simple arithmetic of the public school, as well as how to mix with girls above her social status.

It had not begun well. The headmistress had immediately sensed Bridie's potential and willingness to study, so she earned the name of teacher's pet right away. And along with it the animosity of those girls who had no intention of studying because a good marriage would be arranged for them. There is nothing more vicious than a pack of young girls who sense a weak outsider—as I could tell you, having been educated myself with the daughters of the landowner's family. They took every opportunity to put me in my place and I suspected this was how it was with Bridie, too.

"Some of the girls are all right," Bridie said. "But the snooty ones—they look at me as if I should be shining their shoes. One of them—a girl called Blanche—asked me today why I had worn the same dress to school for a whole week. 'Do you not have other clothes?' she

24

asked. I told her that my family felt that I should dress simply for school as if I was in a uniform, so that I could concentrate on my studies."

"Good answer. That's the spirit," Sid said, smiling.

"But then she said, 'I'd simply die if I had to wear the sort of boring dresses you have. They look as if they came from the poor box.'"

"Ignore her," Gus said. "She's just jealous because she knows you are so much smarter than she is."

"She doesn't need to be smart," Bridie said. "Her family is very rich."

"Well, you do need to be smart to make your way in the world, my dear," Sid said. "Gus and I both went through the same kind of thing in school. Other girls who thought that being keen on studying was unnatural. But when you get to Vassar you'll find everybody is as passionate about literature and science as you are."

Bridie gave a weak smile as if she didn't quite believe this.

"You know we're always willing to have more clothes made for you, Bridie. Even frilly ones if you feel you can't compete."

Before she could answer I intervened. "We all agreed that school attire should be plain and simple, didn't we. She's lucky enough to have several dresses now, which is more than most girls have."

"Another girl, called Helen, told me she has a separate room in her house just for her dresses," Bridie said. "She's even meaner than Blanche."

"You'd better not let me anywhere near these girls," I said. "I'd be too tempted to give them a piece of my mind."

"Oh, dear," Bridie said. "I'm afraid you might be meeting them soon. There is an outing being arranged for this Friday. We are to make a trip to the Statue of Liberty."

"The Statue of Liberty? Isn't it on an island?" I asked.

"That's right. One of the fathers owns a big boat. It should be fun. Better than being in the classroom all day, anyway. And I have to bring a chaperone."

"You know we'd be happy to oblige," Sid said before I could answer. "I don't suppose Molly would feel comfortable bringing Liam on a boat."

I thought for a moment Bridie was going to jump at this and I wouldn't be able to find a way to object without seeming petty. That old jealousy shot through me, but Bridie said, "Thanks, Aunt Sid. It's good of you, but I'd really like to have Molly." She turned to me. "You will come with me, won't you, Mama? If we can find someone to look after Liam?"

"It looks like Liam will have a willing young nursemaid at his beck and call and we'll have moved to the new house," I said. "So yes, I'd be delighted to come with you. And to make sure those spoiled little misses treat you properly."

I could see from Bridie's face that she realized she might have made a mistake inviting me rather than my neighbors. "You won't be rude to them, will you? Because I have to be with them every day."

"No, I'll just let them know that my husband is running for a major political office and that we live on Fifth Avenue," I said. "That should be enough."

And I gave a satisfied smile.

❧ Four ❧

It was late when I finally decided to go to bed. I couldn't settle myself to read. Bridie was at the kitchen table puzzling over several texts and carefully writing and blotting in a copy book. I was listening for the door latch waiting for Daniel to come home.

"Come on, love. Up to bed," I finally said at eleven.

"I can't!" Bridie's face was strained. "I have to have this Latin translation done by tomorrow or I will get demerits."

"Surely they can't expect you to stay up all night?" I noticed the dark circles under her eyes. "You need your beauty sleep."

"They do expect it! The Latin teacher is very strict. It probably doesn't take everyone this long. The other girls have already had years of Latin, and French, and mathematics. I started Latin this spring with Aunt Sid and Gus, but then they decided that we had to study French Impressionists. I'm having to look up every other word in a dictionary."

"Well, I can't help you there. I learned a little Latin when I was a girl but I have forgotten it completely myself. At least you have a good brain." I smoothed her hair and laid my hand on her shoulder. "I'll tell you what. I'll make you a cup of tea and keep you company." I made the tea and put the biscuit tin on the table with a steaming mug of tea. "Have a bikkie, then, for strength." Bridie smiled gratefully at me and went back to her work, being careful to keep the biscuit crumbs off her book. I was not happy with the stress this new school was putting on her. Of course the other girls had received a proper foundation, not just a local school and then the passionate whims of Sid and Gus. I wondered again if Daniel and I were doing the right thing. At the thought of Daniel my mind started to whirl again. I couldn't sit still. I picked up my teacup, then paced around the house until I settled in the back parlor sipping my tea and staring at the fire.

I must have nodded off because I woke up feeling cold. The fire had burned down and the kitchen was dark. Bridie must have finished and gone to bed. I was just about to bank the fire and head up to bed myself when I heard voices outside. The key turned in the latch. I rose and walked into the front hall just as Daniel came in the front door.

"And what time of the blessed night do you call this to be coming home?" I heard my mother's words coming out of my mouth before I could stop them. How many times had I heard her say that to my da as he stumbled in through the front door? I had never used that tone with Daniel before. In fact, I had often waited up for him when he came home late and cold from police business, but I suppose I was still angry from the shocks of the day. "Did the meeting go on into the wee hours, then?"

"You shouldn't have waited up, Molly." Daniel turned up the lamp in the front hall and I could see that he wasn't alone. The man framed in the doorway was tall and muscular. As he stepped into the light I saw he had on a longshoreman's cap and boots and a belt holding the traditional hook all longshoremen wore. "Come on in," Daniel invited, "don't stand on the doorstep, man. She won't bite no matter what it sounds like. Molly, may I present Brendan Finnegan. Finn, may I present my wife."

"Pleased to meet you, Mrs. Sullivan." Finnegan's voice had a pleasant Irish lilt and was surprisingly soft and gentle.

"Won't you come in, Mr. Finnegan?" I offered, instantly embar-

28

rassed to have shown my temper in front of a stranger. "There is a fire in the back parlor."

"No, thank you, Mrs. Sullivan. I don't want to impose." He touched his cap to me and the old-fashioned gesture softened me toward him instantly.

"You must come in," Daniel insisted. "Take off your coat, come in and have a drink." Finnegan agreeably allowed his coat and cap to be removed and we walked into the back parlor, where I quickly put more coal on the fire. He sat as Daniel pulled a rather dusty bottle of whiskey out of the cabinet and poured out two glasses. He handed one to Finnegan.

"Slainte." Daniel raised his glass to Finnegan.

"Your health," he toasted back and downed it in one big gulp.

"So, Mr. Finnegan, were you at the political meeting as well?" I asked as Daniel poured him another shot and indicated that he should sit in one of the armchairs in front of the fire. Daniel took the other and I perched on its arm.

"Please call me Finn, Mr. Finnegan is my father." He laughed. "Yes, I was one of the men to officially nominate your husband for the Democratic slate. I'm one of the district captains. It's my job to help get out the vote and to protect the candidates. Which is why I am bothering you at this late hour."

"Finn walked me home to make sure I got here safely," Daniel explained. "It seems that Tammany candidates sometimes run into trouble after leaving the meetings."

"Thank you." I studied Finn's face, liking what I saw. It was a freckled, weather-beaten face. His nose looked as if it had been broken and set badly. Strangely that didn't make his face unattractive. He reminded me a bit of my own brothers, big and open-hearted. "That was very kind of you."

"It's my job, Mrs. Sullivan. Big Bill will have my hide if anything happens to Captain Sullivan. There's a young strong lad watching at the corner right now and you'll have someone outside day and night. Just give a whistle if you need anything and I can be down here in ten minutes."

"Is that necessary?" Out of everything I had worried about that day our physical safety had never occurred to me.

"Probably not," his voice was that of a strong man reassuring a little lady, "but better safe than sorry. Once you are in the brownstone your cook can do your shopping, but until then please just let me know and I can have someone accompany you."

I glared at Daniel with a look that said, "In a pig's eye!" but my curiosity made me continue. "Mr. Finnegan." I stopped as he shook his finger at me. "Finn, I mean, how do you know about the brownstone? Does everyone at Tammany Hall know about our domestic arrangements?"

He chuckled again. "No, indeed not, just myself. You see, it is in my district so it is my responsibility. You wouldn't expect the Grand Sachem to be concerning himself with domestic arrangements, would you?"

"The what?"

"The head of Tammany Hall, Big Bill himself." He turned earnest brown eyes on me and spoke seriously. "I have to thank you for taking the house, Mrs. Sullivan. I was desperate to think it would be all shut up. You see, I had only just gotten the job for Aileen. She's ever so grateful to have the employment and I would hate to turn her out." That was a new thought. It hadn't occurred to me that the maids might be let go if we didn't take the house. "And Mrs. Paolino, that's your cook. Her husband passed away this year and without this employment she will be back living with her sister in a small tenement apartment." I grimaced, remembering those small and crowded tenements from my first years in New York. I didn't wish them on anyone. "And Mary has been in that house for ten years, since she was Aileen's age. So, as I say, I'm grateful to you."

"How do you know so much about everyone?" I asked, surprised.

"That's my job, Mrs. Sullivan. I know every family in my district. When someone is out of work or in trouble with another family or with the law they come to me."

"And that is a job?" I was truly curious.

"It's a bit of a political position," he said with a smile.

"You don't look much like a politician, if you don't mind me saying so."

Daniel put his hand on my arm. "I hope I don't look like a politician either."

Finn laughed, "Just wait until you meet Big Bill! He worked his way up from the docks same as me." His look turned serious again. "That's what we stand for, Mrs. Sullivan, and why it's important that we win. When Tammany is in charge the little guy gets a fair deal. Hard work can help you get ahead." He grinned. "Oh, now I sound like a campaign slogan. That's a good one for you, Captain Sullivan."

"Will I be meeting Big Bill?" I asked Daniel. "Or is that another part of politics not suitable for women?"

"You will indeed." He was studying my face to see if this was good or bad news to me. "We have been asked out to dine with his wife and him tomorrow night at Delmonico's."

"Oh, most amusing!" I snapped. "It's too late at night for silly jokes, Daniel."

"No, I mean it, Molly. Big Bill has invited us to dine with him tomorrow at Delmonico's."

"Jesus, Mary, and Joseph!" I exclaimed, making Finn smile.

"I'll call at six to bring you over to the restaurant," Finn put in. "I've been invited to come and have a drink with you and then I'll come back after dinner to make sure you get home safely." He rose and set his glass down on the mantel. "But it's late and I have kept you up long enough." He turned to Daniel. "I appreciate the drink, Captain, or should I say Sheriff Sullivan."

"Not yet," Daniel laughed and rose to see him out.

Not ever, if I have anything to do with it, I thought rebelliously.

I rose to shake hands as they said their goodbyes but stayed in the parlor until I heard the front door close and footsteps walking down the path. I was waiting as Daniel came back into the room.

"Let me make this clear, Daniel Sullivan, in case you get any ideas. I will go where I want and when I want without needing permission or a minder. I have never lived in fear and I don't intend to start now."

"Molly, it's late. Can we argue about it in the morning?" Daniel ran his hands through his hair and across his face tiredly. "I think this Finn fellow is nice enough, don't you?"

"Yes, he seems nice enough in general. But in the course of two days I've gone from a safe life in my little house with a police captain for a husband to the wife of candidate for a position with the ridiculous title of sheriff who has to be guarded day and night."

Daniel looked at the clock with a wry smile. "I believe it is in the course of three days by now." I remained stone-faced. "Come on, cheer up, Molly." Daniel walked over and put his arms around me. "I'll work it out, I promise. Now please let's go to bed. I'm meeting the police commissioner in his office early tomorrow to discuss how we will handle my leave of absence. I need to make sure my job is safe if I'm not elected sheriff."

"Well, I hope that your next stop is at the bank and that you have a lot of money saved, Daniel Sullivan." I pushed away from him and put my hands on my hips. "Because if I am going to be meeting with Grand Poo-Bahs and the like and dining at Delmonico's I shall need some very expensive new clothes!"

❧ Five ❧

Tuesday, October 8

Even if Daniel had agreed to fund an extravagant shopping spree for me, there would be no time for even one new outfit before tonight. There might be stores now selling off-the-peg clothing, but it was always of the cheaper variety—shirtwaist blouses, colorful skirts, maybe even summer muslins, but certainly not dresses suitable for a dinner at Delmonico's. That would require Sid's little Jewish dressmaker and a multitude of fittings so that the silhouette fitted me like a glove. I opened my wardrobe door and studied my meager collection. At one time I had owned some fancy clothes—a selection of Gus's cast-offs, and, when I came back from Paris, some stylish gowns, which were, alas, destroyed in a fire.

Now I would definitely look like the poor relative when we met Big Bill and his wife.

"Don't worry about it, Molly," Daniel said, as I poured him a cup of coffee. I had risen early to make sure he went off with a good breakfast inside him. I might be mad at him, but I was still a dutiful wife! "I'm sure you'll look quite delightful, whatever you wear."

This just shows you how unobservant men can be. Women notice every single detail of other women's dresses.

33

"Is Mrs. McCormick also Irish?" I asked. "Also from the old country?"

Daniel chuckled. "Quite the opposite. McCormick married well. She's the daughter of a railroad baron. She grew up with money and brought plenty into the marriage."

"Oh, no. Then that's even worse," I said. "She'll be wearing the latest fashion and be loaded with jewels. This is a stupid idea, Daniel. Why don't you go alone?"

He looked worried. "I can't do that, Molly. The whole idea is for his wife to meet you and to like you." He put a hand on my shoulder. "We're in politics now, whether we like it or not, and I'm afraid wives will be on show. And before you tell me again that you've nothing to wear, I'm sure I can wheedle some funds out of the committee to get you some suitable clothes."

"But not before tonight," I said.

He slipped his arm around me. "You'll be fine," he said. "They'll notice that magnificent red hair and those beautiful green eyes and be entranced. You'll see."

"You're full of the blarney, Daniel Sullivan," I said, pushing him away, but laughing as I did so. "And you had better get those trunks out of the attic if you expect me to pack up all of our belongings in two days."

After he had gone I went upstairs and began pulling clothes out of the closets and laying them aside to pack. I opened my wardrobe door and studied my meager collection, remembering wistfully those dresses that had been destroyed in a fire. I did have Sid's former evening gown, a rather sumptuous purple affair that Bridie coveted. I had worn it to a theater opening, but it was a little too flashy to make a good first impression at a dinner. There was nothing for it—I'd have to swallow my pride and see if I could borrow a gown from my neighbors.

As this thought crossed my mind I realized what a blow it would be not to have them across the street from me. I was so used to popping in for a coffee, asking them to watch Liam while I was off on some escapade or other, or being summoned to meet some fascinating guest, from playwrights to suffragists. I knew I wouldn't be too impossibly far away, but the intimacy and immediacy would be gone. Whether I liked it or not, a new chapter in my life would be starting.

I kept packing until I heard Liam stirring and went into his room. He was lying in the crib that he had really outgrown, having a conversation with his bear. We had talked about getting him a big bed but had put it off because the room was so small. Now he'd have a big nursery with all the toys he might want. And a nursemaid who already seemed to adore him. Why was I still complaining? He scrambled to his feet when he saw me. "Up, Mama?" He held out his chubby little arms to me.

I lifted him from his crib, noting he was getting very heavy. And he was three years old. No longer a toddler but a little boy. Soon the crib would be empty with no new baby to fill it. I felt a great rush of sorrow that I had been unable to have a second baby, since my miscarriage eighteen months ago. My picture of a family was a large noisy group filling a house with laughter and teasing. Was my family always just going to be Liam, and Bridie—already a young lady with a mind of her own and a fine life ahead of her?

I put such thoughts aside and tapped on Bridie's door as I went past. "Time to get up, my darling," I called.

After they had both eaten a good breakfast of porridge and brown sugar, as well as toast and dripping, I handed Bridie her school bag.

"I'm afraid you'll be in charge of Liam this evening," I said. "Papa and I will be eating out—meeting his new boss."

Bridie nodded solemnly. As she reached the front door she turned back to me. "Everything is going to change, isn't it?" she asked. "I know I can visit the ladies when I want to, but nothing will be the same."

"I'm afraid that's true," I said. "I'm not thrilled about it either, but we have to make the best of it, for Papa's sake."

"What will happen to our house?" Bridie asked, as if this had just occurred to her. "Will you sell it?"

"Goodness me, no," I said. "I bought this little house myself, before I married Daniel. And I like it. I suppose we'll have to rent it out until Daniel is done with politics." If and when that would be, I asked myself.

Later that morning, at a time when I knew both Sid and Gus would finally be awake and ready to receive visitors, I took Liam across the alleyway. He needed no urging and ran across, ahead of me, on his sturdy little legs, shouting, "Aunty Sid, Aunty Gus!" at the top of his voice.

Gus opened the door before I could even knock. "Goodness me," she said. "I thought a whole army was invading us. Who has that great big voice?"

Liam grinned, suddenly shy.

"Well, come on in. There's fresh rolls from the bakery and Sid has made coffee," she said.

Again Liam ran ahead of me, through to the kitchen. Gus smiled fondly, watching him.

"So have you made peace with Daniel?" she asked. "Or is his mutilated body lying upstairs, dead with a thousand cuts?"

I had to laugh. "You don't know how close I came," I said. "And I'm still not thrilled, Gus. Do you know we are now to have a minder watching over us—to keep us safe? Have you ever heard of such a thing?"

"Then I have to say I'm glad you're moving out," Gus replied. "I don't think Sid would take kindly to big, burly Irishmen lurking outside at all hours."

"And neither will I," I said. "I've told Daniel I intend to go where I want, when I want."

"That's right. You tell him, Molly."

We went through into the kitchen, where Sid was reading the *New York American*, one hand holding a cup of coffee. "Hearst's newspaper really is a sensational rag," she said. "Listen to this: man sires twenty-four children with different women, boasts about his virility!"

"More fools the women," Gus commented. "I suppose he must be terribly handsome."

"The article says he twirled his fine mustaches in court."

We chuckled.

"And why is he in court?" I asked.

"A husband is suing for alienation of affection because the blaggard lured his wife away. The blaggard then claimed he could have any woman he wanted because he is more desirable than the husband."

"Fascinating," Sid said. "But I expect Molly would rather Hearst keep publishing rubbish like that than starting attacks on Daniel."

"Holy Mother of God!" I exclaimed as this just struck me. "You don't think he'd do that, do you?"

"Bound to. He'll have a man running against Daniel so he'll dig up any dirt he can to make Daniel look bad. You must prepare yourself, Molly."

My heart was beating rather fast. This had all been sprung on me so suddenly that the full implications of Daniel running for political office had not yet hit me. Daniel had led an exemplary life. I knew that. But as I thought about it now I realized that dirt could be dragged up—he had been in prison, wrongly accused, of course. He had once been betrothed to a rich man's daughter. He had clashed with the former police commissioner . . . all sorts of minor incidents that could be twisted nicely by a corrupt newspaper. And me? I found myself wondering. What could they dig up on me? Would they ever find out that I had been on the run for my life? That I had been involved in a jailbreak in Ireland? That my brothers died, connected to the Irish Republican Brotherhood? It seemed as if suddenly my whole life could come crashing down.

"Don't worry about it, Molly," Gus said gently. "I'm sure you two have led blameless lives and the most they'll be able to come up with is 'wife of candidate burned toast at breakfast this morning.'"

I tried to smile, but it wasn't easy. Liam felt he had been ignored long enough and tugged Gus's skirt. "Aunt Gus, Liam wants a cookie!"

"Of course you do, little man," Gus said, sweeping him up into her arms. "But how about a fresh roll with lots of butter instead?"

She put him on the high stool he always used in their kitchen and cut open a roll for him, adding butter and jam before she gave it to him. He set to work right away. I pulled up a chair.

"Actually I came begging a favor," I said. "I've told Daniel that I have no outfits suitable for a sheriff's wife and he agreed that I can have some things made. However . . ." I paused, taking a breath before continuing, "I now find I am to dine tonight with Big Bill and his wife at Delmonico's of all places, and I have nothing that would be suitable. So I was wondering . . ."

"Go through our closets, by all means," Sid said. "I don't think I have much that would be suitable for Delmonico's—I doubt the harem pants would be appreciated—but Gus still has dresses from her former life among the Boston elite, don't you, dearest?"

"Oh, absolutely," Gus said. "Come on up and try some on, Molly."

"I really hate to do this," I said, blushing, "but I can't look like a rag bag in front of Big Bill's wife—who is not from the bogs of Ireland like her husband but from a rich family, so Daniel informed me."

"That's right," Sid said. "I remember reading about her once. Her father was in railroads, wasn't he? I believe she is his second wife, and brought a large infusion of cash when he needed it most."

"Now you see why it's important that I look halfway decent, don't you?" I said. I headed up the stairs with Gus right behind me. We went up past the first-floor bedrooms to the second floor, where there was another wardrobe containing dresses Gus no longer wore.

"I'm afraid some of these are hopelessly old-fashioned now, Molly," Gus said as she opened the door. "This pink one I haven't worn since my debutante days. Far too girlish for you. I don't know why I keep it, but it may be suitable for Bridie with some alterations. However"—she paused and reached for another dress—"this may do the trick." And she brought out a sleek and simple number in pale mauve. "I had to wear this when we were in mourning for my grandmother," she said. "Purple and mauve were deemed suitable mourning colors for a young girl. You still have a girlish figure, Molly. It should fit you. Try it on."

Feeling self-conscious about undressing in front of Gus, I put on the mauve dress with her help. She did up the buttons up the back. It was a little tight around the bosom, but the overall result was satisfying. It looked classic and good quality, just right for a wife who didn't want to make a spectacle of herself.

"You look marvelous," Gus said. "Elegant. And I have a purple feather somewhere you can wear in your hair. You'll wow them, Molly."

"I'm not hoping for any wowing," I said. "I'd settle for making them decide I wasn't an absolute pauper."

Gus laughed. "Now take a look at the rest of this stuff. If there's anything else that catches your eye, then take it. I doubt I'll ever use it again."

She insisted on taking out every gown, making me try on the ones she thought might do, and I left, feeling mightily embarrassed but grateful, with two ball gowns and a tea dress. I knew they were a tad old-fashioned now, but they looked good quality, and that was what would matter.

❧ Six ❧

I'm not usually the sort of person who cares or worries that much about how I look. I've certainly never been in competition with other women when it comes to dressing—having never had the means to be. But I have to confess to being really nervous when it came time for me to dress for dinner at Delmonico's. Only the rich and famous dined there. I'd be in full view of everybody's scrutiny when I entered through those doors. And I'd have to make sure I held on tightly to Daniel's arm. I wouldn't want to trip down the steps into the restaurant as I came in.

I had enlisted Bridie to help me dress. She was doing up the silk-covered buttons that went all the way down the back. At times like this I realized why women who habitually wore such dresses needed a maid. No husband would be that patient! Bridie did up the top button and I turned to examine myself in the mirror. The dress did indeed make me look tall and willowy—quite satisfying, I thought.

"You look all dolled up," Bridie said.

I turned to stare at her. "Where did you get that expression?"

"Helen Belmont says it all the time," she replied seriously. "I'm learning all sorts of new, peachy words. And you should hear what Ruth Depew said at recess . . ."

"Mercy me," I said. "I just hope we're doing the right thing with this school." Then I wished I hadn't said anything. This was the first time that Bridie had opened up about the girls at school and I was curious to hear more.

"It's not so bad," Bridie replied. "I'm pretty behind in some subjects, and I don't think I'll ever fit in with those girls, though. Margaret Wilson said that she had spent every summer of her life in Newport and wasn't it so boring. And Julia Cooper agreed and said that everyone was going to the Riviera next summer. Her brother is at Harvard and her older sister is a debutante. All the girls talk about is how much they will spend on their dresses when they are debutantes and go to each other's balls."

"Not all of them, surely?" I asked.

"Not all, I guess. Judy Lowenstein just gets on with her work. She's the top student in Latin and Margaret calls her a grind. I know she goes to the Catskills every summer, but the girls kind of snub her. I think maybe because she's Jewish, but it could be because her father is only a doctor. Isn't that terrible?"

I nodded. "It is. You'd think that people come to New York to be free of prejudices. Lord knows the Irish have suffered enough here, as have the Chinese, and now the Jews. And why can anyone be against them? I have more respect for a doctor than a man who makes his living buying buildings, or taking bribes," I added, thinking darkly of Tammany Hall.

"I suppose because they are not Christian," Bridie said. "That's another thing. I've been careful not to say I'm Catholic. Julia said that Catholics are papists and can't be real Americans because they would overthrow the government if the pope told them to. Blanche said that's not true. I think she's Catholic because she wears a crucifix sometimes, but the girls don't bother her because her father is very rich. I don't want to tell her I'm a Catholic, though, because she is the most hoity-toity of all." All of this information came out in a rush. Bridie was clearly caught up in the lives of these schoolgirls already.

I shook my head. "Well, give the school a try this year and then we'll think again. Clearly Sid and Gus are determined you'll go to Vassar and want you to be educated, but there must be schools that are not breeding grounds for snobbery too."

The clock in the downstairs hall chimed the three quarters, reminding me I needed to hurry.

"Help me put this feather into my hair," I said, handing it to Bridie. After several attempts and a few giggles we managed to get it right. I picked up my shawl and my gloves and went downstairs. Daniel came out of the parlor, looking very dapper in his evening suit. The way his eyes lit up when he saw me was most reassuring.

"Very nice, Mrs. Sullivan," he said. "So we'll be off, then?"

I turned back to Bridie. "Your dinner is in the pot. Make sure Liam behaves himself and goes to bed at a good time. And if you have any problems the ladies across the street are home."

She nodded and waved as we stepped out into the street.

Finn was waiting for us, along with a burly type who could have been a prizefighter.

"This is Jack," Finn said. "He'll be looking after you from now on. Did you get us a taxicab, Jack?"

"I did, sir," Jack replied in a voice more Irish than my own. "It's waiting at the end of the alleyway."

I took Daniel's arm over the cobbles as I didn't walk too steadily in my dainty evening shoes. At the end of Patchin Place I saw that an automobile was waiting and glanced at Daniel in surprise. The front seat was open to the air. A driver sat in front of the wheel. The back seats were covered and had doors to make a private compartment.

"This is the latest thing," Finn said. "A man has started a motorized cab service. He's calling them taxicabs. What next, eh?"

I was helped into the back seat and we drove, slowly and sedately, up Fifth Avenue until we came at last to the restaurant on the corner of Forty-Fourth. I'd seen it from the outside, of course. I'd even been inside once, when I was following someone in the course of my detective work. But I'd never actually sat at a table and dined there. It was an absolute palace of a place, situated on the corner with a pillared portico like a Roman temple jutting out of the curved façade. Our taxicab came to a halt right in front of this and instantly two flunkies in uniforms with so much braid that they looked like generals, at least, rushed to open the door of the motorcar for me. Finn hopped off the front seat and helped me to step out gracefully, which I appreciated. Then Daniel offered me his arm, the glass doors were opened for us, and we followed Finn into the brightly lit interior.

The first thing that greeted me was the noise. There were so many tables, all of them occupied by people who were having a good time, by the sound of it. I looked around, taking in the silk-covered walls, decorated with swaths of fabric, the chandeliers hanging from the high ceiling. It was almost an overload for the senses.

"You have a reservation, sir?" A maître d' with an impressive Italian mustache appeared out of nowhere. Before we could answer we heard a booming voice calling, "Daniel, over here, my boy!"

I saw where the voice was coming from and that a man had risen to his feet and was waving violently, not caring that diners at nearby tables stared at him with distaste. As we approached him I could see why he had earned the nickname Big Bill. He was a giant of a man—not fat but big-boned with a large round, red face and a shock of gray hair above it. The face had an unmistakably Irish look to it and reminded me of the boys I'd had to contend with at home—great lumping louts who had trodden on my toes at village dances and wanted to kiss me behind the church hall. I supposed that Big Bill had been one of those boys once. I wondered, as we navigated among the tables, whether he had come from Ireland as a young man or had been born here, a child of those who escaped the famine.

"Welcome, welcome!" Big Bill yelled as we approached. "Thanks for bringing them, Finn. Daniel—looking sharp!" He held out a meaty hand to my husband and pumped it vigorously, then he turned to me, running an appraising eye over me. "So this is the little woman, Daniel. What a little beauty! You chose well, I can see. And an Irish lass if ever I saw one." He held out both hands to me. "Mrs. Sullivan, so good to meet you. Welcome, welcome." He took both my hands and squeezed them so hard I thought my fingers might fall off. Then he pulled out a chair for me.

"Take a seat, do. Park your carcass."

"Billy, that's such a crude thing to say. You'll shock Mrs. Sullivan," said a quiet voice from the other side of the table. Big Bill had been so overpowering that I hadn't even noticed his wife until now. I had expected the daughter of a railway magnate to be dripping in jewels and furs, but Mrs. McCormick was what could only be described as rather plain. She was a thin, rather bony woman with light brown hair piled in a coil on her head. She wore gray silk, with a simple high neckline and around her neck a cross made of pearls and rubies on a heavy gold chain. She had a pale, washed-out sort of face with large, rather bewildered-looking eyes that now focused on me.

"I assure you I'm not too easily shocked, Mrs. McCormick," I said, giving her my most reassuring smile, which she returned. When she smiled she looked quite different—younger, almost girl-like.

"I'm Lucy McCormick, Mrs. Sullivan. I'm delighted to meet you. Billy has talked nonstop about how impressed he is with your Daniel." She reached out a gray-gloved hand to me and I shook it.

As we took our places, Finn hovered awkwardly beside Big Bill. "Well, I should leave you to it, sir," he said. "Do you want me to return to escort Mr. and Mrs. Sullivan home?"

"Oh, for heaven's sake, Finn," Big Bill said. "You're like family. Grab a chair and I'll get them to set an extra place for you."

"If you're sure . . ." Finn still hesitated. "I wouldn't want to intrude on a private conversation."

"Good God, boy," Bill said. "If I wanted a private conversation it certainly wouldn't be with half of New York listening in. Besides, we've already had our little talk, haven't we? I think Daniel understands where we're going. Now sit, for heaven's sake, sit."

Bill McCormick snapped his fingers and a waiter came running. "Set an extra place for this gentleman," he commanded, "and bring us something to drink. We'd better start with champagne, since we are celebrating," he said. "And a couple of dozen oysters."

"Oh, not oysters, Billy," his wife said. "They are poor people's food."

"That's as may be. Damned good eating, if you want my opinion, and the same goes for lobster. They do it marvelously here, you know. Cook it in a special sauce. In fact I might order it as the fish course. You'll see."

The champagne arrived, amazingly fast. The cork was popped and five glasses were filled. Big Bill raised his. "A toast," he said. "To the winningest ticket Tammany ever came up with, and despair and destruction to Mr. Hearst and his cronies, who don't have a chance now we've got young Daniel on board."

Oysters arrived. I had never acquired a taste for them, but dutifully ate a couple. Big Bill didn't even seem to notice and downed the rest, one after the other, tipping them into his mouth and swallowing with one easy movement. More champagne was ordered and Bill selected the rest of the meal, not waiting to consult us as to what we might like to eat. The restaurant seemed to be a meeting place for the rich and famous. Several women, one I thought I recognized from the society columns of a lady's magazine, were walking from table to table greeting their friends effusively. A man and his wife walked up to our table and the men rose politely.

"O'Brien! How good to see you." Big Bill seemed to have the same hearty greeting for everyone he met. "Mrs. O'Brien, you look radiant! A picture of loveliness."

"Is this the new protégé?" O'Brien didn't sound nearly as friendly as Big Bill. He looked to be an elegant man, with an expensive suit well tailored to his slender frame. His hair was thinning but still a bright red color and he had a thin, well-groomed mustache.

"Yes, Daniel Sullivan meet Sean O'Brien, the heart and soul of Tammany Hall." Daniel shook hands with the man. "And this is the beautiful Mrs. Sullivan." As Mr. O'Brien shook hands with me I noticed that his hands were soft and manicured, not the rough dockworker hands of Finn and Big Bill. Was that the tension I sensed even though the words of both men were jovial and friendly?

"A pleasure to meet you both. Daniel, I'll be seeing you at Tammany soon. I want to keep a close eye on your career." There was a slightly awkward pause. Mr. O'Brien seemed to be wondering if Big Bill would invite him to sit down. When it was clear he would not, Mr. O'Brien went on smoothly, "Well, I mustn't keep you from your dinner." He gave a slight bow. "A pleasure."

"Let's have a drink sometime this week." Big Bill's hearty tone was back, but Mr. O'Brien's back was stiff as he walked away.

"I didn't see him at the political meeting. Was he there?" Daniel asked. "Is he very involved at Tammany?"

Big Bill lowered his voice a little. "He thinks of himself as my number two. He was a little put out that I didn't offer the sheriff's position to him, and let me know it. I suspect he came here tonight just to get a glimpse of you. But he is better off in his current position." Big Bill shared a knowing look with Finn. "I have my reasons and he will like it or lump it!"

He launched into political discussion with Daniel and Finn. I turned to his wife. She raised her eyebrows. "Don't you find politics quite utterly boring, Mrs. Sullivan? I know I do."

"It's quite foreign to me," I said. "I've no experience of it until now."

"I'd stay well clear if I were you," she said. "How these men can talk strategy for hours on end is beyond me. Frankly I hope Billy does not become mayor or there will be no stopping him. He'll have his eyes set on governor and then president, you'll see. The man is consumed with ambition. To think he started off poor as a church mouse, working as a deckhand on a coastal steamer—then saved enough to salvage and refurbish a boat that had run aground. From there he has built up what he has today. One has to admire him for it, but his energy is overwhelming at times."

"What about you?" I asked. "You come from a different background, I understand."

She gave a tired little sigh. "I most certainly do. My early years were a convent school, summers at our house on Long Island. I suppose I fell for Billy because he was so different from the boys I danced with. He made a promise to keep me in the style I was accustomed to and he has certainly delivered with that. I was quite taken with the thought that he might be an alderman someday. I knew a lot less about politics in those days."

"You have children, I gather?"

Again the smile made her face look so much younger. I realized now that she was probably not more than forty. "Two. A boy and a girl. My son, Cornelius, is currently a student at Columbia. His father wants him to learn the business as soon as he graduates so that he can take it over someday, but Cornelius is anxious to rush off to Europe and live in Paris. He has no wish to be tied down to menial work. It has caused great friction as his father has set all his hopes on him, since the older boy . . ."

I looked up in surprise. "He is not your eldest son?"

"Not my son, Mrs. Sullivan. I am a second wife. Junior, Bill's son from his first marriage, was too old for me to be a real mother to him when we married. Bill had hopes early on for him to go into politics as well, but he is, alas, incapacitated and confined to a wheelchair."

"How tragic. An accident?"

She shook her head so that her long pearl earrings rattled. "No, a wasting disease, I'm afraid. Hereditary. His mother died of the same thing. It will eventually rob him of all his faculties. A sweet, quiet young man who bears his infirmity with great stoicism."

She paused, staring at the glass she held in her hand.

"And you have a daughter?"

Again her face lit up. "I do. A sweet, pretty little thing. Billy has high hopes for her making a good marriage. He's already talking of a trip to Europe and hitching her up with a lord or a French marquis. Always dreams really big, does my Billy."

She broke off as the lobster arrived, smothered in a creamy, bubbling sauce.

"Here it is. Lobster Newburg, invented here at Delmonico's, so they claim," Big Bill said. "Manna made in heaven. Panis angelicus."

"Billy, that is close to blasphemy," Lucy said, wagging a scolding finger at him and making Big Bill giggle like a naughty schoolboy.

"My wife is afflicted with an overdose of religion," Big Bill said. "Too much influence from nuns at an early age. Did you also suffer with nuns, Mrs. Sullivan?"

"I did indeed," I said. "But mine were the Irish sort, too generous with the cane and the paddle."

"How barbaric," Lucy said. "Mine were sweet, gentle things. Quite unworldly."

We set to eating our Lobster Newburg and I had to admit it was delicious. To follow it came the steaks—bigger than any piece of meat I had eaten. I stared at mine with dismay. How was I supposed to eat all this? Big Bill ordered red wine. I tried to refuse, as the two glasses of champagne had already gone to my head, but he wouldn't hear of it. "Not allowed to eat steak without a good claret," he said and thrust the glass at me.

We had just started on the steak when a couple approached our table. The woman was dressed in a revealing gown, showing generous bosoms and a tiny waist. Her neck sparkled with diamonds and she carried an ostrich feather fan. As they came close to our table she gave a little squeal of delight.

"Well, lookie who we have here," she said, and tickled the back of Big Bill's head with her fan. He spun around, startled. The woman giggled, then wagged the fan at him.

"You are a naughty boy," she said. She gave a long, meaningful pause, then said, "You haven't been to see my new show yet."

"I'm too busy for theater these days, Gertie," he said. "Haven't you heard? I'm running for mayor."

"Oh, I've heard, all right," she said. "But don't they say all work and no play makes Jack a dull boy?"

"It will make Bill McCormick the major of New York," he said. "Now, if you'll excuse us, we're letting our steaks get cold."

The woman latched on to her escort's arm. "Come on, Teddy. Let's leave these boring people to their food and go somewhere more fun," she said.

I noticed that Big Bill's face had gone rather red. He picked up his wineglass and took a long gulp. "Odious woman," he said. "These theater types, no decorum at all. I don't know what she's doing here. Not her sort of place."

There was an embarrassed silence. Then he laughed. "Come on, everyone. Drink up. The night is still young."

I turned to look at his wife. Her face was frozen into a look of utter disgust.

It was almost midnight by the time Finn escorted us home.

"So what did you think of Big Bill?" he asked me as he climbed into the back seat of a taxicab beside me. I saw Jack nod to him and then turn and walk down the street. Had he been waiting outside the whole time just to make sure we got safely into the cab?

"Rather overwhelming," I said.

Finn laughed. "I know. He has more energy than anyone I ever met. And few boundaries. Mrs. McCormick, on the other hand . . ."

"Seems his exact opposite," I said. "Quiet, well bred, and horrified by his ribald jokes." Bill had told quite a few as the evening wore on and the wine had its effect. His wife had rebuked him, but it only seemed to goad him into being more and more risqué. It was almost as if he was behaving that way to hurt or punish her. What a strange marriage, I thought as I glanced across at Daniel. I was lucky that I had married a man I could truly admire. I just prayed that politics wouldn't change him too much.

❧ Seven ❧

Wednesday, October 9

The next day began the work of packing in earnest. Two days to pack up my entire life! Mercy me! We were not going to be bringing any furniture with us, just our clothing and personal effects, but all the same there was enough to keep me busy. I couldn't put Liam's items away as he was likely to spill down his front and require a complete change of clothes at any moment. I packed my dresses and toiletries, then turned to Bridie's. She could wear the same dress for one more school day, I decided. Her books were another matter. She had acquired a great number, mainly from Sid and Gus. I wondered if these were just lent and if it would be all right to take them to a new house. I decided to go across the street to ask them.

I washed Liam's sticky face and was heading for the front door when the doorbell rang. I opened it to find Gus there.

"We are dying to hear about the dreadful Big Bill," she said. "Come on over for coffee. I've just been to the bakery on Greenwich and they had chocolate croissants today. Who could resist?"

"I was just coming over to you," I said. "I'm in the throes of packing and wanted to return your dress. It was a big hit, by the way. Quite right for the occasion."

"Oh, goodness me, keep it, my dear," Gus said. "It reminds me of ghastly months of mourning. And if I have to go into mourning again I shall look stunning in black." She grinned. "Well, not quite as stunning as Sid, of course. Black is absolutely her color." As she finished these words she swept up Liam into her arms and set off across the street with him. Soon we were settled in the kitchen dunking chocolate croissants into coffee. Pure heaven.

In between bites I related the events of the evening to them—the overwhelming Big Bill and his quiet, subdued wife, then the incident with the woman who had tickled him with her ostrich fan and called him Billy.

"So Big Bill has an eye for the ladies, does he?" Gus said. "I don't suppose that went down well with the religious Mrs. M."

"If looks could kill that woman wouldn't have walked three more steps," I said.

"Do you suppose she's his mistress?" Gus turned to Sid.

Sid shrugged. "Who knows. Men like that usually have one, don't they? Power attracts certain women. But I should think he'd have to give her up if he's running for office. Newspapers have a field day with such things, and politicians do like to run on the God, home, and family platform."

"It seemed, from what she said, that he hadn't seen her for a while, so maybe that's true," I agreed.

"So the big question is did you like him? Because Daniel will be closely tied to him from now on."

I paused. "He's quite likeable. Very charming. A little too flirty. But I wouldn't trust him and I'm not at all thrilled that Daniel will be working with him."

"Interesting," Sid said. "You're a good judge of character, I'd say, Molly. Let's hope Daniel can keep his distance."

I nodded, finished my croissant, and went to retrieve my son. "I should get back. I have all the packing to do for the move on Thursday. I came over to ask if you mind if I bring Bridie's books with us. She seems to have a little library now of books you've lent her."

"Of course," Gus said. "She will need her books."

"So it's packing day already, is it?" Sid asked.

I nodded. "I'm really not sure how much to take. If we are only to be there for six months at the most, should I leave our summer clothes? And what about kitchen things? I know we are to have a cook, but should I bring our jars of flour and sugar, and our laundry soap? I don't want to seem like a poor relative, arriving with nothing."

"I would say if there is a cook there is already a fully equipped kitchen," Gus said. "And if she needs flour, she goes out and buys it."

I chewed on my lip nervously. "That's another thing," I said. "I'm really not sure how this is to work. I know the servants' wages are paid by our benefactor, but should I give the cook a weekly budget for food? What if she's used to fancy meals and wine all the time? I have no experience of these things."

"I would give her what you normally would spend and she will have to plan her meals around that."

"I don't want her to look down on us," I said, "but I've no idea where the money is coming from right now. Daniel has resigned from the police and is not elected yet, so how are we supposed to live? I asked Daniel and he told me not to worry about it."

"Then don't," Sid said. "If it's being financed by Tammany, then there is plenty of money in the pot."

"So have you decided what is to be done with your own house while you are away?" Gus asked.

I shook my head. "Daniel suggested his mother might want to use it during the worst months of winter. She's quite cut off up in Westchester County."

"Good idea," Gus said. "Better to have someone in the house so you don't attract the criminal element."

"But in the meantime we had a suggestion," Sid chimed in. "Ryan has a new friend coming into town. He was going to put him up at a local hotel, but if you let him use your house he'd pay you rent and keep it running nicely for you."

"A new friend?" I asked, raising an eyebrow and making Sid laugh. I knew what the friends of Ryan O'Hare, our flamboyant playwright, were like. Male and very artistic.

"You know Ryan! He always has new friends, but this one, I gather, is special."

"Aren't they all?" I asked, making her chuckle again.

"Listen to this. He's a Russian ballet dancer. Nikolai Noblikov. He's over here performing at the Metropolitan Opera House on Broadway at Thirty-Ninth. We saw him the other night. He's absolutely amazing—so fluid you'd think he had no bones. And when he died of a broken heart at the end of the ballet I don't think there was a dry eye in the house."

"I'm sure he'd want something more grand than my house," I said.

"Oh, no. This is exactly what he'd want," Sid went on. "Ryan was going to put him up in a hotel, but he's terrified he'll be mobbed by his fans every time he leaves his room."

"Goodness gracious," I said. "So he's really famous, is he? I've never heard of him, but then I've never been to the ballet."

"Ryan says he's very big in Russia," Gus said. For some reason Sid found this funny and spluttered into her coffee.

"Anyway, we think he'd be a perfect tenant," Gus said. "He wouldn't make a mess and he'd only use the place to sleep. He can come over to us for coffee and I'm sure they'll eat out every night."

"I'll mention it to Daniel," I replied hesitantly, thinking of his usual reaction to Ryan. "It might conflict with his ideas of bringing his mother down for the winter."

"Dear God, Molly," Sid exclaimed. "Surely you don't want his mother living in your house? You know what will happen then, don't you? She'll be around on Fifth Avenue organizing Daniel's social life for him, reveling in the fact that he's going into politics and pointing out to you where you are falling short."

This was all too true. Daniel's mother had wanted him to go into politics since I had known her. I wondered how long it would be until she showed up wanting to be a part of Daniel's new political life. "So, a tenant in the house might be a perfect solution," I said. "I'll speak to him tonight and perhaps you could have a word with Ryan."

"Absolutely," Gus said. "He'll be at the theater this afternoon. There's a matinee today. One gathers the show is a great hit and may run for months and then tour. Ryan finally has success on both continents."

"There will be no stopping him now," Sid commented dryly. "He always thought he was God's gift to the world. Now he'll just see himself as God."

On those wise words Liam and I departed to return to the packing.

Even with only our clothes the task took all day. I couldn't imagine what it would be like to pack up a whole house with furniture as well to move. I had just finished when two big bruisers who looked as if they could be Tammany thugs showed up to take the last of our trunks over to the new house.

I think all of us had trouble sleeping that night. I know I did. My mind could not settle and Liam kept climbing out of his bed. I couldn't bring myself to be stern with him since I felt so out of sorts myself. I finally drew him into bed between me and Daniel and we all drifted off.

❧ Eight ❧

Thursday, October 10

Thursday morning we had a quiet breakfast in a house that felt very empty. Liam, still sensing the uncertainty and my tension, became clingy and whiny, meaning that either Bridie or I had to amuse him and thus slow down our progress. I had kept Bridie home from school so that she could help with Liam. I could tell Bridie was not happy about the move either.

"I suppose it will be a good thing, really," she said in a quiet little voice. "The girls at school might even talk to me if they know I live on Fifth Avenue."

"And you'll have a lovely big room of your own with a dressing table and a mirror," I said.

"But I look forward to visiting the ladies when I come home every afternoon and telling them about my day," she said.

"You can still do that. It's not a long walk. And besides, they do like to travel. Before we know it they'll be off to Morocco or somewhere. They've been talking about it."

Bridie nodded, taking this in. She had already learned that our dear friends were not always reliable and were prone to whims. Daniel also seemed tense as he came down the staircase carrying yet another big box. "I'm not sure we need to bring Liam's blankets," he said. "I'm sure the nursery is well equipped."

"But he needs his own blankets to fall asleep," I said. "At least he needs his own things to feel safe. So do I, for that matter."

Daniel looked at me as if he were seeing me for the first time. "I'm sorry. This move is hard for you, isn't it? Don't worry. It won't be forever."

I felt tears well up in my eyes. "Oh, and if you're elected sheriff, then it will be deputy mayor, or state senator, then Congress . . . I know how these things go."

"I promise you they won't go that way for us," he said. "I've no desire for power, unlike our dear benefactor." He carried the box past me and placed it on the street.

A horse and cart arrived and our possessions were loaded swiftly by the same two big bruisers. When one of them said, "Lord love you, ma'am," in the most Irish of voices, my suspicions about their identity were confirmed. The cart was backed up with difficulty, since Patchin Place was not wide enough to turn a horse. After the cart had departed I went around the house, staring fondly at my little kitchen, the scrubbed pine table, the stove that gave such good warmth. What happy days we had shared here. Would I ever sit at that table again?

"Should we not get going?" I asked Daniel. "There's no point in lingering any longer and making ourselves miserable."

"We have to wait for Finn," Daniel said. "He is to escort us to the new place."

"Saint Michael and all the angels," I exclaimed. "Are our whole lives to be dominated by that blasted Finn?"

"Do you not like him? He seems agreeable enough to me," Daniel said.

"He may be agreeable, but there is such a thing as too much closeness. Is he to come everywhere with us? Should we not buy a bigger bed in case he wants to share it?"

Daniel gave an awkward smile. "It's how Tammany works, Molly. Now the world knows I'm running on the Tammany ticket I could meet some unpleasantness. Just an abundance of caution, if you ask me. But Finn was given the task of making the house ready for us, so I think he wants to show us around personally."

There was nothing I could say without sounding churlish, but it was gradually dawning on me that our lives would no longer be our own.

"I'm going to take Liam and Bridie across the street to say goodbye to our friends," I said.

"You make it sound as if we're heading west on a wagon train," Daniel said. "It's a five-minute walk, Molly."

"I know," I said. "But I need to leave them the spare key in case the Russian ballet dancer wants to take a look at the place."

"Let's hope this Russian fellow doesn't fill the place with refugees or arty types," Daniel said. I had managed to convince him it would be a good idea to have someone living in the house for now. His mother wouldn't want to come for more than a quick visit before Christmas at the earliest. In spite of his distaste for Ryan and his circle he agreed a lone ballet dancer would be an ideal tenant—at the theater every evening, sleeping all day.

We had tearful goodbyes with Sid and Gus. Bridie wept. I think I wept a little too. Liam, not wanting to be left out, started crying as well. Daniel came to tell us that Finn had arrived and looked in horror at a room full of wailing women.

"I could understand if we were all in Ireland, about to sail for the New World," he said.

"It's not the distance," Gus said. "It's the realization that Molly's life will no longer be her own. Maybe she won't have time for us."

"Of course she will. She won't be asked to do the campaigning. Maybe some entertaining will be required, but on the whole women are best kept out of politics."

Sid looked at me and raised an eyebrow. "Just wait until we have the vote," she said.

Finn was waiting patiently in the alleyway. Daniel put a protesting Liam into his buggy and we set off. I tried not to look back when I reached the corner and turned onto Sixth Avenue.

"I think you'll be happy with the arrangements, Mrs. Sullivan," Finn said as we crossed to Fifth Avenue and approached the house. "Mary has been there for a while and comes highly recommended. Aileen is newly arrived and untrained but seems willing enough, and I've appointed a cook for you so there will be no need to do any kind of household tasks."

I didn't like to ask what I would be doing all day. Sitting at my embroidery, no doubt!

"So what do you think, Bridie?" I asked.

She was staring up at the house, I couldn't tell whether in admiration or horror. "It looks big," she said.

Daniel removed Liam from the buggy and handed him to me while he and Finn carried it up the front steps. Finn opened the front door, then stood aside to let us enter first. Mary, Aileen, and a large woman with an impressive coil of gray hair were standing in a line, like soldiers waiting to be inspected. I had seen this kind of thing when I visited the landowner's house in Ireland, but the thought of me inspecting a line of servants made me want to giggle. It seemed so improbable.

"Here is your staff, Mrs. Sullivan," Finn said. "I believe you met Mary and Aileen earlier."

Mary dropped a little curtsey. "Welcome, ma'am," she said.

Aileen bobbed an awkward one and gave me a shy smile that I found quite endearing. The woman at the end did not curtsey or smile.

"And this is your cook," Finn said. "Constanza. I'm afraid her English is not too good yet, but she'll learn quickly."

The cook now held out her hand. "Buongiorno, Signora," she said. She still did not smile.

"Constanza's husband was killed in an accident at the docks," Finn said. "We try to take care of our own."

"I'm sorry," I said to her. She nodded.

"This is our ward, Bridie." I took her hand. She was hanging back shyly. "And you've already met our son, Liam. Now if you'll all excuse me, I should go and unpack."

"It's all done, ma'am," Mary said. "We've put everything in the right place."

So it seemed I was not to have a say over where my own stuff went. I was beginning to feel like a prisoner in a very elegant jail. But I didn't want the servants to know that. "Then I'll do a little inspection," I said. "Get the lie of the land. And Aileen can take Liam up to his nursery and let him get settled in properly."

"Very good, Mrs. Sullivan," Aileen said. She scooped up Liam. "Come on, little man. Let's go and find that rocking horse."

"Horsey?" Liam went with her without a single look back.

Bridie took a hesitant step forward as if she might be expected to head for the nursery too.

"Come and look at the rooms with me, Bridie love," I said. "You'll have some good suggestions about things we might want to change."

She gave me a grateful smile.

"I'd better leave you to it," Daniel said. "Finn and I have a meeting at noon. So I won't be home for lunch."

He didn't wait for me to reply, but nodded to Finn and they took off. Mary was looking at me—I couldn't tell if it was a friendly smile or a smirk that I was now in her power. I decided I was being fanciful and went ahead of her into the front parlor. As I had seen before, it was an ornate room—the sort of room one keeps for entertaining important visitors, not for the family. Certainly not the sort of room I was going to feel comfortable in. I noticed no fire in the grate.

"Is this room just for visitors, Mary? You don't usually light the fire in here?" I asked.

"Oh, but ma'am, remember I told you we have the steam heat. You'll notice the radiators in every room. I'll only be lighting a fire when you ask for one."

"I do like a fire in the evenings," I said. "It makes the place look cheerful, don't you think?"

"Then you'd probably want it in the back parlor, which is more like the family sitting room," she said, and led me down the foyer to the room we had been shown before. This room was indeed more homely, although with more knickknacks and drapes than were my taste. "That stuffed bird will have to be put somewhere," I said, pointing at the object under a glass dome on a side table. "Liam will have that knocked over in minutes."

"Very good, ma'am," she said.

"And what else is on this floor? The dining room is across from this one, is it not?"

She didn't reply, but opened the door to a room with a long mahogany table and eight chairs around it. It looked out onto a small square of back lawn. At least Liam would have a safe place to play. It felt horribly formal to me and I had a vision of myself hosting dinner parties at that long table. Mercy me! How on earth would I know what to do, never having held a proper dinner party in my life?

"And the kitchen, where is that?" I asked, leaving the gloomy room hurriedly.

"It's downstairs, ma'am. In the basement. You'll have no need to go down there. If you want to speak to Cook you can ask me to fetch her for you. The food comes up on the little dumbwaiter, if you noticed the little cupboard on the wall?"

Goodness, what next. I tried to look as if I had been used to dumbwaiters all my life.

"So is that all the rooms on this floor?"

"No, ma'am. Across the hall is the library." She opened the door for me and I stepped into a room that was floor to ceiling lined with books. I had never seen so many in my life, not even at Sid and Gus's house. Bridie will have a field day here, I thought. Even as the words passed through my head Bridie stepped into the room behind me and gave a little gasp.

"Oh, look at all these books. Can I read any of them I want to?"

"You can read them all," I said, smiling at her excitement.

"Wait till I tell the girls at school," Bridie said. "Now I have a real library in my house. Just like Julia and that stuck-up Blanche."

"Come up and see the bedrooms. You can choose which one you want." I put an arm around her shoulders, noticing that she was now almost as tall as I was. We started up the stairs.

"I've put the young lady's things in the bedroom at the back," Mary said, coming up behind us. "I thought it would be quieter with less distractions from the street."

I felt annoyance rising, but when I saw the room I really couldn't say anything. It was a pretty room and it had a little desk in the window, looking out onto the backyards. There was even a tree to one side that would look pretty when it was in leaf. But I wasn't about to let Mary dictate to me.

"What do you think, Bridie?" I asked. "Is this the sort of room you'd feel happy in?"

"Oh, it's lovely," she said. "Nice and quiet for me to do my homework." She turned and gave Mary a grateful smile. "Thank you for getting it ready for me."

"You're more than welcome, Miss Bridie," Mary said, giving her a nod of approval.

"And Liam?" I asked. "Where is his bedroom?"

"The nursery is on the top floor, ma'am. He'll be sleeping up there."

This didn't go down so well with me. "Oh, I don't know if I want him sleeping so far away from us," I said. "He likes to climb out of bed and who knows what trouble he can get himself into if I don't hear him."

Mary's face remained impassive. "Don't worry, ma'am. Aileen is sleeping next door to him. I've told her she'll be acting as his nursemaid as well as helping me around the house and she's happy to do so. She misses her own young brothers and sisters, apparently."

So it seemed as if all my needs were to be taken care of. I should be delighted, so why wasn't I? I went across the hall to the bedroom that would be ours. My toiletries and hairbrushes were now arranged on the vanity in the dressing room. My underwear in the drawers and my clothes hanging in the wardrobe. There was even a nightgown laid out for me on the bed. Holy Mother! So this is what it was like to have proper servants. I wasn't at all sure that I liked the idea.

"Is it all to your liking, Mrs. Sullivan?" Mary asked.

"Yes, thank you, Mary. You must have worked hard," I managed to say graciously.

"I think it's a lovely room. Just like the rooms the girls at my school have," Bridie said, examining the frills on the bed and the swathes around the windows. I couldn't very well say that I disliked such froufrou and it would be coming down as soon as I felt comfortable here. At least Bridie was pleased.

"We should feed Liam his lunch soon or he'll be cranky," I said.

"Aileen will take care of it," Mary said. She put out a hand and almost touched me. "You really don't have to worry, ma'am. We're all quite competent. We'll make sure your life runs smoothly here. It's our job."

"I'm sorry," I said. "You have to understand that this sort of lifestyle is foreign to me. I've never lived in a big house nor had servants."

"That's all right, ma'am. It's true of many people in New York, isn't it? They come across from Europe with nothing and they make good. I think it's wonderful. We can all dream, can't we?"

"Have you been here long, Mary?" I asked. I presumed she was Irish because of the Tammany connection, but she sounded like an American. "Were you with the original family here?"

"No, ma'am. I came a year ago when the last gentleman moved in. The one who was supposed to be taking the office your husband is now running for. Such a nice man he was too. Never gave me any trouble."

"What happened to him?" Bridie asked. "Did he die?"

"Oh, no, miss. That Hearst devil dug up dirt on him and he had to leave town in a hurry. Now he has to wait it out up in some heathen part like Vermont or Maine until the scandal has died down."

I found myself shivering. Was Hearst at this moment trying to dig up dirt on Daniel or, worse still, on me?

❧ Nine ❧

Luncheon proved to be the first of the interesting meals. Mary informed us that the meal was ready to be served and it would be cold since they didn't know at what time I'd be arriving.

I retrieved Bridie from the library, where she already had a pile of books around her, and we went through to the dining room. On that vast table two places had been laid at one end. Between them was a platter containing several unidentifiable items—little round white balls, slices of odd-looking meat, vegetables in oil, and tomatoes. Beside it was a platter of bread. I gave Bridie an encouraging smile and we sat down. The white balls seemed to be some kind of bland cheese, but Bridie took one of the cuts of meat and gave me a horrified glance. I tried it and had to agree—it was slightly spicy and so heavily laden with garlic that it took my breath away. I had learned what garlic and spices were through Sid and Gus's experiments, but finding this for my own lunch was a bit much.

I rang the bell and Mary appeared. "Mary, what are all these things?"

She shrugged. "I really couldn't tell you, ma'am. Constanza, she is Italian. She has only ever cooked for her family, so I expect all the food would be what they are used to. Do you want me to send for her?"

I was loath to make trouble on my first day. I shook my head. "No, let's just see how we get on, shall we? Tomorrow I'll have a talk with her and we can plan the menus for the week." Which brought up another point in my mind. "And speaking of menus, Mary, am I supposed to give Cook money for the food and she does the shopping? Because . . ." I broke off, not wanting to say that it would certainly be a limited budget if my husband had no job until he was elected to an office.

But Mary smiled and shook her head. "Oh, no, Mrs. Sullivan. Mr. Finnegan has arranged all that. Cook will be getting the weekly housekeeping money from him and she'll do the shopping, or we can send Aileen out for her."

"I see." I was beginning to see, rather clearly. I was not even to have the pleasure of pushing Liam around the shops. We finished our meager lunch that was mostly cheese and bread with a slice of tomato—something else I had never quite learned to like, since it was unknown in my childhood and a luxury since. Then Bridie fled straight back to the library and I went up to see how Liam was getting along. I found him sleeping peacefully. I tiptoed down again and went through to my own bedroom. What in God's name was I to do now? To do every day? I was tempted to go over to Sid and Gus to report on the move, but my pride wouldn't let me admit defeat so soon. Lucky Bridie, I thought. She'd be in her element—a whole library to work her way through and a house that would seem more normal to her schoolmates. As for me, I'd never been a great reader. I'd been good at my studies and learned quickly, but having not had a book in the house except the Holy Bible and the Catholic Missal I'd never learned the art of leisure reading. Let's face it, I'd never had any leisure until now. It was probably about time I learned to become a lady.

I went down to the library to find Bridie deep in a book. "So what would you recommend for me?" I asked.

She frowned. "I'm not sure what you might like here. There's a translation of Homer's *Odyssey* that Aunt Gus said I ought to read, but they have the whole of Dickens over there."

I didn't want to show my ignorance in front of her, so I grabbed a random book from the shelf. It turned out to be *A Tale of Two Cities*. I went to sit in the back parlor and started reading. The language was hard going for me, but soon I was hooked. Until I remembered Liam. I had hardly seen him all day. I put down the book and went to the nursery, where I heard singing. Aileen was singing an Irish song in her soft, gentle voice. I hardly liked to barge in. Liam was sitting on her lap with his thumb in his mouth while she swayed him gently and sang. It was such a sweet scene. She looked up as I opened the door.

"Oh, hello, Mrs. Sullivan. The little one woke up."

"That's good," I said. "I thought I might take him out for a while in his pram, maybe down to Washington Square."

"Oh, I can do that for you," she said. "I've finished my chores for the moment."

I decided it was time for some straight talk. "Aileen, I'm delighted Liam's getting along so well with you, but I'm not one of these high-class mothers who hands over their child to the nursemaid and only sees them for an hour at teatime. I enjoy being with my son."

"Oh, I understand that, ma'am," she said. "And if you don't mind me saying so, I think it's wonderful that someone like yourself can come over from Ireland with nothing and turn into a fine lady so quickly. It gives hope for the rest of us."

I had to smile at this. "I wouldn't say I've reached the rank of fine lady yet," I said, "but I do have a good life here." I bent to pick up my son. "Come on. Let's go for a walk, shall we?"

Liam struggled. "Horsey," he complained. "Liam wants to ride horsey."

"I think the horse needs a rest," I said. "I'm sure you've worn him out. Don't you want to take some bread for the birds in the park?"

"Bread for birds." He looked more cheerful now. But by the time I had put on his jacket and cap the sky had darkened and it looked as if it might rain at any second. I admitted defeat and watched him ride the horse instead.

When the ornate clock on the mantelpiece chimed four I realized I hadn't had my cup of tea. I hesitated, not sure how to summon somebody and feeling awkward about doing so. So I found a door at the back of the hall with stairs leading downward until I came into a large dark kitchen. Constanza was sitting on a chair, mouth open and snoring.

Good, I thought. I'd make myself a cup of tea without having to ask. The kettle was full, so I put it on the stove and looked around for a teapot. My rummaging woke Constanza, who jumped up, startled. "Madonna mia!" she exclaimed.

"It's only me, Constanza. I came down for a cup of tea."

"Cupatea?" She looked puzzled.

"You know. Tea. To drink." I pantomimed lifting the cup to my lips.

"Ah. Tea."

"That's right. But I can't find the pot."

"Como?"

"The pot. Teapot. You know."

"Ah. No pot for tea. Only coffee."

"Well, let's make it in the coffee pot for now, then, shall we," I replied, thinking that I'd be going back to Patchin Place to retrieve my teapot and my tea caddy. And if Mr. Russian ballet dancer wanted tea he'd have to supply his own pot.

"I make-a the caffè for you?" she asked.

I shook my head. "I don't like coffee in the afternoon. Never mind."

I stomped up the stairs again, now in a thoroughly dispirited mood. I attempted to go back to my reading but I couldn't settle, waiting impatiently for Daniel to return. What if he was out for dinner? What if this was to be the new normal in our lives?

He returned just after five.

"Had a good day settling in?" he asked cheerfully as we sat in the unfamiliar back parlor.

"Oh, never been better," I replied. "For lunch I had to eat disgusting cold meats laden with garlic and chewy bread. My son doesn't need me anymore because he has a new love. Bridie will never come out of the library again and there is no teapot in the kitchen so I've had no tea."

"Sounds like the end of the world," Daniel said with a sardonic smile. "If you'd come with me you'd have seen people who really do have something to complain about. We visited docks on the East River—docks not owned and run by McCormick. You should see how those men work—backbreaking loads. Dangerous conditions. Men falling and getting crushed every week. Tammany is trying to help them organize a union."

"Or to lure them away to work for Big Bill?" I asked sweetly.

"Big Bill has all the workers he needs," Daniel replied. "And I have to say, his docks do seem to run smoothly, even if the odd bit of cargo goes missing and shipping companies might have to pay for protection."

"Goodness. So he is a crook?" I asked. "You are working alongside a crook, Daniel. That must tar you with the same brush."

"Don't worry," Daniel said.

"Of course I worry." I snapped out the words. "One minute you're a respected policeman and the next you're fraternizing with the enemy. You've always told me how you despise the way Tammany works and now look at you."

He put a hand on my shoulder. "Molly, it's going to be all right. I have good reasons for what we are doing."

What could I say? I did trust Daniel, but I got the feeling that there was more going on than he wanted me to know. I would get to the truth one way or another. "Were you there to do those workers any good or to get publicity for Tammany?" I asked, not ready to give up yet.

"A bit of both," he answered honestly. "Finn was there. He seemed to know every man's name and their families. I think he has done a lot of good, judging on the reception he got." He smiled wryly. "That Mr. O'Brien showed up just when the newspapers did. He is the publicity hound, I think. Big Bill seemed none too pleased."

"It's all right for you," I said. "You're busy with your new pals. But what in heaven's name am I supposed to do all day? The nursemaid entertains Liam. The maid cleans and shops. The cook cooks. I'm not used to being idle, Daniel. And I'm not about to take up embroidery."

He had to laugh at this. "I'm sure you'll be a great asset as the campaign goes forward," he said. "You'll be entertaining the wives of wealthy sponsors."

"Holy Mother," I muttered. "And what would I know about entertaining wealthy women?"

"You managed that tea party at Miss Van Woekem's," he said. Then he paused. "We could always invite my mother down to instruct you. She's mixed with plenty of wealthy folk during her life. She could be a big help."

"Instruct me? Daniel Sullivan!" I rounded on him. I'd opened my mouth to give him a piece of my mind when there was a soft knock on the door and Mary came in.

"Excuse me, Captain Sullivan. Cook says that dinner is ready and she is not sure what time you would like to eat."

"Well, not five fifteen." I looked at Daniel. "Heaven only knows what dinner will be. This cook has no idea what we like to eat at all." I turned to Mary. "We normally eat at seven if Captain Sullivan is not working, and seven thirty on a day Captain Sullivan works."

Then a thought struck me. "Which he won't be doing anymore, so seven will be fine every day."

"I'll tell the cook. And I'll have dinner ready for you on the table at seven." Mary gave a little bob of a curtsey and left the room.

"You see how you handled that? Just like a lady of the manor." Daniel grinned at me and I didn't feel like fighting with him anymore.

I took Daniel up to the nursery so we could both be with Liam while he ate his supper, then had his bath and a story. He was not going to forget that he had loving parents! Then Daniel discovered an amply stocked liquor cabinet and we both had a sherry before dinner. I had to admit the new situation did come with a few privileges, such as someone else clearing away my meals and doing the laundry. Really, I had nothing to complain about if I could just find a way to amuse myself.

At seven o'clock on the dot Mary summoned us to the dining room. The table was laid for two. There were candles in silver candlesticks and they threw a soft light, making the room look less severe. I took my seat opposite Daniel. Mary opened the dumbwaiter and lifted a casserole dish onto the table. She took off the lid and again the smell of garlic hit me. She spooned a red, congealed mass onto my plate and then his. Then she gave a little bow and went to leave.

Daniel stared at his plate. "Mary, wait a minute. What is this?"

"Cook says it's rigatoni, sir. A kind of pasta."

Daniel prodded it suspiciously with his fork. "And what sort of meat goes with it? And green vegetables?"

Mary looked a trifle embarrassed. "I'm afraid it's just the pasta, sir. No meat. There is some sort of shredded cheese to go on top of it."

Daniel gave me a look, and I couldn't tell if it was of warning or despair. I spooned some of the cheese from the dish onto the red blob on my plate. The dish might have been palatable at five o'clock. By seven it had overcooked, congealed, and dried out. We ate, bravely, but I can't say I'd ever eaten anything as disgusting, even my mother's tripe and onions, which was my least favorite dish.

Instead of a dessert there was another sort of cheese, this one hard and acidy, and some of the bread from lunchtime, now quite dry and impossible to chew. I had grown up eating meat and potatoes. Sid and Gus had broadened my tastes, but I confess that at home I like to eat what I know. Surely Italian food must be delicious when prepared by an expert cook, but I was beginning to suspect that Constanza had never worked as a cook before.

As we ate, I noticed Bridie picking at her food. She was normally a healthy eater. "Is something wrong?" I asked.

She shook her head. "I'm just nervous about the outing tomorrow. I don't know what to wear."

"It will be cold on a boat. Wear your cape over your warmest dress."

"But that cape looks old," she said. "It doesn't have any fur or anything."

"Bridie, we can't be what we are not," I said. "If the other girls judge you by what you wear, then shame on them."

"You're probably smarter than the bunch of them," Daniel added.

"Maybe, but they don't care about being smart. They care about looking fashionable."

"Then this may be the wrong school for you," I said. "The last one wasn't right because those kids didn't want to learn, and this one is too hoity-toity. There must be a middle ground."

Her cheeks flushed. "Oh, I like the school all right. The teachers are wonderful. I'm learning so much. It's just . . ."

"I understand," I said. "Give it time, Bridie. You've only been there a month. You will make friends."

"I don't know about that." She stood up. "May I be excused? I have homework."

As she went, Daniel turned to me. "We should never have allowed your friends to interfere," he said. "Now the girl is miserable."

"But they are paying for a good school for her, Daniel. We should be grateful. They want her to get into Vassar."

"I think we should learn to be grateful for what we have," he said, "and not reach for what we can't have."

"Oh—thus speaks the man who has given up a promising police career to run for office?" I demanded. "Who has stuck his family into a strange house with a cook who can't cook?"

Daniel looked at me for a second, then smiled. "It will all work out, Molly. I promise. It won't be forever. Just be patient."

"When have you ever known me to be patient?" I demanded, making him laugh out loud.

As we left the dining room Daniel drew close to me. "You need to have a word with that woman in the morning," he said. "Tell her that cooks are ten a penny in New York and she'd better pull her socks up or she'll be gone."

"But your darling Finn put her here," I reminded him. "He wouldn't allow her to be sacked."

Daniel gave a cross between a sigh and a groan. "You're right. Of course, our hands are tied. But for heaven's sake show her what we like to eat. Teach her how to cook it, if necessary."

"Oh, and you're putting this on my back now, are you? Nice of you."

"You were just complaining that you had nothing to do all day," he said sweetly. "Now you have a challenge to keep you busy."

There were times when I'd have liked to clobber him one.

That night we lay in our big new bed in the unfamiliar room. I wasn't used to such a large space around me, nor to the noises coming from a major thoroughfare outside our window. Hansom cabs clattered past, automobiles honked their horns. In the distance I heard the fire wagon sounding its bell as the horses galloped to a fire. I tried to sleep, but sleep would not come. *What am I doing here?* It felt as if I had stumbled into a dream and didn't know the way out.

❧ Ten ❧

I suppose I must have drifted off to sleep eventually, because I opened my eyes to cold gray morning light. When I first woke, I wasn't sure where I was. It was strange to wake in a warm room. It took a whole minute of staring at the ceiling to remember I was in a new house. As soon as I remembered that, I realized that it was the day of Bridie's outing. She had only reminded me about it a hundred times the night before. Luckily, I had found my warm two-piece the night before and Bridie had laid out her clothes. We dressed quickly. I decided I would not risk whatever Constanza might prepare for breakfast. Surely they would give us something on the boat. I left Daniel to the mercy of the maids and the cook and Liam playing happily with Aileen in the nursery.

It was just after eight when we came down the steps onto Fifth Avenue. Even though it was bright and sunny I had made sure that Bridie and I had our warmest capes on. It was sure to be freezing in the harbor. We were just setting off when Jack, our Tammany minder, came running up to us. "Excuse me, Mrs. Sullivan." He stopped, panting, beside us. "Where you headed?"

Really, I shouldn't have to explain my business every time I leave

74

the house! "We are going on a school outing for Bridie." I tried to remain patient. It wasn't his fault he had been given this assignment.

"Finn told me to get you a taxicab and take you wherever you need to go." Jack started looking down the street as if searching.

"We are perfectly capable of taking the el and not likely to be accosted on our way to the Chelsea Piers," I said frostily, although come to think of it I had been badly injured in an el accident once before.

"The docks?" Jack's eyebrows lifted. "I gotta take you there, missus, or Finn will have my head."

I was about to reply that I refused to be taken all over the city as if I couldn't take care of myself when Jack stepped out into the street and gave a piercing whistle. A shiny red taxicab pulled over right in front of us, and Jack opened the door. I looked at Bridie and shrugged. It would seem rather ridiculous to leave a perfectly good taxicab empty while we walked to the el. I assumed that Jack was going to pay for it since he had called it, and I was right.

"Did you say the Chelsea Piers, Mrs. Sullivan?" he asked.

"Yes, please. It's a day cruise so it will be one of the smaller piers for ferries, I think."

"Yes, I know which pier the harbor ferries go from." Jack gave directions to the taxi driver and climbed in beside us. We shot off up the street.

Jack kept up a running commentary all the way to the pier; the people going by, the current chance of the Tammany Hall ticket against "that corrupt Hearst fellow," his wife's cough and his mother-in-law's rheumatism. It hadn't occurred to me that Jack had a wife, much less a mother-in-law, but I heard all about them with not a chance to get a word in edgewise. To my surprise I started to find him likeable. I had only thought of him before as a silly imposition. As we neared the docks he described the big steamers that were currently in and the cargo they carried with great excitement. "There are a lot of happy lumpers heading for that ship, they'll have work for days on that one."

"Jack, were you a longshoreman?" I asked, curious. "Is that why you wear that hook on your belt? And what about Finn, he wears that hook but he doesn't seem to have anything to do with ships anymore."

"I was a lumper, an unloader, before I came to work for Finn," he explained. "If you don't have your hook on you won't get hired for a single job. Finn was my stevedore before he had anything to do with politics. Now I guess we both wear the hook to show we're on the side of the longshoremen. Even Big Bill puts one on for rallies, and I would bet he hasn't unloaded a ship in twenty years! Well, here we are, missus," he added.

As he was speaking the taxicab slowed to a crawl and had to weave in and out of the crowded dockland scene—piles of cargo, carts, and barrows carrying unloaded luggage from a big liner, the whole place busy with commerce like an anthill. Adding to this was the cacophony of hoots, of whistles from tugboats and coastal steamers, the grinding of winches and cranes and shouts of longshoremen. We came out to the waterfront and pulled up at a small pier. The boat that was moored there was actually quite large, although it was dwarfed by the steamer the next dock over. "I have a job to do this afternoon, missus," Jack said as he opened the door and helped us out, "so Finn will be by to collect you. I assume you will be in by three if this is a school outing."

I started to tell him that I would not need collecting as I was not a piece of mail, but before I could take a single breath he had climbed back in the taxicab and was gone. Other automobiles pulled up, not taxicabs but chauffeur-driven fancy autos. We walked down the dock toward the ferry and then stopped, looking at the view across the Hudson to New Jersey before turning back to see who else was arriving.

"Do you see any of your friends here yet?" I asked.

"I'm not sure I exactly have friends." Bridie looked nervous. I put my arm around her shoulders.

"I'm quite excited to meet the other mothers," I said to Bridie.

"It might be interesting to have some other women to talk to." But the women getting out of the autos and helping out the beautifully dressed young ladies looked much too young to be mothers of teen-agers. And I saw uniforms peeking out from under their coats. Bridie looked at me, stricken. "They've all brought their maids," she said. "Quick, let's get aboard before they see us."

"They have to see us sometime, we are going on the same boat. I'm sure some other mothers will have come to chaperone," I said, but I let her hurry me down the dock and onto the boat. It was a white pleasure cruiser with the large paddle wheel at the rear of the boat. I could see the windows of cabins on the lower deck below us. CITY OF TROY was printed on her front bow. We were helped across the gangplank by a handsome young man in uniform and directed toward a seating area under a bright blue canvas awning on the top deck. I imagine two hundred people could have comfortably gathered there, but there were tables set out for about sixty. They were small round tables that looked as if they would be more useful for a garden party than a boat. I hoped we wouldn't run into any big waves or they might all tip over! Bridie hurried to an empty table in the farthest corner and sat looking at her feet. I pulled out a chair and took a seat beside her. There were plates of pastries put out for us. I offered one to Bridie, and took one myself. Another young man in uniform offered us some coffee, which I gratefully accepted.

"Who is this, Bridie?" A pleasant-looking woman of about fifty walked up to us. She had a bright, alert face and it lit up when she smiled at Bridie. Bridie stood up quickly and I followed.

"This is my mother, Molly Sullivan, Miss Jones. Mama, this is Miss Jones, our history teacher."

"I am so glad to meet you, Mrs. Sullivan." Miss Jones turned her beaming smile on me. "Bridie is such a lovely addition to our school community."

"Pleased to meet you, Miss Jones." She held out her hand and I shook it. "Are you leading the school outing today?"

"Oh, yes. We are going to be learning about the history of immigration in our country. First we will go by the Battery, where the settlers met with the Indians. Do you remember which tribe it was, Bridie?"

"The Lenape," Bridie said confidently and I silently thanked this nice woman for making sure she felt welcomed.

"And then we will pass by Ellis Island, of course, and talk about the waves of immigrants who have come through there, and then finally Lady Liberty herself." She beamed as if no one could possibly think of a more enjoyable way to spend a school day. "Oh, I think we're pushing off," she said as I felt the boat lurch slightly. "I'll wait until we are out in the middle of the river and then call you girls together."

"She seems really nice," I said to Bridie as Miss Jones walked out of earshot.

"She's peachy!" Bridie said fervently.

The girl at the nearest table looked up and saw us. She had pale yellow hair tucked under a fashionable dark blue hat that was threatening to come off in the wind from the Hudson. She was wearing a silk day dress in the same color with a matching heavy wool cape with silver buckles. She looked more like a lady's dress advertisement than a schoolgirl. She was seated with another similarly dressed girl. I could see why Bridie had been complaining about her school clothes. These girls looked like little fashion plates out of *Ladies' Home Journal*. She nudged the girl next to her. "Good morning, Bridie," she called across to us, "did you bring your nanny with you? I miss my nanny, don't you, Helen? She left when I was ten, but perhaps your parents don't feel you can get about the city with just a maid yet." Her voice was perfectly polite and smooth but caused Helen to burst out into a laugh that she turned into a cough.

I hoped Bridie would stand up for herself, but she seemed tongue-tied and I was not going to let the girl's rudeness go without comment. "I am Mrs. Sullivan, Bridie's mother," I said pleasantly. "What is your name, young lady?"

"That's Blanche," Bridie said in an embarrassed whisper.

"Well, Blanche, I do think it is a shame your nanny left you quite so early because I have heard they are quite good at teaching young ladies manners." I locked eyes with her and she was the first to look away. I realized that she was even younger than Bridie. As she blushed she looked like a little girl in her mother's clothes and I was glad that I dressed Bridie as a regular schoolgirl. We would have a long talk when we got home, I decided. I wasn't going to have her idolize silly little girls playing dress-up no matter how much money their fathers had.

"Come on, my darling, let's go for a walk," I said. I took Bridie's hand and led her to the front of the boat. The wind was very strong as the boat moved quite quickly through the gray waters, steaming ahead. As far as I could see on both sides brand-new piers stretched out into the river from the New York and New Jersey shores. Good for commerce, I supposed, but it made the river look dirty and cluttered. A huge steamship passed us heading for the Chelsea Piers and I thought of Jack and the longshoremen waiting with their hooks to unload her. If I hadn't met Daniel I might be the wife of one of those longshoremen, living in a tenement and waiting each night to see if he had gotten enough work to keep us going another day. Here I was on a pleasure cruise with upper-class young ladies. Honestly, I was still not sure which life suited me better. I could still hear my mother's voice in my head, "You've got ideas above your station, my girl, and they will get you into trouble someday."

Miss Jones called all the girls together as we approached the Battery and started giving a lecture on the original inhabitants of Manhattan and the first Dutch settlers. I found that two other mothers had come along and we sat together at a table drinking coffee and making polite conversation about the weather. I could hear Miss Jones's lecture change to the topic of immigration as we approached Ellis Island. I couldn't pass it myself without remembering my feelings of fear on first arriving and the complicated business with Rose McSweeney a few months ago. I saw Bridie looking at me and gave her an encouraging smile. And then we were docking at the Statue of Liberty. She looked absolutely enormous from below. The girls were allowed to climb the many steps to her crown while the chaperones stayed gratefully below. We could hear their excited voices. They sounded like young girls enjoying themselves after all.

Bridie sat with me on the way back while most of the girls stood around the rails, chattering excitedly. "Don't worry, you'll make friends," I assured her. "It just takes time." I patted her lap.

We were startled as a loud bell clanged.

"Excuse me, may I have your attention." A muscular uniformed man I assumed to be the captain was standing at the front of the boat with a serious expression on his face. "I'm afraid that we have a small emergency—a little fire on board. Now, please don't panic." He raised his hands palm down to calm us as girls rose from their seats as if looking for a place to run to. "Panic is the only thing that could do us any harm at this moment. Please believe we have it under control, but I need you to sit here on deck and be ready to disembark as soon as we dock."

"I'll keep them calm." Miss Jones stood and came up to the captain. "Julia, stop your screaming immediately. Winifred, sit calmly and quietly. The captain has this under control." Under her now stern gaze the girls obeyed and sat quietly. I realized then that I could smell smoke and had been smelling it for some time, taking it for a fire coming from the bank somewhere. I could see no sign of flames, but I did see a thin trail of smoke escaping from the back of the ship. My heart began to race.

"Trust me, ladies, I'll get you home safely," the captain said, then ran to the back of the ship, disappearing below deck. I hadn't paid any attention to how many crew members were on board, but now I saw four or five men lowering buckets for water and disappearing down the stairs in the back of the ship. I supposed the engine room was below deck. Bridie and I were the closest to the engine room, and I heard the men swearing unreservedly as they pulled up buckets of water.

"Jesus Christ, I told you this was going to happen," I heard an older man say to a younger as they rushed past. "You can't keep pushing a boat like this without maintenance and improvements."

I felt the boat swing around. We were still in the middle of the harbor but now headed straight for the nearest pier on the New York side of the river. The men continued with the buckets for about ten minutes and then seemed to give up on their attempt to put out the fire. They came up on deck and stood, two by the gangplank and three on either side ready to man the lifeboats. I noticed there was a small rowboat on either side that could be lowered down. Perhaps eight people could fit in either rowboat, not nearly enough for all of us on board. I hoped the crew weren't planning on using them to desert us and save themselves. I have to confess my heart was thumping, although I tried to look calm and unworried for Bridie's sake.

All eyes were on the pier as it came closer and closer. Everyone was standing now and pushing toward the gangplank wanting to be the first off once it was lowered. Now we could hear the crackling of the flames behind us and started to feel the heat. I began to plan my escape. "Take your cape off," I ordered Bridie. "And be ready to go overboard if we need to."

❧ Eleven ❧

"Take my cape off?" Bridie looked terrified. "Why?"

"In case we have to swim to shore. Your cape will only drag you down." I took mine off and contemplated my skirts. I was in my sturdy two-piece wool suit and I was sure the wool would be impossible to swim in. I looked up and saw how white Bridie's face was.

"Now don't tell me you didn't join your cousins in the East River growing up. I know you can swim."

She removed the cape obediently and I led us closer to the rails and out of the crowd of pushing and shoving girls. One part of my mind thought this was crazy. It didn't seem possible that these well-dressed and well-behaved people who had been sitting calmly on a deck moments ago were facing a life-and-death situation, but I wasn't going to risk dying just to appear well behaved. I would swim if I had to.

The pier was much closer now and it seemed we were going to make it.

"Don't crowd the sailors, girls," Miss Jones called, keeping them in a group so that the crewmen could get ropes ready to throw. The pier was five yards away, then four, three, two. We bumped against it and the boat rocked so violently that some of the ladies who were standing fell into each other. Several girls screamed. The men at the gangplank were struggling to slide it down. The boat seemed to be at a strange angle and the gangplank kept falling short each time they tried.

"We can't make fast here. We need to go downriver," one of the men yelled over the screams and sobs of the girls and maids. A crewman fended us off and we started backing into the stream. I stared at them, incredulous. How could we not make fast? Why were we headed back out? I started forward toward the gangplank to see for myself what had happened. Surely we could tie up on a pier?

I heard a wailing scream and turned back. Flames ran up the ropes holding the awning and in seconds the entire structure was engulfed and fell to the deck. A screaming crowd pushed me back and I fought to catch my breath. Only three people were caught on the other side of the flames. Blanche, her maid, and Bridie.

I struggled to push forward, terror surging in my chest. I had to get to Bridie. Then, as I watched in horror, Blanche's silk dress caught on fire. The flames began at the bottom of the skirt and ran quickly up the flimsy fabric. She screamed a high wail and seemed frozen in terror. Her maid backed up away from the flames to the rail, then, realizing that they were on every side of her, she climbed the rail and jumped off.

"Man overboard," cried one of the crewmen, struggling to get to the lifeboat to let it down. But the terrified crowd would not be moved a step closer to those flames. The boat gave a huge lurch again. All my attention was on Bridie and then, as I watched, she calmly picked up her cape where she had laid it across the back of the chair. Holding it out in front of her, she leaped on Blanche, tackling her to the ground and beating at her until the flames on her skirt were out.

"Ladies, off the boat, quickly." Miss Jones's voice, loud as only a teacher could make it, cut across the noise of screaming, and I realized that the lurch had been us arriving at the next pier. The gangplank was down and girls were being thrown down it with speed and no elegance by the crewmen. They staggered onto the pier and ran along it. The captain, coming up from below to witness the deck in flames, stood in the doorway for a minute, considering what to do. Now that the wind was no longer keeping them at bay, the flames were burning the ropes with great intensity. The awning was still lying across the deck—a carpet of flickering flames—making a wall between the girls and me. But it was burning itself out and the deck had not yet caught beneath it. I grabbed the side of one of the tables and pushed it so that the legs caught against the burning canvas. I pushed with all my might, dragging the material to one side, creating a gap of several feet between the flames and the side of the boat. I jumped back before my skirts caught on fire.

"Bridie!" I screamed. "Through here." Bridie was helping a sobbing Blanche up to her feet and didn't hear me, but the captain did. He rushed forward, pushing the two girls in front of him between the table and the rail, shielding them with his own body. Then Bridie saw me and rushed into my arms.

"Come on, let's get off." I had to raise my voice above the crackle of flames. The table that I had used was now engulfed.

"Blanche!" Bridie yelled. "She's not moving." And Blanche was standing immobile just as the captain had left her. We both rushed back and each grabbed an arm.

"Come on!" I urged as we pulled her onto the gangplank and down onto the pier. We were the last off the boat except the captain, who, true to tradition and decency, made sure everyone was safe before leaving. I watched him run down the gangplank and call to the crew to help push the boat out into the river. They untied her and worked with long poles, pushing her back out into the river. I realized they were trying to save the pier, but it was too late. The tarred pilings were already burning. Continuing to drag Blanche, Bridie and I staggered down the pier, not stopping until we were safely on land. There we watched the boat drifting out into the harbor. There was an explosion, the boat rocked, and flames shot into the air as it was completely engulfed.

"Blanche, are you hurt? We must get you to a doctor immediately!" Miss Jones rushed up to us. She bent to examine Blanche's legs. The silk dress and petticoat below now ended in a long line of char at her knees.

"I'm okay." Blanche sounded stunned. "Bridie put it out." She squeezed Bridie's hand that she was still holding. "Thank you. I was so scared. I thought I was going to die."

"You don't seem to be burned, which is a miracle," Miss Jones said, straightening up. "That was very brave." She turned to Bridie. "And just the right thing to do. Well done."

Bridie flushed. "I remembered my papa telling me what the firemen do if someone is on fire."

Just then we heard the sound of bells and several fire engines arrived, the firemen unloading hoses and pumps, trying to stop the fire on the pier from spreading to the wooden buildings on the dock. We were on a small dock, probably a private one. I was amazed and grateful that such a big boat had been able to moor here at all. I suspected that the owner would not be as grateful. Who could expect a flaming ship to tie up and burn your jetty to the ground? I wondered where in the city we were. We had not yet reached the Chelsea Piers, but I suspected we were not far. I turned to Bridie. "I think I would like to just go home. Are you feeling well enough to walk to the el and catch it home?"

She nodded, but Blanche tightened her grip on her hand. "Please don't leave me alone. My chauffeur won't know where to find me. Stay with me, Bridie." I glanced at Bridie, who looked back at me with surprise. I had heard nothing about Blanche except how rude she was to Bridie. This was a strange development. Then for the first time I remembered Blanche's maid. What had become of her? Poor Blanche must be feeling traumatized by the whole affair. And she was, after all, just a little girl, however grown-up she acted.

"Can you contact her parents?" I asked Miss Jones. "I can stay with her until they come."

"I would appreciate that, Mrs. Sullivan. I need to round up all the girls and see what I need to do to get them home safely." Miss Jones gave me a grateful smile and hurried off.

Blanche was now shivering uncontrollably and her face was ghostly white. "Come on, let's see if we can find her somewhere to sit down." I put my arm around the girl and led her away from the dock, looking for a place to sit. I couldn't take her into a tavern, but perhaps we could find a café to get her off her feet. She was still clutching Bridie's hand as if it were her lifeline.

"Mrs. Sullivan! Mrs. Sullivan!" I realized that someone had been calling my name for a while. I looked up to see Finn running toward me. "I'm so glad you're all right," he began as he drew level. "I was waiting at the Chelsea Piers and heard that the *City of Troy* had gone up in flames." He looked panicked, and I was touched that he had been that concerned for us. Surely we were just part of his job, weren't we?

"Thank you for finding us. We really want to get home," I said gratefully. "And can we help this young lady get home too? She's had quite a shock. Her maid jumped into the river and left her and her dress was burned in the fire."

"Of course. We can take her to your house if you don't mind and call her parents from there. I'll just go and find a taxicab." He left as quickly as he had come.

"Stay here, I have to let your teacher know you are leaving," I said to Bridie as I went to find Miss Jones. I let her know that I would be taking both girls home and placing a call to Blanche's parents from there.

"Thank you so much, Mrs. Sullivan. That would be the best. I think she may be in shock and I would imagine they would want a doctor to see to her."

The taxicab was pulling up just as I got back to the girls, and Finn jumped out to hold the door for us. Blanche was still shaking, and he

86

held out a hand to help her in. As he looked at her his face changed. "Miss Blanche?"

She looked up and seemed to come to herself for the first time since the fire. "Finn? Are you taking me home to Mama and Papa?"

"Yes, we'll get you home. Don't worry. Everything is going to be all right." He spoke gently and then looked around. "Where's Mary Jane?"

"She jumped off the boat. She left me all alone." Blanche's face crumpled and tears sprang into her eyes. "I don't know if she can swim. Did she die?"

Finn turned to me. "I think Miss Blanche may be in shock and I think she should be in a quiet place and have a hot drink. I had better find out what happened to her maid so she doesn't worry." He spoke gently to Blanche. "Take this taxicab to Mrs. Sullivan's house and I'll go and talk to the crewmen to try to find out what happened to her." He turned to me. "Can you take her home? I will find her mother and bring her to your house." I nodded and he was gone before I could ask any more questions.

We climbed into the taxicab and I gave the driver my address. I almost told him to go to Patchin Place before I remembered the new address on Fifth Avenue. Then I turned to Blanche.

"How do you know Finn?" I had a suspicion but needed it confirmed.

"He works for my father. I'm Blanche McCormick. My dad is Big Bill."

❧ Twelve ❧

Blanche would not let go of Bridie's hand for the whole ride home.

"Let's telephone your mother right away," I said to Blanche as Mary opened the door for us. She stared in horror at the blackened ruins of Blanche's dress but was too well trained to say anything.

"I think she is out for the afternoon." Blanche now sounded like a scared little girl, nothing at all like the scornful rich girl who had confronted us on the boat.

"We will leave a message, then." What I wouldn't give for a good cup of tea right now, the Irish medicine for everything from surgery to shock. But alas my teapot was still residing in Patchin Place. "Mary, we have been in a terrible accident. Please bring us all a small dose of brandy. We have had a bit of a shock. And then have Aileen run a lukewarm bath for this young lady." We walked into the front parlor and Blanche hesitated to sit on the sofa, obviously not wanting to mark it with the soot on her dress.

"Go ahead and sit. You've had quite an ordeal." Blanche sank into the sofa right beside Bridie. "Here's what we are going to do." Mary appeared with a tray with some small glasses on it and a brandy decanter. "You are going to sip this and feel a little better." I handed both of the girls a glass. "Then we will get you upstairs into a cool bath. You shouldn't put hot water on your skin in case you have any burns. Then we will lend you one of Bridie's dresses to get you home as soon as someone can come for you." I wondered if I would hear an outburst about having to wear one of Bridie's dresses home, but instead Blanche sipped her brandy obediently and managed a little smile.

"How does your family seem to know just what to do? First Bridie knew how to save me from the fire and now you know just what to do to make me feel better."

"We've had to take care of ourselves for most of our lives, having had no servants to do it for us," I said, thinking that those rich girls could learn a thing or two from Bridie. "I'm so glad that Bridie's father taught her what to do in a fire, and I'm just doing for you what my mother would have done for me." Probably while telling me what a fool I was and how I would come to a bad end, I thought to myself.

The color came back into Blanche's face as she sat and sipped the brandy. When Aileen came downstairs to say the bath was ready, Blanche followed her meekly.

"Run upstairs and look for one of your school dresses," I instructed Bridie. "Nothing fancy, just with soft fabric in case her skin is raw." Bridie gave a delighted grin at the thought of Blanche McCormick in one of her unfashionable school dresses and went upstairs herself.

I went into the back parlor and lifted the telephone to my ear. "Central 355," I gave the number that Blanche had given me and waited while I was connected.

"McCormick residence," a rather smooth and snooty voice answered the phone.

"May I speak to the lady of the house, please."

"I'm afraid she is out at the moment," the voice said. "Would you care to leave a message?"

I left the message that Blanche had been in a fire but was safely at my house. I stumbled a bit giving our house address and felt a bit of a fool. If the voice on the other end of the line was shocked by my news or disbelieving, I had no idea. He merely said he would inform Mrs. McCormick in those formal unflappable tones.

I was just hanging up when Mary walked into the room, followed, to my surprise, by Finn. She might have at least warned me that he was here or given me a chance to say I was resting. My head was now aching terribly, probably from the smoke and the fact that I had had only one small bun to eat yet. But I supposed that in Mary's eyes this was Finn's house more than mine and he would be given admittance whenever he wanted.

"How is Miss Blanche?" he asked immediately.

"I think she is physically all right," I said, motioning for him to sit down, "but very shaken up. She is upstairs washing the ash off. Did you find her maid?"

"I did. One of the crewmen pulled her to shore. She has been taken to a local hospital, but I think she will be okay. I don't like her chances with Big Bill, though, when he learns she left his daughter on a burning boat."

"I think she panicked," I said sympathetically. "The flames were all around her."

"How did Blanche get out of there, then?" Finn asked. I described what Bridie had done to save Blanche and the brave captain who had dragged the girls out of the flames. I might have been a bit too descriptive, because Finn looked quite sick. The same panicked look I had seen on the dock came back into his eyes. He actually swayed as he sat.

"Finn, are you all right?" I asked, concerned. "You look white as a sheet."

"Yes, I have just been running around a lot today with no food since breakfast."

"You had better have a brandy as well." I led him back into the front parlor, poured a glass, and handed it to him. He downed it in one gulp and put the glass back on the tray.

90

"I'd offer you something to eat but I don't know where anything is yet. Are you sure you are okay?" I asked again. He was staring at the unlit fireplace as if in a different world.

"Yes, I'm sorry." He seemed to come to himself and focused on me. "Molly, I'm sorry. I've had a bit of a shock. My older brother was killed in a boat fire on the Hudson, and hearing you describe your ordeal, it brought it back to me." He tried to smile, but it came out as more of a grimace.

"I'm so sorry. What a terrible loss. Do boats catch fire often on the Hudson, then?" I was afraid I was babbling a bit and not offering the condolence I knew I should. In my defense my head was aching quite badly and I desperately wanted a cup of tea and something normal to eat.

"Just twice now that I know of. I suppose that is why it was such a shock." He stood up abruptly. "Have you been in contact with Blanche's parents?"

"I left a message at the house for Mrs. McCormick but I am not sure the person who answered realized the importance of the message. He seemed completely unconcerned."

"That will be the butler, Roberts. He would sound unconcerned if the Lord was descending from heaven with all his angels. And I doubt if he knows where Mrs. McCormick is, but I do. I'll go and fetch her. Unless you want me to take Blanche home."

"I would feel better if her mother saw her first." The offer was tempting, but I had to consider what the girl had just been through. "She may think Blanche should be seen by a doctor before she goes rattling around in a taxicab."

"I'm sure she'll come over in the Pierce Motorcar." He smiled now and was starting to look more like himself. "And it won't rattle, I assure you. I'd give up politicking any day if Big Bill would let me be the chauffeur and drive that thing around!"

"It looks to me like you're pretty valuable to him just as you are."

I smiled back. "You seem to have a finger in every pie." My smile faded. "Including my domestic arrangements, and I want to talk to you about that."

"I think I had better go and fetch Mrs. McCormick." Finn suddenly seemed very eager to leave. "I'll just see if Mary can get me my hat." And he was gone.

I made my way down to the kitchen. Constanza was nowhere to be seen, but I did find the bread box, toasted and buttered some bread, then sprinkled some sugar on it. I carried it up on a tray and set it on the dining room table. Mary must have heard me, because she came hurrying in.

"I could have done that for you, Mrs. Sullivan." She looked quite shocked. I suppose her former employers had not cooked for themselves. Of course, if they had employed Constanza, I was sure they had eaten out a lot or starved.

"I didn't know where you were or how to get you and I was hungry." I was too tired to play the lady of the manor. I took a big bite of the toast.

"The bell in the parlor rings in my room," Mary said in a tone that indicated I should have known this.

"Well, now that you are here, can you see if the girls are dressed and ask them to come down? I'm sure they are hungry too. And if you can find Constanza, please ask her to make us some coffee. I didn't know where to find the pot."

Blanche looked much younger as she came down dressed in Bridie's school dress. Her cheeks were clean and red. Her hair was wet and tied back with a ribbon of Bridie's. Her face lit up when she saw the toast. "I'm starving," she said.

"Me too," Bridie said, coming into the room after her.

"Well, this is all there is for right now until I sort out the kitchen." I handed out the toast and Mary came in with the coffee. Blanche and Bridie sat side by side whispering to each other and giggling.

With something in my stomach my headache was starting to recede, and I looked at the girls with a smile. If it took a boat fire for Bridie to make a friend perhaps the morning had been worth it. Neither of them seemed worse for wear.

It was almost five o'clock when Mary came in to announce that Mrs. McCormick was at the door. She came in breathless with a panicked look and rushed over to Blanche.

"Oh, my darling!" Blanche stood up and her mother swept her into her arms. "Are you hurt? Finn said you were in a fire."

"I was," and Blanche, who just minutes ago had been laughing happily with Bridie, burst into tears. "My dress caught on fire and I was almost burned up. Mary Jane jumped off the boat and left me all alone. Then Bridie threw herself on me and put out the flames."

"Are you burned?" Mrs. McCormick stood back to look at Blanche. "And what are you wearing?"

"Bridie let me wear one of her dresses. Mine was all burned up. Mrs. Sullivan brought me home because I was half-naked!" I could tell now that Bridie and Blanche were destined to be friends. She had the same gift for exaggeration. "But my skin wasn't burned. Just the dress." Mrs. McCormick looked as if she wasn't sure if she should laugh or scream with panic. She decided on laughter and her face relaxed. She seemed to be aware of Bridie and me for the first time.

"I'm so sorry, Mrs. Sullivan." She held out her hand. "Please put my rudeness down to a mother's concern. It is so nice to see you again. I had no idea that our daughters were at the same school when we had dinner together. I'm afraid I don't remember you mentioning a daughter at all."

"I am not sure I mentioned my children. And please call me Molly." I took her hand and shook it. "I was a bit startled to find myself at Delmonico's! Not usually the society that I move in. This is Bridie." I gestured for Bridie to stand up and greet her.

"Nice to meet you, Mrs. McCormick," Bridie said, offering her hand and giving a little bob of a curtsey. She didn't take it and instead put both of her arms around Bridie. "You brave girl, thank you for rescuing my Blanche." Bridie looked embarrassed but pleased.

"Mrs. Sullivan," Mrs. McCormick began.

"Please call me Molly," I interrupted.

"Then you must call me Lucy. Since our husbands will be endlessly talking politics together we will have to be allies. Does Bridie have any brothers or sisters?"

"That's a bit complicated. Bridie is actually my ward whom I am hoping to adopt." I gave her a smile. "And I have a little boy, Liam, who is upstairs with his nursemaid." A pang of guilt shot through me. Was he upstairs? I hadn't even been up to check that he was all right.

"I am so thankful that you rescued Blanche and it was so kind of you to take her home. Finn has been telling me all about it. At first I couldn't understand at all why we were coming to Bill's first house, but now it makes perfect sense." She gave a charming little laugh.

"This was Mr. McCormick's house? Wouldn't that make it yours as well?" I asked, puzzled.

"No, this was his house with his first wife, Elsie. He lived here when I first met him. He had business with my father and we came to dinner over here several times." She looked around the room as if trying to see if it fit her memories. "I haven't been here since."

"What was his first wife like?" I couldn't contain my curiosity. Lucy McCormick seemed so opposite of her big, brash husband I wondered if his first wife had been the same. I realized as I asked that the question was rather rude and flushed, but she didn't seem to notice.

"I'm afraid I never met her. She had died before I met Bill. I gather she had been an invalid for some time, with a wasting disease that got progressively worse. Of course it was very sad for Bill and little Junior. That was his nursery upstairs where your little boy's is." There was a knock on the open door of the parlor, and Mary came around it.

94

"Mr. Finnegan is outside with the motorcar. He asked me to remind Mrs. McCormick that she has guests expected for dinner soon."

"Can you tell him I will be right there?" Lucy said to Mary and then turned to Blanche. "Do you have all your things? Are you ready to go?"

"All my things are burned up. I had such a nice little handbag too, although there was only a dollar in it."

"We can get you another handbag. I am so thankful you weren't hurt. We will have to light a special candle to Our Lady on Sunday to give thanks." Lucy turned to me. "Thank you so much again, Mrs. . . . Molly. I hope we will be seeing you soon in more pleasant circumstances." Lucy started walking out of the room, but Blanche hesitated.

"Mom, wait." Lucy turned back to look at her daughter. "Can Bridie come over to dinner?"

"Not tonight, Blanche. We have guests."

"But then I'll be up in my room all by myself and I won't even have Mary Jane with me. Please, Mom. Please." Her voice was pleading. Clearly she was used to doing this to get what she wanted.

"Tonight you can come down and eat with us," Lucy began in a placating tone.

"Not with Papa. He'll be talking about boats and taxes and railroads all night." Blanche's voice was now whiny.

"Then you can eat in your room. It's your choice." Lucy's voice was firm. Blanche took Bridie's hand and held it tightly, refusing to be moved. She had her father's Irish fire and stubbornness, it seemed. Poor upper-class Lucy McCormick would have her hands full with those two.

"But, Mom, she saved my life. We have to have her over for dinner. If it weren't for Bridie your daughter would be nothing but a pile of ashes."

"I think we are free tomorrow." Lucy squinted her eyes as if trying to see an imaginary date book in her head. "It's Saturday, isn't it?

No school. Why don't we take Bridie out to lunch? That is, if Mrs. Sullivan gives permission," she said, turning to me.

"Yes, of course," I said. "I'm glad for Bridie to have a school friend. Where shall we meet?"

"We will come around tomorrow in the motorcar about eleven to pick Bridie up. There is no need to inconvenience you." She turned a smile on Bridie. "I can tell that Blanche has taken a liking to you. She is very passionate about her friends."

With this treat for tomorrow planned, Blanche dropped Bridie's hand and gave her a swift hug. "See you tomorrow then, Bridie," she said. Lucy and Blanche walked out the door arm in arm. "Can we go to Macy's first to get a new handbag?" she asked her mom as they were leaving.

Bridie and I exchanged a look.

"I wouldn't like my chances if I talked to you or Papa that way," she said with a grin. "I think Blanche is a little spoiled but very sweet."

"Let's go and check on Liam, shall we? I've been neglecting him terribly all day." I practically ran up the stairs to the nursery. A terrible vision of Liam alone and soiled up in the nursery came to me. But as Bridie and I reached the top landing we could already hear his laughter. I opened the door to the nursery and saw Aileen sitting on the floor with Liam. They were building a large tower of blocks and then Liam was knocking them down and squealing with laughter. He looked up as I came in and ran to me with a big smile on his face.

"Mama. We've built towers. And Liam knocks down his blocks!"

"I can see that." I smiled. "It looks like you had a wonderful morning, Aileen. Thank you for taking such good care of him. I would have been up earlier, but we have had a bit of an adventure."

"It was a pleasure, Mrs. Sullivan. He's a grand little man. What was your adventure?" I let Bridie tell her all about the morning while I sank into a nursery chair and put Liam on my lap. I could tell my dramatic little girl was enjoying the gasps of horror that Aileen gave as she described the boat fire.

"Mercy me, thank the blessed saints that you weren't all killed!" Aileen said when Bridie finished. "And how brave of you to rescue Miss Blanche. Mr. Finnegan has told us all about the family. He takes care of them like they were his own. Mr. McCormick will be so grateful."

"Yes. Mrs. McCormick was already here and expressed her gratitude." I reflected that I was doing a poor job of being the mistress of the house. I was actually enjoying chatting with Aileen much more than I thought I would with the wives of political muckety-mucks. I wanted to sit down with Aileen, have a cup of tea, and a chat about home. But I was the lady of the manor now and that wouldn't do.

I turned to Bridie. "Are you sure you want to go to lunch with Blanche?" I asked. "After all, she did treat you very badly before today."

"Oh, I do!" Bridie said fervently. "I think she needs me. She's had an awful shock and she needs a friend. And today she was very nice to me."

"And you'll get a good lunch and a ride in a fancy motorcar," I laughed. "Speaking of good lunches, I can't find a thing in the kitchen. Let's go to the soda fountain as a treat and then you can help me shop for dinner."

Bridie liked that idea and we had a lovely afternoon. We walked over to my regular butcher to choose some pork chops and the market to buy potatoes and some sprouts. Liam alternated between his pram and holding Bridie's hand. Bridie chattered excitedly and didn't leave my side for the rest of the day. She even helped me cook dinner, searching the kitchen for the pots and pans we needed, laughing as I literally shooed Mary and Constanza out of the way saying I would damnty well cook for myself tonight.

When Daniel got home he seemed relieved to see me smiling and an actual dinner on the table. I let Bridie tell him the adventures of the morning. They seemed a little more harrowing at every telling.

"Molly, why didn't you telephone me as soon as you were home?" he asked when she finished. "I would have come home right away."

"I had no idea where you were, and we were both fine. No harm done. To me the greatest shocker of all was that the Blanche who has been tormenting Bridie at school is Big Bill's daughter. Can you believe it?"

"But she's nice now," Bridie put in. "And I'm going out to lunch with her tomorrow."

For the first time since setting foot in the house I felt the tension in me relax a little. I looked around at my family. I would have preferred my little table in my dear house in Patchin Place. But didn't today show me how precious and fragile life could be? We were all safe and all together and I had to be grateful for that.

✖️ Thirteen ✖️

Bridie was bursting with energy all the next morning. She was up and down the stairs a dozen times trying on all of her dresses to decide which would be the best to wear to lunch. When the grand automobile finally pulled up and Bridie rushed out the door I decided I would walk over to Sid and Gus's to pay a call. Daniel was "canvassing the district," whatever that meant, and would not be home for hours. I was just about to go up and put my hat on when Mary came in.

"There are two persons here to see you." She put an emphasis on the word "persons." She sounded quite doubtful. "They say they know you. Should I send them in?"

I was curious. "Yes, of course." I waited as she went back to the front door wondering who the people might be.

Sid walked in first in a purple smoking jacket and black pants. She had topped the outfit with a purple Moroccan fez. Gus was wearing a matching purple fez, and a red tunic-type top over a flowing peasant-style skirt. I could see why Mary had been doubtful.

"Sid, Gus, I was just coming to see you!" I jumped up to give them both hugs.

"We just had to come as soon as we read this!" Gus held out a copy of the *New York American*. A banner headline read, BIG BILL'S BOAT BLAZES—PENNY PINCHING BILL BURNS LOCAL PIER. "It says that girls from Bridie's school were on the boat. Was this the school trip? Are you hurt?"

"As you can see I'm fine. And I certainly wouldn't be calmly sitting around the house if Bridie were hurt. Won't you sit down?" I gave yet another account of the fire on the ship with frequent interruptions and exclamations. I ended with the news of Bridie's new friendship.

"Three cheers for Bridie," Sid said. "She is the heroine of the whole affair."

Sid and Gus sat, looking curiously at the pictures and curios dotted around the room. For the first time, feeling like I was playing the lady of the manor, I rang the bell sitting on the table in the parlor. Mary appeared promptly.

"Mary, could you ask Constanza to make us some coffee and bring up the biscuits I bought yesterday?" I asked.

"Yes, Mrs. Sullivan," Mary replied and then hesitated. "And will these people be staying?" She looked at Sid and Gus in a way I found quite impertinent. I hadn't realized that servants would have their own opinions of my behavior and my friends. It appeared Mary was a bit of a prude. "Does Mr. Finnegan know them?"

"These are my friends," I said, firmly emphasizing the word "my," "and they are welcome in my house any time."

Mary looked doubtful, but gave a very small curtsey and left.

"So you have a maid and a cook? You're moving up in the world." I couldn't tell if Gus was happy for me or disapproving.

"Two maids, actually, the upstairs maid is acting as a nursemaid for Liam. I feel like a complete fraud and I think they know it." It felt so good to have friends to talk this over with. "But they come as part of the house. And it's such a big house it would be awkward for me to go down to the kitchen and make us coffee myself."

"Of course, we both grew up with servants," Sid said thoughtfully. "They can be quite as snobbish as their bosses."

"I'm afraid that Brendan Finnegan, Bill's right-hand man, is their boss," I said. "They know they have to answer to him and not me."

"The thing is to not let them get the better of you." She stood up, rang the bell, and sat back down again.

"You must let them know who's boss," Gus said seriously. "Don't let her run over you."

Mary came back in and looked at me quizzically. "Yes, Mrs. Sullivan? Did you want something?"

I pointed at Sid.

"Mary," she said in a languid voice with an upper-class drawl, "I would like my coffee black with two sugars and some brown bread to go with it, lightly buttered." She turned to Gus. "That is what Mrs. Vanderbilt has each morning. She says it helps one keep one's figure."

"If that is what Mrs. Vanderbilt suggests then I shall have brown bread as well," Gus replied seriously.

"I'm not sure if we have brown bread, Miss . . ."

"Miss Augusta Mary Walcott of the Boston Walcotts," Gus said in equally posh tones. "Not have brown bread? How can you not have brown bread?"

"The cook is Italian, Miss Walcott," Mary said, squirming with embarrassment now. "I'll go and ask her."

"It's all right. I bought a loaf myself when I did the shopping," I said, turning to Gus. "You shall have your brown bread."

"Thank heavens for that. And do have Cook cut the crust off of mine, Mary," Gus said. "I can't stand to eat crust. Oh, and bring the biscuits as well," and she winked at me.

"Yes, Miss Walcott." Mary gave a much deeper curtsey in Gus's direction and walked out swiftly.

Sid and Gus burst into laughter.

"I love Italian food! You must have us over for dinner," Sid said.

"I'm afraid this cook has only produced congealed dough with raw garlic so far." I made a face. "I seem to have as much luck with her as with the other servants. You did marvelously, though!"

"Next time we visit we will dress in the latest fashion as befits Fifth Avenue," Gus promised. "We were just so worried we rushed right over to see if you were all right."

"Like I said, they are snobs," Sid laughed. "Just drop a few names and be extremely demanding and she will be eating out of your hand. You are too nice."

"I suppose I have always identified more with the servants than the ruling class," I mused.

"And we love you for it. We are socialists, after all. But you can't let that young lady rule the house. You must be strong. I wouldn't be surprised if she has been put here to tell your Mr. Finnegan about all your movements."

"Or Mr. Hearst. She could be a spy for his newspaper hoping to get dirt on Daniel," Sid put in cheerfully.

"You've been reading too many novels," I laughed. But then I had a sudden doubt. Mary did seem much more loyal to Finn than to me. Was she a spy? Then something struck me from the headline that Gus had read.

"So the boat that we were on, it belongs to Big Bill?"

"Yes, the paper says it is the second fire on one of his boats." Gus opened the article again, but she stopped speaking as Mary entered with a tray of coffees, biscuits, and buttered brown bread with the crust cut off. She served each of us and gave a curtsey before leaving.

Gus took a sip of her coffee and sighed with pleasure. "Two sugars, perfect." Then she looked back at the paper. "There is a whole account of a terrible fire in which dozens of people died on one of Big Bill's pleasure cruisers, the *Lady Liberty*. I remember reading about it, don't you, Sid?"

Sid nodded. "It made the headlines, I remember. Shocking loss of life."

Gus glanced down at the newspaper again. "According to the paper there was an investigation into whether his poor maintenance had caused the fire, but he was declared innocent. The paper suggests that he paid off the commission."

"But take it with a grain of salt because that is Hearst's paper and he hates Big Bill. He's been trying for years to bring him down." Sid peered over Gus's shoulder, reading along.

I remembered something I had heard on the boat. "I think Hearst might be correct this time. I heard one of the crewmen complaining about the lack of maintenance while they were trying to put the fire out."

"Or Hearst planted a crewman to tamper with the wiring so the boat would catch on fire. Then he could run this article and remind everyone of Big Bill's previous scandal," Gus mused. "This is bare-knuckle politics and I wouldn't put anything past either of them." It crossed my mind that I could probably ask Finn to see if any crewman who had been scheduled to be on the boat had missed work that day. I didn't expect that anyone would be stupid enough to set fire to a boat they were on. But hadn't Big Bill done essentially that with his own daughter on board? Surely it had to be a horrible accident, nothing more.

"If it was poor maintenance that caused the fire I can't believe he would let his own daughter go on one of his boats," I said, angrily. "She could have been killed! We could all have been killed."

"Perhaps he didn't even know. Don't mothers normally handle the school outings?" Gus put down her coffee and turned the page. "And who would know that this would be the fateful trip?"

"I bet he got an earful from Mrs. McCormick last night." I smiled grimly, picturing the scene. "She doesn't seem too happy with his political ambitions. Come to think of it she didn't seem too happy that night at Delmonico's. I think I told you about that rather scantily dressed actress type who stopped to talk to Big Bill, and you should have seen the look she gave him. If looks could kill, Big Bill would be dead by now."

"You know all these political types have their mistresses." Sid looked up from the newspaper and Gus folded it back up. "It comes with the money and power."

"So now Daniel is helping a philandering, corrupt murderer. I can't believe that this is happening." My voice rose with emotion. How could Daniel be involved with a man like this?

"I am sure that Daniel has honorable intentions." Gus was clearly trying to calm me down. "Also, it is quite nice to have a big house with a cook and two maids. The wages of sin are quite lucrative." She raised her eyebrows so expressively that despite myself I had to laugh.

"Speaking of sin," she went on. "Ryan's friend Nikki will be moving into your house on Monday. He'll come by our house to get the key. I'm quite fascinated to see him. Ryan seems besotted."

"He always is," Sid put in, "especially with these temperamental artistic types."

"I thought Ryan was the temperamental artistic type," I commented. "I don't think he likes being upstaged, but I'd like to meet the ballet dancer too." It felt like a band was loosening across my chest talking to good friends like this. They made everything seem like such an adventure.

They stayed chatting until Bridie got home from lunch and listened to her excited description of how fancy the restaurant was and the different courses they tried.

"We must go," Sid said, finally rising. She walked over and rang the bell.

"Do you need something?" I asked.

"No, you do. Now before that girl comes in, think of something you want. I want to see you in charge before we go."

Mary came in. "Yes, Mrs. Sullivan?" I shot Sid an annoyed look, trying to think fast. She and Gus made being in charge look so easy.

"Mary, I'm going to have lunch now and then a rest," I said, finally collecting myself. "Miss Bridie has already eaten with Mrs. McCormick, so it will be just myself in the dining room. Also, please go up and make sure that Aileen has fed Liam and put him down for his nap."

"More," Gus mouthed at me from behind Mary's back. I tried to imitate their confident manner.

"Ask her to dress him in that little blue jacket when he wakes up. It is his father's favorite. I will need my bath drawn for me by three, and lay out my blue dress, as I will need to change." I was gaining confidence with every word. "Oh, and tell Constanza she is not to put any garlic in the dinner tonight. I expect it to be freshly cooked and hot when Captain Sullivan comes home." I put as much authority into my voice as I could. To my surprise Mary took my commands as a matter of course.

"Very good, Mrs. Sullivan." She bobbed a little curtsey and hurried out the door. Sid and Gus burst into applause.

"We can leave you without worry. Well done," Gus said as they took their leave.

Daniel and I sat down that night to a dinner of limp soggy pasta. I did notice that the watery tomato sauce had no garlic in it, so I supposed I was making some headway. Mary was in and out of the room serving so I didn't want to mention what Sid and Gus had read today about Big Bill. I couldn't shake the idea that she was a spy for Big Bill or at least for Finn. But as soon as Daniel came into our bedroom I accosted him. I was sitting in front of the dressing table pulling the pins from my hair.

"Did you know that your pal Big Bill almost killed your wife and daughter?" I said, standing to face him and jabbing a hairpin in his direction.

"What do you mean?" he asked warily.

"The paper today says that the boat fire was caused by poor maintenance and that it is the second such fire on one of Big Bill's boats. The first fire killed people! We could have been killed."

"I know." He put his arms around me and pulled me close. "I am so glad you are okay," he said. He pulled a pin out of my hair and it fell down around my shoulders.

"Daniel Sullivan, you let me be mad at you." I tried to push away. "Stop trying to soften me up." He just pulled me closer.

"Molly, I couldn't live without you," he whispered into my hair. "Thank God you are safe. And believe me, if Big Bill is responsible for that fire I want him to be held accountable as much as anyone."

"Well, how are you going to hold him accountable when you are beholden to him?" He let me pull back now.

"You will just have to trust me. Don't doubt me now." His eyes were pleading as he looked at me.

"Do you know how many times you have asked me to trust you?" My voice was tense. "I do trust you, Daniel, but I also know you well. There is something you are not telling me. You are the last person who would want to get ahead by corruption. I suspect you think you are doing something noble to protect me." I couldn't stay angry any longer. I let him pull me close. He took the last pin out of my hair, smoothed it back behind my shoulders, and kissed me on the forehead.

"I won't let anything happen to you." I was going to retort that he hadn't done much about saving me from a burning boat, but I decided to let him kiss me instead.

❄️ Fourteen ❄️

Sunday, October 13

I woke up on Sunday morning to soft light coming through my window. I like to have a quiet Sunday morning. Just not this morning, however, as we had to go to church. Finn had suggested to Daniel that we be seen at St. Michael's, which was where the fashionable Catholics worshipped in this part of the city.

Breakfast was a dismal affair of coffee, stale bread, and jam.

"This morning!" Daniel muttered, wagging a finger at me. "The talk."

"I don't see why you don't have the talk with her," I replied.

"It's something the lady of the house does," he said. "Besides, Finn is coming over to lunch."

"Jesus, Mary, and Joseph," I muttered. "You've invited someone to lunch on our first Sunday here, with a cook who only cooks Italian peasant food? Is our whole life going to be with Finn now? Are you sure you don't want him to move into the spare bedroom? Or would you rather share the room with him and have me move out?"

Daniel grinned. "Not my idea. Finn is grooming me in a hurry so we have to play along. Besides, if he has a chance to eat Constanza's food we may find ourselves with a new cook."

"Oh, yes." I nodded agreement.

Summoning all my courage, I went down to the kitchen to see Constanza.

"Constanza, Mr. Finnegan will be coming to lunch," I said. "What do you plan to serve for him?"

It took some hand waving and repetition before she even understood this. "Ah, Signor Finn," she said. "I make the ravioli."

"No meat?" I asked. "We usually have a roast on Sundays. Captain Sullivan likes his meat."

"Roast beef?" she asked, looking horrified and waving her arms in dramatic fashion. "Meat cost much money."

"We have an allowance, apparently," I said. "And I expect to eat the food we like. Tomorrow I'll go to the market and bring back what Captain Sullivan likes to eat. And if you don't know how to cook it, then I'll show you."

She gave me a defiant stare as I left.

We went to church, where Liam behaved like an angel. Finn arrived in time for lunch and we sat down in the dining room. Mary served from the dumbwaiter, putting a mound of what looked like dumplings onto each plate. Finn looked up expectantly, waiting for what came next. Nothing did.

"It's another pasta, apparently," I said sweetly. I watched the men's faces fall. "Finn, we appreciate having a cook, of course, but this one is a bit of a disaster."

Finn glanced around before saying, "We can't get rid of her. Her husband was a big noise among the Italians at the docks. It was unfortunate he was killed and we need their vote."

"So we're to eat no meat for the foreseeable future?" Daniel asked.

"I've offered to teach her how to cook food the way we like it," I said, "but she didn't seem to like that suggestion."

"She's your cook, Mrs. Sullivan," Finn said. "It's up to you. And if it really doesn't work out in the end—well, we'll see what we can do."

"I'm happy to cook our own food," I said. "I know what Daniel likes to eat."

Finn shook his head. "That wouldn't be right and proper. You'll be expected to entertain—maybe powerful donors. It wouldn't be right for you to have to serve your own food."

I gave a sigh. "Very well. I'll give it a try."

"Big Bill is very grateful to you for taking care of his daughter on Friday. He said to tell you that we have heard nothing but praise for Bridie and Mrs. Sullivan all weekend." Finn took a mouthful and ate it determinedly.

"Bridie has been full of stories about lunching with Blanche. I'm so glad they have made friends. How is the maid?" I realized that I hadn't heard a thing about that poor girl.

"She is out of the hospital, but she won't be welcomed back at the McCormick house. Bill was livid when he realized she had deserted his daughter, just like I thought," Finn said.

"Poor girl." I pushed my food around my plate. "She saw the flames and panicked. Anyone would have."

"You wouldn't." Finn looked at me with admiration in his eyes. "You stayed on deck and helped rescue both girls."

"Yes, well . . ." I stopped, a bit embarrassed, and then changed the subject. "Does Big Bill know what caused the fire? Could it have been sabotage?"

"I can't think anyone would be cruel enough to sabotage a boat with schoolchildren on it," Finn mused, "although I don't think Big Bill has ruled it out yet. The investigators found the first spark came from the kitchen."

"Was it poor maintenance like they reported in the paper?" I asked.

"Molly, don't cross-examine the man," Daniel put in, embarrassed. "He's not on the stand."

Finn did look uncomfortable. "Let's talk about something more pleasant. Daniel will be meeting with some longtime supporters in the next few weeks and we thought we might have a gathering with wives included. When do you think you might be ready to host a little party?"

I held up a soggy ravioli. The filling had leaked out and was congealed on the bottom of the bowl. "If we don't want to poison off Daniel's supporters," I said dryly, "I don't think it will be any time soon."

After Finn had taken his leave, I had to reflect that he was quite good company. He had told some funny stories at lunch and kept us laughing.

"What terribly important meeting do you have to rush off to now?" I asked when Daniel and I were alone.

"Nothing." He smiled. "Fancy a stroll?"

"That sounds like a marvelous idea. We can stroll to Patchin Place."

"Oh, not to visit your friends, please."

"Not my friends. My old house. I am not going another day without my teapot!" I declared.

Daniel shook his head. "Very well, we can visit it on our way to the park. That Russian ballet dancer won't have moved in yet, will he? I have no desire to have to converse with him."

"He's not coming until tomorrow, so you'll be quite safe."

Bridie was up in her room poring over her Latin homework, but we decided Liam needed some fresh air. Aileen insisted on pushing Liam in the buggy while Daniel and I walked behind arm in arm as we set off for Patchin Place.

"Don't you miss our own dear little house?" I asked mournfully as I let us in the front door. Liam insisted on coming in and immediately ran up to his bedroom. I found my teapot and caddy and gave one last look around with a sigh. If Ryan's friend was moving in on Monday I might not be back for a while.

"Come down, Liam, my love," I called up the stairs.

"This is Liam's house." He appeared at the top of the stairs with a frown on his sweet little face. "I don't want to go. I want my supper here." I noticed how quickly his language skills had progressed since he had Aileen to talk to all day, and wondered if I had been neglecting him before.

"Good idea," I played along. "You stay here and I shall go and ride the horsey." I pretended to call outside. "Aileen, Liam is going to live here now and I shall have the room with the horsey."

"No!" Liam came bounding down the stairs and ran behind me as I walked to the front door, pretending I would leave without him. "That's my horsey," he said forcefully to Aileen as she lifted him back into the buggy. I handed the teapot and caddy to Daniel and locked up the door.

"What was that all about?" Daniel asked as we walked away.

"I may not be the smartest woman in the world," I grinned, "but I can still outsmart a three-year-old."

We walked back past a little Jewish shop that stayed open on Sunday afternoon and I bought some fresh bread, cheese, and pastrami. I marched straight down to the kitchen to put the kettle on as soon as we arrived back at the brownstone. Constanza was already chopping onions and garlic for whatever food she was planning to prepare.

"Let's save that for another night," I said with a shudder. "We will have a cold supper tonight," I told her. "Please help me slice this up." And, rather sulkily, she did. I determined that tomorrow when the shops were open I would finally be able to buy the type of food that we liked and I would teach her to cook it.

It seemed a bit strange to have the four of us sitting in the fancy dining room eating cold meat and cheese. I had insisted that Liam join us for dinner. I didn't like him being away from me so much, far up in the nursery. I knew that society mothers let the servants raise their children and just saw them for a little while in the evening. I was not a society mother and I didn't ever want to be no matter what Daniel or Big Bill had planned.

Still, I reflected as I was lying in bed that night, I had begun to take control of my situation. Thanks to Sid and Gus, I knew how to make Mary respect me. I was taking charge in the kitchen and determined to insist on my way there. Although I hadn't chosen this situation, I was beginning to find my feet. And lunch with Finn had actually been enjoyable. He was no upper-class snob. But the thought of Finn took my mind back to the question I had asked him. What had caused the fire on the boat? Was it Big Bill's poor maintenance? Did he cut corners and risk people's lives? Or was it his enemies? Had they tried to discredit him or, the thought struck me, even known that his daughter would be on that boat? Finn had warned me that Tammany's enemies played rough, but it was just now coming clear to me. Were they willing to kill?

❧ Fifteen ❧

Monday, October 14

The next morning, after Bridie had set off for school and Daniel to God-knows-where, I put Liam into his buggy and prepared to right the wrongs of the previous day. The most important one was buying food that Daniel would actually eat. Whether I could teach Constanza to cook it was another matter.

As I started down Fifth Avenue a man stepped out of the shadows. It was the burly Jack, who had driven us to the docks.

"And where would you be heading, lady?" he asked, making it quite clear that he intended to come along with me.

"Just to the market," I said.

"Oh, right you are, then," he said. "And where will we be doing the shopping, then?"

"*We* will not be doing the shopping," I said. "I am quite capable of visiting a few stores on my own, thank you."

"Oh, but I've been given me orders," he said, shaking that prizefighter's head. "Don't let her out alone. That's what I've been told."

I fought to keep my face calm. "Really this is quite ridiculous," I said. "I'm going to my old neighborhood where everyone knows me and I'm in no danger at all."

"All the same," he said, "I have me orders, ma'am."

"Then if you must follow me, you'd better do it several steps behind so that it's not obvious."

"Right you are, then, ma'am." He gave me a grin that revealed several missing teeth. I was right about the former prizefighter, then!

Liam had been observing this interaction with alarm and now decided he wanted to be picked up. "Pick me up, Mama," he said.

"No, my darling. You need to stay in your pram," I said. "Mama can't carry you all the way to the shops."

He looked as if he were about to bawl. "We might have time to stop in the park and you can run around," I said, "but only if you're good now."

"I'm not sure you want the little one running around Washington Square by himself," Jack said. "Too easy to snatch him and hold him for a hostage."

"Mercy me," I snapped. "This is beyond ridiculous now. Who would want to take my son? Or harm me, for that matter?"

"The other side has no scruples," he said. "They'll do whatever it takes to discredit your husband or make him drop out of the race." He saw my face. "You've no idea, have you? People who cross Mr. Hearst and his cronies have a way of winding up dead or disappeared."

"I still intend to let my child play," I said. "If you want to you can hide behind a tree to leap out to save him, but you're not going to scare me into being a prisoner in my own home."

With that I set off resolutely. Liam still looked worried. Perhaps he was picking up my anxiety. I didn't believe, or didn't want to believe, what Jack had told me. If Daniel really thought this world of politics was so dangerous, surely he wouldn't have put his family in harm's way?

My first stop was stocking up on vegetables from the Jefferson Market and then shopping for food that Daniel liked before going to Washington Square for Liam to chase the pigeons, his favorite occupation. All the while I was conscious of Jack, lurking behind a tree and watching. But since the only other occupants of the square were children, students, and a constable I didn't think he had much to worry about. I arrived home feeling quite satisfied and set about showing Constanza how to cook an Irish stew.

"Ah. You like zuppa!" she said, nodding. "I make zuppa."

At dinner that night Daniel gave a satisfied smile. "So you managed to teach her how to cook, did you?"

"Not exactly," I replied. "I made the stew. She stood and watched."

Bridie was excited and full of stories from school. Not only had she recovered from her frightening ordeal on the boat with apparently no lasting effects, but the incident had turned her into something of a heroine at school. What's more, the dreaded Blanche had now become her best friend.

For the rest of the week we heard nothing at dinner except what Blanche had said or done that day, how they had sneaked out of school at lunchtime and gone to a soda fountain together and Blanche had treated her to an ice cream sundae.

All the same, I was surprised when a stiff vellum envelope arrived, addressed to Mr. and Mrs. Sullivan and Bridie. Inside was a gold-rimmed invitation:

You are cordially invited to join us in the celebration of Blanche's thirteenth birthday. Saturday, October 19, at 7 P.M. A late supper will be served. William and Lucy McCormick.

I showed the invitation to Bridie when she came home from school, expecting her to be thrilled, but she shot me a horrified glance.

"I can't go. I have nothing to wear that is suitable." Before I could answer, she shook her head. "And please don't suggest my white party dress. It would be quite wrong for evening. Blanche said so.

She said the dressmaker is designing her first long dress for her. The girls will all be in proper party dresses."

"Well, I'm sorry you don't want to attend your friend's party," I said. "But I do understand the clothing situation. I feel the same way myself sometimes."

"You do?" She looked at me in surprise. "You always sound as if you don't care what other people think."

"Maybe that's because I'm good at covering up what I'm feeling," I replied. "But you'd want to go to Blanche's party if you had the right dress, would you?"

"Oh, yes." Her face lit up. "Blanche is my best friend. She really wants me there, because there will be all these important people and she hates having to talk to them. She says her parents parade her around like a prized doll. She thinks they are already trying to find a husband for her. Can you imagine? She's only going to be thirteen."

"I suppose that's what rich people do," I said. "They make good matches for their children. It's all about holding on to their wealth."

"How horrible," she said. "That's another reason not to get married. I wouldn't let anyone choose a husband for me, if I even wanted one."

I gave her a gentle smile. "You'll meet the right man one day, I promise you. And then you'll feel quite differently. I had no intention of marrying those uncouth boys back home in Ireland, but luckily I brought you to America, met Captain Sullivan, and fell hopelessly in love with him." I didn't add that when we first met he was the policeman and I the suspect in a murder case.

She nodded. "You're so lucky," she said.

I turned my attention back to the matter of a dress. "I might have an idea," I said. "Aunt Gus has several ball gowns with lots of fabric in the skirts. Hopelessly old-fashioned now, of course. And she'll never wear them again. But she did say they have a good dressmaker. Perhaps she could use the fabric from the skirt and make you a dress."

"Really?" Bridie's face lit up again. "Do you think Aunt Gus would agree?"

"I don't see why not. We'll walk over and ask her, shall we? The aunts haven't heard about your school progress for a few days."

I went up to retrieve Liam, who had been enjoying his tea in the nursery. I was amazed how quickly he had adapted to this new routine, actually protesting when I wanted him to come down from the nursery and spend some time with me. He thought Aileen was just marvelous, as indeed she was—kind, playful, and with boundless energy. I had to confess my own energy had been sapped recently, with all the turmoil of the move and then the drama on the boat.

We had a pleasant visit and I put my request hesitantly to Gus. She nodded and promised to have the dressmaker there the next afternoon to take measurements. I should have known, of course, what Sid and Gus were like. When we went to meet the dressmaker the next afternoon we found a bolt of beautiful turquoise silk that my friends had purchased for Bridie.

"So perfect with her coloring," Gus said. "The fabric in my skirts would have been quite wrong."

"I can't let you dress my children all the time," I said, feeling my cheeks glowing. "It makes me feel like an abject failure."

"But, Molly, we love doing it," Gus said. "We have no children of our own. This is the closest we'll ever come to having a daughter and we're so proud of her. And look at her face—she loves the fabric. She's excited about how she's going to look."

I turned to Bridie and saw that this was true. She was trying not to smile, but the excitement showed in her eyes. She nodded and said, a little breathlessly, "Wait till Blanche sees me in this. And Helen and Julia. They won't think I'm the poor relation then."

"Of course not," Sid said. "You'll be the belle of the ball."

And so it was settled. Bridie went for a fitting on Thursday, and, amazingly, by the morning of the party the gown was complete. I was not sure what to wear myself—the subdued mauve dress I had worn to Delmonico's, or one of the ball gowns Sid and Gus had bestowed upon me. I decided my pride would not let me be seen by Mrs. McCormick wearing the same dress twice in a row, so I opted for the least flamboyant of the ball gowns—it was a burgundy red and somehow complemented my hair. I was pleased and surprised at the overall effect. So was Bridie.

"You look so pretty," she said. "I bet you'll look as pretty as Blanche's mother, and her dress was made in Paris."

"I once had a dress made in Paris," I said wistfully, because it too had been quite lovely. "But it was burned in the fire last Christmas."

Daniel nodded when he saw Bridie and me come down the stairs. "Am I to have the honor of escorting two elegant ladies?" he asked. Bridie giggled.

Jack was waiting outside, having already found a taxicab, and we set off uptown. A cold wind was blowing in our faces, threatening to yank out my carefully placed feather. I hunkered down behind Daniel, who was sitting up in front, next to the driver. Bridie snuggled close to me.

"I hope she likes my present," Bridie whispered. After much debate we had settled on a book of poetry, leather-bound. I thought it wouldn't matter much what Blanche was given as she probably already had two of everything. It seemed to take forever as we passed the bright lights of theaters then moved into the rarified atmosphere of Central Park. At Sixty-Eighth Street we turned between two enormous mansions. I had been to this part of the city before, when I once solved a case, but Bridie gasped.

"Are these places where people really live?" she whispered. "They are like palaces."

"I expect we'll find that your friend lives in such a house," I whispered back. And even as I said the words, we crossed Park Avenue and then came to a halt outside another towering structure. Lights twinkled out from windows. An automobile had pulled up ahead of us and we watched a chauffeur hurry around to open the back door for an elegant couple and a younger person.

"That's Julia," Bridie whispered. She gave me an anxious look. "Do you think it will be all right?"

"It will be fine. You look as pretty as a picture."

In truth I wasn't feeling too confident myself. I suspected there might be a lot of new money here, and such people like to show off their wealth. Our turn came and Daniel opened the door for us. Two attendants in smart livery stood on either side of a broad flight of marble steps. At the top we were greeted by an older man—a butler, I presumed.

"Captain and Mrs. Sullivan and Bridie," Daniel said.

The man nodded graciously and a maid rushed forward to take our outer garments. Then we joined a reception line in a doorway. Big Bill and Mrs. McCormick were standing just inside a large drawing room, on either side of Blanche, who looked dazzling in a pink dress embroidered with pearls. When Mrs. McCormick saw us, she whispered to her husband.

"So this is the little girl who saved our daughter's life," Big Bill said. "We can't thank you enough, young lady. Such a brave thing to do. And to think she's Daniel's adopted child too. You see—it all ties together. It was all meant to be. Fate."

Blanche's eyes lit up as she saw Bridie and she reached out to grasp her hands.

"I'm so glad you came," she said.

"Happy birthday," Bridie said, and handed her the gift, which was then handed off to a maid to join the pile.

"Wait until I've greeted everyone and then we can talk properly," Blanche called after Bridie.

We joined the rest of the partygoers. There were a couple of dozen people in the room, including several girls of Bridie's age. One of them came up to Bridie.

"Bridie, fancy seeing you here," she said. She was going to say something cutting. Then she examined Bridie's dress, and said, with obvious surprise, "Nice dress. Quite fashionable."

"Thank you, Helen," Bridie said smoothly. "I had it made just for tonight."

I gave a little grin. My girl was learning to hold her own.

❧ Sixteen ☙

Saturday, October 19

Daniel and I were exchanging pleasantries with Helen's parents when Blanche and her parents came over to join us. "So, I see you've brought your brother, Helen," Mrs. McCormick said. "Blanche has been dying to meet him. Alfred, isn't it? Blanche, you must meet Alfred. I gather he's a good golfer and tennis player."

A tall and rather gawky young man gave a little bow. Blanche grasped Bridie's hand.

"And do we hear that you're heading off to college next year?"

"That's right, ma'am."

"Off to Yale, our boy is," Helen's father said.

"What a pity it's not Columbia or Cornelius could have shown him around," Mrs. McCormick said. "Where has the boy got to?"

Their eyes searched the room. "Cornelius. Get over here," Big Bill boomed.

An elegant and stunningly attractive young man detached himself from a group in the corner and came over to us, champagne glass in hand. "What is it now, Father? Did you know Mr. Templeton lived in Paris? I've been pumping him for suggestions."

"Cornelius, we have already had this discussion, now drop it. You're not going and that is that," Big Bill said.

"I am twenty-one. I can do as I darned well please and you can't stop me," the boy said, his eyes flashing angrily.

"Except with the purse strings, young man. And don't forget it."

There was an embarrassed silence.

"So you were at Columbia," Daniel asked, smoothing troubled waters.

"I was." Cornelius gave him a challenging stare, almost a sneer. "Good school. You are familiar with it?"

"I am a fellow graduate," Daniel said. "Class of ninety-two."

For the second time that evening I had an urge to grin. Instead, I looked around and spotted a man standing off in a dark corner. He was not wearing evening clothes and there was something furtive about the way he was observing the room. As I watched he took out a pad and scribbled something. I tugged on Daniel's sleeve.

"That man is writing something down. Who is he, do you think?"

Daniel looked around, saw Finn, and beckoned to him. A few whispered words, then Daniel calmly resumed the conversation. Suddenly there were raised voices in that corner and we watched in horrified fascination as the man was escorted from the room by Finn and one of the male servants.

"We'll get you yet, McCormick," he shouted as he was dragged out. "One day we'll find out what happened to Ronnie Walker. And what about your latest ship disaster? How many more ships are going to catch on fire, eh? How many more people are you going to kill?"

The voice echoed into the night air. There was a moment of stunned silence. Finn came back and had a word with Big Bill and Daniel. Mr. O'Brien appeared and came to consult with them as well. Big Bill glared. "One of Hearst's men? How did he get in here? Roberts?" He yelled the name.

The butler appeared in the doorway. "You want me, sir?"

"Who the devil let in the enemy?" Big Bill shouted. "Works for Hearst's rag. Now we'll be on his front page tomorrow. How did he get in—that's what I want to know."

"I'm deeply sorry, sir," the butler said. "I don't know how he managed to slip past. I can only assume he came in when several families arrived at once, and I took him for the son of one of them."

"Lock the front door," Big Bill snapped. "And there better not be any more traitors lurking here tonight or I'll have your guts for garters."

He took his wife's arm firmly and led her away. I turned to Daniel. "That man worked for Hearst?" I asked. "What did he mean about Ronnie Walker?"

Daniel glanced around, as if wanting to make sure nobody else overheard. "He was a newspaper reporter, working for Hearst. He disappeared on an assignment at one of Bill's docks."

I remembered then that Gus had mentioned his sister. Daniel made it clear that he didn't want to say any more. He handed me a glass of champagne, then moved away to talk to Finn. They were swallowed up into the crowd. Bridie was already off with Blanche and other schoolmates. It appeared that the other parents seemed to know one another and were chatting with animation—except for Mrs. McCormick, who stood like a statue, a sort of fixed smile on her face. She was not having a good time, I thought, and wondered why when it was an occasion to show off her beloved daughter.

I stood there alone for a moment, looking around with that slight panic one gets from not knowing anybody and feeling out of place. Then I caught the gaze of a young man, sitting in a wheelchair beside the bar. He gave me a sweet smile. I went over to him.

"Hello, I'm Molly Sullivan," I said.

"I know. I've met your husband several times and heard all about you," he said. "I'm Junior. William McCormick Junior, that is." I could see then that he resembled his father. He had a shock of dark hair and the same large features. But where his father was portly, Junior was painfully thin. His lower half seemed shrunken and twisted and was partially hidden under a blanket.

"Oh, you're the older son, of course," I said. "I'm pleased to meet you." I began to hold out my hand to shake hands with him but stopped when I realized his right arm was very thin and held close to his body.

"You clearly find this sort of occasion as tedious as I do," he said, "but alas I am required to put in an appearance. Placed suitably out of the way so as not to be an embarrassment." His speech was slightly slurred. He patted a chair beside him with his left hand and I sat.

"My brother, or should I say half brother, laps up the attention, you'll notice," he said. I remembered then that his mother had died from a similar disease to the one afflicting him. We glanced up as Cornelius gave a loud laugh. "He's all sweetness and smiles now, unlike an hour ago when they were at each other's throats again."

"Oh, dear," I said. "I got a hint that all was not smooth sailing a few minutes ago. Your brother wants to go to Paris, is that right?"

"He wants to be a writer, I believe. To experience the world. Father wants him to learn the business—to take over someday. Corny refuses. Although, unfortunately, I should be the rightful heir, being the son of the first wife. Not much use when it comes to running docks and ships. But then Father has his sights set on bigger things now. First mayor, then governor, then . . ." He gave a brittle laugh. "And I gather he'll take your husband along for the ride."

"Saints preserve us, I hope not," I blurted out before I realized this was not a wise thing to say.

"My dear lady, anyone who is caught up in my father's whirlwind gets swept along with no way of escape," he said. "He is a force of nature."

He looked up and broke off speaking as Big Bill came in our direction. At first, I thought he was coming to speak to us, but then I saw he was heading for an older man, wearing a dark suit and not in formal dress like the rest of us. The man had been making for the door, but Bill took his arm and drew him aside.

"You're not leaving?" he asked.

"I don't think there is anything more I can do until you draw up a rough draft, Mr. McCormick."

"Then stay until I've completed it."

"Now? In the middle of a party?" the other man asked. "Surely it can wait until morning?"

"I have my reasons for getting it done as soon as possible," Big Bill said. "I intend it to be the trump card in settling this matter."

"Very well, then." The man nodded. "Do you want me to come with you to your office?"

"Give me a while to put everything down first," Bill said. "It's all really simple. It won't take long. Have another drink." He picked up a glass from the bar and pressed it into the man's hand.

"You're not having one yourself?" the man asked, amused. "I've never known you to turn down an opportunity for a drink."

Big Bill chuckled. "Sure. Why not. Drink a toast to our accomplishment, eh?"

He turned around. "Here, Father," Junior said and handed him a glass.

"So you're the bartender now, are you, son?" Bill asked, in what I thought was not a nice tone. "Found a way to be useful?"

Bill took the glass, clinked with the other man, then downed it in one swallow, making a face as he put down the glass on the bar. "Luckily I have the good stuff up in my study. My secret stash, you know. The best Irish whiskey, not namby-pamby ferret's pee like this champagne." He gave the man a hefty pat on the back. "And stick around for supper. It should be good."

The man nodded as Big Bill headed toward a doorway.

"Where are you going, Bill?" Mrs. McCormick called sharply. "You can't run off in the middle of your daughter's party."

"Don't go, Papa," Blanche pleaded, rushing over to grab his hand.

"I'll only be gone for a few minutes, darlin'," Bill replied. "I'll be back in time for the cutting of the cake, I promise you. And anyway, it's time for party games. Everyone head to the ballroom. Corny, you're master of ceremonies. Get the games started." He looked around the room. "Off you go, then. Prizes for everyone!"

The girls ran ahead, sounding for once like excited schoolgirls and not bored young ladies. Their parents followed. I couldn't see where Daniel and Finn had gone to. I exchanged a glance with Junior. "Are you coming to join the fun?" I asked. "Would you like me to push you?"

"Oh, no, thank you," he said. "I have my trusty Charlie, who maneuvers me around. Besides, I can handle the wheelchair quite well on smooth surfaces. It's just all these darned rugs and carpets that stump me." He gave me a smile. "You go and enjoy yourself. I'm not too thrilled with the idea of watching spoiled little girls battle to the death for the prize of a new handkerchief!"

I had to laugh then. Whatever the disease was doing to his body, clearly his brain was intact. I left him and followed the others into a lavish ballroom, the walls lined with mirrors, decorated with velvet swags. Electric chandeliers were suspended from the ceiling, providing twinkling light and sparkling from the polished floor. Cornelius was in his element as the center of attention. The girls played statues, then musical chairs, then hot potato, each game accompanied by squeals and laughter. Prizes were handed out. Bridie won a mother-of-pearl comb for her hair and she was mightily pleased, rushing over to show it to me and insisting that I place it in her hair right away.

When the girls paused for lemonade, declaring they were exhausted and when was supper going to be ready, Blanche looked around. "Where is Papa?" she asked. "He said he'd only be a few minutes and we've been playing for ages."

"You know what your father is like when he gets involved in any kind of business," Mrs. McCormick said. She beckoned to the butler who was hovering in the background. "Where is Charlie? Send him up to fetch my husband for supper."

"I believe he just helped take Mr. McCormick Junior upstairs a few minutes ago," the butler said. He had just finished speaking when the young footman appeared, out of breath as if he had been running.

"Mr. Roberts, the pass key if you please," he said. "Junior is concerned about his father. He found the study door locked and Mr. McCormick won't answer."

"He may be on the telephone," Mrs. McCormick said. "You know how he likes these late-night business calls."

"But Mr. McCormick Junior banged on the door and called his father's name several times. I heard him. He's quite worried."

"Just a minute. I'll get the pass key." The butler hurried off, followed by Charlie.

We waited. The girls begged for the phonograph so they could dance. Mrs. McCormick looked unconcerned. "Junior does get worked up about things."

"I'll go up and see, shall I?" Cornelius asked.

"Yes, all right." Lucy looked annoyed. "Your father's probably just on the telephone. Tell him to come down. We'll be serving supper in just a few minutes." She chose a record, put it on the phonograph, and began winding the spring.

"I'll go and tell him he has to come down and dance!" Blanche said. "It is my birthday."

Cornelius left the ballroom. Daniel followed him without being asked. So did Finn. I was sorely tempted to go up and see for myself. I went as far as the foyer, watching them heading for the sweeping staircase. I heard the music begin in the ballroom.

Then, over it, I heard a trembling voice that had to be Junior's. "I knew something was wrong. Take me in to see him. Has he passed out? Is he all right? Father? Pops?"

Cornelius sprinted up the flight of stairs. "Let me get past!" he muttered. "Move out of the way, you cripple!"

There was a moment's silence, then Cornelius's voice, high-pitched and strained, "Oh, my God. I think he's dead."

My first instinct was to rush up the stairs to see what had happened. But then I thought of the girls down in the ballroom. I could hear them laughing as they danced. I didn't think they could have heard Cornelius over the music. Surely it would be better to keep them from panicking, but Lucy needed to know something was wrong. I went back into the ballroom. She was standing by the phonograph staring rather absentmindedly at the dancing girls.

"Lucy"—I laid my arm on her sleeve—"you need to come upstairs. I think something has happened."

"Happened?" She looked at me quizzically.

"With Mr. McCormick. Please come now."

A look of fear crossed her face and she ran out of the room and up the stairs. I confess I followed.

Across a broad landing and along a hallway to where a door was now open, with light streaming out. Junior's wheelchair was still in the doorway and he was craning forward trying for a better view, now blocked by the men who had gone into the room.

"Oh, Bill!" Mrs. McCormick exclaimed as she saw her husband slumped over the desk. "Is he really dead? Was it a heart attack? His doctors warned him about his heart."

"Not a heart attack, I'm afraid," Daniel said. "He's been stabbed in the back."

❧ Seventeen ❧

I crept toward the open door, trying to see in around the people assembled there. I was looking into a small room dominated by a huge polished mahogany desk on which papers had been arranged. On the back wall was a portrait of Big Bill, looking prosperous and smug with the harbor and a big steamship in the background. Big Bill had been sitting at the desk, facing the door. He was now slumped forward, sprawled across the desk, but from my position I couldn't see where he had been stabbed. Cornelius, Finn, and Daniel were standing at the desk.

"Oh, Bill! No! No!" Mrs. McCormick tried to reach her husband, but Daniel came forward to prevent her. "I'm so sorry, but you can't come in," he said gently.

"He's my husband. Let me pass. I want to go to him." She struggled to move past Daniel.

"This is now a crime scene, Mrs. McCormick. We have to wait until the police arrive," Daniel said calmly. "Cornelius, please take your mother downstairs and get her a brandy." He ushered her to the door. "Everybody out. Now!" he commanded. "Finn, please go downstairs and call the police," he said. "Nobody touch anything in this room and nobody is to leave the house." He turned to the butler, who was staring white-faced with shock. "Mr. Roberts, can I assign you to make sure nobody goes out the front door? And we'll need a list of all those attending the party. I suggest that we tell no one what has happened until the police arrive. Why don't you send them in to supper to make sure nobody tries to leave."

Mrs. McCormick turned back to Daniel. "You will find out who did this terrible thing, won't you?"

"I'm no longer a policeman, Mrs. McCormick," Daniel said. "But I'll do my best to make sure the case is handled properly."

"It was that man who gate-crashed the party. The one we threw out. He came back to get revenge," she gasped, sobbing now.

"Come along, Mother," Cornelius said. "Let's get you a nice glass of brandy. God, I need one myself."

"I don't want brandy. I want to find the man who killed my husband." She was close to hysterics as she was led away. I stayed in the shadows out in the corridor, feeling sick and uneasy, as the others filed past me.

Only Junior stayed, leaning forward for a better look at the scene. Daniel went over to him. "Tell me what happened," he said. "From the beginning."

"I was feeling tired," Junior said. "I don't handle being in company too well these days. I had Charlie take me up to my room. I was going to have my supper brought up to me."

"He carries you up the stairs?" Daniel asked.

"No. We had a little elevator put in for me," Junior said. "Charlie takes me up in it."

"And where is your room?"

"On the other side of the landing, at the far end," Junior said.

"So how did you happen to be passing your father's room?"

"I wasn't passing it. I wanted to have a word with him before I went to bed," Junior said. "Something that had been troubling me. I needed to ask him about it."

"And what was that, may I ask?"

"No, you may not," Junior snapped. "None of your damned business. As you just said to my mother, you are no longer a policeman."

"Hey, calm down," Daniel said. "I am only trying to help. You want to find out who killed your father, don't you? That means I have to start with the movements of everyone in the house."

"You can rest assured that my question to my father had nothing to do with this," Junior said. "Anyway, Charlie took me up in the elevator and was going to take me to my room, but I had him take me in the other direction, to Father's study. I can move up and down the hallways just fine as they are not carpeted, but as you can see, I can't make it over the threshold and across the carpet of this room." He looked up at Daniel, who nodded.

"And what happened then?"

"I knocked on the door and was surprised to find it was locked. I jiggled the handle and it wouldn't open."

"Does your father often lock himself in?" Daniel asked.

"Sometimes when he is making an important telephone call or it is imperative that he not be disturbed," Junior said, then he grinned. "Usually when he's doing something underhanded or illegal."

"And do you have any reason to believe that he might have been conducting something underhanded tonight?"

Junior looked up at him. "I am not privy to his business dealings," he said. "He sees me—saw me—as a poor specimen not worthy of his attention."

"Continue," Daniel said. "The door seemed to be locked."

Junior nodded. His face was lined with grief, and the nod seemed to cause him pain. "I called his name. I asked, 'Father, can I come in?' He didn't answer. So I banged louder. I thought he might have drunk too much and fallen asleep. But no amount of banging roused him. So I sent Charlie to get the pass key. Mr. Finnegan came up with Charlie. I asked to be handed the key and put it in the lock. I couldn't insert it to start with, because, I presume, the rightful key was in the lock from the other side. Charlie tried to help me. Then I got the key into the lock but I couldn't turn it. I lack strength in my right hand, you see. So Charlie opened the door and saw my father slumped over. I thought he might have passed out from drinking too much."

"Does that happen often?" Daniel asked.

"Not often. Usually he can put away a good amount before he's incoherent, but I have seen him passed out before."

"And then?"

"I called his name again, loudly, and told Charlie to push me into the room, but before that happened my brother came running up and shoved me out of the way, as usual. And then you came in and said he had been stabbed."

"Thank you," Daniel said. "You've been most helpful."

"I have?" Junior said. "I don't think I've helped you solve the case, have I?"

"You're often in the role of observer in this family, I'd imagine," Daniel said. "Do you have any ideas yourself?"

Junior gave a sort of lopsided grin. "You want me to rat on my family? Someone who was clever enough to kill a man in his own house in a locked room? I think you'd need to look for Houdini. But if you want motives, I think you'll find plenty. My stepmother is up in arms because she found out that my father has resumed his relationship with a certain actress. My brother is mad as hell because my father won't let him go to Paris and has cut off his allowance until he gives in and agrees to learn the business. Only my little sister is blameless. And I don't think she'd have the strength to stab a big man like my father anyway."

"That's an interesting point," Daniel said. "Your father was a big and powerful man and yet he allowed someone to come up behind him in a small room and stab him. One does not die instantly from most stabbings. Why didn't he turn around and wrestle with his attacker? He must have been comfortable enough to allow that person in the room with him and not watch his back."

"But the door was locked from the inside. Did the attacker go out the window?" Junior asked.

Daniel walked over to the window. "It's a long drop," he said. "And the window appears to be shut."

"So how did Father's attacker manage to leave the room?"

Daniel shrugged. "Your guess is as good as mine." He put a friendly hand on Junior's shoulder. "Thank you. You've been helpful and I'm sure this has been a terrible shock. I'll find Charlie and have him bring you up some supper. Do you need help getting to your room?"

"No, thank you. I can manage the hallway, and my room is not carpeted." He nodded, then backed his wheelchair away from the door and set off down the hall. I noticed that the wheels were rubber and made no sound. Daniel was about to go back into the room when he noticed me, standing in the shadows between light sconces.

"I thought you wouldn't be able to stay away," he said. "So what do you think? This is strange, isn't it? A man who goes everywhere with bodyguards is killed in his own house."

"It may be precisely because of that," I said. "If there are bodyguards everywhere else his own house might have been their only chance."

I followed him into the room. Now I could see clearly the hilt of a knife stuck into his back. He had removed his jacket and it hung over the back of his chair. There was a ring of red stain on his white shirt.

"He didn't bleed much," I commented. "It looks like quite a small knife. So the killer must have been a professional—known exactly where to stab to strike an organ."

"Or been very lucky." Daniel looked up with a grin. "But I agree with you about the lack of blood."

I looked at the desk. A whiskey decanter had been knocked over and the contents had spread over the surface, saturating much of the paper that lay there.

"Whatever was on this desk won't be of any use now," I said. I tried to read. The ink had run, creating ugly black blotches, but I thought I read the words "And Test . . ."

"It looks like a will," I exclaimed. "He was going to change his will."

"If that was his intent he didn't manage to do so," Daniel said. "Look—the blotter hasn't been used." He came over to me and put an arm around my shoulders. "You should go downstairs. In fact we should both go down, since I have no official reason to be here now. We don't want to find ourselves as prime suspects. God, I hope the police send someone capable. This will be a high-profile case."

"Do you think that one of Hearst's men managed to sneak up here and stab him?" I asked. "That newspaper reporter managed to get in easily enough." A thought struck me. "Perhaps he was a diversion, allowing an assassin to sneak upstairs."

Daniel turned and stood staring back at the body. "There's nowhere really to hide in this room," he said. "Bill would have seen an intruder the moment he came in, and probably been able to subdue most men. Besides, if you were Hearst and you wanted to get rid of your opponent it would be much easier to wait until he was in a crowd at a rally and kill him then. Maybe shoot him from a rooftop. His own house seems like a tremendous risk. If he's captured and made to divulge who sent him it would be the end for Hearst."

Daniel ushered me into the hall and went to lock the door. "I wonder if there was a key in the door, locking it from the inside?" he said. "Or did the killer leave the room, lock the door after him, and take the key?"

"Junior said it was hard to get the key into the hole, suggesting that there was a key on the inside."

"For him. You'll notice he has little control over his limbs."

I glanced down at the floor. "Look, here it is on the carpet." I bent to retrieve the original key. "He was right. It was in the keyhole."

"Careful touching that," Daniel said sharply. "We may be able to get a fingerprint. I hope they bring a kit with them. This whole room must be checked. Unless he's a pro, he'll have left a print somewhere." He took out his handkerchief, turned the key in the lock holding it, then wrapped both keys, depositing them into his pocket.

"Now, I don't know about you, but I could use some supper," he said.

"Isn't that rather heartless?" I asked. "How can we sit down to dinner when there is a man lying dead in his office?"

"You married a policeman, Molly," Daniel said, "and I know that we will be here a long time and we are going to need something to eat."

We started down the stairs. "Poor Bridie. She'll worry where we've got to," I said.

"She'll be busy tucking into her supper, I expect," Daniel said. "The young don't let much keep them from their food."

"So they still don't know?"

"Probably not, unless all the shouting and Mrs. McCormick's hysterics have given it away. Let's hope they just think he's been taken ill."

We heard the sound of voices and the clink of cutlery and followed them into a dining room. In the center was a long table, now spread with all kinds of enticing dishes: cold chicken, salmon in aspic, oysters, lobster, salads, fruits, cheeses, all beautifully displayed. Guests were helping themselves and then taking their plates through to the sitting room. If they thought it was odd that the hostess was missing no one mentioned it. Daniel went to follow suit. I looked for Bridie.

"Do you know what happened to Bridie?" I asked one of the girls who was now tucking in happily to a large plate of food.

"Bridie?" She looked around. "I think she must have gone with Blanche up to her mother's room. Those two are very thick now, you know. I gather Mr. McCormick has been taken ill, somebody said, and Mrs. McCormick was upset."

135

I decided to leave well alone and joined Daniel at the table. We had just put food on our plates and were looking for a place to sit when Finn came over to us.

"The police are on their way," he said quietly. "I tried to stress the importance of handling this properly." He moved closer to Daniel. "You saw him. You saw the room. What do you think?"

"All I can tell you right now is that it must have been someone he was comfortable with. Someone he allowed to walk behind him."

"So one of the family members?" Finn asked.

"Or servants. Or someone he trusts, like his lawyer."

"His lawyer is hardly likely to have gone to the trouble of writing a new will for him, only to kill him," Finn replied dryly.

Daniel looked up. "So you knew about this will?"

"Oh, yes. He told me he was going to do it."

"And did you know what was in it?"

Finn shook his head. "I'm not privy to family matters. He just said that it was time he set things straight."

"I wonder why now during a party?" Daniel asked. "What was the urgency?" He put down his plate. "Stay close, Finn. We may have to let the guests know what has happened soon. People will want to leave."

"The butler is guarding the front door like a bulldog," Finn said. "I don't think anyone can have left."

"Unless they did so before the body was discovered. The murderer would certainly have slipped away if it was an outsider."

"Do you think it was an outsider, then?" Finn shook his head sadly. "What a disaster. I can't believe it. Big Bill murdered in his own home. I've no idea who they will get to replace him. Tammany has nobody with his kind of clout."

"So Hearst will just take the job. No contest?" Daniel asked.

"I can't see the Tammany bigwigs allowing that to happen." Finn looked at Daniel.

"Oh, no. Don't look at me," Daniel said. "I have none of the populist clout you were speaking about. In fact I've probably arrested some of the types who would be needed to back me. Besides, I have no desire to be mayor."

"Perhaps O'Brien—" Finn began, but broke off when Roberts, the butler, approached the men.

"I'm sorry to disturb you, sir," he said to Finn, "but I'm having a bit of trouble with some of the guests. They want to leave. They are important men and they don't like being told what to do by a servant. If you'd come to the door and speak to them?"

Finn turned to Daniel. "Will you give me a hand? I'm sure you're more skilled at this sort of thing."

Daniel put down his plate on a nearby table. "Watch my food for me, Molly," he said. "Though I can see I won't get the chance to eat."

I stared after him as he went. The thought that someone was now suggesting to put Daniel up for mayor to replace Big Bill was making me feel thoroughly sick. Why did he have to get involved in this mess in the first place, I asked myself. We were perfectly happy where we were. He liked his job. He was good at his job. And I . . . I liked my life just the way it was.

⚜ Eighteen ⚜

O ut in the foyer I could hear raised voices. Someone was wailing. A deep male voice was demanding, "Do you know who I am, young man? You can't keep me here against my will. Your superiors will hear about this."

Then a woman's voice. "I never heard of such a thing, not being able to leave a party. What is going on?"

"I'm sorry, madam, but there has been a murder," came Daniel's firm voice. "The police have been called and I'm afraid they will want everyone to stay until they get here."

"Who's been murdered?" the man boomed so loudly that other guests heard and began to walk over.

"Are we safe?" said his wife. "When do you think the police will get here?"

As if in answer to her question there was a thunderous knock on the front door. I didn't have a clear view from where I was as the escaping family was blocking my vision, but I heard the voice clearly enough: "Police. Stand aside."

The foyer filled with uniformed men.

"Who is in charge here?" a rather unpleasant male voice asked. "Where's Mr. McCormick?"

"It is Mr. McCormick who has been killed," Daniel replied.

I inched toward the open doorway. This was too good to miss.

The man who had just entered was older than Daniel and sported a droopy mustache that added to his sad, bloodhound look. He stared at Daniel, frowned, then said, "Good God, Sullivan. What in God's name are you doing here? We heard you'd resigned."

"Hello, Doyle," Daniel replied. "I am on temporary reassignment, actually, but any help I can be . . ."

"What are you doing here in the first place?"

"I happen to be a guest at this party," Daniel said. "And until an hour ago I was running for sheriff on the same ticket as Big Bill in the upcoming elections."

"Police department not good enough for you, huh?" The voice was grating and gravelly. The man was considerably shorter than Daniel, but he had that belligerence you often see in small men.

"That's neither here nor there," Daniel said. "Now, would you like me to fill you in on the details of the crime?"

"Where was he killed?"

"In his study, inside a locked room," Daniel said. "I have secured the crime scene. Nobody has touched anything as far as I know."

"As far as you know?" the man said.

"I locked the door and the keys are in my pocket, wrapped in my handkerchief. I suggest you take a look at the crime scene and have one of your men dust for fingerprints."

"Fingerprints?" Doyle made a disparaging noise. "And what use are they? Stupid newfangled things."

"Doyle, they will change everything!" Daniel said. "For the first time we can definitively identify someone."

"But they are not admissible in a court of law. We can't use them as evidence, so why bother?"

"Why bother? My dear man, they'd identify who might have been in that room who had no business to be there. They might find your killer for you."

"And I can't pin the crime on him based on that evidence," Doyle snapped. "And you'd better not speak to me in that tone. You are no longer my superior, nor do you have any official status in this case. In fact you're a suspect like everyone else. But if you want to help, why don't you make yourself useful and round up everybody in one room for me to question them."

"I suggest you send some of your men to do that, since I no longer have authority," Daniel said in a calm voice. "The guests are already complaining about being held against their will. I gather there are some pretty powerful types among them. People you wouldn't want to anger."

"I'll want to start with the family," Doyle said. "There is a wife? And children?"

"There is a wife," Daniel said, "two sons, and a daughter."

"And where will I find them?"

"I think the wife and daughter are in Mrs. McCormick's bedroom," Daniel said. "One of the sons is in his room. I couldn't tell you where the younger one is."

"Johnson—go and round them up," Doyle said. "Tell them I want them down here right away."

I decided it was time for me to act. "Excuse me," I said, stepping forward, "but Mr. McCormick's widow was absolutely distraught. So was their daughter. Might I suggest you speak to them in the privacy of her boudoir? She wouldn't want to be questioned with other people listening in."

Those droopy eyes focused on me. "You're a family member?"

"No, I'm Captain Sullivan's wife, but our daughter is up with Blanche McCormick, comforting her. I think it would be most painful for them to have to appear in public at a time like this." I gave what I hoped was an appealing smile. "Do you think you could talk to them first, alone, in her room? I know they'd appreciate it."

He stared at me for a long moment. "Very well," he said. "You go ahead and tell them to make themselves ready and I'll be up there in five minutes."

"Thank you so much," I said.

"Don't you want to take a look at the scene of the crime first?" Daniel asked, giving me a quick look of appreciation.

"Of course," Doyle said. "But it won't take that long. My men will take the details."

"Then follow me," Daniel said.

"They don't have servants who can show me the way?"

"The servants are busy serving supper to the guests, I'd imagine," Daniel said. "Besides, since I was one of the first on the scene I can describe to you how the body was discovered."

"It seems I'm to be stuck with you whether I like it or not," Doyle said. "Go on, then. Lead the way. And Johnson and Byrne, you'd better come with me."

Daniel started up the stairs. The policemen followed. So did I, staying well back and keeping out of the way. I knew I was supposed to pass along the message to the family, but I could do that in a minute.

"It's down this hallway," Daniel said.

"What was this man doing upstairs when there was a birthday party for his daughter going on below? Taking a quick nap or a quick dalliance with a maid?" He laughed at his own joke. I could tell why Daniel didn't like him.

"It's his office," Daniel replied. "His lawyer was present and I gather he went up there to sign some papers. From what I saw it looked like a will."

"A will, eh? There we have a motive for murder if ever I saw one. Someone's cut out of the will and doesn't like it. Did he actually sign?"

"He's slumped forward over the desk, but from what I could tell he didn't," Daniel said. "What's more the whiskey decanter was knocked over and the whiskey has soaked into the paper, spoiling it."

Daniel paused outside the door, took out his handkerchief and unwrapped the keys.

"So he was first found by his older son," Daniel said. "He wanted to speak to his father but found the door was locked. He sent a servant for the pass key and when the door was opened he saw his father slumped over the desk. He thought his father had passed out and called for help."

"He didn't see the knife and realize he was dead?"

"He didn't go into the room," Daniel said. "He is confined to a wheelchair so he couldn't go any further than the doorway. When he called out the younger son ran up the stairs. I followed hot on his heels. We went into the room and saw the knife."

"Ah, so nobody had a chance to tamper with the room before you got there?"

"They did not," Daniel said. Then he held the key carefully in the handkerchief before turning it in the lock. "Just in case you decide on testing for fingerprints at some stage," he said. The door swung open. The smell of whiskey floated out toward me, mingled with a less pleasant odor—I recognized it as the smell of death. I'd smelled it before. The men went inside. I moved nearer.

"So what killed him?" Doyle asked. "Do we know?"

"If you come around here, he has a knife in his back," Daniel said.

"Ah, stabbed from behind," Doyle said. "That would indicate he knew his killer, right? It would be almost impossible for an intruder to sneak up behind him at his desk and stab him. And certainly nowhere to hide in this room."

"Precisely," Daniel said. "And you see, he's a big man. He would have turned and grappled with an assailant. From what I can see it doesn't look like a very impressive knife."

"It does not," Doyle said. "He must have been lucky and pierced the heart."

"Not much bleeding, that we can see," Daniel said.

"Punctured a lung, then?"

"Possible." Daniel paused. "You'll do an autopsy, of course?"

"No need, is there? The guy was stabbed. He's dead. Doesn't really matter what organ the knife found, it did its work."

142

Daniel chose not to reply. I couldn't see his face, but I imagined his jaw was clenched.

"So let's take a look at these papers on the desk," Doyle said. "Too bad the whiskey has stained them so badly and made the ink run." There was a pause while presumably he moved Big Bill's body aside. "It does look like a will. I'll have my men dry it out when we've moved the body. Byrne, arrange for a stretcher to transport the body to the morgue. And, Johnson—we'd better take photographs. Did we bring the necessary equipment in the vehicle?"

"Yes, sir. Corelli has the camera and flash equipment."

"Then get him onto it. I need to talk to this guy's family. It's clear enough it's an inside job. All we need to do is find out who is left out of a new will and we have our suspect."

✂❧ Nineteen ❧✂

I didn't want to be caught snooping and realized I was supposed to alert Mrs. McCormick. I didn't wait another second but walked quickly down the opposite hallway. I could hear voices coming from behind a door at the far end. I tapped on it, then didn't wait to be given permission to enter. Surprised faces looked up at me. Lucy McCormick was lying on her bed. Blanche and Cornelius were sitting on either side of her. Bridie was perched on a low chair nearby.

"What is it?" Cornelius asked, standing up as he saw me. "What do you want? My mother should not be disturbed."

"I came to warn you. The police are here and they want to question everyone," I said in a low voice. "I persuaded them not to make you come downstairs with everyone else so the lieutenant is coming to this room. He's not the most pleasant of men."

I went to leave, but Mrs. McCormick held out her hand. "Please stay, Molly," she said. "I need an ally right now. And your help. Bridie tells me that you were once a real detective and you've solved murders before. You'll help us, won't you?"

"If I can," I said. "And I know my husband will do his best to get to the truth."

"It can't be that hard," Cornelius said. "It was obviously one of

Hearst's men, sent to eliminate the competition. He's been trying to find a way to get my father out of the race since he announced his candidacy. He's a ruthless man, Mrs. Sullivan. He'll stop at nothing."

I looked directly at him. "The only question about that theory is how did he make his escape? Apparently the window is closed and it's a long way to the ground."

"He snuck down the stairs, of course," Cornelius said, giving me a scornful sneer. "We were all in the ballroom playing party games. It would have been perfectly easy to come down without being seen."

"Except that the room was locked from the inside," I replied, rather enjoying scoring a point against him. I have never liked being patronized by arrogant men.

We had no time to continue the discussion, as we heard voices outside the door.

"Is this the room?"

And then Daniel entered, followed by Lieutenant Doyle and one of his assistants.

"You're Mrs. McCormick?" Doyle asked.

"I should think that was obvious." Cornelius came toward him. "I am Cornelius McCormick, her son. And may I point out that my mother has had a terrible shock and needs to rest. She is in no state to speak to anyone."

His aggressive tone seemed to have knocked the wind out of Doyle's sails. "Sorry to disturb you, ma'am, but I do need to ask you a few questions. And your children as well."

"I don't know what I can tell you." Mrs. McCormick sounded close to tears. "It's all so unreal."

"You can recount the events of the evening until the time when your husband's body was found."

"That's easy enough," she said. "It's my daughter's birthday. We spent the afternoon preparing for the party. The first guests arrived at seven. We had a receiving line at the door to welcome them.

When everyone had arrived, champagne was served to the adults. Then we went through to the ballroom to play party games before supper. Cornelius was master of ceremonies."

"And I have to say I did a brilliant job of it too," Cornelius said with a grin. "Isn't that right, Blanche?"

"You were all right," she replied. "A little too bossy in trying to enforce the rules."

"That's because your friends cheat."

I studied him, looking quite pleased with himself. Didn't he realize his father had just been murdered? But then I decided that people handle grief and shock differently. Maybe going back to the happier time earlier in the evening was all he could handle right now.

Doyle cleared his throat. "So how many guests are there?"

"Twelve families, I believe, making around fifty guests."

"They are all friends of yours?"

"Not really," she replied. "The girls are school friends of my daughter. I had not met some of the parents before now."

"Aha," Doyle said. "So you don't know exactly who they are. A stranger might have gained entrance among them."

"Highly unlikely," she said.

"Actually there was a stranger earlier," Daniel said. "My wife spotted a man hiding in a corner taking notes. It turned out he was a reporter working for Hearst and he was thrown out."

"So it would have been possible for anyone to have crept in at any time," Doyle said. "Make a note of that, Johnson."

"Oh, I don't think . . ." Mrs. McCormick said quickly. "I mean, we have servants in the house, coming and going all the time. And the butler has to open the front door."

"Yet the reporter got in." Doyle nodded with satisfaction.

"I've no idea how that happened," Mrs. McCormick said. "He must have attached himself to one of the arriving families."

"So let's come to your husband," Doyle said. "Where was he all evening?"

"He was beside me, until he had a word with his attorney and then said he had to go up to his office to handle some papers."

"I didn't want him to go," Blanche said. "I didn't want him to spoil my party."

"And why would his leaving spoil your party, little girl?" Doyle asked.

Blanche gave him a withering look at being addressed as "little girl." "My father was often called away on business from family gatherings," Blanche replied. "I thought he might not come back and I wanted him there at my party."

"Did you have an idea what these papers were, Mrs. McCormick?"

"I think he was updating his will," she said. "He had not made one for many years. In fact I believe he had not made a will since my marriage to him. He thought he was immortal, you know." A spasm of pain crossed her face. "Anyway, we had never discussed such matters. I abhor talking about money, but I did want to make sure my children were well provided for."

"And why was it so important that he update his will in the middle of a party?"

"That's exactly what I asked him. Even his attorney said it could wait until the next day."

"And he replied?"

"You don't know my husband, Lieutenant. When he has something that needs to be done, he'll not rest until it is done. He's that sort of man." She paused, collected herself, then said, "Was that sort of man."

"Is the lawyer still here?" he asked.

"I really couldn't tell you," Lucy McCormick replied. "I forgot about him when the girls were playing their games and having such a good time."

"Thanks to me," Cornelius said.

"You got tired before we did," Blanche countered. "You left us while we were playing hunt the slipper. I saw you!"

147

"Nature does call from time to time, dear child," he said. "And I had drunk rather a lot. I just went to the cloakroom on this floor."

I glanced up at this, wondering if Lieutenant Doyle had also picked up on the fact that Cornelius had left the room.

"So Mr. McCormick goes upstairs and you are all playing party games. Did you notice anyone else leave the room?"

"It's hard to say," Mrs. McCormick said. "Servants were carrying around trays of lemonade and champagne, so I presume they went in and out, but we were all watching the girls rushing around and having a good time."

"When did you notice your husband had not returned?"

She sighed. "I remember thinking he'd been gone awhile, but I knew better than to interrupt Bill while he was working. He could get quite hot-headed about it. But then Blanche asked where he was, and at that moment our footman, Charlie, came rushing in, demanding the pass key, as Mr. McCormick's older son suspected something was wrong and couldn't get into his father's study. Then we waited, we heard raised voices, sounding upset, and someone said Bill was dead. Then we all rushed upstairs and saw for ourselves."

"I went ahead, because I can move faster," Cornelius said. "My older brother couldn't get into the room because of his wheelchair, but he was blocking the doorway. I had to shove him aside. I went in and saw my father slumped over the desk."

"And I went around the back of the desk and saw the knife in his back," Daniel said.

Doyle looked from one face to the next, then he said, "Thank you, that will be all for now. But you are not to leave the house until I give you permission."

"As if I'd want to leave this room," Mrs. McCormick said. "I simply can't face anyone at this moment. Corny, I'll rely on you to bid farewell to our guests. And Blanche, darling, perhaps you can be brave enough to go downstairs and thank them all for coming."

"Yes, Mama, I can do that," Blanche said. "But they are not allowed to leave yet, are they?"

"Lieutenant, please notify us when our guests are free to go," Lucy McCormick said. "It would be quite improper if we did not bid them farewell."

"Very well," he said. "So I think I can leave you in peace now. But I'll need to speak to your older son. William McCormick Junior? Is that his name? Where can I find him?"

"He'll be in his room. Across the hall from this one," Mrs. McCormick said. "And he is my stepson, the child of the first wife."

"What happened to her? Divorce?"

Tact was clearly not one of Lieutenant Doyle's strong points.

"She died when Bill Junior was a small child," she said. "Of the same wasting disease that he has unfortunately inherited. I married his father later that year."

Doyle turned to Daniel. "You said the older son was the one who went to his father's room first. He thought something had happened to his father? He was the first on the scene?"

"That's right," Daniel said.

"But I think you can dismiss him as a suspect, Lieutenant," Cornelius said, with amusement in his voice. "His hand shakes when he tries to lift his teacup. And he is trapped in that wheelchair unless Charlie carries him."

"And who is Charlie?" Doyle asked.

"Our footman," Mrs. McCormick replied.

"I'll need to speak to him too. All of your servants, in fact."

"I hope you're not going to bully or upset them," Mrs. McCormick said. "I don't want them leaving us. It's hard enough to get quality servants these days."

"Must be terrible for you," Doyle replied in a dry voice as he strode from the room, followed by his sergeant. Daniel gave me a swift glance, then followed him. I stayed with Mrs. McCormick.

149

"Lucy, would you like me to have some supper sent up to you?" I asked.

She shook her head, lying back onto her pillow. "I couldn't possibly eat a thing. I'm too distraught," she said.

"But what about the young ones?" I asked. "They must be hungry after all those boisterous games."

"We can go down and help ourselves," Cornelius said. "It will be every man for himself since that little man will be bullying our servants into confessing all kinds of untruths about this family."

"Cornelius, this is not a joking matter," Lucy snapped. "I don't think you realize but someone has killed your father and we are all suspects."

"Sorry, Mother. Just trying to lighten the mood," Cornelius said. "Come on, girls. Let's see if the guests have decimated the supper table."

I went over to Lucy. "Would you like me to stay?" I asked.

She shook her head. "You are very kind, but I'll take one of my sleeping powders. I think I need to sleep." She reached out and took my hand. "But you will do your best, won't you? You'll find out who did this?"

"Even if the truth might be painful?" I asked.

Her eyes opened wide in shock. "What are you saying?"

"Only that someone may have wanted to stop your husband from signing a new will."

"But you can't think it was one of us?"

"I hope not," I said. "I really hope not."

❧ Twenty ❧

I slipped out of the room as Lucy lay back. In truth I was feeling sick and scared now that the first rush of excitement had left me. I had not taken to Big Bill and was still annoyed at my husband for getting involved with him, but nobody deserves to die like that. And the more I thought about it, the more I worried that someone close to Big Bill had been responsible. But who could have locked the door from the inside? How, then, did they escape? I was still mulling this perplexing problem when I heard voices coming from the room across the hallway and saw that the door was not quite shut. Of course, I went over to hear what was being said.

"So what made you decide you had to speak to your father at that moment? Did you know he was about to sign a new will?" I recognized Doyle's antagonistic tone of voice.

"I did not," Junior's voice replied. "I wanted to ask him about something quite different."

"Which was?"

"A new treatment I had read of for my type of condition. Using electric shocks to stimulate the legs to enable me to walk again. I hoped he would agree to pay to send me to Berlin where it is being done." His voice was surprisingly strong, given his frail physique, and even had a touch of his father's brogue to it.

"So why ask at that moment?"

"Because, Mr. Policeman, I had been thinking about it all week. Trying to talk to him is like trying to harness a tornado. He's never still for a minute. So when I knew he'd gone up to his office and would be alone I decided to take my chance. I had Charlie bring me upstairs and I waited until I thought he had been in there long enough, then I went to his door."

"Charlie is the servant who looks after you, right?"

"He is. I couldn't really get around without him."

"So he was with you when you went to your father's door?"

"No, I was alone. I can maneuver along the hallways quite easily because they have wooden floors. It's just thick carpets that are a problem, and trying to get over the edge of them."

"Go on. You got to his door and . . ."

"I tapped and called, 'Father, it's Junior. May I come in?' But there was no reply. I thought he might be on the telephone. I listened but heard nothing. I banged louder. If he was busy he'd have yelled for me to go away and leave him in peace. But he didn't answer. That's when I became concerned. I thought he might have passed out."

"Passed out?" Doyle asked. "Is he liable to pass out?"

"He has done a few times when he drinks too much."

"And had he drunk too much?"

"I couldn't tell you. My father always drank a lot. He had a champagne glass in his hand every time I saw him all evening. He had a decanter of whiskey in his room and he'd get through that quite quickly. So I thought it was possible he'd maybe nodded off to sleep."

"So what did you do?"

"I yelled for Charlie and sent him to get the pass key. He came back with the butler, who gave me the key."

"Why give you the key?"

"Because I asked for it. It's only right and proper that a family member open the door first. But I couldn't get it into the slot properly and Charlie had to help me. At last it felt as if something gave way. I presume a key was in the door on the inside and we pushed it out. We opened the door and saw my father slumped over. I assumed he was sick and told them to get a doctor, but then other people came up. My brother pushed past me into the room and declared my father was dead."

"All right, Mr. McCormick. Thank you. I can't think of anything more to ask you tonight, but we know where to find you." Doyle's voice became louder as he must have turned toward the door. "Now let's get downstairs and see what the guests have to say."

I ducked back into shadow at the end of the hall as Doyle came out, followed by the policeman he had called Johnson. Daniel followed them, not noticing me. Instead of going downstairs with them, he headed back along the hallway to Big Bill's office. I tiptoed behind at a suitable distance. A flash and smell of sulphur greeted me, and I heard Daniel say, "Taking photographs. That's good, Corelli. But no fingerprints? That is so infuriating. How does he plan to make an arrest?"

And a voice from the room said, "I'm of your mind, Captain Sullivan, sir. I wish you were on this case."

"Well, I'm not, Corelli, and we have to make the best with what we have."

"Tell you what, sir," came the other voice. "We have the kit in the police wagon. If I happened to bring it into the house and forget to collect it, you might just happen to find it."

"I like your thinking, Corelli," Daniel said. "Only God help you if Doyle suddenly wants it later."

"He won't, sir. He's dead against fingerprints. Doesn't believe in them, even though we've tried to show him how useful they are. But then there are enough judges who think like him, aren't there? Never been allowed as evidence even though one person's prints show up on the handle of a revolver. Doesn't make sense to me."

"Me neither," Daniel said. "So if you could leave it in a suitable corner when you take out your photographic equipment . . ."

"I will, sir. The umbrella stand? And may I say I'm sorry you're not with the department anymore. The guys were all really put out when they heard you'd left and were going into politics."

"It won't be forever, Corelli. And thank the guys for me."

Daniel nodded then came back toward the top of the stairs. He saw me standing there.

"Oh, hello, Molly," he said. "You stayed with Mrs. McCormick?"

"I have. Poor thing is just devastated. Have they found anything useful yet?" I asked innocently.

"Not that I know of. Did the family say anything of interest?" he asked.

"Just that a lawyer was here to help draw up a will. That must be what Big Bill was writing out," I said, then remembered a conversation I overheard. "Actually, I just realized I heard Big Bill telling a man he was going to write a first draft of a document and the man should come up to his study in about an hour. It meant nothing to me then, but that must have been the lawyer he was addressing."

"I wonder if he knows what Big Bill intended to write."

"I think the police lieutenant had the same idea. He asked for him."

"At least he is not totally useless." He lowered his voice. "But do me a good turn, will you? Keep Doyle occupied downstairs for a while."

"What are you going to do?" I spoke in the same low tones.

"Do a little snooping of my own before they take the body away. And I want to make a telephone call to somebody where I can't be overheard, so I'll use the extension in McCormick's office."

"Don't you worry about smudging the prints on the receiver?" I asked, again innocently.

"Don't worry. I'll handle it," he said. "Off you go. If Doyle looks as if he's planning to come back up here in a hurry offer him some supper. And a glass of champagne. That usually does the trick."

As I turned to go downstairs I almost bumped into Finn, coming up.

"Ah, there you are, Daniel," he said as he walked past me with an apologetic nod of the head. Daniel paused and turned back. "I've been on the telephone to Tammany, to let them know. It's terrible, isn't it? I can't quite believe it. But then he did have his enemies, poor man. Plenty of folks who wished him dead. Never went out without a bodyguard and now they find him at home."

"You think it was an outsider, then?" Daniel asked.

"You don't?"

"He was in the process of drawing up a new will, Finn. And I don't see how anyone could have made it up to his study and then down again without being seen."

"That newspaper guy got in earlier easily enough."

"That's true," Daniel agreed, "but it would take a particularly brazen type to kill the host in the middle of a party."

"I suppose you're right. Tammany will be putting out feelers. If it was the other side, someone will be boasting about it." Finn paused. "So do you need me to do anything now?"

"You can help Molly keep that police detective occupied downstairs. Any minute now they're going to take the body away and the crime scene will be spoiled."

"Right. Come on, Molly. Let's go down and face the music."

Finn put a hand on my shoulder and steered me down the stairs.

I sensed the tension as I entered the ballroom, where the guests were assembled on chairs around the perimeter. They had obviously now been told about the murder and were in the process of being questioned. Doyle's assistants were going around, getting details from each family. Several girls were crying. Several parents arguing.

"When can we leave? It's past my daughter's bedtime."

"This is outrageous. To treat us as if we are suspects. Your superiors will be hearing about this in the morning." That was Mr. O'Brien,

I noticed. His wife was looking pale and anxious. They didn't have any children with them. I wondered why he had come. To solidify his role as Big Bill's number two? I wondered if that made him number one now.

"No, I don't know much about Bill McCormick except what I've read in the papers," said another man. "Never met the man before tonight. I didn't even realize Julia was in the same class as his daughter until we got the invitation."

I tried to listen in to as many of the complaints as I could. I looked from one prosperous face to the next. Did any of them look anxious or uneasy? Some of the women looked stunned and worried, but the men mostly looked annoyed at being inconvenienced. People who hardly knew Big Bill and with no motive to harm him. I realized at that moment that it might be possible that we would never come to the truth about who killed him, unless Daniel was having any luck upstairs. And I had promised Lucy McCormick that I would help. Although how I was going to do that, I had no idea.

It was several hours before the obnoxious inspector decided that he had enough information and the guests were free to go. Blanche came down with Cornelius, Bridie following behind. Blanche's eyes were clearly red with crying, but she bravely said goodbye to each family in turn, thanking them for coming in a small choked voice. Cornelius tried to play the man of the family, bidding goodbye to the guests in a tone that seemed to imitate his father's. Almost all of the guests had left when Daniel came downstairs. I tried to ask him with a look if he had managed to get the fingerprints, but he rubbed his eyes tiredly. "I've sent someone to hail a taxicab or hansom," he said. "We should let the family be alone."

Bridie did not want to leave. "Blanche needs me," she protested. "She's been crying since that policeman questioned her." Blanche had said goodbye to the last guest and came over to join us, grabbing onto Bridie's hand.

"Oh, please don't go, Bridie. Can't you stay?"

Daniel spoke gently, "Not tonight. Bridie needs sleep and so do you." Tears welled up in Blanche's eyes again.

"I can't bear to be here alone. Mama is in her room crying, Corny is lording it over everyone acting like he is in charge. And Papa's dead." The tears threatened to turn into sobs.

"I understand how you feel," I said, putting an arm around her, "but you can't do anything tonight except sleep. Why don't you come to lunch at our house tomorrow? That way you'll have something to look forward to. That is, if your mother allows you."

"She will, I'm sure." She hugged Bridie. "We normally have Sunday dinner together, but I don't think Mama will leave her room. I'll see you tomorrow, then." She looked back at Bridie and waved again as she left the foyer.

As the taxicab pulled up the fog was swirling in. It was after two and the streets were quiet. Bridie sat between us in the automobile and fell asleep with her head on my shoulder in about five minutes.

"Did you get the fingerprints?" was my first question to Daniel.

"Yes, Corelli has taken them back to the station. And he passed on to me the information that Doyle questioned the lawyer but that he had no idea what was to be in the will. He only knows that Big Bill summoned him out of the blue today, wanting it drawn up and signed immediately. Corelli will let me know if they manage to recover the writing after it is dry. He's a good man," Daniel said approvingly.

"But what will you compare the fingerprints to?" I asked. "I imagine Doyle didn't ask the family for their fingerprints."

Daniel nodded. "As it stands now, I have no authority to ask the family for their prints. But I put in a call to the police commissioner while Doyle was out of the way. I can't stand back and let him botch this investigation. I want the commissioner to put me on the case."

"So you'll be giving up politics and going back to police work?" This sounded too good to be true. How did I know that Daniel could still go back to the police department? It hit me that he had just lost his Tammany Hall patron and the man who had lent us a house. If Daniel had no political career, would he still be welcome in the police force? "Are you sure you haven't burned any bridges leaving as you did?"

"Quite the contrary. I did all of this as a favor for the police commissioner." Daniel lowered his voice to make sure the man driving the taxi did not overhear.

"What?" I blurted out the word and it sounded unnaturally loud in the night air.

Daniel put a finger to his lips in warning. "I'm so glad I can tell you now," he continued in a low voice. "I hate keeping secrets from you, Molly, especially since you are so damned perceptive it is hard to fool you."

"What secret were you keeping, then?" Was this going to be good news or bad? I thought we had no secrets between us. Well, I knew I kept things from Daniel sometimes, but I didn't think he kept anything from me.

"The police commissioner wanted me to investigate the reporter who went missing at the docks while writing a piece for Hearst on corrupt practices. I think he may have been getting some pressure from Hearst. But it was impossible to do any investigating from the outside. He knew that Tammany would just close ranks, and he would have made a powerful enemy to boot." There was no traffic on the road and Daniel's face looked eerie in the light of the street lamps we passed. "So he asked me to go undercover. I was thinking of getting a job at the docks, changing my name, and getting work as a lumper."

"Oh, Daniel," I interjected, "I can't believe you would even think of that if one man has already gone missing."

"As I said, I was thinking about it, but then Big Bill asked the police commissioner to recommend a candidate to run for sheriff. He came to me right away. It seemed the perfect way to get into his inner circle quickly."

Daniel's behavior over the past few weeks was beginning to make more sense. "And why wouldn't you just tell me? This makes much more sense than me thinking you had suddenly become Tammany Hall's best friend. Do you know what you put me through?" I started to raise my voice and then lowered the tone again, not wanting the driver to overhear.

"The commissioner insisted nobody know for my own safety," he said. "One man had already been killed, or at least has disappeared for investigating. And I know you. If I gave you a mystery you would not stop until you solved it. I couldn't bear for you to put yourself in danger. And then, what if I had won? Could you really have played the sheriff's wife while all the time trying to investigate Tammany Hall? I just couldn't take the risk."

"I don't like you keeping secrets!" I wanted to be angry, but all that I could think was that I was going to get my life back.

"I tried to tell you that there was a reason for what I was doing. Something I couldn't share with you yet." This was true. He had asked me to trust him. My head was spinning from the lateness of the hour. Should I be angry? Or just glad it was over. And I had so many questions.

"Do you think Big Bill had the journalist killed?" I asked.

Daniel sighed. "I just don't know. And now I may never know. It takes time to be trusted by a man like Big Bill. I don't think he was ever unguarded with me. Maybe after some months together he might have taken me into his confidence, but all I saw was his political friendly face."

"And now he's dead." I wasn't sure if I should mourn or not. Had he been a corrupt murderer or just a normal politician? I decided I could at least be sad for Lucy and poor little Blanche. "And you can give up politics?"

"With all my heart." Despite the late hour Daniel sounded newly energetic. "And I want Big Bill's murder to be my first case back. The police commissioner owes me that." The rush of joy that I felt made me feel quite guilty. The McCormick family's tragedy was going to put my life back together. As we pulled up to the brownstone I was already wondering how quickly I could ask Ryan's friend to leave Patchin Place. I couldn't wait to get back to my life there.

Daniel fished for a key in the pocket of his suit as I stood with my arm around a shivering Bridie. Before he could find it, the door opened. Mary was standing there.

"You didn't have to stay up, Mary," Daniel said, surprised. We walked gratefully into the warmth of the foyer.

"I didn't want to lock up until you were home, Captain Sullivan," Mary said, helping me off with my cloak. "Was it a nice party, Mrs. Sullivan?"

My eyes met Daniel's. "It was interesting, Mary." I wasn't sure that I wanted to even talk about the murder at this time of night. "Can you help me take Miss Bridie up to bed?" Mary and I helped a very sleepy Bridie up to bed. When she was in her nightdress and tucked into bed I sent Mary to bed herself and came downstairs. Daniel was in the family parlor pouring himself a drink.

"I suppose I should have told Mary about Big Bill," I said, coming over and sitting down by him. "Everyone will know tomorrow."

"It was a good idea to let her go to bed without worrying. This is Big Bill's house, after all. When we go back to Patchin Place we don't know what will happen to her employment." The certainty with which he mentioned going back to Patchin Place made my heart swell. Going home! Daniel must have mistaken my silence. He put his drink down and took my hand.

"Are you all right, Molly? It's not every day you are at a house with a murder."

"I am a little shocked, I confess. And very sad for the family. Honestly, I want to put all of this politics behind us and go back to our normal life."

"My normal life includes dead bodies and crime," Daniel reminded me, "but at least we know who the bad guys are. With Tammany Hall I am not really sure."

"I'm so glad to know your life's ambition is not really to be the sheriff of New York." I rose. "Shall we go to bed?"

Daniel stayed seated. "Actually, I'm waiting up. I called the police commissioner while I was at the McCormicks'. I don't like the way Doyle is handling this at all. He said he would call tonight."

I stared at him. "If you haven't noticed it is not the night but the wee hours of the morning. Why don't you just go to his office tomorrow?"

Daniel shrugged. "He asked to meet here tonight. I can only assume that he either wants to tell me something that he doesn't want overheard or he wants me to do something that can't wait until tomorrow." There was a quiet knock on the door. "That will be him now. Why don't you go up to bed?" But I was already heading for the door. There were going to be no more secrets in our marriage if I could help it. Daniel followed.

The police commissioner looked startled to see me as I opened the door. "Oh, Mrs. Sullivan, you're still up. How do you do?" He stammered the words as he held out his hand.

"Police Commissioner, won't you come in?" I stood back to let him enter. There was another man with him. They were both dressed in dark suits as if coming home from a night at the theater or a nice restaurant. "Can I take your hats? Our maid has gone to bed," I said, playing the hostess. I hung the commissioner's hat on the hat stand. The other man raised his hat to me politely before holding it out. He had neat blond hair and I could see as he stepped into the light of the foyer that his suit and the hat he handed me were very high quality.

"Commissioner Bingham." Daniel stepped forward to shake

161

hands. He looked inquiringly at the other man. By his dress he was clearly not a policeman. He was in his forties and slightly portly, though not unattractive.

"Daniel Sullivan," Daniel said, holding out his hand.

The other man shook it firmly. "William Randolph Hearst," he said. I dropped his hat.

❧ Twenty-One ❧

Sunday, October 20

I f Daniel was shocked he didn't show it. "Please come in, Mr. Hearst, Commissioner," he said, and led the way into the front parlor. Without asking he poured them both a drink of whiskey. "Please have a seat."

"Thank you, Sullivan." The police commissioner took the drink and sat. He was younger than I had expected with hair parted in the middle and a handlebar mustache. My gaze went to the other man, the power-hungry Mr. Hearst I had heard so much about. He was also younger than expected, clean-shaven and wearing a rather gaudy tie and a large-stoned ring on his little finger. I hovered in the doorway, not sure if I was welcome in their conversation but determined to hear anything that might impact our life. "I'm sorry to come by so late, but Mr. Hearst and I needed to talk to you before the news gets out about Big Bill."

"I'm actually very glad you came," Daniel said. "Doyle is not up to a high-profile case like this. I was hoping that now I will be taking my hat out of the ring for sheriff I could help with the investigation."

"That's what we wanted to talk about, I'm afraid." The commissioner turned to the other man. "Mr. Hearst? Would you like to take it from here?"

"Yes." Mr. Hearst cleared his throat. "Sullivan, I think you might have known or at least guessed that I was behind the request for you to join the Tammany ticket. I appreciate that you put yourself at some risk and inconvenience to infiltrate Big Bill's inner circle. Has that paid off? Do you have any idea what happened to my reporter?"

"I'm afraid I don't, Mr. Hearst," Daniel said. "Big Bill was friendly toward me, but I don't think he trusted me. I do have enough evidence already to bring some serious corruption and bribery charges. My feeling is that he was capable of having your reporter murdered if it suited his interest, but I have no proof. Now that he is dead, it is a moot point."

"Not at all," Mr. Hearst spoke forcefully. "It is more important than ever that we find out what happened to Ronnie Walker. He is not the only one who has disappeared. He was investigating the deaths of dockworkers who appeared to cross Tammany Hall. He had statements from three wives whose husbands met with accidents after they had a dispute with Big Bill or one of his flunkeys. Now I don't give a damn what political party you vote for at the end of the day, excuse my language, Mrs. Sullivan." I started. I had been standing as inconspicuously as possible, not wanting to be asked to leave the conversation. He saw the shock on my face and took it that I had been upset by the use of the word, not at being discovered. Then, to my continued amazement he smiled, and I could have sworn that he winked at me. A ladies' man, then! That was interesting.

Now I was sure that Mr. Hearst at least was free to speak in my presence, so I came all the way into the room and sat down. "But don't you see, if some individuals are willing to resort to murder it has to be stopped. I want a newspaper that gets to the truth!" He banged his glass down on the table so loudly that I jumped. "And how can I do that if my reporters have to risk their lives to get it."

"But surely now that Big Bill is dead that avenue of investigation is closed," Daniel said, trying to sound reasonable. "And, with no disrespect meant, I think there are those in the city who will believe you may have had something to do with it."

"I am no murderer." Hearst sounded resigned rather than angry. "I don't deny that I fight dirty and I like to win, but I would never stoop to murder."

"Perhaps as I investigate Big Bill's murder I will uncover more about what happened to your reporter," Daniel began. Mr. Hearst looked at the police commissioner.

"I'm sorry, Sullivan, I can't put you on this case officially." My heart sank. Once before Daniel had been betrayed by the police department, even ending up in jail. Was this commissioner going to go back on his promises to Daniel?

The color rose in Daniel's face. "Commissioner, you promised me my job back when this investigation was over."

Commissioner Bingham put up a hand. "You will have it, you will," he said soothingly, "but that is the point. The investigation is not over. I can't be seen to be investigating Tammany Hall. If I do I won't survive as commissioner for a week. You are perfectly placed on the inside to see who rises up into the power vacuum. Is there someone above Big Bill who was pulling the strings? Someone has been committing murder, and we need to know who it is."

"Excuse me, Commissioner." I was not going to sit silent. "But aren't you asking Daniel to do something very dangerous? If you can't investigate Tammany Hall, what will happen to him if he is found out?"

Daniel did not look pleased. He never liked it when I interfered with his work. But this time I could argue that it was my life as much as his that he was putting at risk.

"You are quite right, Mrs. Sullivan," Mr. Hearst said, giving me another appraising look. "It is a big sacrifice to ask you to make. I suppose the question is, do you think someone should stand up to corruption so that innocent people can go about their lives without

165

fear?" What could I say to that? Wasn't it exactly what I had been saying to Daniel?

"Your husband is perfectly positioned to do just that," Hearst said. "And you will have my influence and knowledge on your side. I know a lot about what goes on in this city. I promise that as much as it is in my power neither he nor you will come to harm." He gave me quite a knowing look. It made me think that he was well aware of the time Daniel had spent in jail and perhaps some of my other scandals. Was he aware that my brothers had been Irish freedom fighters or maybe even why I came to New York in the first place? Was he truly making a promise, or was it a threat?

Daniel tried to regain control of the conversation. "So, you want me to keep running for sheriff, but what about investigating Big Bill's murder?"

"Officially, Doyle is going to be in charge of it. You can't be seen to be involved. But I'll tell Corelli to keep you informed of all the evidence we have. Knowing who killed Big Bill may bring us closer to finding out what happened to Mr. Hearst's reporter." Commissioner Bingham stood. "I think we need to let your charming wife have her beauty rest. If you need me, send a note through Corelli. He's a good man and very loyal to you, by the way." Mr. Hearst stood as well. He held out his hand to Daniel.

"I know I'm asking a lot, but I have faith in you, Captain Sullivan." He shook Daniel's hand.

"Thank you, sir, I'll try not to let you down." There was a note of respect in Daniel's voice that told me he believed what Hearst had said. We stepped into the foyer, and I handed the men their hats. Commissioner Bingham gave a respectful nod, William Randolph Hearst an almost too friendly smile, before walking down the stairs and disappearing into the night.

"So you are going to do it. Going to keep running for sheriff?" I asked as soon as we were alone in the foyer. I wondered if Daniel would be angry that I had not gone upstairs and left him to his secret conversation. But to my surprise he sounded more like he wanted my approval.

"You heard them, Molly. I'm in the right place for this investigation. It would take them months or even years to get someone else inside." Daniel took my hands. "I don't want to put you and Bridie and Liam in any danger. Will you still be able to play the part of the politician's wife knowing what you know, or would you like to leave the city? You could always go and stay with my mother."

I didn't let Daniel see my shudder at that idea. "No, thank you," I said. "If you are perfectly placed, then so am I. I'm friends with Lucy McCormick. Bridie's friendship with Blanche gives me a natural reason to be over at their house. I'm sure I will find out things that they would never tell the police. I'm going to find out who killed Big Bill while you investigate the journalist's disappearance so we can all go back to our normal lives."

"Molly, don't be foolish," Daniel started.

"How many times have we had this conversation? You know I'm a good investigator. I know that you want to keep me safe, but I'm in no more danger investigating this than just from being your wife. Lucy McCormick has already asked me for help." He still looked doubtful, but at least he was not saying no. Our relationship had come a long way from the days he wanted me to have nothing to do with any investigation. Then I played my winning card. "And you need me to go along with your cover story and be the perfect politician's wife. Which I promise I will do."

"It seems I have no choice. Just promise me you'll stay out of danger." Daniel took me in his arms.

"I always do," I said untruthfully. I always did try to, I thought. "Now let's go to bed." We turned and started up the stairs, but as we paused on the landing, I could have sworn I heard a noise below like footsteps retreating. I peered down into the darkness but saw nothing moving. The house sounded silent. I could hear only the ticking of the grandfather clock in the hall. Had the footsteps been my imagination or had someone overheard our conversation?

I climbed into bed gratefully. It felt like mere minutes had passed when I was jerked to consciousness by the sound of bells. I lay there, half-awake, until I remembered it was Sunday morning and I'd had precious little sleep. At least Daniel wouldn't insist on attending church and making a good impression when there was no longer a reason for it. The full memory of last night came rushing back to me and I felt sick. I hoped fervently that Daniel's attempt at obtaining fingerprints from the crime scene would reveal an outsider, a shady figure from the corrupt world of Tammany and dockland, or even a henchman from Hearst, who had dispatched Bill McCormick and it was not one of his family.

As soon as the thought of Bill McCormick's family crossed my mind I remembered that we had invited Blanche to come to Sunday lunch and thus remove her from the tensions at home for a while. I sat up in bed, making Daniel groan in his sleep and reach for the covers. It had seemed like a good idea last night, but this was Blanche Mc-Cormick, spoiled daughter who had grown up with wealth and until recently had tormented Bridie. If she could switch from tormentor to best friend so rapidly, could the tide not turn again—especially if she was subjected to Constanza's food? I got out of bed.

"There's no rush," Daniel murmured, still half-asleep. "I think we can legitimately skip church today, since we only just went to bed. I'll need to go back to the McCormicks' house, of course."

"What will you be doing?"

Daniel opened his eyes fully, focusing on me now. "I have taken fingerprints from McCormick's office. Now I need them from the family and servants. I managed Mrs. McCormick's brandy glass last night, but now I have to obtain them from the others. Also I'd like a word with the servants when the police are not around."

"How are you going to take fingerprints when Lieutenant Doyle is so much against them? Word will get back."

Daniel nodded. "I'll be subtle."

"You mean sneaky."

He smiled then. "Definitely." He reached out and stroked my arm. "There's no need to get up yet. Come and cuddle for a while."

"I know where cuddles with you end up." I gave him a knowing stare. "Besides, Blanche McCormick is coming to lunch with us."

"Blanche McCormick?" He sat up now. "How did that happen?"

"You know she's now Bridie's new best friend and she was desolate last night. She wanted Bridie to stay, but I thought it wiser to bring Bridie home with us, until we knew more about the situation, so I invited her to luncheon—only realizing afterward, of course, that we have a cook who is liable to poison the girl, thus adding to the demise of the family."

Daniel chuckled. "Perhaps she won't feel like eating much," he said.

"Young people always feel like eating, in my experience," I replied. "So I'd better get up and have a word with Constanza. Not that she understands most of what I say . . ."

His grip tightened on my wrist now. "Don't go." He put on a pathetic face. "How often do we have the chance to just lie together without having to rush somewhere?"

"Not often," I agree. "But just five minutes." I lay beside him, resting my head on his shoulder. "So what do you think, then?" I asked.

"About what?" His hand was caressing my shoulder.

"About the murder? Who was most likely, in your opinion?"

"Molly, I can't give an opinion on that until we know more. When we've examined those fingerprints and tried to match them, and seen the contents of the will, then perhaps we'll have a better idea. But as for now . . ." He pulled me closer to him.

"Mrs. McCormick seemed genuinely upset," I said. "And Junior seemed bewildered. But Cornelius was being quite flippant, I thought. He didn't seem to care that his father was dead."

"Just his personality, I'd guess," Daniel replied.

"And what about the families at the party? Could any of them have a grudge against Bill McCormick?"

"Molly, I didn't question them, so I don't know yet. Now please let's not think about it for five blissful minutes."

Half an hour later I got up, dressed hurriedly, and went down to the kitchen. Constanza was bustling around and the smell of coffee wafted toward me.

"Ah, Signora." She looked up, startled as if any appearance by me meant an attack. "What you need, eh? Breakfast already?"

"We have a special guest coming to lunch today," I said. "An important young lady. The daughter of Mr. McCormick." I remembered as I said it that Constanza had no idea he was dead. None of them did. I'd leave it to Daniel to decide when to tell them. I presumed it would be in the morning papers if Hearst had anything to say in the matter.

"Ah. Signor McCormick." She nodded and I also remembered at that moment that her husband had been a big noise at the docks and had met a tragic and untimely end. Someone who might have complained about how those docks were run, perhaps. How the workers were treated? Someone who might want revenge against Big Bill. I wondered how much she knew and how I could ever question her. I suspected there might be several more dockworkers with a grudge if it had been really true that Big Bill cut corners wherever he could when it came to safety.

"The Italian butcher is open on Sundays, yes?" I asked.

"Sì. He is open," she agreed.

"Then I want you to go and choose some meat for lunch. Meat that you know how to cook well, understand? Make a good lunch for Mr. McCormick's daughter."

A smile spread across her face. "I go. I make good meat."

I could only hope.

❧ Twenty-Two ☙

D aniel left after breakfast, heading for the McCormicks' mansion. Blanche was delivered in the family automobile at noon, looking horribly pale in a mauve dress.

"Isn't this dress absolutely awful, Bridie?" was one of the first things she said after she and Bridie had hugged. "But Mama says we're in mourning and mauve is suitable for a child. At least it looks better on me than black."

"I think it looks very nice," Bridie said.

Blanche gave her a grateful smile. "Do you? Then you shall have it as soon as the mourning period is over."

"Really?" Bridie shot a glance at me to see if this might be allowed.

"How is your poor mother?" I asked, changing the subject.

"Mama just woke up as I was leaving. You can tell how upset she is—she didn't even go to church. Mama never misses church and she was quite horrified when she remembered it was Sunday and we had missed mass. She said we'd all have to go to confession."

"I think this counts as a special circumstance, don't you? A death in the family?" I gave her an encouraging smile, as she looked so worried. She nodded, hopefully.

"Anyway, now the dressmaker is up in her room taking measurements for her mourning attire. I think it's rather silly, don't you? I mean, poor Papa is dead and he won't care what we wear."

"Are the police back in your house?"

"Yes, some of them never left, I think. It's too horrible. I don't know what they think they are going to find, poking into all our rooms. They even came into my bedroom and looked through my doll collection. I mean, really!" She gave a nervous little laugh. "Thank you so much for letting me come over here. Everyone at home is tiptoeing around looking frightened, except my brother, who keeps making silly jokes, just to annoy the policemen." She paused, thinking. "But I suspect that's because he's nervous."

"And your older brother?" I asked. "How is he taking it?"

"I haven't seen him all morning. He's kept to his room and had food sent up to him. But then he often does that. He's no longer very sociable."

"Was he once?"

"Oh, yes," she said. "I remember he used to be a lot of fun when he could still walk. He's always been sort of bookish, you know. Always to be found in the library, but he took part in family games and used to draw me pictures and tell me stories."

"Until the disease struck," I said.

She nodded sadly. "It must be horrible for him, knowing how quickly it killed his mother. It's like a ticking bomb, isn't it?"

"It seems to be. And there is no cure, I suppose?"

"Junior told Corny and me there is a doctor in Berlin who is experimenting with electric shock treatment. He was going to find the right moment to ask Papa if he could go. Corny said if he couldn't go to Paris then Junior certainly couldn't travel to Europe. Junior said that getting his life back was hardly on the same level as having a fling with a Paris chorus girl. Corny almost hit him. It was rather a nasty scene."

"When was this?"

"Oh, about a week ago," Blanche said carelessly. "Corny has become obsessed with Paris. So silly, really. If he just went along with Papa and started to learn the business, he could have found excuses to travel abroad and nobody would have stopped him." Again she paused, frowning. "I wonder what will happen now? Someone will have to take over the company, won't they? And Junior can't do it. And I'm sure Mama won't want to do it. It will have to be Corny after all, whether he likes it or not."

I digested this, still dying to know what was in that will. With any luck Daniel would be home for lunch and might have found out. He did come back just as I was wondering if we should start without him. Knowing Constanza's food was not edible when dried out, I didn't want to risk a disaster with Blanche here.

"I'm glad you're here. We're about to eat," I said. "Blanche is with us."

"Oh, of course. Hello, Blanche," he said, noticing her for the first time. I thought he looked distracted. Well, I could understand that. He had found himself in a situation he would not have chosen in the first place. That situation was now even more dangerous. Someone had been prepared to kill, maybe to stop Big Bill from becoming mayor, and Daniel had been told he could not walk away yet. Now he had even more work to do.

Mary appeared and rang the bell for lunch. We went into the dining room. I decided against bringing Liam to join us, as he could be rather expressive with spaghetti. Besides, he seemed quite happy up in his nursery. I got the feeling that he preferred Aileen's presence to mine these days.

I held my breath as Mary carried in a casserole dish and placed it on the table. It contained spaghetti. My heart sank. But then she returned with another dish emanating a strong herby smell. Inside some kind of meat was covered in a red sauce. Mary spooned some onto a plate. I took a closer look. It seemed to be mostly bone—round circles of bone.

"What is this, do you know?" I prodded it cautiously.

"Cook says it's osso bucco? Veal leg?"

She proceeded to serve us. "We have an Italian cook, Blanche," I said. "I'm afraid we're not quite used to her food yet." And I took a cautious bite. It tasted surprisingly good.

"This is very nice," Blanche said. "And I love spaghetti. We hardly ever have it at home."

Miracles would never cease. I would make a point of complimenting Constanza. As I was leaving the dining room I noticed Daniel lingering. I hesitated outside the door and saw him pick up Blanche's glass, holding it gingerly with his handkerchief. Fingerprints, of course, I thought and smiled.

After the meal Bridie showed Blanche the library and they discussed books they liked. Then they went up to Bridie's room, where apparently Blanche showed Bridie how to fix her hair with the new comb. All the sort of things normal girls do. I was glad we were taking Blanche's mind off the tragedy.

At four o'clock the automobile arrived with Finn in it. The girls were still up in Bridie's room, so I sent Mary up for them.

"So are there any developments at the house?" Daniel asked Finn.

"Not that I know of," Finn replied. "The police are still poking around and upsetting the servants. But you must be feeling really glad that you're out of it now."

"What do you mean?" Daniel asked.

"Oh, come on, Daniel," Finn said. "You were never too keen on the political life, were you? Your heart wasn't really in it. And now you're free to go back to what you really love, which is your police work."

"Sorry to disappoint you, but I'm staying put for the time being," Daniel said. "Tammany will pick somebody else to head the ticket and I'm glad to continue as part of it."

Finn frowned. "You can't be serious. Daniel, I know how you feel about corruption. The next candidate could be worse than Big Bill. You know that Tammany thrives on corruption, don't you?"

"Then why do you stick around?"

Finn shrugged. "I started off with the best intentions, like you. Working with the unions at the docks, wanting better, safer conditions for the men there. Then Big Bill noticed me, promoted me, paid me a good salary, and I found myself winding up as his henchman. Not a job I would have chosen, but once in, it was hard to leave. People who crossed Big Bill did not always walk away safely."

"So now you'll be free to do what you choose?" I said.

Finn nodded. "I'll need to think about it. I suppose I could still help Daniel with his reforms if he is elected. That would be worthwhile. You see, I—" He broke off as the two girls came down the stairs.

"Thank you for a lovely lunch, Mrs. Sullivan," Blanche said.

"We were pleased to have you, Blanche." I put an arm around her shoulders. "You are welcome any time."

"I don't want to go home," Blanche said, grasping at Bridie's hand again. "But I suppose I must because my mother needs me." She turned to me with pleading eyes. "Do you think that Bridie can come and stay with me for a few days? It would mean so much to have her with me at this horrible time."

I glanced across at Daniel.

"I don't see why not," he said. "We'll have to check with your mother first, but it seems like a good idea."

The two girls hugged.

"Until tomorrow, then, Bridie," Blanche said. "I can't wait."

"Neither can I," Bridie replied.

As soon as the motorcar had driven off and Bridie had gone up to her room I moved closer to Daniel. "Do you think that's wise, letting her stay in a house where a murder has taken place?"

"I don't think she's in any danger," Daniel replied. "We have a policeman stationed in front of the house. Also, whoever killed Big Bill had his reasons for wanting him out of the way. It may turn out to be one of Hearst's men after all. Didn't you think he seemed a bit jubilant last night—as if he had scored a victory?"

I considered this and nodded. "You may be right. I do hope that is what turns out to be true. Then none of the family is involved. That would be the worst, wouldn't it?" But when I thought about it, it seemed that the worst had already happened. They had lost a husband and father. Nothing would ever be the same again.

Then I remembered that Daniel had been to the house that morning. "Did you find anything of interest at the house?" I asked.

"Not really. I managed to get fingerprints from Cornelius and Junior without their noticing."

"I saw you getting Blanche's fingerprints from that glass at lunch." I gave him a grin.

"You are too observant for your own good." He smiled too. "But now I have to hope that Corelli or someone at headquarters can process and match them without Doyle seeing."

"You can't honestly suspect poor Blanche?"

"Stranger things have happened before now," he said, "but no, I don't suspect her. I do need to rule her out, however."

I nodded. "But you learned nothing more?"

"I did learn one thing. I expect it's of no consequence, but Mrs. McCormick went out in a hurry that afternoon. She didn't tell anyone where she was going and the butler was quite surprised to find she had gone. She didn't take the family auto or send a servant for a cab."

"She could have been buying a last-minute item for the party, realized that she forgot something important like candles for the cake."

"Surely she could have sent a servant to buy something like that."

"A surprise, then—a surprise for the party that she didn't want anyone to know about."

"That's possible. She was up in her room, and I couldn't really question her. But if you happen to get the chance . . . will you take Bridie over there tomorrow if she's staying the night?"

"I could do," I said. "I'll wait for Blanche to ask her mother's permission first."

"Bridie's a smart girl," Daniel said. "We can ask her to keep her eyes and ears open."

❧ Twenty-Three ❧

Monday, October 21

On Monday morning I sent Bridie off to school. Finn called for Daniel and they went off too—but didn't tell me where. Bridie was bubbling with excitement about going to stay with Blanche. I wasn't so happy about it. A murder had occurred in that house, and while I understood Daniel's point, that it was likely the murderer had achieved his goal, I didn't want Bridie to put herself in harm's way by eavesdropping or snooping. What if she wanted to prove herself to me as a good sleuth? I almost changed my mind and told her that she couldn't stay with Blanche after all, but I did understand that Blanche was in need of comfort, having lost her beloved father.

When Liam was happily playing in his nursery, having decided that morning naps were beneath a busy three-year-old boy, I rang for Mary.

"Mary, who is in charge of the finances for this house?"

"Mr. Finn, ma'am," she said.

"Does he give us a weekly allowance or do we submit bills to him?"

"Until now he has just given me some money and said to ask for more when it is all gone."

"Well, I'd like some this morning," I said. "I'm going to go shopping for the food that Captain Sullivan and I like to eat. Then I'll teach Constanza how to cook it."

I thought I saw a smile twitch on her lips. She had also written Constanza off as a lost cause. "She's an old woman," Mary said. "I don't think she'd take to learning new things very easily."

"Well, since I don't think I'll take to eating congealed spaghetti very easily, I'm going to give it a darned good try," I said, making her really smile this time.

She disappeared then returned with ten dollars. "We can ask Mr. Finn for more next time we see him," she said, then her face clouded. "But where will the money come from now that Mr. McCormick is no more? And will your husband even be running for sheriff now there is no Tammany ticket?"

"I have no idea what will happen next, Mary," I said. "Only that right now he has been asked to help with the murder case."

"Help find out who did it, you mean?" Did she sound worried? Her voice had certainly taken on a sharper tone. "And why would he be doing that, since he's no longer a policeman?"

"People in high places have asked him to. That's all I know. I'm as much in the dark as you are."

"You'd probably like to go home now. Back to your old life, wouldn't you?" she asked.

I should have told her it was an impertinent question and not one that a servant should be asking, but I replied, "At this moment I'd rather that we all work to see that justice is done and the right person is held accountable."

"Oh, yes. Of course," she said, rather too hastily.

I wondered about this as I headed out, basket over my arm, to the shops, the inevitable Jack following behind. Did Mary know more than we did? And then, of course, the next question: Had Mary been planted by somebody to spy on us? In which case, by whom? She seemed on good terms with Finn, but was she really working for

Hearst? For someone within Tammany who wanted Bill out of the way? I understood it was a cutthroat sort of place with an ongoing power struggle. I might suggest to Daniel that it would be worth looking into who might take Bill's place at the top.

I had a grand old time buying sausages, lamb's liver, and lamb chops. I had to stop myself from buying more, but food would only spoil after three days, even outside in a meat safe in this weather. I added eggs, bacon, good bread from the French bakery on Greenwich, then, on impulse, I bought three chocolate croissants to take over to Sid and Gus. Daniel would not approve of my running back to them all the time, but I knew that they'd have heard about the murder by now. It might not have been in Sunday's papers but it certainly was in today's.

TAMMANY HEAD BRUTALLY MURDERED was splashed across a billboard at a newspaper stand.

"Read all about it. Big Bill killed at daughter's birthday party," sang out a newsboy with morbid excitement. I felt the bile rise in my throat again when I went through the events of that evening. How could it have been an outsider? Which meant it had to be a family member, and I was going to let my darling Bridie stay in a house with a murderer. My mind kept repeating the same arguments for and against her stay. Blanche needed a friend. Bridie might find valuable evidence. It must be a family member.

I walked up Patchin Place, feeling the familiar cobbles under my feet. I glanced for a moment at my house. Had the Russian moved in yet? Was he content with my shabby old furniture? Then I knocked on Sid and Gus's front door, hoping that they'd be home. After a few minutes Sid opened the door.

"Molly! We were debating whether we should call on you or not," she said, almost dragging me inside. "But now you're here. Perfect."

From inside the sitting room came the sound of voices and then loud laughter.

"If you've got company, I won't stay," I said.

"Don't be silly," Sid said. "He's dying to meet you and we're all bursting with curiosity about the murder. Do you have any juicy details?"

"Too many," I said. "We were at the party. Daniel was one of those who found the body."

"And now he's investigating. How thrilling," Sid said.

"Don't shut us out of any of the fun. We want to hear too," came an impatient male voice from the sitting room. I followed Sid inside. Ryan O'Hare was sitting in one of the armchairs by the fire, Gus occupied the other one, and the man I identified as my new tenant, ballet star Nikolai Noblikov, was taking up the whole sofa, sprawled in an elegant position. Ryan jumped up when he saw me and opened his arms.

"Here she is, the lady in question. See what I told you, Nikolai? Isn't she divine? Look at that red hair."

"In Russia red hair sign of bad luck," Nikolai said. He extended one languid land to me. "Noblikov. Delighted to meet you."

I almost felt he expected me to kiss it. I shook it. Firmly. "How do you do, Mr. Noblikov."

"Call me Nikki. Everyone does," he said, waving a hand as if granting a royal favor. He made no attempt to sit up or move over for me.

"I won't stay," I said. "I just wanted to see if you had arrived yet. So how do you like my little house?"

He gave a shrug. "Is very small," he said. "Smaller than my dacha. You know dacha? House in country. Away from city. Much peace."

"But you think my small house will be adequate for your stay here?" I asked, giving him what I hoped was a sweet smile because I didn't want him to see that he was annoying me. "It will give you sufficient peace?"

"Don't worry. It will be perfect, my darling," Ryan answered for him. "And don't mind Nikki. He's a spoiled child because everybody adores him. It's the same for every genius. I alone can balance genius with a kind and loving nature, can't I, Nikki?"

"If you think you have genius," Nikki said.

Ryan looked hurt. "My plays are adored."

"Yes, it is easy to please the masses. But for true genius one must suffer. I do not think you suffer when you write your plays."

"I certainly don't," Ryan said. "I have a great old time, chuckling away at the wicked lines."

Nikki spread his hands wide. "There. You see? Each time I dance a part of my soul is ripped apart. I shall die young. The world will only have Noblikov for a short while. This I know."

I caught Gus's eye and I swear that she winked. "So, Molly, we read the paper this morning and we're dying to know . . ."

"She was there," Sid answered for me. "At the party where he was killed."

"And who did it, Molly? Do tell," Ryan said.

I looked from one excited face to the next, realizing that my friends still thought of murder as a game.

"I'm afraid I can't tell you much more than was in the papers," I said. "He went upstairs to sign some papers, which turned out to be a will. When he didn't come down he was found dead in a locked room with a knife in his back."

"How wonderfully dramatic, eh, Nikki?" Ryan asked.

Nikki did that expressive shrug again. "In Russia murder is so common it is boring. The husband kills the wife, the lover kills the husband, et cetera, et cetera. You will find it is one of the above. It always is."

"Oh, I don't think Mrs. McCormick killed her husband," I said quickly. "She was devastated afterward."

"Guilt," Nikki said.

"We were discussing it," Sid interjected. "And we think, given his reputation, it was more likely to be a professional hit man from someone who has been swindled or ruined by Tammany."

"I do hope so," I said. "It would be much easier if it was an outsider. Because if it wasn't it had to be one of his family."

"Ah, the new will, I expect," Gus said. "What did it say?"

"I don't know yet. It had a decanter of whiskey poured over it so it was taken away to be dried out."

"I must go and rest." Nikki uncurled himself from the sofa, stretching like a cat. "Monday, you understand. Theater is dark. My one day of freedom, but alas I must start learning new role. New Russian ballet written for me. I am a satyr, full of sexual prowess and danger, and I lure a poor peasant girl to the forest. Aha! Such fun."

"You'll be wonderful," Ryan said.

"Yes, I will," Nikki replied. "You shall be the first to see it and bring me roses. White roses, remember. Never red."

"Who is the composer, Nikki?"

"A brilliant young man called Stravinsky. You have heard of him?"

"We have!" Gus said, looking at Sid for affirmation. "Remember that lecture we went to about new voices in music?"

"He's written a symphony already," Sid agreed.

"Ah, I am with cultured women, unlike most Americans," Nikki said. "I shall enjoy coming over for coffee here every morning."

"Oh, yes, you must," Gus said.

On that note I made my exit. Sid came with me to the door.

"Isn't he perfect," Sid whispered as she escorted me to the front door. "Thank you for allowing us such a stimulating neighbor, Molly. We were just complaining that we'd sink into a slump without you to brighten our day and now we have Nikki and all his wonderful insights into ballet and Russian culture. I'm going right out to buy a samovar. And maybe he can teach us some Russian peasant dances. We have a great desire to dance."

"You don't find him a little too . . ." I couldn't finish without being rude.

"A little too much?" She looked at me and laughed. "Of course, but that's the charm, isn't it? He shakes us out of our humdrum, boring lives. He's like a character in a play, but he means all those outlandish things he says. You can tell that Ryan is besotted, but I think Nikki will make him suffer, don't you?"

"Serve him right," I replied, making her laugh again.

I had an uneasy feeling in my stomach as I walked away. I knew that Sid and Gus moved easily from one passion, one whim, to the next, but I hadn't realized that included people. Had they dropped me so easily in favor of the more entertaining Nikki? If only Daniel (with my help) could conclude this darned investigation and let us return to our own house and our former lives.

✦ Twenty-Four ✦

That afternoon Bridie came home after school to change and pack a bag to stay with Blanche.

"Blanche told me not to bring too much because I can wear her dresses. She says she has so many that I can probably keep some if her mother agrees."

I didn't want to be thought of as a charity case, but I also didn't want to disappoint Bridie's thought of lovely new dresses.

"They are sending the chauffeur for me," Bridie said.

"Oh, I was planning to take you myself and make sure everything was all right," I said.

"You don't need to do that. Blanche said she'll probably come in the automobile so I'm not lonely on the ride to her house."

I sighed. That plan was stymied. But I'd have an excuse to drop in at some stage with something that Bridie might have forgotten. We packed her bag and I hugged her before the auto arrived.

"Bridie, I want you to be careful," I said. "Don't do anything silly."

"Like what?" She looked genuinely surprised.

"You will be in a house where someone was killed," I said.

Her eyes widened even more. "You think I may be in danger?"

"No, of course not," I said. "I just don't want you to get in the way of the police or even to think of doing any snooping."

"Of course not," she said indignantly. "Blanche and I will be in her room. We will sleep in her bed. It's enormous and has the softest eiderdown!"

We had just finished packing after Bridie rejected almost every item I thought she should bring. "Too ordinary. Too girlish. Too plain."

Finally I said, "You are going to a house in mourning. The plainer the better."

And thankfully she agreed with that.

I heard a knock at the front door.

"Finish putting your washcloth and soap into your sponge bag," I said, and started down the stairs. Mary was letting Lucy McCormick in through the front door.

"Lucy, you didn't have to come out yourself. I would willingly have brought Bridie over to you," I said as I walked down, holding out my hands to her. She was now wearing black and looked more bird-like than ever, and so very pale. She took my hands in hers.

"I needed the air," she said in a low voice. "It was good for me to get out."

"Let me get you a cup of tea before you drive back," I said. "You poor thing. What a terrible strain it must be."

"Tea would be nice, thank you," she said.

"Some tea please, Mary," I said to Mary, who was hanging up Lucy's coat. I tried to use my lady of the manor voice. "Tell Constanza to make it the way I showed her."

"Yes, Mrs. Sullivan." Mary curtseyed deeply and I guessed it was for Lucy's benefit.

I led Lucy through to the front parlor. I took a seat in the chair beside her, wondering what to say. But before I could utter a word she said, in a low whisper, "I came myself because I need advice. Help. Maybe."

"Of course," I replied. "I'm happy to help in any way I can."

She lowered her voice even more so that I had to lean forward

186

to hear. "It's about the afternoon before the party. One of the maids told the police that I had gone out on my own."

I nodded. "That's understandable before a party, isn't it? You wanted to make sure all the details were in place."

"Yes, that is what I said when that horrid Doyle man questioned me. But I'm afraid the truth will come out and it will look very bad for me."

"Go on." I put a hand on her knee, wondering what was coming next.

"I received a note from my husband's mistress," she said, looking around as she said it in case we could be overheard.

"His mistress?" I suppose at heart I was still the naïve girl from the west of Ireland. Then I remembered the encounter. "That woman who spoke to your husband when we were dining in Delmonico's?"

When she saw my shocked face she gave a sad little smile. "Yes, I've known about her for ages. Bill is not the most subtle of men, and another woman's perfume does tend to linger. But Bill promised me he'd given her up and it was all behind us."

"What did the note say?"

"It said, 'I must speak with you. Gravest importance. You don't want me to come to the house, do you?' And it named a tearoom over on Second Avenue." She took a deep breath. "So I went, naturally. I didn't want any upset on the afternoon of Blanche's party."

"You didn't tell your husband or show anyone else the note?"

"Of course not. That would be the last thing I wanted."

She broke off speaking as we heard the sound of footsteps tapping across the marble foyer. Mary came in with a tea tray and we waited while she poured two cups.

"Will that be all, ma'am?" she asked.

"Yes. Thank you, Mary."

She gave a bobbed curtsey and we waited until her footsteps had receded. I let Lucy have a mouthful of tea before I prompted her. "So what happened when you met her?"

Lucy shook her head as if trying to shake away a painful memory. "Anyway, she was sitting there, in the tearoom, looking less flashy than usual. Quite refined, in fact. High neck. Fox fur. She told me that Bill was going to divorce me and marry her, only he couldn't do it while he was running for mayor because he had to avoid any trace of scandal. He had given her money to lie low and not say anything." She gave me an imploring look.

"But why come and tell you? Was she enjoying a moment of triumph?"

"I asked her that very thing," Lucy said. "She said she felt for me and she didn't want it sprung on me when Bill up and left. She thought I should have time to adjust and make plans."

"How despicable. What did you say?"

"I asked her what made her think that I'd grant the divorce?"

"And?"

She looked down at her gloved hands. "She said I knew what Bill was like. Something bad happened to anyone who stood in his way. It had been done once before, very close to home."

"Holy Mother of God!" I exclaimed. "What a terrible threat. Did you confront your husband about it?"

"I did." She raised her voice now. "We had a horrible fight right before the party. He swore none of it was true. I called him a liar. He said we'd discuss it later and we must smooth things over for Blanche's sake." She took a big, shuddering breath. "But don't you see? If they find out any of this, I have the perfect motive for wanting him dead."

I considered this. "Oh, I don't think so, Lucy," I said. "If you wanted revenge how much better to take him to the cleaners—not let him divorce you without making him suffer. Not only paying you handsomely but bringing out the sordid details in the newspapers to wreck any future political career."

"That's true, isn't it?" she said. "I had it in my power to ruin his political ambitions. I should have told him that. Although what Gertie

Grace said made me think twice. Bad things happened to those who crossed him."

"But who was the person close to home she was referring to?"

Lucy shook her head. "I have no idea. Unless she meant someone within Tammany. I'm sure accidents happen to men who step out of line there."

We looked up as Bridie came into the room. "I'm all packed and waiting whenever you are ready, Mrs. McCormick."

Lucy stood up. "Of course, my dear. Just let me finish my tea. And your dear mama must come over to us any time she wants to." She reached out and took my hand. "It's good of you to spare her for a few days. Poor Blanche has been quite distraught. Can't sleep. Plagued with nightmares and worries that someone will come after the rest of us." She gave a shuddering sigh. "Oh, I do hope your husband can find who did this really soon. I don't know how much longer we can go on like this."

"He will do his best, I promise you," I replied. "He's a good detective."

"And so are you, Mrs. Sullivan, so I've been told."

"I will do my best too," I said as I led her to the door.

After Bridie had gone I went upstairs to fetch Liam, who had woken up from his nap and was full of energy. We built towers of blocks and knocked them down again. We made trains out of blocks then sat and ate sugar sandwiches together. It made me realize how much I missed being part of his daily life. To be sure it was sometimes a challenge to get my work done with a lively boy running over my wet floors, but now I realized I was missing so much. His speech was improving so fast. He was counting. Singing songs.

"This will soon be over," I told myself. "We'll be back in Patchin Place and I'll have Liam to myself every day." Which had me wondering whether Aileen might want to come to work for us there. If only this horrid business would hurry up and be concluded so we could go home!

I was just telling Liam a story when I heard my name being called—yelled, rather. Daniel's voice echoed up the two flights of stairs from the front hall. I came to the landing and peered over.

"Up here, Daniel. I'm with Liam."

"Send Aileen up to him. I have to talk to you," he called, sounding like the imperious Daniel of former times, before I had softened him up.

"All right. Hold your horses. I'm coming."

I located Aileen, having her own cup of tea in the kitchen with Mary and Constanza, and sent her upstairs, apologizing as I did so for interrupting her meal.

"It's my job, ma'am," was all she said. Sweet girl.

"Come in here." Daniel opened the door to the library. I followed him in and he closed the door behind us. What on earth could this mean, I wondered. Was I in some kind of trouble?

"What is it?" I asked.

"I've things to report on that I'd rather were not overheard," he said.

"You don't trust the servants?"

"Let's say I wonder if they may have been placed with us for a reason and I'm not sure whose side they are on."

"Surely they came from Big Bill, didn't they?"

"In a way, yes. But that doesn't mean they don't report back to someone else."

"Jesus, Mary, and Joseph," I muttered. "And here was I talking to Lucy McCormick this afternoon about all manner of things."

He started. "Lucy McCormick was here?"

"She was. She came to pick up Bridie, who has now gone to stay with them. But she came because she wanted to speak with me." I related briefly what she had told me. "And she's afraid it will look bad for her if this comes out," I finished.

190

"It could do, especially now that I know the contents of the will. The police have managed to dry it out and read it almost completely."

"You do? And?"

"Big Bill was leaving all his business assets to his son, Cornelius, only on condition that the son took over the running of the business. If he didn't then he got nothing."

"That's harsh," I said. "And the others?"

"Lucy got the house."

"No money?"

"The will states that she has ample funds of her own and will inherit a fortune from her own family. The rest of his income is divided between Blanche, held in trust until she marries, and Tammany Hall."

"Tammany Hall?"

Daniel gave a wry smile. "The benevolent fund at Tammany Hall—which could mean anything."

"What about his older son?"

"A sum is to be set aside to provide for the lifetime care of William Junior, but he has no money of his own."

"That's terrible, Daniel," I said. "They all seem to have a motive now, don't they? Lucy's not getting his money. Cornelius gets nothing if he doesn't do what his father wants, and Junior has no money of his own. They will all be glad it wasn't finished and signed."

"At least we know what we are dealing with now." He ran his fingers through his hair, something he only did when he was agitated. "So Tammany would definitely have wanted to keep him alive long enough to sign. But I have more to report. I was over at the house. The knife was no knife at all, but a letter opener that had been meticulously sharpened."

"Whose letter opener?"

"Lucy McCormick's," he said.

"Lucy's?"

"She claims she mislaid it weeks ago. She remembers leaving it on her desk but then couldn't find it again."

"Convenient," I said. "But I can't see Lucy daring to stab her husband. He was such a big, powerful man and she looks quite frail. Surely she'd worry that he'd overpower her."

"Unless the whiskey had knocked him out first."

I shook my head. "He wasn't up there long enough to have drunk that much whiskey. Besides, Lucy was in the ballroom with us while the girls played their party games."

"All the time?" Daniel raised an eyebrow. "You can swear to that?"

I hesitated. "Well, no. I suppose anyone could have slipped out while the game was going on. It was rather chaotic with the girls rushing around screaming. But she would have no way of knowing in what condition she'd find her husband."

"Neither would anyone else, for that matter," Daniel said. "I'm really hoping this turns out to be an outsider. I'm meeting with some of the top brass at Tammany in the morning. I'll be interested to hear what their grapevine has uncovered."

"Unless it was one of them. After all, his second-in-command was at the party, wasn't he? He might have ambitions for the top job."

"O'Brien? Yes, I suppose he was."

"So was Finn," I pointed out.

Daniel shook his head, smiling. "Can you see either O'Brien or Finn using a sharpened letter opener to kill Bill McCormick? Lucy McCormick's letter opener? Wouldn't they strangle him or have a more reliable knife?"

"Unless whoever did it wanted to incriminate Lucy."

"Come on, Molly. We just agreed that Tammany would want to keep him alive long enough to sign the will and leave half his money to them. No, this has to be something to do with that will and it has to involve his family."

"And then there's Junior. He has a strong motive, cut out of all the money and the running of the business. I wonder if he knew that was in the will?" I mused.

"Could Junior even hold a knife? You saw how he struggled with the key to the door. And he couldn't cross the threshold in that wheelchair," Daniel said. "If he was involved, he had to have had help or have paid someone."

"But with what money? Does he go out or have any money of his own?" The thought just struck me. "Does the family know yet? Has Doyle been over there to tell them?"

"I don't believe Doyle himself knows yet. I just happened to have visited the police lab and saw for myself, so I came straight home to tell you."

"Then we must get over to the McCormicks', Daniel. Before Doyle bullies them and makes them confess to things that aren't true."

"You want to tip off a potential murderer to have time to work on his alibi?"

"Well, I think they have the right to know what is in the will, and I didn't take to Lieutenant Doyle."

Daniel sighed, then nodded. "There may be hell to pay if Doyle finds us there."

"Then we'd better hurry."

I rang the bell, then took down my cape from the peg on the hall-stand. Mary appeared, wiping crumbs from her mouth. "You rang, madam?"

"Yes, Mary. We have to go out for a while. Please make sure that Master Liam has his supper and is put to bed if we are not back."

She looked from Daniel to me. "Does anyone know who killed Mr. McCormick? Is the rest of his family safe? I hate to think of anything happening to Mrs. McCormick."

"The police are investigating," Daniel said. "We don't know anything yet."

"If you ask me," she said knowingly, "it was that Italian gang, the Black Hand."

❧ Twenty-Five ❧

I t was amazing how easy it was to have Mary summon a taxicab and to speed across town. I thought of my early detective days when a horse-drawn hansom cab was far beyond my budget and I often walked to avoid the cost of the el or a trolley. What a strange life I was living now! Roberts took our coats and showed us in as if we were expected. I wondered if Lucy had given him instructions to that effect.

The whole family was gathered in the drawing room, dressed for dinner. Bridie got up as we walked in, a look of concern on her face.

"Is everything all right? You haven't come to take me home?" She moved closer to Blanche as if to prevent this from happening.

"Not at all. We came to visit with the family." I turned to Lucy. "Daniel has some information for you. I don't mean to interrupt your dinner."

"Not at all." Lucy motioned for us to have a seat. "Dinner is not until eight. We always come down early and have a drink. Would you like one?"

Cornelius got up and went to a well-stocked table of different glass bottles. "Scotch, Captain Sullivan?"

"Please." Daniel accepted a glass and sat in an empty armchair. I waved off his offer of a sherry. I needed my head clear. Either one of these people was a murderer or they were all innocent parties whose lives had been turned upside down. Either way, I wanted to have my wits about me. I sat next to Lucy on the settee.

"Bridie, we have to talk to the McCormicks about some police business. Perhaps you and Miss Blanche could . . ."—Daniel seemed to search for something suitable that would take the girls out of the room—"go and see the library. I'm sure they have an amazing one here."

I tried to convey with a look that Bridie should do what Daniel said and I would fill her in later. Whether she understood or was actually excited about the idea of the library, she rose obediently, and she and Blanche went out.

Junior was sitting just on my right. "I'm afraid our library will be a disappointment, Mrs. Sullivan." He smiled, although sadly. "It was my mother who had the passion for books. The library at your house is much better than ours."

"Of course, I remember," I said, "that was your house when you were a little boy." I tried to avoid Lucy's eye. I wondered if she was thinking, like me, about her replacing the first wife the way that Big Bill's mistress had threatened to replace her. But surely disease and death were not the same as divorce. Lucy had stepped in and given Junior a new home and family after his mother died.

"You said you had some news for us?" Cornelius was clearly impatient to hear what Daniel had to say.

"I've just heard what was in the will that Big Bill was drawing up."

Lucy and Cornelius sat forward, listening intently. "Go on," Lucy said. "Don't keep us in suspense."

"To you, Mrs. McCormick, he left this house but no money. He said you had family money and no need of his."

"Very true." Lucy nodded. "That was thoughtful of him to know I would want to stay in this house."

"He left his investment income in trust to be divided between Blanche and the Tammany Hall benevolent fund," Daniel continued. I saw Lucy's lip curl in disgust as she heard Tammany's name mentioned. "Will that mean your daughter is taken care of, Mrs. McCormick?"

"I believe so," Lucy replied. "Of course my husband didn't discuss financial matters with me, but I have always had all I wanted and I imagine she would as well. And she will have her share of my fortune one day."

"And to Cornelius he made a strange condition," Daniel went on.

"I know!" Cornelius interrupted angrily. "He cut me off without a penny if I set foot in Paris and don't follow in his footsteps. He told me often enough."

"Not quite," Daniel said calmly. "He has given you the business. All his assets. The steamship company. The ferries. The docks."

"Holy—" Cornelius started to say, then glanced at his mother and fell silent.

"On one condition," Daniel went on. "You take over the running of the business. If you choose not to then you are cut off without a penny."

"He what?" Cornelius looked shocked. "What about Junior? He is the oldest son. I know Father wanted me to take over, but I assumed Junior . . ." He trailed off as if unable to finish his thought.

"I know what it says about me," Junior put in. "Father and I discussed it. It says that I must be taken care of for the rest of my life." For the first time I heard some bitterness in his voice. "I asked him to put that in there, actually. I have heard from the doctors that my disease will progress rapidly. My being in charge of any business matters would only complicate things."

"But you seem so intelligent and capable," I couldn't help putting in. "Surely it doesn't matter if you can't walk."

He turned to me. "That's kind of you, Mrs. Sullivan. If I had a disease like polio and it had only taken my legs from me I would agree with you. But my disease is progressive. You can hear it is slurring my speech. Soon I will need someone to feed me." He looked over at his brother. "So I hope you don't run off to Paris, Corny, and you do assume the business and take care of me?"

"I think you are forgetting something," Daniel spoke up. "This will was never signed or notarized. Whoever killed Big Bill saw to that. The previous will is still in effect if he had one."

"But how would we know that?" Lucy looked quite bewildered. "And what happens if we can't find a will?" I could see that she was trembling and felt a pang of guilt that we were talking about money matters when she was still in shock from her husband's death.

"I'll search the house." Cornelius came over, sat beside her, and took her hand. "If it's not there we will speak with his attorney, or will find where Father has all his bank accounts and safe deposit boxes."

"I know where he banks, I believe he has a safe deposit box there," Junior put in.

"There you are." Cornelius sounded reassuring. "If not we'll ask Finn for help. Father might keep things in the safe at Tammany Hall. If we can't find it I think we have to go through probate and the court will tell us how to split the money."

"What if we find it and it was written before we were married?" Lucy had clearly not considered this before; her voice was rising into hysteria. "What if we are all cut off?"

"Please be calm, Lucy," said Junior. I noticed he did not call her Mother. "In that case I will inherit and do exactly what Father wanted. Cornelius will run the business, you and Blanche will stay in the house, and I will be looked after. Money is the least of our problems right now." He turned to look at Daniel. "Am I right to think that the police have this information and will use it to question us?"

"They do," Daniel replied. "We thought it only fair that you hear it before they questioned you."

"We hated to think of that Doyle bullying you all," I put in. "But please don't mention that you heard it from us. Daniel has only just learned about it from some police contacts."

Roberts came in and announced that dinner was served. Charlie entered just behind him and stood behind Junior's chair, ready to wheel him through.

"Won't you stay?" All of Cornelius's suspicion and surliness seemed to have gone out of him. "It was so kind of you to come over."

"I don't want to put you out," Daniel began politely.

"Nonsense," Lucy said. "You came all the way here to help us. I'm sure I don't know how I could have gotten through the last two days without your family. Bridie has been such a treasure and you have treated us so kindly." She had a catch in her voice as if she were going to cry. Then she composed herself as she addressed the butler. "Roberts, add two places for dinner."

"Let's go in." Cornelius helped his mother up and took her arm. We followed them into the large ornate dining room. Charlie pushed Junior in and I saw there was a place prepared for him with no chair in it. Roberts left and a minute later Bridie and Blanche joined us. Blanche's eyes looked red and Bridie had a comforting hand on her arm.

"I've asked your parents to stay for dinner," Lucy said as they sat. The room fell into an uncomfortable silence as Charlie and another servant served the food. It seemed hard to know what to say. What is polite dinner conversation when the patriarch of the family has been murdered? I thought of Saturday night when the party guests had been cheerfully eating at this dining table not knowing that Big Bill was lying murdered upstairs and shuddered.

"Are you looking forward to getting back to school tomorrow, Blanche?" Lucy was struggling to play the hostess.

"Oh, not yet, Mother, I couldn't possibly." Blanche's eyes welled up with tears again. "My daddy is dead. How can I go to school?"

"It will take your mind off it," Lucy suggested. "I don't like thinking of you here dwelling on it."

"But I won't! I'll have Bridie with me." Blanche looked at me for confirmation.

"Well, I don't want Bridie to miss school," I began. "She's quite behind as it is."

"We can ask the school to send over our work and I can tutor her," Blanche put in eagerly. "Please, Mrs. Sullivan, I just can't face leaving the house and having all those girls asking me questions and pitying me."

"That sounds reasonable," Daniel answered. "The funeral is on Wednesday. Why don't we let them study at home for now then go back and start fresh next week."

I had some misgivings. Bridie was already struggling. But I reflected that having Blanche as her best friend would solve the social problems she had been having and she could use some tutoring.

"All right, but I expect you to do your Latin every day," I said. "Bridie never had a chance to study that in school before."

"We will," Blanche promised. "Perhaps I could come over to your house one day this week as well? Bridie says you have a much bigger library than ours and you are an easy walk from Washington Square."

"I'm not sure about that." Lucy frowned. "I'm not sure I want you out in the city until you have a new maid. I suppose I will have to hire a new one, but I just can't think about that now."

"Our maid Aileen would be happy to chaperone, or I could bring them over myself," I offered. Honestly until this murder was solved I would feel happier with Bridie and Blanche at our house.

"But you promised I could stay here." Bridie was clearly not wanting to give up the novelty of staying at a friend's house for the first time.

"Stay tomorrow, then." I looked at Daniel to make sure he agreed. "And the next day is the funeral and wake so we will all be over here. Why doesn't Blanche come on Thursday?"

"Mrs. McCormick, I wonder if I could invite myself along," Junior spoke up. "You remember I grew up in that house. Losing my father has made me remember some of the happy times and I would love to see it again while I'm able." I thought of the stairs leading up to the front door. Obviously so did he, because he went on, "Charlie can carry me in, and bring my chair from the automobile. Of course I won't ask him to carry me all the way up to visit my old rocking horse"—he gave a lopsided grin—"but I would like to see the library. I wonder if any of my old books are there. I used to love adventure stories."

"I think there are," Bridie said. "I saw a book with 'Billy' written inside the front cover. *The Adventures of Sherlock Holmes*. Would that have been yours . . ." She hesitated as to what to call him, clearly unsure if she could call this grown-up man Junior as his sister did.

"Call me Junior, you're one of the family now," Junior said. Bridie flushed with pleasure. "Although I may go back to Billy." A look of sadness crossed his face. "We used to be Big Bill and little Billy you know." He looked at me. "May I visit, Mrs. Sullivan?"

What could I say? "Of course. Come to tea on Thursday. I would invite you to lunch, but I'm afraid of what our cook would serve you. Tea is safer."

"I thought her spaghetti was very good," Blanche put in. "We never have pasta at home."

"Then you can stay and spend the night after your brother goes home," I said with a smile, "and you shall have all the pasta you want for dinner."

"Why did you choose an Italian cook?" Lucy asked. "Do you enjoy spaghetti and garlic?"

"I suppose I could if they were cooked correctly," I started diplomatically, "but I'm not sure this woman has ever been a cook before. Finn gave her the job as a favor to Tammany."

"Perhaps she is the wife of that dockworker who died in an accident last month," Cornelius mused. "Tammany likes to take care of their own."

"Yes, well, that is a lovely sentiment as long as you don't have to eat her food," I said, and everyone laughed. But it did make me think I was being rather hard on Constanza. Poor woman was alone in the world now and having to earn a living with no husband. If I could teach her how to cook for us she would have a skill she could use. Then a thought struck me. What had Mary meant by the Black Hand? Wasn't that an Italian gang that blackmailed and murdered people? Had they been at odds with Big Bill as well? This was going to be a difficult case to solve. It seemed that half of New York had had a motive to want him dead.

❧ Twenty-Six ❧

Tuesday, October 22

O n Tuesday morning it was strange to not have to rush to make sure Bridie got off to school on time. No last-minute drama when she couldn't find her hair ribbon or her book. Daniel and I enjoyed a quiet breakfast.

"I hope this isn't the calm before the storm," I said. "I hope Bridie's all right."

"I'm sure she'll be fine, Molly. She'll be enjoying the new experience of being waited on hand and foot by servants. Let's just hope she doesn't come home and expect the same."

I nodded, feeling distracted. "Is there anything I should be doing today?"

"I don't think so. There's not much more we can do until we get the various results from the police. I have the unpleasant task of being grilled by O'Brien and others at Tammany. They will want to know all the details and presumably to make plans about where we go from here."

"Don't you dare volunteer to run for mayor," I said, making him chuckle. He got up from the table and gave me a kiss on the forehead. "Enjoy a morning with your son for once," he said. "He hasn't seen enough of you lately. He'll begin to think that Aileen is his mother."

"I agree. I've been feeling guilty about that. But when I go up to see him he's clearly so happy having a playmate on the spot. You must hear the songs she's taught him in Gaelic."

Daniel glanced at his watch. "I had better put my hat and coat on, then. The automobile will be here at any moment with—"

On cue the doorbell rang. We heard voices in the hall, then Mary appeared, dropped a curtsey, and said, "Mr. Finn is here for you, Captain Sullivan."

Of course, I thought. He wasn't allowed to go anywhere without Finn. I followed Daniel out into the front hall, where Finn was standing.

"Ready to go, then, Daniel?" he said. "We don't want to keep them waiting. They are in a big enough tizzy as it is with their entire plans in limbo. I'm probably going to get an earful for not protecting him better."

"How were you supposed to protect him in his own home?" Daniel asked. "Who would have thought that something like this could happen?"

"I know. It beats me," Finn said. "If a man's not safe in his own study, where is he safe?"

Their voices continued as they walked out onto the steps and shut the front door.

"Goodbye, Molly, my darling. I'll miss you every second," I said to myself, since he had gone without turning around. That seemed to be how it was when he was with Finn. Which made me think that maybe he had needed a close friend. It couldn't have been easy being the youngest police captain, more educated than most of them. Perhaps that was one of the reasons he so objected to Sid and Gus. He was jealous. This new insight made me think as I went up the stairs to see Liam.

"Look, Mama!" Liam jumped up as I came in. "We made a zoo."

And they had made a zoo with an upturned chair as a cage, a laundry hamper on its side as another, and stuffed animals inside them. So delightful. So creative. Aileen would be a hard act to follow when we moved back home.

"I've come to take Master Liam to the park," I said. "Would you get him ready, please, Aileen."

"Aiyeen come too?" he asked hopefully.

It would have been churlish to say I wanted him to myself, but Aileen shook her head. "I should be helping Mary more. I'm spending too much time entertaining you, young man. But there are rugs to be beaten in fine weather. And no doubt washing to be hung too."

So half an hour later Aileen helped me carry the pram down the steps and put Liam into it. He objected to this strongly. "Liam wants to walk. I'm a big boy."

"You really are," I agreed, "and you can walk as soon as we've crossed the busy streets. We'll go to the park and take your ball, shall we?"

He was quite happy with this and held his ball. I hadn't gone two paces before Jack appeared. I had no idea where he had been lurking before, but suddenly there he was.

"Where are you off to this time, missus?" he asked, falling into step beside me.

"Only to the park, Jack. You really don't have to come along."

"Not have to come along? After what happened to the boss?"

"You surely don't think an enemy killed Mr. McCormick?"

"Of course. Who else? There's plenty who would want him dead, and not just Hearst's men either."

"Who might the others be?"

"There's enough who have grievances," he said. "He hasn't always treated men fairly. Cut too many corners, if you ask me." He looked around, as if he expected to be overheard. "But I shouldn't go on like this, God rest the poor man's soul."

It was no use telling him he didn't have to come to the park with us. He had his orders and he wasn't going to deviate from them. I set off with Liam, with Jack several paces behind. When we reached the park I released Liam from his prison and he started kicking his ball around. His aim wasn't too wonderful and the ball headed for a group of students enjoying the morning sunshine between classes at the university. One of the young men obliged by kicking the ball back to Liam, who thought this was the start of a great game and promptly kicked it back to the student.

"Liam, come over here," I called. "Leave the young men alone."

"Oh, no, it's good to have a chance to play," the student said. "We can become too serious with all the studying. And he's got a strong leg on him. He'll grow up to be a good athlete." He kicked the ball back to Liam again, who had to run this time and pick it up. As I turned to watch him I caught sight of someone I thought I recognized. Surely that impressive coil of black hair belonged to Constanza. She was crossing the street at the far side of the square, but I was sure it was her. She had a big basket over her arm. Off doing the shopping, I presumed. Then I saw a man step out from behind a tree to intercept her. She stopped. A few words were exchanged and she handed him the basket. Then she turned back in the direction she had come. As she crossed the square I saw her start, as if in fear, pull her shawl over her head, and literally run away. Had she seen me, I wondered, but then I saw Jack, standing on the path by the arch.

The episode unnerved me. What was in that basket, I wondered. Was she giving away my food? That would explain why we had been eating so poorly. I knew she was trying to support a fatherless family, but Finn had found her a position. She was getting a wage. No need to steal from her employer. But something had made her run away. Was it seeing Jack or me? It looked to me that she had been doing something wrong. I'd have to speak to her about it, although it wasn't up to me to dismiss her.

I realized I hadn't been watching Liam and spun around, my heart beating fast. I need not have worried. He was now part of a group of students, who were patiently throwing him the ball. I retrieved him after a while and then he had fun with the piles of fallen leaves, running through them and throwing them into the air with whoops of delight. How easy life is for the very young, I thought. They have no fear. They take delight in the simplest things. Whereas we are always burdened with larger worries.

At last I rounded him up and we headed for home, with me deciding what I should say to Constanza. I handed Liam back to Aileen, then found that Constanza hadn't yet returned. There was a soup bubbling on the stove for our lunch, but no sign of her. I paced impatiently until I heard the front door slam shut. Surely she hadn't the nerve to come in through the front door? I stepped into the hallway in time to see Daniel removing his hat.

"You're back quickly," I said. "How did the meeting with Tammany go?"

"Interesting," he said. "They were rather cagey. Asked lots of probing questions about what the police might have found and whether I had managed to get to his private papers first."

"So they are not weeping for their leader?"

Daniel smiled. "From what I could gather O'Brien is not at all unhappy that Big Bill is out of the way. I think he now sees himself as the obvious choice for mayor—less confrontational, less scandal, more a middle-of-the-road sort of guy."

"You said they were worried. Do you think it's possible that it was Tammany who decided to get rid of him after all?" I asked. "They did have Finn on the spot."

"It did cross my mind," he said. "But not Finn. I'd have said he was more loyal to Bill than to Tammany." He reached out to touch my shoulder. "I've got more news. How would you like to go to the theater?"

I looked at him as if he'd gone mad. "Are we not in the middle of an investigation?"

"Precisely." He paused. "I stopped by at police HQ to see if they

206

had managed to work on matching fingerprints. Corelli said he was trying to get to it when Doyle wasn't around but it wasn't easy. However, he did show me what they had taken from McCormick's desk. First of all, a large amount of cash, tied into bundles."

"Ready to bribe people if necessary?" I asked.

He nodded. "A good guess, I'd say. But there were papers too. The ones Tammany were so concerned about. We don't know what they all refer to yet, but among them was a letter from a Miss Gertie Grace."

I tried to place the name. "Oh, the actress. His mistress? The one he was planning to marry?"

"The same woman, but he wasn't actually planning to marry her, according to this letter."

"What did it say?"

"She'd go to the papers and tell them all about their affair unless he paid her off handsomely. Ruin his chances of becoming mayor."

"No, that doesn't sound like happily ever after," I agreed. "A blackmail note. But would that give her a motive to kill him? If she was blackmailing him he'd be worth more to her alive."

"And if he refused to be blackmailed? He sent someone to threaten her?"

I considered this. "I suppose that might have upset her enough to want him dead. So we are going to have a chat with her at the theater?"

"I thought we'd take in the first matinee at two, and then catch her in her dressing room afterward."

"I wouldn't say no to an afternoon at the theater," I said.

"Then we'll grab a bite to eat and be on our way."

"Good luck with that," I replied. And I told him what I had seen.

"So the poor woman was taking some food to her family, Molly. I think we can overlook that, don't you?"

"I suppose so," I said. "But I'd like her to know that I saw her doing it. And she knew she was in the wrong because she looked terrified when Jack stepped out from behind a tree."

"Interesting," Daniel said. "So if she's not home, do you think you

207

might forget about being lady of the manor for a second and go and make us a couple of sandwiches?"

I laughed and went to oblige. When I came back I found him seated in the dining room.

"One more thing that turned up among his papers," Daniel said as he took a plate from me. "There was a bill coming from an address in Mount Vernon, with a note saying it was the final one, as the patient had now passed away."

"Another of his charitable acts, I suppose." I sat beside him. "Taking care of someone who used to work for him or for Tammany. He did have a good heart, so it seems."

"When it suited him." Daniel went to work on his sandwich.

✨ Twenty-Seven ✨

I t isn't often I go to the theater with my husband. Actually I couldn't remember a time when we had been together. Maybe when a former case involved strange goings-on, but then I'd had to become a member of the chorus, rather than sit in the stalls. Sid and Gus had taken me a few times so I wasn't exactly a neophyte, but I still got a thrill as I stepped from the lighted foyer into the dimly lit stalls and saw the balconies rising in tiers to an elaborately decorated ceiling. That thrill intensified when the orchestra started to warm up.

"We should do this more often," I whispered to Daniel. "It's exciting, isn't it?"

"Saints preserve us," he replied. "I don't mind a good, tense drama, but a lot of women wailing and kicking up their legs is not what I enjoy." He leaned closer to me. "Molly, you do realize this is vaudeville and some of it might be a little risqué, to say the least."

I was touched but amused by his desire to protect me from the big wicked world. "I'll suffer for the sake of our investigation," I said. "I'm anxious to have a word with Miss Gertie Grace. Although I don't see why we couldn't have gone to her apartment instead and cornered her there."

"Because we'll take her by surprise here. She'll think I'm an admirer."

"Don't play the part too realistically," I warned.

The house lights dimmed. The conductor appeared. The orchestra struck up a lively polka and the curtain rose to reveal a farm scene with milkmaids wearing rather less than the average farmhand. There was also a fake cow with large udders. The milkmaids sang a song about life on the farm and what they did after dark in the hay. A comedian came on and there were jokes about udders. The audience roared with laughter. I saw there were many more men than women. Gertie was not in that first scene, but then she came on stage and sang a sweet love song about the boy she left behind. She really looked rather beautiful and I could see why Bill had fallen for her. She had a vitality about her that kept you riveted to her and she moved in a sensuous way.

After her came jugglers, a contortionist, and a man who played drums, violin, and mouth organ at the same time. All amusing, but I was getting impatient. Then Gertie came on again, this time dressed as a French maid in a white frilly apron and cap, very short black skirt, and fishnet stockings with the suspenders showing. This got a roar of approval from the men in the audience. I think Daniel leaned a little forward in his seat. Then she sang an extremely crude song in a French accent about her duties as a maid, how she kept the master happy, full of innuendo, some of which went over my innocent head. The rest of the audience got it, all right.

She appeared in several more scenes, including one in which she appeared to be naked behind a huge ostrich feather fan. It was cleverly done, as she didn't really reveal anything more than a hand or foot at a time. Then there was the big finale at a fairground with a realistic merry-go-round. I have to say that I enjoyed myself. I'm sure Daniel did too, given the amount of female flesh that was exposed. As they were taking their second bow Daniel grabbed my hand and jerked me from my seat.

"Come on. Let's get round to the stage door before the crush," he whispered. We made our exit, treading on some toes, and stood blinking for a moment in the late afternoon light. Daniel led me around the theater to a side alley and an open doorway. As he was about to step inside he was stopped by an elderly doorman. "Hey, where do you think you're going? You wait your turn with the rest out here," he said.

Daniel produced a warrant card from his pocket. "Police," he said in a low voice. "We need to question one of your performers. She might do a bunk rather than talk to me, so I'd like to catch her when she comes off stage."

"I don't suppose I can stop you," the old man said. "But we don't want no trouble here. We run a respectable establishment."

"Sure you do," Daniel replied. "And don't worry. Nobody's done anything wrong, but this person might have important information for us."

"And who is this?" The doorman turned his gaze to me.

"A fellow detective in plainclothes, as I am."

"Go on." The man gave a disbelieving laugh. "They allow lady detectives these days?"

"They do. And very useful they are too. Come on, Detective Sullivan, let's go." He strode ahead of me down a dark, narrow hallway and up a flight of rickety stairs. I remembered the smells from when I unwillingly joined the chorus: greasepaint and sweat and hot lights. Past a communal dressing room where half-naked girls were getting changed. One saw us.

"Where the hell do you think you're going?" she demanded.

"I'm Miss Grace's new friend," Daniel replied.

"Oh, really. She doesn't waste any time, does she?" The girl chuckled as she shut the door on us.

We passed other doors with names on them and then came to hers. We went inside, only to find a startled older woman dresser. "Hey, you can't come in here," she said, trying to shoo us out as if we were chickens. "Miss Grace doesn't let anyone in until she's changed and taken her makeup off. Go on. Beat it."

"We're police. Here to talk to her about Mr. McCormick's death," Daniel said quietly. "I suggest you disappear for a few minutes."

"She doesn't know anything about that," the woman said. "Quite cut up she was when she read it in the papers. 'I always knew he'd come to a bad end.' That's what she said. 'Someone was bound to get to him. And serves him right.'"

That didn't sound to me like a broken-hearted fiancée. Daniel produced a dollar bill from his pocket. "Here, go and get yourself a cup of coffee. We won't take long."

"Thank you kindly, sir," she said. "And be gentle with her, won't you? I reckon it hasn't sunk in yet about Mr. Bill. She's in disbelief."

Then she went. Daniel motioned me to sit on the small armchair in the corner, next to the screen on which her outfits were hung in order. He himself paced up and down.

"Won't you get in trouble for claiming to be a policeman when you are not?" I asked.

"And who is going to report me here?" he laughed. "They all have something to hide in places like this. Peddling drugs, or on the run from something or someone."

I realized I wasn't usually allowed to watch him interviewing a suspect. It would be educational for me. As soon as these thoughts had passed through my mind the door burst open and Gertie came in.

"Great house for a Tuesday afternoon, Sadie. God, I need a drink." She broke off abruptly as she caught sight of Daniel.

"Who the devil are you? And how did Sadie ever let you into my room? You better have a good explanation before I call the cops."

"I am the cops, Gertie. Here to ask you a few questions about Bill McCormick."

"Never heard of him." She threw back her head defiantly.

"I might believe that, only I was sitting beside him at Delmonico's when you stopped by our table and ruffled his hair," Daniel said.

"So. I'm friendly with a lot of men."

Daniel looked across at me. "And I'm a good friend of his wife, I mean widow," I said. "She was distressed about what you told her in the tearoom."

"Shit," Gertie said. "Look, I just wanted to get back. To throw the cat among the pigeons, don't they say. I knew she'd go home and there would be a big fight. I wanted him to suffer."

"Why would you want him to suffer, Gertie, when according to what Lucy McCormick said, he had told you he was going to marry you?" I asked quietly.

She gave me a scornful sneer. "You don't think he'd really marry the likes of me, do you? Not with his political ambitions and all her money? No. He came to see me a couple of weeks ago and told me it was all over. He couldn't see me again because it would damage his reputation. He wasn't paying the rent on my apartment any longer." She gave a dramatic sigh. "I knew it had to end sometime. C'est la vie, right? Kismet. Fate. On to the next one. There are plenty of men lined up outside, all wanting to treat me nice."

"So you thought you'd make a bit of cash out of him, did you?" Daniel asked. "A letter from you was in his desk. It looked an awful lot like a blackmail note to me."

"Blackmail? Nah. Just a friendly request for a helping hand, after being so long together." She gave a defiant smile.

"A friendly request? You'd go to the papers and share all the details of your affair? And other things you knew about him?"

She shrugged.

"You were playing with fire, Gertie. You might have wound up floating in the Hudson."

"Yeah. I realized that afterward. But I was fighting mad," she said. "I didn't expect him to dump me like a sack of coals." She looked around, nervous and vulnerable for the first time. "He sent one of his bully boys to warn me off. Told me Bill was prepared to overlook my threat for old times' sake, but just this once. And if I ever breathed a word, he couldn't vouch for my safety."

"So when was the last time you saw him?" Daniel asked.

"You were there. That night at Delmonico's."

"But you did take another risk, sending that note to his wife," I said. "What on earth made you do it?"

"Pure spite." She gave a derisive laugh. "I read that they were having a big party and I thought I'd just stir things up nicely. Did it work?"

"Somebody killed him that evening, Gertie. Stabbed him in the back."

She hesitated, then opened her mouth. "Hey. Don't look at me. Do you know where I was that evening? I was performing in front of a packed house. Lots of witnesses. Besides, I'd never have harmed the old goat. I was too fond of him. We had a good time together for quite a while. I've got some nice jewelry and furs. I ain't complaining."

Daniel handed her his program. "No hard feelings, Gertie. Do you think you could sign my program, as a keepsake?"

She looked surprised, then laughed. "Sure. Why not?" She took it from him, put it on her counter and signed. "So how did you like the show?" she asked, handing it back to him.

"I thought you were the cat's whisker," he replied. He turned to me. "Come on, Detective. We have to be going."

And we left her.

"You had her sign your program?" I demanded as we came around to the front of the theater. A fine rain was now falling and I turned up my collar, wishing I had brought an umbrella.

"How else could I get her fingerprints?" He smiled at me. "And congratulations. You asked good questions. I think we work well as a team."

"We certainly do," I replied.

We turned onto a crowded sidewalk. I hesitated, taking Daniel's arm, and glanced back at the theater. Big posters outside had Gertie's name splashed all over them. THREE SHOWS DAILY! And in smaller letters: MATINEE ONLY ON SATURDAY. I tugged at Daniel's sleeve and pointed to it.

214

"So Miss Gertie wasn't quite honest with us. I am surprised," he said. "Let's see if her fingerprints show up anywhere. Although someone as striking-looking as her would surely have been noticed among the crowd at the party."

He ushered me through the crowd and hailed a hansom cab.

"Who is paying for this now that Big Bill is not funding us?" I asked as he helped me climb up.

"I expect Tammany will foot the bill, or if not them then Mr. Hearst."

"You're playing both sides. Isn't that dangerous?"

He gave that cocky little grin that had so attracted me to him in the first place.

As the cab set off, the clip-clop of the hooves echoing up from a damp pavement, I sat in silence, trying to digest what had just happened. She had a motive now, I thought. He had broken up with her. Stopped paying her rent. There is nothing like a woman scorned, and a stab in the back would be the sort of thing she'd do. But how could she have gained access to his private office in a house milling with people? Then a picture came into my mind. There were several maids hovering in the background at Blanche's party. Handing around food, clearing away glasses. Perhaps they had hired extra help for the evening and one more maid would not have been noticed. And Gertie had been good at playing a maid!

❦ Twenty-Eight ❦

When we arrived home we were greeted in the hallway by Mary.

"You just missed a gentleman who called to see you, Captain Sullivan," she said.

"What sort of gentleman?" Daniel asked.

"If you ask me, I'd say it was a policeman. You can always tell the look. Big, swarthy Italian type."

"Did he leave a message?"

"He left an envelope. He said he'd managed to take care of the things you were interested in." She indicated the hall table where a large manila envelope now lay. Daniel almost sprinted over to it.

"Thank you, Mary," I said. "Is Constanza back?"

"I didn't know she'd gone out," Mary said. "She's down in the kitchen, as far as I know. In fact she was rather put out that she'd made a good soup for your lunch and then you weren't there to eat it."

"Ah, well. It will keep for tomorrow," I said, not sure if I found it annoying or amusing to be put in the wrong if she was the one who was stealing my food. "But I think we could do with a cup of tea. And some toast."

As she went off I turned to Daniel, who had opened the envelope and was staring at the contents.

216

"What is it?"

"The results of the fingerprint analysis." He was still scanning the page. "Quite interesting."

"We'd better not say any more in the front hall," I said. "Come on through to the sitting room." I led the way. Daniel came to sit beside me on the sofa. "Well?" I asked.

"No prints from an outsider, which I suppose rules out Gertie and Tammany, and Hearst's boys for that matter, although there were no prints on the knife handle, meaning the perpetrator either wore gloves or wiped it clean." He scanned the page further. "Finn's prints in several places, which one would expect since he was often called to the office. A couple of the servants had been in there, to clean, one supposed. Not a sign of Lucy McCormick's. Clearly she wasn't welcome in his private sanctum. Nor any sign of Junior's."

"He couldn't get across the carpet in his wheelchair," I pointed out. "So Bill McCormick didn't welcome the family into his private office. But what about Cornelius?"

"Here we come to the interesting part." Daniel's gaze met mine. "Cornelius's prints were on the whiskey decanter and the handle of the desk drawer."

"Then he was in there recently and saw the will, and didn't want it signed." I waved a finger excitedly. "Remember Blanche commented that Cornelius slipped away during the games?"

Daniel stood up. "I think we should pay a call on the McCormicks right away, don't you? We may catch Cornelius off guard and see what he has to say for himself."

We ran into Mary coming up from the kitchen as we headed for the front door.

"You're going out again?" she asked. "What about tea?"

"I'm afraid we have to forget about it for now," I said. "And we may be late for dinner. Tell Constanza to keep that soup warm, just in case."

I didn't wait to see her expression but followed Daniel out of the front door. Jack appeared as always, touching his cap to Daniel.

"That's okay, Jack," Daniel said mildly. "I can take care of myself and my wife." To my surprise Jack didn't argue but just touched his cap again and slouched over to the side of the house.

"I think it's just as easy to take the el at this time of day," Daniel said, walking ahead of me at a great pace. It wouldn't be easy to locate a taxicab and the hansoms take forever. He cut across to Sixth Avenue and up the steps to the el platform. The carriage was crowded and we had to fight our way on board. It was only when I was standing there that I realized that I avoided traveling on the el for a good reason—I had been on the el when it came around a corner too quickly and plunged off the tracks. The car I was in hung in the air at a sickening angle and we were lucky to be rescued. I didn't think about it often, but now the memory came rushing back, making it hard to breathe. I couldn't tell Daniel I wanted to get out so I shut my eyes and clung to a pole until we came to Fifty-Eighth Street—the last stop on the line.

As we came down the steps my legs didn't want to hold me up.

"I have to stop for a moment," I said.

Daniel looked at me with concern. "Is something wrong? You've gone quite white."

"Not enough air in that carriage, I suppose," I replied, not wanting to show weakness to my husband.

"A walk past the park will do you good, then," he said, and we set off, past the new Plaza Hotel and along the railings that separated the park from Fifth Avenue. We were in a different world. Elegant carriages passed us, with ladies in furs and gentlemen in top hats. A bitter wind swept toward us, reminding me that winter was on its way, and I wouldn't have minded a fur coat myself.

There were two police constables standing guard outside the house. One of them saluted Daniel.

"Is Lieutenant Doyle in there?" Daniel asked.

"Haven't seen him today, sir," the young man replied.

"It's okay to go in, then? We need to confirm something with the family," Daniel said, and the constable nodded.

"Sure thing. Go right ahead."

Roberts opened the front door. "Oh, it's you, sir. Do come in. The mistress will be glad to see you both. This not knowing is playing havoc with her nerves."

We were shown into the drawing room and soon Lucy appeared, her face ghostly white against the high-necked black dress.

"Daniel, Molly, how good of you to come," she said. "Do you have any news?"

"We have several things that might be of importance," Daniel said. "Could you have your butler summon your sons? I'd like to talk to them."

"Of course," she said. "You'll take tea, will you? It's become very cold suddenly."

"Thank you. We'd appreciate it," I said, before Daniel could answer that it wasn't necessary. Men tend to forget about their stomachs, but I was still feeling unsettled from that train ride.

"How are the girls getting along?" I asked.

Lucy's tired face broke into a smile. "Oh, wonderfully. Every time I pass Blanche's door I hear them chatting and laughing. Your Bridie has been helping Blanche with her mathematics. She never was good at figures and Bridie is so patient with her. And of course they both like to read so they've been down in the library discussing books." She looked up as Roberts entered. "Our visitors will take tea, Roberts. And please tell my sons that we wish to see both of them right away."

"Very good, ma'am."

I waited until he'd gone and then glanced at Daniel before I said, "We do have one piece of news that might reassure you. We saw Gertie Grace today."

Instantly her face became guarded again. "You did. And what did she say?"

"That Bill never intended to marry her. In fact he had broken off all contact with her."

"Then why did she tell me . . ." Lucy's cheeks had now flushed bright red.

"She knew you were having a party and she wanted to upset the apple cart. To find a way to get back at Bill."

"How very silly," Lucy said. "And to think that—" She broke off as we heard voices in the foyer.

"Wants to see me? What is it now? Can't a fellow have a minute's peace?"

And Cornelius came into the room. "Really, Mother, how long is this going to go on?" he asked. "I'm not allowed to go and meet my friends. I'm stuck here with the police poking in every corner. It really is the utter end."

"Until we find who killed your father, I'm afraid this is the way it's going to be," Lucy said. "Captain and Mrs. Sullivan have come with news."

Cornelius noticed us sitting on the sofa. "Really? You've found who did it. Don't policemen match fingerprints these days?" He walked over and took the armchair beside the fire.

"They do indeed," Daniel said.

"Fascinating. I just love all the advances in science. I suppose I should have gotten a degree in chemistry rather than the humanities. But I was determined to be a writer. Still am, although God knows where this mess now leaves us. Has anyone found the original will?"

"I couldn't tell you that," Daniel said. "Perhaps he didn't have one."

"In which case the estate would be divided between the wife and children," Cornelius said. "Let's give Blanche the docks. That will keep her busy. And she'll enjoy looking at all those brawny types in their undershirts."

"Don't be facetious, Corny," Lucy scolded. "This is no matter for joking. Can't you see that I am going out of my mind with worry?"

"Sorry, Mother. You know I like to make light of things," Cornelius said. "So what news do you bring, Captain Sullivan?"

"Let's wait for your brother," Daniel said.

220

"He could take all day to get here. When last seen Charlie was chatting with Annie on the back stoop."

"Then go and get him, darling," Lucy said.

"What exactly do we have servants for when a fellow has to run his own errands?" He started for the door, then stopped, looked back, and said, "No need. Here he comes now."

And Junior came into the room, his face red from exertion as he maneuvered the wheelchair on his own.

"I don't know where Charlie has got to," he said. "I had to come down in the elevator by myself. I had to use my stick to reach the handle."

"Well done, dear. You did it," Lucy said, looking at him with obvious kindness.

"Right, now the suspects are assembled and the grilling can begin," Cornelius said with a chuckle. Lucy frowned at him.

"Is this what it is? A grilling?" Junior asked.

"Not at all," Daniel replied. "I came because I took fingerprints from the scene of the crime. Lieutenant Doyle does not believe in fingerprints, so I had to take them behind his back."

"Which means they'd never be admissible in court," Cornelius said quickly.

"They never have been yet," Daniel replied. "But they are useful, nonetheless, in homing in on a suspect."

"So what did these fingerprints show?" Lucy asked. "Do we know who took my letter opener?"

"That was the one item with no prints on it," Daniel said. "It was presumably wiped clean. And it seems the family did not often visit Mr. McCormick's study."

"He made it very clear that we were not allowed in there," Lucy said. "We kept well away. He could have a savage temper at times."

"If the family kept well away, whose prints do show up there?" Cornelius asked. "Have you identified the murderer? How jolly clever."

"The prints that we have found in the study belong to you, Cornelius," Daniel said.

"What?" Cornelius sat forward in his chair. "There must be a mistake."

"No mistake," Daniel said.

"Cornelius, how could you . . ." Lucy burst out.

"But I didn't, Mother. I didn't kill him."

"Nobody said you killed him, Cornelius," Daniel said quietly. "Your prints were taken from the whiskey decanter and from the handle on the desk drawer, where it turns out he kept important papers and a large amount of cash."

Cornelius now turned bright red. "All right. You've caught me out. I confess." He looked from one face to the next. "I have been known to come into Father's office to help myself to the odd swig of whiskey. He kept the good stuff for himself, you know. And as for the drawer—I knew he kept bundles of cash in there. Well, he kept me very short of cash. A pitiful allowance when he was rolling in it. A fellow has to live. So I did help myself to the odd bill from time to time. But not recently. I swear I haven't been near for weeks."

"May one know what other fingerprints you discovered, Captain Sullivan?" Junior asked.

"None that would arouse suspicion, Mr. McCormick," Daniel said.

A slow smile spread across Junior's face. "I have just realized. I am William McCormick. I am no longer Junior. How about that."

"And a lot of good it may do you, old fellow," Cornelius said. "At least you'll get some money out of the estate, since he didn't sign the will cutting you out."

"But he didn't cut me out," Junior said. "I kept telling you. He arranged for me to be cared for and that's essentially all I need. I'm afraid you're going to have to take control of those docks and ships, Corny, whether you like it or not."

"I'll sell the whole lot," Cornelius said. "Then we can all go and live our own lives, as we choose."

"You realize, Cornelius," Daniel said quietly, "that you are not off the hook, I'm afraid. You had the means. You left your prints and you have the motive."

"What do you mean? What motive?" For the first time Cornelius looked rattled.

"That new will would have tied you to the business forever. His murder stopped him from signing it."

"But I didn't do it!" Cornelius spat out the words. "I told you. I didn't go near his room that evening. And don't tell me you found my fingerprints on his door handle, because when I came up there the door was already open."

"No. We found Junior's prints on the door. And Charlie's."

"Of course. We were trying to get in," Junior said. "I tapped on the door. I called his name and then I got worried and we shook the handle."

"Precisely," Daniel said. "We did find Charlie's prints inside the room, but I presume he had to come into that room occasionally."

"He had to replenish whiskey glasses, bring up the mail—all sorts of reasons," Junior said.

"So we are none the wiser," Cornelius said. "If only we could have a séance and get the dagger to speak. Or summon Father's ghost."

"Corny!" his mother warned.

"But it's all the rage these days, isn't it? One of the fellows at Columbia went to a séance recently. He said it was as spooky as hell. This white thing floated across the room."

"I think you'll find most of them are clever fakes," Daniel said.

"Should I bring in the tea, Mrs. McCormick?" The butler put his head around the door, making us all jump and look up, so intense had the atmosphere become.

"By all means. I think we could all do with some refreshment at this stage," she replied. A tea trolley, laden with cups, saucers, plates, and a variety of cakes, was wheeled in. Lucy poured tea. "So are we any further ahead in this investigation?" she asked. "If the fingerprints don't point to a culprit how will we ever find out who is responsible? We may never know."

"I'm sure the police are following up on various leads," Daniel said. "They may be getting tip-offs from informants."

I looked from one face to the next to see if this statement made any of them look smug. It's been my observation that murderers like to think of themselves as clever and superior. But I didn't notice any change in expression, except Cornelius shifting uneasily in his seat. "Look, Mr. Sullivan, you're no longer with the police, are you? Do you have to let them know about the fingerprints?" He gave a nervous laugh. "I have a horrible feeling that insensitive blighter will leap to pin the crime on me and not bother to look any further."

"I give you my word, Cornelius," Daniel said, "that I shall keep working until we have solved the case and justice is served."

"We shouldn't keep you any longer," I said. "But I would like to give Bridie a hug before we go."

"Of course," Lucy said. "Enjoy your tea first. The chocolate cake is remarkable, by the way."

We ate in silence, with me wishing that I was home and not in this strange sitting room with tension still thick in the air. There was nothing that tied any of them to Bill's death. Corny's explanation of his prints seemed quite reasonable and natural. And yet someone had known where Bill's private office was, had gone up the stairs in the middle of a party and stabbed him in the back.

We went up to see Bridie, who was clearly having the best of times. There were books all over the room, and ladies' magazines with fashionable dresses circled, while a sketch pad showed the girls were trying their own hand at dress design. Bridie looked worried when I came in.

"You haven't come to bring me home, have you?"

"No, just to say hello," I said. "You can go back to your fashion designs."

She gave me a beaming smile, ran over to give me a quick hug before returning to her seat on the day bed beside Blanche. Daniel was waiting in the hallway as I came down the stairs.

"All well?" he asked.

"Couldn't be better. They are designing new outfits for themselves."

"The young are very resilient," he said.

At that moment there was a thunderous knock at the front door. Roberts hurried to open it. Lieutenant Doyle pushed his way in, striding into the front hall. When he saw Daniel he stopped, glared.

"You again? What are you doing here? You better not be poking your nose into police business or I'll have you arrested on the spot."

"We were visiting our daughter, who is staying here to comfort her friend," I said sweetly. "And we were just leaving."

"Where are the family members? They need to hear this," Doyle said.

"In the sitting room, I think," I replied.

Doyle stormed in without waiting to be introduced. "I came right away," he said. "We've just had the results of the autopsy and it changes everything. Bill McCormick was heavily drugged before he was stabbed. In fact he may have already been dead."

❧ Twenty-Nine ❧

L ucy McCormick gave a little gasp of horror. My brain had raced back to the scene when we found Bill's body. So that had explained the lack of blood from the stab wound. He was already dead. Ah. Now it made sense.

"Do we know what was used to drug him?" Daniel asked.

"We do," Doyle said. "It was morphine. Large amounts of morphine."

There was something that sounded like a strangled sob from Junior. Doyle spun to face him. "You know something about this, do you?"

"I am the one who uses morphine," he said. "There is a bottle of the stuff on the shelf in my bedroom, over the sink."

Doyle gave something like a smirk. "So you use morphine, do you, sir?"

"My doctor prescribed it for me," Junior said. "I have occasional bouts of intense pain, owing to my condition. When the pain makes it impossible for me to lie comfortably or to sleep I take a couple of drops in a glass of water."

"I see." Doyle looked back at the door. "Johnson. Have the boys search the house. Especially the room belonging to this gentleman. Look for the morphine bottle over his sink. Bring it down carefully, mind you."

"Try not to handle it," Daniel said.

"Back to your fingerprints again, are you?" Doyle said. "I don't know what you think you might do with them, since you are not a policeman and I will not consider them."

"You want to be careful, Doyle," Daniel said. "Hasn't it occurred to you that with Bill McCormick dead the Tammany ticket has fallen apart and I might well want my old job back?"

"And you think they'll give it to you?"

"I'd say there's a fair chance," Daniel said.

"But in the meantime . . ." Doyle started to say when Johnson came into the room, holding a small glass bottle in his handkerchief.

"This is what you wanted, sir?"

Doyle took the bottle and placed it on the side table. "This is your morphine bottle, Mr. McCormick?" he asked Junior.

"It certainly is."

Doyle held it up to the light. "It's empty."

"No, that can't be right," Junior exclaimed. "It was almost full. I have been doing well recently and I haven't had to take any for weeks."

"So when was the last time you checked it and noticed it was still full?"

Junior frowned. "I can't really remember. I had a bad turn when the weather turned hot at the beginning of September, but I'm not sure whether I took any morphine then."

"And who else would have known about this bottle?" Doyle asked.

"All the family, I presume. They know I have relapses when I can't get out of bed and the doctor comes to me. Someone has to bring up my prescriptions when they are delivered."

"I presume the servants also knew," Doyle said. "Johnson, round up the servants. I'm going to need another word with them."

"Surely you can't think—" Lucy began, but Doyle cut her off.

"Does it occur to you, Mrs. McCormick, that someone deliberately drugging your husband and then stabbing him is very different from rushing in, catching him unawares, and killing him? The latter could indeed have been carried out by an outsider, but the former—it had to be someone in the house who knew where the bottle was. It had to be one of you or one of your servants."

"There is one thing I'd like to point out, Lieutenant," I spoke up, hearing my voice sounding strangely loud. "That evening at the party, am I right in thinking that you employed extra staff for the evening, Mrs. McCormick?"

"We did indeed," Lucy said. "How clever of you to think of that, Molly. We always use the same agency when we host a big party. They send over extra maids and footmen."

"So you really would not have known who the extra servants were?" As I said this I had a strange feeling. I remembered taking a drink from a tray handed around by a handsome young Italian man. And I was pretty sure I had seen that man since—he was the one who met Constanza in the park and took the basket of food from her. I was about to blurt this out but then decided I'd mention it first to Daniel. That description fit a number of people and I might be mistaken. But the agency would know who they sent.

"So the name of this agency, Mrs. McCormick?" Doyle asked.

"Grand Central Domestics," she said. "On Forty-Fourth Street."

I stood up. "We should be leaving, Daniel. These men have work to do and we don't want to be in the way."

"Right." Daniel held out his hand to Lucy. "Thank you for the tea. We will see you at the funeral and the wake. And chin up. We will get to the bottom of this."

She gave a brave little nod. "Those two girls are such a comfort to me. Thank you for lending us dear Bridie."

How strange life was, I thought as we stepped out into the bitter night air and walked toward the park to hail a cab. Not long ago Blanche was Bridie's worst enemy, Daniel was happy with his job in homicide, and I did not know that the McCormicks existed. I was about to share my thoughts with Daniel when I heard the sound of running feet behind us. Daniel turned, ready to defend me, I suspect, but it was Cornelius running up to us.

"Sorry. I couldn't let you go without telling you," he said, gasping for breath. "About that bottle of morphine. You don't think that obnoxious fellow will examine it for prints, do you?"

"He may not, but I may get permission to do it behind his back," Daniel said, "Why the concern?"

"Because I'm afraid you'll find my prints on that bottle!"

"You are confessing to me that you killed your father?"

"No!" The word echoed out in the night air. "Of course not. It's just that I helped myself to a little of Junior's morphine from time to time. When Father was having a go at me, horrible shouting matches, calling me all sorts of names, I needed something to calm my nerves. Just a drop or two, you know. But it worked like a charm."

"What sort of names did he call you, Cornelius?" Daniel asked.

"If you must know, he called me a loafer and a namby-pamby in his good moods. In his bad moods he called me a bastard." He looked at me. "Excuse me, Mrs. Sullivan, but it is true." He turned back to Daniel. "There. Now you know it. It will probably come out soon and I'll be suspect number one."

"You may be lucky if Doyle refuses to test the bottle for fingerprints," Daniel said.

"So you won't tell him?"

"I am conducting my own investigation," Daniel said. "I rather suspect that I'll get to the truth before he does."

"Thank God for that. You're a good fellow, Sullivan. A credit to Columbia." He slapped Daniel on the shoulder and ran back to the house.

Daniel looked at me. "What did you make of that?"

"I'm beginning to think there are rather too many coincidences," I said. "Cornelius admits to being in his father's study but was only there to help himself to an occasional whiskey or the odd bit of cash. And he admits to touching his brother's morphine bottle because he needed to calm his nerves occasionally. Do you think he takes us for fools, Daniel? Do you think he's back home, already chuckling at our gullibility?"

"On the other hand," Daniel said, "all those explanations do seem to ring true. So the question is, has Cornelius simply found himself in the wrong place at the wrong time?"

"How will you ever prove that? How will Doyle prove that?"

"I suspect his tactics will be to bluster and threaten and hope one of the servants confesses to seeing something incriminating."

"Oh, dear," I said. "Can't you do something?"

"I intend to, but not while Doyle is present. While you were hugging dear Lucy I slipped outside and had a quick word with one of Doyle's team. I asked him to make sure that samples were taken from the whiskey decanter and the glass for testing. He said he was pretty sure that Doyle would do that, but if he didn't, he'd remind him."

"That would be logical, wouldn't it?" I said. "The killer would know that the first thing Bill would do would be to help himself to a whiskey."

Daniel stepped out into the street and waved down an approaching hansom cab. He helped me inside. "So what do you think, Daniel?" I asked him. "Who do you think killed Bill McCormick?"

"It's hard to tell," he said. "Now that we know he was drugged this turns into a crime planned well in advance, so not a sudden fit of rage or passion. I think that must rule out Miss Gertie."

"It would rule out anybody who didn't know where the morphine bottle was kept," I pointed out.

"True."

"Which brings it back to family."

"Or servants."

"What possible motive could they have?"

"Being paid well by a rival or an enemy."

That brought me back to the young man I had seen. "Daniel, I told you I saw Constanza handing over what I took to be a basket of food to a young man. Well, something just came to me. I think that man was one of the extra servants handing around champagne on the night of the party."

"Was he?" Daniel said. "I suppose that would make sense. If he's related to Constanza and Finn has been trying to look after her family since the accident to her husband, it's possible he employed her son or her nephew whenever he could."

"Yes," I agreed. "That does make sense. But what if they are actually in the pay of an enemy? The Black Hand, for example."

"That doesn't sound much like their method of operation. Drugging someone? They are usually more violent. A bomb thrown in through the window, like they did to our house. Or a shot fired when Bill was walking to his auto. That would be more like them. Besides, if this man was extra hired help for the evening, how could he possibly know about the morphine bottle in Junior's room?"

"You're right," I agreed. "I guess I don't want to face reality that it was one of the family."

A fierce wind had blown up as we arrived home, swirling up piles of dead leaves on the sidewalks. It was good to be in the warmth of our house. I had to admit that central heating was a lot more desirable than the heating in our home at Patchin Place, which was decidedly chilly in winter. It turned out that Constanza didn't know whether we'd be coming back for dinner, so we had to be content with more of the soup. It was quite flavorful, made with lots of beans and tomatoes, and fit the bill for a cold evening. I was going to have my talk with Constanza about giving away our food, but frankly I had had enough emotion for one day. I felt incredibly tired and only wanted to crawl into my bed. I went up to say goodnight to Liam, again fighting back feelings of guilt that I had left him so much recently, but as I opened the door quietly I heard Aileen's soft voice telling him a story, while he lay in his bed, gazing up at her adoringly. I had clearly been relegated to second place!

❧ Thirty ❧

Wednesday, October 23

I don't think I slept very well. Images haunted my dreams—Lucy holding a bloody knife and saying "of course it's mine." Junior's wheelchair plunging down a staircase while Blanche stood at the top laughing. Cornelius stuffing his pockets with cash. Each time I woke up with my heart thudding. Were my dreams trying to tell me something? There were times when my Celtic sixth sense had warned me of danger, but in this case I realized that my dreams were telling me that someone in that family was guilty. I just had to find out who.

I woke at first gray light, hearing the rattle of milk bottles as the milkman carried them to our doorstep. The day of the funeral, I said to myself. At least it wasn't raining. Daniel still lay in contented sleep. I got up, bathed, and decided what outfit I had that might be suitable for a funeral at St. Patrick's and then in the bitter cold of the cemetery. I did own a heavy black skirt, and my winter cape was such a dark green that it looked almost black. I did not have a black hat, however. I'd have to keep wearing the mantilla after church so that my head was covered for the funeral. I thought wistfully that in the past I'd have popped across the street to see if Sid and Gus had a black hat to lend me. Then I decided that they probably wouldn't possess such a thing anyway. If they went to a funeral it would probably be in bright colors to cheer everyone up.

I came down to a silent house. If no one was up yet, then I'd make myself a proper cup of tea. Constanza still felt that it was wasteful to put in more than a spoonful of tea leaves, and the result was pale amber. As I went down the stairs to the kitchen I heard voices. Voices speaking in Italian. I froze on the staircase. Two voices, a female one, presumably Constanza, and a male. I had no idea what they were saying, but I could hear the urgency in their words. Whatever was going on I needed to find out. Maybe it was as harmless as taking extra food to a family member. Maybe it was more serious. I took a deep breath and barged into the kitchen.

"All right," I said firmly. "What is this? Who is this in my kitchen?"

Constanza put her hand to her bosom. "Madonna mia," she muttered.

The young man's eyes darted to the door, as he thought to make a bolt for it, I suspected. I moved between him and the back door. I noticed there was a basket on the table, filled with items wrapped in greaseproof paper. There was also a note tucked into the side of it. I couldn't read the Italian, but I did see the word "Sullivan" and what looked like dates and times.

"What is this, Constanza?" I demanded. "You steal from me? You take my food and give to someone else, eh?"

"No, Signora," Constanza said, sounding equally angry. "Not your food. When I do the shopping I buy also for my family. My children. They still live in our apartment on Mulberry."

This threw me off guard. "Your children? They live alone now?"

"Not alone. I go home to them at night. After I finish your dinner."

"How many children do you have?" I asked.

"Five. Three girls. Two boys. Youngest is ten." She turned to the young man. "This my oldest son. Gianni."

The young man nodded solemnly. "Buongiorno, Signora."

"How do you do, Gianni," I said. "So are you in charge of the family or do you work?"

"My sister, Sofia. She takes care of the family. I work when I can. Signor McCormick, he gave me work."

"You were helping out at the party, weren't you?" I realized I was treading on dangerous ground, but I reminded myself it was my own house and Mary and Aileen were within hailing distance. "The party when Signor McCormick was killed?"

"I was there," he said.

"My husband is helping to find out who killed him. Do you have any ideas?" I held his gaze. He looked away.

"Why should I have ideas?" he said. His English was better than his mother's, with only a slight accent. I wondered if he had been born in this country.

"The police wonder if the murder was the work of an enemy," I said. "Someone who wanted to make sure that Bill McCormick never became mayor. Someone like the Black Hand."

Constanza gave a gasp and put her hand up to her mouth. I turned to her. "You know something, Constanza? Something you'd like to tell me? About the Black Hand? About Bill McCormick's death?"

"Mama. Silencio," Gianni warned.

Constanza was shaking her head. "I did not want this," she said. "It was not right."

"You mean that you and your son were helping the Black Hand— helping them kill Bill McCormick?"

"And why shouldn't we?" Gianni said. "He killed my father."

"No, Gianni. It was not right," Constanza said.

I turned to the young man. "You know that Bill McCormick killed your father? It wasn't an accident? Just a horrible accident?"

Gianni shook his head. "My father. He was an honorable man. A man of honor. He tells us he does not like what goes on at the docks. My father, he says too many accidents because they don't follow the rules. Also, sometimes things are stolen from a shipment. Sometimes things like guns, liquor are smuggled and the customs men are paid not to look. One day this newspaper man—he comes to the docks, asking many questions. And my father, he sees what happens to him. These men, they take him behind the piles of cargo and he does not come out again. And my father is sure they have killed him and gotten rid of his body. He is so shocked he goes to Big Bill himself and tells him what he has seen. And Big Bill tells him he is a good man and he will promote him to supervisor. My father is so pleased. Then the very next day a load of cargo falls from a crane onto him. He is killed. Crushed." He looked up at me and I saw tears in his eyes. Constanza gave a little sob and crossed herself.

"You don't think it was an accident? You just said that accidents happen all the time at the docks."

Gianni looked across at his mother and shook his head. "No accident," he said.

Constanza let out a stream of Italian, her hands waving in the air as she became more and more animated.

"Everyone is 'so sorry,'" Gianni said. "The man who works for Big Bill—Mr. Finn, they call him. He come to our home. He tell us not to worry. Big Bill will take care of us. He give money to my mother."

Constanza nodded. "Mr. Finn. He good man. He look after us. He give me job here."

I waited, wondering what to ask next. I filled the kettle and put it on the stove while I thought. "So you were taken care of and it sounds as if Big Bill was sorry for what happened."

Gianni gave a disparaging grunt. "These men come to our home," he said. "Italian men. They tell us that it was no accident. They know it was arranged for the cargo to fall upon my father. And they say it was commanded by Big Bill himself."

"And you believed them."

"They are fellow Italians," Gianni said. "They are even fellow Sicilians—why would they lie to us? And they said if we wanted revenge we could help them. We could spy on Big Bill and help to bring him down."

"They were the Black Hand?" I asked.

"They never say this. No one ever says that they are the Black Hand, but they asked for our cooperation. We were afraid to say no," Gianni said.

"So you've both been passing information about us?"

Constanza gave another little sob. "I tell my son about the birth-day party. I ask Mr. Finn if my son can help out and he says yes. And my son tells these men about the party and now Mr. Big Bill is dead."

"Are you telling me that one of these men came in and killed him?"

Gianni shrugged. "This I do not know. But this is what my mother believes. Now she is regretting she ever said yes to these men."

Constanza let out another stream of Italian, waving her arms dramatically again.

"My mother, she feels guilty that she might have aided in the death of Big Bill. She wants to stop speaking to these men. Now that Big Bill is dead she hopes she can never see them again, never talk to them again. It is all behind us, finished. But then also she have no job. You will go back to your home and we will starve."

I didn't know what to say to this. It was probably true. The kettle was boiling and there was silence while I scooped the tea leaves into the pot and poured the boiling water into it.

"Sit down," I began. "We'll have some tea and talk about this." They sat, Gianni somewhat reluctantly, at the kitchen table. I poured some tea, adding milk and quite a lot of sugar. I felt we had all had a bit of a shock.

"Constanza, you know that my husband was a policeman," I began. She shrank back as if I were threatening her with prison.

"No, Signora Sullivan. No police," she said. Gianni stood up. He looked at me angrily and it suddenly occurred to me that no one upstairs could hear if I screamed. I stood up as well.

"I want to help you, Gianni," I said placatingly. "Hear me out." I locked eyes with him until he nodded and sat back down.

"My husband is going to keep running for sheriff, at least in the short term," I began. "I don't know who will pay your wages, but I believe that Tammany will somehow or other so I don't think you will be destitute." I grimaced inside at the thought that I had just willingly decided to keep Constanza on as my cook.

"Thank you, Signora Sullivan." Constanza looked grateful.

"The police commissioner is investigating crime at the docks," I continued. "I will ask my husband to arrange a meeting with him in secret. If you tell him what you told me he may be able to help you."

"We can't go against the Black Hand." Gianni sounded scared now. "We will be dead if we do that."

"I understand, believe me," I said. "I've had my own dealing with the Mafia. But if you give information that can help the police they can keep that secret—from Tammany Hall and the Black Hand. The police commissioner is not in the pocket of either. I promise you. It's your best chance to get away from both."

Constanza looked at her son. "We may be assassins, Dio ci perdoni, we go to confession and help the police."

I hoped she didn't confess to a priest in the pay of Tammany, but decided that was less likely in an Italian church.

"Will you come to the funeral this morning?" I asked. "I think Mary is going."

"Sì, Signora." She nodded. "I make you breakfast first. Then we go. Mr. Finn ask us to."

I went back upstairs to find Daniel getting dressed. I quickly told him about my conversation. "This might be it, Daniel!" I said excitedly. "If they know what happened to the reporter the investigation will be over. We can get back to our lives."

"Lower your voice," he said. "It occurs to me that Constanza might not be the only person in this house spying for someone. If anyone finds out what they know they will be in great danger. Too many people have died already. I'll make an appointment with the police commissioner for tomorrow morning, but we have to act as if everything is normal until then."

"I think you have a strange definition of normal, Daniel Sullivan," I said, raising my eyebrows, "if going to the funeral of your murdered boss who may be a murderer himself is normal for you."

We went down to a breakfast that was thankfully scrambled eggs on toast with no garlic in sight. Perhaps Constanza really was grateful and trying to show it. Mary, Constanza, and Gianni set off to walk up Fifth Avenue to St. Patrick's Cathedral while I fed Liam and took him upstairs.

"You don't mind staying with him, Aileen?" I asked again. "It looks like rain outside and I don't want him in a drafty church or out in a graveyard."

"Nor do I want to be in either of those places!" she said emphatically. "I'd much rather be here with my little Liam."

So would I, I thought as I headed downstairs, reflecting that right now the life of sixteen-year-old Aileen might be much nicer than that of Molly Sullivan.

❧ Thirty-One ❧

The morning was perfectly suited to a funeral. It was so gray and gloomy that only the mantel clock in the parlor let me know it was past nine o'clock. There was a knock on the door and Daniel opened it himself.

Jack was standing outside. "I came with a hansom cab, Captain Sullivan," he said, touching his cap. It was drizzling already and we hurried into the back of the cab, Jack jumping in with us. I felt sorry for the poor cabby and horses out in the rain. The ride was not a long one, straight up Fifth Avenue. The street became crowded with automobiles and hansom cabs as we neared the cathedral. The sidewalks were also crowded, a sea of umbrellas as the drizzle turned into a steady downpour. Traffic came to a standstill as we waited to be dropped off in front of the cathedral.

"It seems Big Bill was very popular," I commented to Daniel. "Half of New York is coming to his funeral." I watched the people streaming up the steps, lowering their umbrellas and closing them as they entered the ornate doors. I reflected that politics in New York seemed to be the great leveler of classes. Men and women in tattered overcoats or patched shawls were entering alongside those climbing out of Daimlers in fur jackets and exquisitely tailored suits.

"Everyone loved Big Bill. He was the same in a tenement room or on Park Avenue," said Jack, surprisingly echoing my own thoughts. As we came up to the front of the church we saw a black platform with the coffin on it drawn by two beautiful black horses. Their harnesses were decorated with brass medallions and red, white, and blue ribbons. Someone was draping an American flag over it. Jack jumped out of our cab and held out his hand to help me down, handing me my umbrella as he did so. I saw as I got out that it was Cornelius draping the flag. He was standing with a small group of men dressed all in black. Finn was in the group as well. The pallbearers, I realized. Then Daniel took my hand and we walked up the steps and into the cathedral.

I had not been inside St. Patrick's Cathedral before. The wealthiest New Yorkers of Irish descent attended mass at the cathedral. I crossed myself as we entered, then spoke softly to Daniel. "Should we sit at the back, do you think?"

"Why?" He raised his eyebrows quizzically.

"We can see everyone as they come in. I've heard that murderers like to attend the funerals of their victims. If it was a political opponent maybe they will show up and give us a clue."

"Not a bad idea." Daniel nodded, and we sat on the center aisle at the back of the church. I looked around curiously. The cathedral was huge and open. With its towering ceilings it looked as if it was made for giants rather than people. Stained glass saints looked down from all around the top of the walls, although they were not lit up today since the sun was not shining. The marble floors made the whole inside sound hollow and the echoes of footsteps and whispered voices sounded quite eerie. An organ began to play and the pallbearers walked in with the coffin on their shoulders. The congregation stood to watch it pass. Cornelius was on our side of the aisle walking slowly under the weight of the coffin, and I could see that he had tears in his eyes as he walked down the aisle. Junior followed the coffin, being pushed in his chair by Charlie. Lucy came after, dressed in black. Her normally plain face looked quite lovely offset by the black fur collar and a netted veil that hung from her hat that shaded half her face. Two ladies walked behind her holding hands dressed in matching burgundy. Their little veils hid their faces from me and I strained to see who they were, peering around Daniel, who was at the end of the pew. Then one of them stopped and looked right at him.

"Hi, Papa, why are you all the way back here?" It was Bridie. The other young lady was Blanche. Lucy turned and saw us when Bridie spoke.

"Captain Sullivan, you belong up in the front pews," she said in surprise.

"We don't want to intrude," Daniel said politely. "After all, we didn't know Big Bill for very long. It's not like we are family."

"Please, I insist," Lucy said. "Mr. O'Brien and all his supporters are taking up a whole pew at the front. Bill chose you and I would like to see his wishes respected today." Her voice broke and she dabbed at her eyes with a lace handkerchief.

People in the church had turned to see who Lucy was talking to, and I felt embarrassed now as many eyes were on us. "Go on," I whispered and nudged Daniel. "People are staring." He exited the pew and stood behind Blanche and Bridie. I tried to do the same, but Lucy reached out her hand to me.

"Come and walk with me, won't you, Molly? I can't bear it." Tears were now running down her face. I took her outstretched hand and held it as we walked up the aisle. Where were her friends and family that should be gathered around her in her hour of need, I wondered. As we walked up the aisle I tried to see who was there in the church. I was quite annoyed that my plan had been ruined. If we sat in the front pew I would have to turn all the way around to see who was in the church and I couldn't do that during mass. Most of the back pews were filled with working people. I noted Mary and Constanza, Gianni by Constanza's side. The grander folk were sitting in the front pews. I saw a lot of faces I recognized from Blanche's party

241

and tried to remember who was who. Was that the lawyer that Big Bill had talked to that day? Or was it the man who had been thrown out of the party? I did recognize Mr. O'Brien in the front right pew sitting with his wife. He had been there at the party. I wondered if he was really sad that Big Bill had been murdered or if he saw this as a fantastic opportunity.

We genuflected and sat in the family pew on the left side of the aisle. Cornelius came over to sit by his mother after the coffin was placed on a table at the front of the church. Junior was placed right beside the pew in his chair. Four priests came down the aisle, one of them swinging a brazier full of incense so forcefully I could hardly see across the church as the mass started. They were all dressed in long white robes with green stoles embroidered with gold thread. Behind them came the bishop, dressed the same but with a tall golden hat. I have been to a number of funerals, I'm sorry to say, and this one was grander but not different. "Requiem aeternam dona eis, Domine." The ancient Latin words echoed around the church. We stood, and sat and kneeled. The bishop gave a short homily extolling William McCormick as a champion of the poor and a follower of the words of Our Lord, "Whatsoever you do to the least of your brothers, that you do unto me." When the mass was over the organ played a final hymn. I expected to leave, but instead Mr. O'Brien rose and came to the front of the church.

"My friends," he began, "on this day of tragedy I have been asked by the family to say a few words about our great friend and benefactor William McCormick." I looked at Lucy. She shook her head angrily.

"I didn't invite him to do anything!" she whispered. "Must politics spoil even the most sacred day of his funeral?"

"William McCormick was known as Big Bill to most of us," he went on. "Just about everything was bigger about Bill." There was a slight chuckle in the congregation and Lucy glared at the speaker. "His appetite for life, his generosity, his fight for the worker and the citizen of New York. They were all larger than life." There were murmurs of agreement. "And now, that fight continues. We cannot let the spirit of Big Bill die. While one man fights on for the righteous cause, the life of Big Bill will not have been in vain." He turned grandly to the coffin, his hand over his heart. "I swear to you, Bill, that I will continue your fight. I will not rest until we have made of this earthly city a heavenly paradise in which the regular working man can live with decency and dignity." His supporters in the front row burst into applause. One of the priests walked over quickly, looking scandalized. O'Brien put his arm around the priest in a friendly gesture and walked him to the side of the church. They were right in front of me so I saw as he pulled an envelope out of his breast pocket.

"For all of your good works, Father," he said, putting it into the priest's hand. "And God bless you." The priest seemed to know exactly what was happening because he smoothly took the envelope and tucked it away under his vestments.

"God bless you, my son," he said in a soft Irish lilt. O'Brien walked back to the front of the church.

"There will be a second offering today for the charitable works of St. Tammany. Think of your poor brothers and sisters living in squalor and the poor working man."

When I had met O'Brien before I had thought him quite refined with the clipped tones of the New York upper class. Now I noticed he was speaking with a bit of an Irish brogue, imitating the working man's rough burr. I looked at Daniel.

"Politicians!" I said, giving a derisive sniff. Finally, after baskets full of money had been passed to the front of the church (and I'm sure into O'Brien's pockets), we filed out of the church. Most of the crowd waited respectfully on the sidewalk outside until Big Bill's coffin was carried out of the church and placed on the platform again. Then, giving their condolences to the family, they melted away.

It was a much smaller group that started out for the cemetery.

Daniel and I, much to my annoyance, were offered a place in the O'Briens' automobile. Mr. O'Brien was driving himself and Daniel sat in the passenger seat. Mrs. O'Brien and I sat behind. Bridie and Blanche, still inseparable, accompanied Lucy in the family vehicle. I saw Cornelius helping Charlie lift Junior into a third black car as we pulled out. We crawled down Fiftieth Street behind the coffin. People stopped to watch. Men took off their hats in respect and women crossed themselves as the coffin passed.

"We're having a special meeting at Tammany at noon," Mr. O'Brien said, turning to Daniel. "We'll want you there for it now that you have joined my ticket." I noticed the tone of confidence. It seemed O'Brien was more ready to step into Big Bill's shoes than Finn had thought. From what Finn had said no one had chosen O'Brien to any position of leadership yet. I half expected Daniel to remind O'Brien that as yet he was the only one chosen to run for office. Instead he replied mildly.

"Isn't there a wake at the McCormick house?" Daniel asked.

"We'll go by there later. We need you in the meeting to make some decisions."

Daniel nodded, his face noncommittal. I felt my temper rising. Who was this man to order Daniel around? Then I remembered that I wanted Daniel to leave this life anyway. He was probably going to try to go along with Mr. O'Brien to get as much information as possible. O'Brien had seemed very much a background figure at Tammany to me until now, but his behavior made we wonder. Could he be behind the reporter's disappearance and could Big Bill have been innocent?

"It is all over the papers that Big Bill was murdered," O'Brien continued. "We need you to let us know where the investigation is going so we can manage it to our advantage. You know that Hearst is going to try to use it against it somehow." He took his hand off the stick shift and patted Daniel on the back familiarly. "You have an inside track to the police, my boy, you can let us know what they're thinking."

"I'm not with the police department anymore, Mr. O'Brien," Daniel reminded him. "In fact the investigator on the case has no great liking for me, I'm sorry to say."

O'Brien's face darkened. "You can always remind him what happens to the police when they cross Tammany," he said. I leaned forward at that.

"What happens to them, Mr. O'Brien?" I asked innocently, thinking of the reporter who had disappeared.

"Why, we cut the contributions to the Police Benevolent Fund of course, little lady." O'Brien's tone had the false Irish brogue back in it. He winked at Daniel. I gritted my teeth. I have never enjoyed being called "little lady." Daniel looked back and gave me a warning look and I swallowed the comment I was about to make.

I wracked my brain for something polite to say to Mrs. O'Brien. "Do you have children, Mrs. O'Brien?" was the only thing I came up with as being a safe subject.

She turned to me briefly. "No," she said, her face expressionless, and turned back to look out the window. So much for that!

When we reached the East River we climbed out of the cars and boarded a ferry. The crew took off their hats respectfully as the coffin was brought on board. Luckily the rain had stopped or we would have been drenched, as there was only an open deck with no cover. The sun had not yet come out and the water looked gray and menacing. A freezing wind blew up off the river and the rocking motion of the boat made me feel sick. I was normally a good sailor, but I supposed the choppy side-to-side motion of the little river waves was different than the big ocean swells. Daniel offered his arm. I took it and gazed out at the approaching riverbank.

The cemetery as we came near was like an island of green in the middle of the gray city. The marble mausoleums rose like miniature palaces. As the ferry docked the pallbearers put the coffin on their shoulders once again and we all marched somberly behind it. A guide appeared to direct us through the maze of headstones. A priest, not the bishop I noticed, accompanied the group. We had to leave the path and walk over the grass that was quite wet with the rain. I noticed that Charlie was having a hard time pushing Junior in the wheelchair through the muddy ground. I nudged Daniel. "Shall we help?" I asked quietly.

We walked back toward them. I had to tread carefully, as the ground was becoming slippery and the mud was clinging to my shoes. Good thing I had worn my stout Oxfords. The wheelchair had one small wheel at the back that had become hopelessly mired in the mud. Daniel took one of the wooden armrests while Charlie took the other and together they lifted it onto a less muddy patch. From there they worked to keep the back wheel clear and pushed it, somewhat precariously, on the big front two wheels. Junior looked quite embarrassed at being lifted around. I walked beside them and tried to think of something to say to make the situation more normal.

"Will your father be buried beside your mother?" I asked.

"No, her grave marker is over there." He gestured in the direction of the old cemetery. "Cornelius and Lucy arranged for a new family plot on top of the hill." He nodded in the direction of the top of the gently sloping hill we were climbing.

"I'm sorry," I said, realizing for the first time that Junior had no real family left. Cornelius and Blanche were half siblings to be sure. I wondered if they considered him their true brother or an interloper in their family.

"It doesn't matter," he said, gazing off into the distance. "She's not there anyway. She won't mind." The words were said so blankly that I couldn't tell if they were the words of a son convinced his mother was in heaven or a true atheist who thought she was gone from this world for good.

There was no gravestone yet for Big Bill. Just an open grave with a pile of dirt beside it. The pallbearers lowered the coffin down into it and stood up panting a bit. It had been a hard climb up the hill and Big Bill had been well named!

The family clustered around the grave. Cornelius had an arm around Lucy, who was crying into her handkerchief. Blanche stood beside them, hand in hand with Bridie. We pushed Junior up to join them and Cornelius reached out and put a hand on his shoulder. I stood back, wanting to be able to look at the crowd. Who had chosen to come to the gravesite? Could the murderer have come? As I had told Daniel, murderers thought themselves clever and sometimes showed up at the burials of their victims. I noticed the police commissioner was here and guessed that was the reason. I knew he had not been a big fan of Big Bill. The priest took his place in front of the grave. The O'Briens stood right beside him and I wondered if Mr. O'Brien was going to make another stump speech from the grave. Finn stood with the poorer folk; dockworkers and Tammany toughs with their wives. I recognized Jack among them. One woman in the crowd had a black mantilla still on. She was dressed in a simple black cotton dress and I guessed she was a house servant of some kind. But something in her bearing was familiar. I decided to get closer to her as we walked back to the ferry. Mary stood with Constanza and Gianni. I knew that Constanza was there out of guilt. Unless she had not been telling me the truth.

The priest began the prayers, "I am the resurrection and the life, sayeth the Lord." When he had finished and blessed the grave the family each threw in a piece of dirt from the pile. As the group started back down the hill to the ferry it started to rain again. Daniel rapidly opened the umbrella over us.

"Can you keep Bridie from getting soaked?" I asked him. "There is something I want to check." He walked over to the two girls and held out the umbrella, keeping the worst of the rain off them. I looked around for the woman I thought I recognized. It was hard to see through the crowd with the rain in my eyes and many people under big black umbrellas. Cornelius, I saw, was helping push Junior back to the path. I picked up my skirts and ran in the direction of the path. Some of the men without umbrellas had gallantly taken off their jackets and were holding them over their wives, trying to stave off the worst of the rain. I craned my neck looking for the woman in the black mantilla.

Lucy, I saw, was the last to leave the gravesite. She looked forlorn walking down the hill alone, seeming not to care that the rain was soaking her. As I watched, a woman approached her and pushed a black mantilla off her face. There she was! How had I missed her? She must have called Lucy's name, because Lucy turned and looked at her. I couldn't tell if they said anything to each other. I was too far away. But I saw Lucy turn and continue her lonely walk down the hill. The woman walked off in the other direction. I wondered where on earth she was going. Wasn't the ferry the only way on or off this part of the cemetery? It was too late for me to catch her even if I ran, but I had seen what I needed. I had recognized her walk and I could swear that the woman walking away from the crowd was Gertie Grace.

✥ Thirty-Two ✥

The rain was coming down in earnest as we boarded the ferry to go back across the East River. I thought about huddling under Daniel's umbrella, but I was much too wet already. I didn't want the girls to get sick. The wind blew the rain sideways under the umbrellas and everyone on the ferry stood quite miserable. The waves, which had been choppy on the way over, were much bigger on the way back. I felt sick to my stomach again and suddenly weak enough that I had to clutch at the rail to keep from falling over.

"Are you all right?" Finn was at my side, steadying me.

"I feel a bit sick, actually," I admitted.

"It's no surprise," he said touching my hand. "You're frozen to the bone. Where's Daniel? He needs to get you home as soon as we dock."

"I think he is meant to go to a meeting with Mr. O'Brien, actually. Don't worry about me, I'm a tough Irish girl, not a lady, whatever I'm pretending right now. I'll take a hot bath when I get home." I managed a smile.

"I'll take you home, then." Finn took off his own overcoat and put it around my shoulders. I tried to protest.

"You'll be freezing. I'm already too wet to warm up." But he paid no attention. The coat did make me feel a little warmer. I was sure I looked a fright draped in an overcoat that was much too big for me. But, I reasoned, everyone huddled under their umbrellas was too busy trying to keep from getting drenched themselves.

"There's something worrying me," I said, remembering what I had wanted to talk to Finn about. "Who is paying for my staff now? We have no income to pay them from. I don't mind keeping house myself, but it would be very hard for them to be out of a job."

"Don't worry about that yet," he said. "I already have their wages for this month. I'll talk to whoever becomes the Grand Sachem next about a stipend for Captain Sullivan. I would imagine the McCormicks won't mind you staying on in the house, especially since you are now friends of the family. But please don't worry yourself. Let me get you home."

"Won't you be going to the meeting?" I asked. "I think they're talking about Tammany politics."

He stared disconsolately out at the river. "They won't ask for my opinion. I'm thinking of getting out of politics."

"Really, what would you do?" I asked.

"I don't know. That's the problem. I can't work on the docks if I walk away from Tammany. I don't know what else I'm fit for."

"What would you like to do?" I asked curiously.

"I like being a district captain. People come to me with their problems and I have some way of solving them. I can find jobs and do favors, but I just can't go on with it. I was tied to Big Bill. Now that he is gone, I can't seem to get any enthusiasm for this O'Brien character." He looked around scornfully in the direction of the O'Briens, who sat under two enormous umbrellas in the stern of the boat.

"Was Big Bill really a good person, then?" I asked the question that was foremost on my mind. It was the key to this whole investigation and perhaps the key to his murder.

"He really cared about the little person. He really wanted to make life better for them." Finn turned to me. "But he cut corners. He took money for himself and his family. He crushed people who disagreed with him." He stared out at the river again. "Do you remember I told you my brother died in a boat fire?" I nodded, suddenly putting together Finn's story with a newspaper article I had read.

"That was Big Bill's boat, wasn't it?" I asked. Finn nodded.

"The crew all said that the maintenance checks had been skipped. The boat had been pushed too hard. It was only a matter of time before there was a fire on board. The money that was saved lined Big Bill's pockets and paid his way to the top of Tammany Hall." His voice was bitter.

"Why on earth would you work for him, then, if you knew he was corrupt?" I couldn't help asking.

"When my brother died, Big Bill came to our house. My brother's wages had been paying the rent on a tiny tenement apartment. I was the oldest now of five children. Big Bill found us a better place to live and paid the rent for the first six months. He gave me a job on the docks and told the foreman to look after me. Molly," he looked at me, "I can't answer your question because I don't know the answer. Maybe Bill didn't know the answer himself. He was a bastard." I'm afraid I flinched. Of course I had heard rough language before, but not coming from Finn with such venom.

"Excuse me," he said, seeing my shock. "He was evil, but he was also kindhearted. If you were close to him, he took care of you."

"And if you crossed him?" I asked.

"Then God help you." The boat bumped against the dock and I swayed against Finn. Damn, I didn't want to end this conversation just yet. I felt like I was meeting the real Finn for the first time. He also was kindhearted and good to those close to him. Was he warning me that he was also dangerous to those who crossed him? The crew tied up and pushed the gangplank across to the dock. I noticed that a number of people looked as sick as I felt coming off the boat wet and shaken.

Daniel was quite concerned when he saw how wet I was and wanted to come home with me. "You'll catch your death," he said.

"Finn will see me home and I'll get into a hot bath. I feel fine," I promised, which was not exactly true. I still felt sick from the boat ride and my head was spinning. Breakfast seemed a long time ago. I wondered if I should bring Bridie home with me, but she was already climbing into the McCormicks' motor.

"If you're sure," Daniel said, giving me a quick peck on the cheek. "I won't be long." Mr. O'Brien honked his automobile horn, making us all jump.

"Come on, Sullivan," his voice boomed out.

"Odious man!" I said to Daniel darkly. "I hope you find evidence he killed Big Bill and we can send him to the gallows."

"Now, now," Daniel said, and grinned at me. "Unfortunately, being an ass is not a criminal offense in New York yet." He ran over to the automobile and climbed in beside Mr. O'Brien. Mrs. O'Brien was in the back looking straight ahead. I reflected that I had not heard her say more than a dozen words yet. What a strange wife for a politician.

Finn managed to flag down a taxicab and I climbed in out of the rain gratefully. I was now shivering violently. Luckily the trip down Fifth Avenue did not take long and we were soon pulling up to the brownstone. Finn helped me out of the taxicab and up the stairs. Mary answered the door.

"Oh, Mrs. Sullivan, you're soaked," she said. I walked into the foyer feeling the warmth of the house with gratitude. "Let me run you a warm bath and help you out of those wet things."

"Thank you, Mary," I said gratefully. "Could I have a cup of tea and a biscuit while it's filling? I'm feeling quite faint." I turned to Finn. "Thank you so much for seeing me home." I realized I still had his overcoat over me. What a sight I must look! I slipped it off and handed to him. "Thank you for everything. You take good care of me." I smiled at him.

"I'll see you at the wake this afternoon, then?" He made it a question. "Do you think you will feel well enough?"

"I'll be there," I promised. "I think Lucy could use my support." After Finn went back out into the rain Mary helped me off with my wet things.

"I can't believe Captain Sullivan let you get so wet," she scolded. "You're soaked to the bone."

"All my own fault," I assured her. "I asked him to keep Miss Bridie dry and I ran around in the rain looking for someone I thought I knew."

"Well, funerals do make everyone a little crazy, I suppose," she mused, almost talking to herself. "Come into the parlor and stand by the radiator while I get you something. Constanza is not home yet." I realized guiltily that Constanza had gotten off the ferry at the same time I had. She was walking home through the rain. I should have offered her a ride home with me. I wasn't sure if that was how one was supposed to behave with one's servants, but it would have been the kind thing to do nonetheless.

I stood right in front of the radiator, feeling my clothes begin to steam and glorying in the heat. The tea and biscuits that Mary brought up seemed the most delicious meal I had ever eaten. I was ravenous and even licked the crumbs off my fingers. I felt more myself as I climbed the stairs and even better as I sank gratefully into a warm bath. I was just climbing out when there was a gentle tap on the door.

"Yes?" I called.

"Mrs. Sullivan, there is a telephone call for you," Mary called through the door. "He says it is urgent." I threw on my robe and ran downstairs in my bare feet, getting another scolding look from Mary as she saw me go past. I was tempting fate and it would be my own fault if I got sick. I ran into the parlor and picked up the receiver.

"Hello?"

"Mrs. Sullivan, this is Cornelius. Is Captain Sullivan home?" Really! I thought. He could have asked Mary that and saved me the trip downstairs. But his voice sounded strained.

"No," I answered. "He's at a meeting. Is something wrong?"

"I need to tell him something." Cornelius's voice definitely showed emotion now. "It's very important. Can you ask him to come over today?"

"We are planning to come over for the wake," I reminded him.

"Yes, but I have to talk to him alone. Please ask him to come over as soon as he gets home." Was it my imagination or had Cornelius lowered his voice as if he didn't want anyone to hear? I tried to imagine where he might be calling from. I knew there was an extension in Big Bill's office. Was there also one in the butler's parlor?

"Should I have him call as soon as he gets in?" I asked.

"No." This time I was sure Cornelius was almost whispering. "I can't tell him on the telephone. Please ask him to come over."

"I will." I was extremely curious now. "Can you tell me what it is about?" But there was silence on the line. Cornelius had hung up.

I walked back upstairs slowly, wishing Cornelius had confided in me. I knew that he was looking for his father's will. Had he found something that shed some light on Big Bill's murder among his papers? That sent my mind in another direction. One thing that had always bothered me was the locked door. How had the killer left the room if the door was locked? Perhaps Cornelius had discovered a way in or out of the room. Whatever it was, I was now impatient for Daniel to come home. I dressed quickly. The only black clothing that I had was soaked. I draped it over the radiator in my room to dry and put on my blue wool suit. I realized with relief as I smoothed my hair back into a bun in front of the dressing mirror in my room that I was feeling much better. My cheeks were still red from the heat of the bath. Hopefully I would avoid catching a chill. I couldn't afford to be sick until I had solved this murder and we could go back to our dear little house and the life I had made for myself.

When Daniel came home he found me already dressed and sitting impatiently in the parlor. I told him about the phone call from Cornelius as soon as he set foot in the door.

"Molly, I'm dead tired," he protested, sinking into the sofa and rubbing his eyes. "The wake will go late into the night. I was thinking of having a little lie-down."

"You didn't hear his voice, Daniel," I insisted. "Something is wrong. We have to get over there right away."

"All right," he sighed, and started to get up. I stopped him.

"Stay there. I'll call a cab and make you a sandwich while it comes."

"Can't Constanza do it?" he asked.

"I'm not sure she is back from the funeral yet. I haven't seen her." I called a cab, marveling a little at how easy it was to get around the city when one had the money to call cabs. I ran downstairs, sliced some bread, slathered on butter, topped it with some leftover pastrami, and added a little pickle. I ran it back upstairs. Daniel had just finished eating when the taxicab pulled up.

It was still drizzling out and there were few automobiles or carriages on the streets. We made good time.

"Tell me about your Tammany Hall meeting," I said.

"Mr. O'Brien clearly sees himself as the next Grand Sachem," Daniel said with a grimace. "He has most of the support that he needs among the money people, but I don't feel the rank and file like him very much."

"I got that feeling from Finn," I said. "He wants to get out of politics altogether." I told him about the conversation I had had with Finn on the boat.

"Molly, has it crossed your mind that Finn might have been one of the men that Gianni saw with the reporter?" Daniel looked at me seriously. "I know you are friendly with him, but he may be dangerous."

"I'm friendly with him?" My voice rose. "And who brought him and this whole business into our lives, then?"

"As part of an investigation." Daniel looked pained. "And I'm sorry I ever got you involved."

"It had crossed my mind, actually," I said. "I like Finn and I want

255

to trust him. And I don't think Constanza would have accepted his help if she thought he was a murderer. But he might have had a grudge against Big Bill because of his brother's death and he might have felt trapped and unable to get away."

"Either way I would prefer you to stay away from him until we know who killed Big Bill and what happened to the reporter," Daniel said as we pulled up at the McCormick house. A black-clad young man ran out to open the door of the taxicab and hold an umbrella for us. Daniel paid the taxicab and we got out.

The door was slightly open and we walked right into the foyer. We could hear loud voices coming from the parlor. Of course, Finn was the first person I saw when we walked in. He was standing in the middle of a group of men, a whiskey in his hand, talking animatedly. Knowing this was an Irish wake, I wondered if he had already had too much to drink.

"I'll find Cornelius," Daniel said, "and see what this is all about."

"I want to find Bridie and make sure she is still happy to be here." I glanced around. The parlor was filled with men, all with drinks in hand. Some were even smoking. The puffed-up Mr. O'Brien was in the back of the room holding forth to a group of men who were loudly agreeing with him. I suspected that many of them, like Finn, had already had a drop too much to drink. I couldn't see anyone from the family.

Roberts hurried up to me. "Excuse me, where is Mrs. McCormick?" I asked.

"I'm so sorry, Mrs. Sullivan, that no one was there to greet you and tell you. The ladies are all in the upstairs parlor paying their respects. The . . ."—he hesitated—"gentlemen are down here." His tone told me what he thought of the Tammany Hall crowd. Poor Roberts, I thought. Looking around, I noticed only Charlie in uniform moving among the men. It was a big step down from the night of the party. I wondered if some of their staff had left because of the murder.

"Thank you, I can find my way up," I said. He gave me a grateful look and hurried off. As I reached the landing I looked down the corridor to the left leading to the family rooms and Bill's office. I shuddered remembering the night of the murder and Big Bill sitting in his office dead with a knife in his back as the party went on below. I surmised that the upstairs parlor would be to the right and turned that way. The room was at the end of a small hallway. I heard voices coming from it and pushed the door open. It was bright and feminine. The far wall had large bay windows. The window seats were ornately carved with pretty blue velvet cushions. There were several couches in the same blue velvet and highly embroidered little Queen Anne chairs. A table was laid with a silver tea set and an assortment of pastries and cakes. A dozen women all dressed in black were sitting in the parlor talking softly. Bridie and Blanche were sitting together on a window seat talking. Junior was the only man in the room. He was sitting along the far wall staring out the window. I didn't blame him for not wanting to be downstairs right now.

"Oh, Molly, I'm so grateful that you came." Lucy rose to greet me when I came in. I took her outstretched hands. "Please come and save me, these women are awful," she said softly as she leaned in to kiss my cheek. I looked around at the women, and the first person I saw was Mrs. O'Brien staring straight ahead in her usual strange manner. I didn't know anyone else in the room. Lucy introduced them all as wives of the political men downstairs, but I confess I didn't remember a single name.

"So, your husband is running for sheriff, is he?" asked a rather stout woman in a two-piece bulging at the seams. "Is he a longtime Tammany man? I don't remember having met you before."

"No, he has spent his career in the police force, which is why I suppose Mr. McCormick thought he would make a good sheriff," I answered.

"A policeman with no political experience." The woman sitting beside her was as thin as the first was stout. Her face was set in severe lines. "That was Big Bill, always championing the poor and downtrodden." She gave Lucy what she meant to be a sympathetic smile, but on her harsh face it came off as a grimace.

"A police captain," I corrected. I could see what Lucy meant about these women being awful. "And what does your husband do?"

She looked shocked that I did not already know. "He is in the state legislature." She turned pointedly away from me toward the stout woman and began asking after some mutual acquaintances.

I smiled at Lucy. "That's me put in my place," I said softly. "Are they all political wives?"

She nodded. "They've come to offer their false sympathy and their husbands have come to drink my whiskey," she said with bitterness in her voice. "I'm doing this out of respect for Bill, but it's the last I ever want to do with politics. I think I may go and stay with my parents for a while until the will or lack of a will is sorted out. This is too much for me." She brushed away a tear. She seemed a woman who was barely holding it together. I tried to imagine myself at Daniel's wake trying to make conversation with a bunch of stuck-up political women. I decided that I would throw them all out with some very unladylike words. Lucy was a lot more genteel than I.

"Has Cornelius still not found a will?" I asked.

"No, he was looking for it after the funeral. He knows I'm a little worried about how to manage. Bill always handled everything, of course, and gave me spending money. The police have kept the cash that was in his desk. Finn said that Tammany Hall would pay for the funeral and wake, but I don't know where to get the money to pay the servants. Half of them have left anyway because there was a murder in the house."

"Surely the bank can give you some money out of Mr. McCormick's accounts?" I said.

"Yes, that is what Cornelius said. We are going down together to the bank tomorrow. If only we could find his will it would make it so much easier." She saw the worried expression on my face and patted my hand. "I'm afraid I am overstating my troubles," she said with an attempt at a smile. "I have my own money, of course. It's just in funds and investments that Bill managed so I'm not sure how to get at it. My parents have plenty of money and they will welcome me home at any time. They just didn't approve of Bill so they won't help me keep this house."

"Is that why they are not here?" I asked. I had wondered why Lucy seemed so alone at the funeral.

"Yes, there was an awful fuss when I married Bill. They said I was marrying beneath me. They are old-fashioned, you know. Prejudiced against trade, and Bill had had some scandals that had been in *The New York Times*. They told me I was always welcome in their home as their daughter but not as Bill's wife. So going back to their house feels like I'm going back to being a little girl. But I'm not sure what else to do."

"You can march down to that bank and ask them to give you your own money." I had never held with helpless women and I didn't like seeing Lucy becoming one now. "Make the bank manager explain where your money is invested and how to get some ready cash."

"Do you think so?" She looked as if she were wondering if she could be so daring.

"I do. I'll come with you if you need, but I think Cornelius would be a better choice. Where is he, by the way?"

"I think he is downstairs with all the men."

"He's not thinking of going into politics, is he?" I asked.

"Oh, God, no," she said with a shudder. "I suppose he will have to take over Bill's businesses, unless they belong to Junior. It's so maddening to not know!"

There were footsteps in the hall and Daniel appeared in the doorway.

"Excuse me for barging in, ladies," he said as he took in the room full of women, "Mr. McCormick," he nodded to Junior. "I'm looking for Cornelius. He wanted to speak with me."

"Good afternoon, Captain Sullivan," Lucy said. "I believe he's downstairs."

"He's not down there and no one has seen him, which is why I came up here to look. I thought that he might prefer your company like his brother." Daniel looked puzzled.

"Maybe he's still looking for the will," I said softly to Lucy. "He knows how much it means for you to find it."

Lucy rose. "I'll go and find him for you."

"I couldn't possibly take you away from your guests, Mrs. Mc-Cormick." Daniel looked embarrassed now.

"I insist," Lucy said. I thought privately that she wanted a little break from these particular guests. "The only servants in the house I trust up here right now are Roberts and Charlie and they are using up my whole liquor supply on the distinguished gentlemen downstairs." I thought I saw a flush on Mrs. O'Brien's cheeks at that remark. Lucy went out of the room to search.

"May I present my husband Captain Sullivan?" I turned to the state senator's wife with the same slight emphasis on the word "captain." "Daniel, this is Mrs. . . . ." I paused because I had completely forgotten her name.

"Johnson," she put in, and held out her hand stiffly. "Pleased to meet you, Mr. Sullivan."

"Mr. Johnson is a state senator," I informed Daniel. "I am not up on my politics, but I think that means he will be counting on you to make sure his constituents can vote fairly when you are sheriff. I can hardly believe it, but I have been told that without the sheriff to protect them ballot boxes are often stolen or stuffed with votes for the wrong party. Have you heard that, Mrs. Johnson?" I turned to look at her.

"Yes, I believe that is true." This seemed to have given her something to think about. "So we will be counting on you, Captain Sullivan." I noticed her use of "captain" and gave a triumphant grin. It may be petty of me, but I was not going to let anyone put down my husband, even if he was only going to be sheriff over my dead body.

I looked up at the sound of quick footsteps in the hallway. Lucy came into the room.

"Captain Sullivan, I need you," she said a little breathlessly. "Could you come?"

"Of course," Daniel said, and rose to follow. I, of course, went too, filled with curiosity. We followed her over to the hall with the family's rooms. She stopped outside a door I guessed was Cornelius's.

Lucy turned to us, a look of panic on her face. "I can't wake him up," she said. "I've called and shaken him and he won't wake up." We rushed into the room. Cornelius was lying curled up on his bed, still fully dressed for the funeral. He looked as if he were peacefully sleeping, but as Daniel shook him and called his name he didn't stir.

"Is he drunk?" I asked, thinking of the men downstairs. I looked around for a bottle or glass.

"I think we would smell it if it were whiskey," Daniel said, sniffing the air near the bed. Cornelius's room was large with a curtained four-poster bed against one wall and a beautifully carved fireplace on the other side. The fire had been lit and was burning down to the embers. I walked over to it. On the mantel was a folded piece of paper and next to it was an empty morphine bottle.

🦋 Thirty-Three 🦋

D aniel, look at this," I said, softly but urgently. Lucy was still by Cornelius's side trying to wake him.

"Don't touch it," Daniel said quickly as he saw the bottle and realized what it meant. "There might be fingerprints." He fished a handkerchief out of his pocket and used it to open the paper. It was a typed letter with a signature at the bottom.

"To the authorities," it read, "I confess to the murder of my father. Please tell my mother that this is the best way. I put morphine in my father's whiskey. May God forgive me. Cornelius McCormick."

"I'll go and call the police," Daniel said softly. "See if I can get Corelli here so the fool Doyle doesn't ruin the fingerprints on the bottle. Can you stay with Lucy and make sure nothing is touched? And I'll have Roberts call a doctor. He might still be saved." I nodded. Was it better that he slip away quietly or wake up to a trial and a noose, I wondered.

"Lucy," I said gently, sitting on the bed beside her. She was holding Cornelius's hand and crying.

"Why won't he wake up?" She turned a blank face to me.

"I'm afraid it's morphine. He tried to take his own life."

She gave a despairing cry. "No, he wouldn't. Why would he?"

Daniel had left the note untouched beside the morphine bottle.

"There's a note on the mantel. No . . . don't touch it," I said quickly as she rose. "It is evidence."

"Evidence of what?" She turned an uncomprehending face to me. I hated to be the one to tell her. But I supposed I would be kinder than the police and they would be here soon.

"He says that he killed his father," I began.

She looked bewildered. "He didn't do that." Her voice rose. "I know he didn't." She looked at me, explaining, "It's not in his nature. I know my son."

"He said it was an accident. Why don't you read the letter? Just don't touch it." I held it out with the handkerchief. She read it and her face crumpled.

"What was he thinking? Why didn't he tell me? He didn't have to do this." She turned back to her son on the bed. "Oh, Corny, don't be gone." She sat on the bed, stroking his hair. "Come back to me, Corny, we'll face this together." Tears rolled down her face. I had to turn away from the utter heartbreak. I was relieved when Daniel entered the room again followed by Doyle. He snatched up the letter and read it.

"You'll want to get fingerprints from the letter and the bottle, Doyle," Daniel said.

"Not that again, Sullivan," Doyle sneered. "Even if I believed in fingerprints I would see no reason to take them when a man has confessed to taking his own life. Of course his fingerprints will be on the bottle." He picked up the bottle and examined it. "Looks like another of the bottles meant for the crippled brother. We will ask the chemist when this was filled."

"Cornelius did admit to us that he sometimes took Junior's morphine," I put in. "He could have taken this at any time from his brother's room." Something occurred to me. "Why would he type a suicide note? Isn't that suspicious?"

Doyle looked scornfully at Daniel. "So your wife has taken over as the detective, has she?"

I opened my mouth to retort, but the look on Daniel's face made me close it again.

Just then the doctor arrived. He was a stern-looking older man with spectacles, a long black coat, and an enormous black bag. He took one look around the room.

"Out," he said firmly. "Everyone out. I will try to save this boy's life."

"This is a murder investigation, Doctor." Doyle swaggered up to him, his large belly almost bumping into the doctor. "And this boy is a murderer. I'll say who goes and who stays."

The doctor wagged a finger in Doyle's face. "I am going to save this boy's life and you can kill him later if that's what some archaic law allows you to do. I don't hold with policemen in my sickroom. Now get . . . out." His voice was deep and powerful, and amazingly Doyle obeyed. We followed him. I guided Lucy by the arm and she came with me unresisting. She seemed in a trance.

"Right," Doyle said, looking pleased with himself as we walked down the hall and onto the landing. "That's the murder solved, then." He turned to Lucy. "I will be posting a policeman at your front door. If your son pulls through he will make sure you don't try to take him away anywhere. Good day." And he walked down the stairs actually whistling.

"Odious man," I said, turning to Daniel. "I can't believe he is a lieutenant."

"He won't be for long if I am reinstated," he said softly. Lucy swayed.

"Look out, she's going to faint." I turned and steadied her before she could tumble down the stairs. "Why don't you go and lie down. I'll ask your guests to leave," I suggested.

"I want to be with Cornelius." She staggered back down the hall and into his room. I didn't hear the doctor yell at her to get out so he must have allowed her to stay.

Daniel turned to me. "I'll see if I can get the drunken fools downstairs to leave if you can convince the ladies."

I nodded. "I will. And I'm taking Bridie out of here right now. I can't believe I let her stay in the house with a murderer. Who knows what could have happened?"

I walked back into the upstairs parlor. It took me quite a while to explain to the ladies that Mr. Cornelius had been taken ill and Mrs. McCormick wanted to be at his side. I thought I would try to protect the family's privacy for as long as possible, although I was fairly certain the police coming and going would be noticed and they would eventually read about the scandal in the news. When they were finally gone I sat down with Bridie, Blanche, and Junior.

"Bridie, I need you to come home now, please go and pack your things," I said firmly.

"Oh, but why, Mrs. Sullivan?" Blanche put in immediately. "I love having Bridie here. Please don't separate us. Is what Corny has contagious, is that why she has to go? I remember when I had the mumps no one could visit."

I debated how much to tell her. "You will have to ask your mother." I decided it was better to let Lucy tell Blanche and Junior whatever she wanted them to know. If Cornelius died it was possible that the police could quietly close the case and his brother and sister would never have to know what he had done.

"You and Junior are still welcome tomorrow for tea and then you can spend the night with us." It came to me that it would be a good idea to get Blanche out of this house. First her father was murdered and now her brother had confessed. I really wanted to spare her all I could. I hoped Bridie would not get behind missing school this whole week, but some things were more important.

"That would be wonderful." Bridie brightened. "Maybe I can take her out to lunch at the soda fountain. I'll go and pack." She looked down at the burgundy dress she was still wearing that matched Blanche's exactly. "Would you like your dress back, Blanche?"

"Oh, no, you keep it. We'll fix on a day to wear them together to a school function and come in like twins." Blanche smiled at Bridie.

It struck me that schoolgirl friendships could be as sudden and passionate as love affairs. I had missed out on this sort of friendship by being with two rather horrible and snooty upper-class girls during my time in the schoolroom, but I had seen village girls be inseparable friends one day and enemies the next. I hoped that didn't happen to Bridie. I was afraid it would crush her if her first real friend turned on her.

"I don't have much stuff here, I'll run and get it," Bridie said, and walked out.

Daniel walked in with a sigh. "The men are all gone, finally. A few of the gentlemen had to be carried out to their cars." He grinned. "The wives were most disapproving. Shall we go? I've asked Roberts to call us a cab."

"Bridie is getting her things. Let's wait on the landing for her," I said. "We will see you tomorrow, Blanche, Junior." I shook hands with each and we walked out to the landing. We stood looking down into the marble foyer where Roberts was coming in and out clearing up after the party. I wondered what would happen to Roberts now. What would be left of the McCormick legacy with the master gone and the son facing murder charges if he even lived. I suddenly felt dizzy and clammy all over.

"Are you all right?" Daniel looked at me with concern as I hunched over, feeling nauseous.

"I'm sorry." Tears sprang into my eyes. "Just thinking of him lying there. And what will happen to the family now. I feel afraid for them. And for us." I didn't know what had come over me. I was normally adventurous and levelheaded. Perhaps these occurrences were just too close to home. I straightened up and tried to smile as Bridie came out of the hall.

I must not have done a good job because Bridie instantly knew something was wrong.

"Is Cornelius very sick?" she asked.

"Yes, I'm afraid he is," I said. "I'll tell you more on the way home."

266

"I like Cornelius," Bridie said as we descended the stairs. "He treats me like a little sister."

As soon as we were in the taxicab and headed home I told Bridie what had happened.

"Oh, poor Blanche," were her first words. "First her father and now her brother. I don't believe for a second that Corny is a murderer."

"I admire your loyalty," Daniel said gently, taking her hand. "But I absolutely forbid you to visit that house again until the investigation is over. I won't have you in danger."

"But, Papa!" Bridie looked as if she wasn't sure whether to cry or explode with anger. "Mama?" She turned to me with an appeal.

"I agree with Daniel on this," I said firmly. "But Blanche can come and stay with us for as long as you like. We will keep her out of danger as well."

"But how can we be detectives if we are not at the scene of the crime?" she asked hotly.

"What do you mean, 'detectives'?" I asked warily.

"Blanche and I have been reading Sherlock Holmes. We decided it would be the best way to become detectives like Papa . . . and you," she added. "We've been writing down clues in her notebook."

"What kind of clues?" I knew I shouldn't encourage her, but I wondered what she had found. She and Blanche could have been all over the house.

"Well, we started by checking the soil on everyone's boots," she said. "Because Sherlock Holmes always does that. He can tell what county of England someone comes from by the mud. But it just looked like dirt to us so that didn't help much. Then we checked everyone's clothes for bloodstains."

"You went into their closets?" Daniel seemed shocked.

"Yes, but we didn't find anything and Mrs. McCormick's maid found us and was annoyed." Bridie laughed as if this had been a fun adventure.

"We did find a bloodstained cloth in the laundry."

"You did?" Now I was shocked. My eyebrows shot up.

"Yes, but Cook said she had used it to clean up after she cut up lamb chops."

"Now I absolutely don't want you to go back there. Leave the investigating to the police." Daniel's voice was firm.

"Yes, Papa." Bridie gave him a submissive smile. As she turned away from him her look changed to one of determination. I could tell that she planned to keep investigating no matter what the cost.

"Saints preserve us," I muttered under my breath. This was my fault. We might not be related by blood, but I was raising my daughter to be exactly like me. And if I was honest, I was quite proud.

The rest of the ride home was a quiet one. We were each lost in our own thoughts. Bridie excused herself and ran off to the library to see which Sherlock Holmes books might be there. I was glad when we headed up to bed.

"There are two things that are puzzling me, Molly," Daniel said after we had tucked Liam in together and walked back to our room. "One is why Cornelius didn't wait to talk to me when he called me and asked me to come over immediately."

"Perhaps he had already taken the morphine," I guessed. "And he realized he didn't want his mother or sister to be the one to find him and the letter. He panicked and called you so you would be the one to find him."

"Perhaps." Daniel sounded doubtful. "But he was searching the house for documents. I get the feeling he found something important."

"That was my thought when he called. What is it you are saying?" I asked, a feeling of unease creeping up inside me.

"The note tells his mother this is the best way," he mused. "Do you think he might have confessed to protect someone he loves?"

"Confessed to murdering his father when he didn't do it? I can only think he would do that for Lucy or Blanche," I said.

"Or Junior?" Daniel queried.

"I'm not sure they were that close, they were only half brothers," I said. "What was the second thing?"

"What?" Daniel asked.

"You said there were two things. What is the second?"

He looked thoughtful. "The note he left says the morphine was in the whiskey, but I got a look at the police report. There was no morphine in the glass or the decanter."

❧ Thirty-Four ❧

Thursday, October 24

My first thought when I woke Thursday morning was of Cornelius in the hospital. I wondered if we could call and find out if he had survived the night. They might not tell us anything, but perhaps Daniel could use a police connection. I could presumably call Lucy, but I guessed she would be at the hospital by his side.

"Can you let Constanza know that we have an appointment with the police commissioner at eleven?" Daniel asked as we rose and began to dress.

"What?" I looked at him blankly, not understanding.

"I set up an appointment with the police commissioner so they can tell their story. It may be what we need to get to the truth about what happened to the missing reporter."

My thoughts had been so full of last night that I had forgotten this was happening. But it quickly occurred to me that solving the reporter's disappearance was the key to getting our own life back. The police commissioner must take this seriously to have agreed to meet with them so quickly. It might also shed some light on who had killed Big Bill and if Cornelius was a murderer or a victim.

"I have to go out first," Daniel continued, "but I will be back to escort her."

"Good luck getting out of here without being seen," I replied. "I have not managed to go to the shops once without that Jack fellow tagging along."

Daniel looked worried. "That is a very good point. We can't have anyone from Tammany suspect where we are going, for Constanza's safety."

I thought about it. "I'll send Constanza back home this morning after breakfast. I'll have her write down the address for you and you can meet them there. She comes and goes from there all the time so it shouldn't be suspicious. I'll go out to the shops for the cakes and breads I want for tea and Jack can follow me there."

He looked at me. "I'm sorry to take away your cook when you are entertaining."

I smiled. "I'm not. Who knows what she would think is appropriate to serve rich people at tea time? Probably garlic dumplings, from previous experience." Daniel laughed. "Although Blanche did say she likes her spaghetti," I said, trying to be fair. "I'm of the opinion that everyone likes cake, so I'll get plenty and we'll have a grand old time." A new thought struck me. "And even if she was the best cook in New York and I was feeding the five thousand, I wouldn't mind the work if it helps you to solve this case and gets us back to our normal life."

"I think it just might," Daniel said with a smile. "Molly, I don't know how many other wives would be so eager to move down in society, but in this case I'm with you. I don't say I might not want to run for office with my own ideas someday, and I don't want to live in Patchin Place forever"—I gave him a look at this statement, but he went on—"but in this instance I am as eager as you are to go back to being plain Captain and Mrs. Sullivan."

"Amen to that!" I said. I went all the way down to the kitchen, making sure first that Mary was up on the second floor making the beds. I wanted to trust her, but I also wanted to be careful. Constanza's life might be at risk. The kitchen smelled heavenly. Constanza was frying bacon and breaking eggs into a bowl ready to scramble. It seemed she was going to turn into a good cook just as I was ready to go back to my own life. At least it would help her to get a new job when we left. She was very quiet as I relayed Daniel's message.

"Is dangerous, sì?" she asked, finally. "Visiting police. Is dangerous for my son. What if police think he is killer?"

"Captain Sullivan will go with you and I know he believes you." I put my hand on her arm. "It is more dangerous if you don't tell what you know. Someone might try to silence you or your son before you can report it." That made her look even more scared, but in the end she agreed to go and wrote her address down for Daniel.

Bridie was still quiet and thoughtful at breakfast. I was sad that a murder and now an attempted suicide would come so close to her. I supposed it was good that she saw herself as a detective rather than a victim. She should not be worrying about anything more than her studies and friends.

"Do you think that Cornelius really killed his father?" she asked me, after Daniel had left for his meeting and Mary was cleaning up the breakfast. I saw Mary start with surprise and keep cleaning up, deliberately not looking at Bridie. I waited until she had gone to answer.

"Careful what you say in front of Mary," I warned her. "No one but the family knows about the note yet." I continued, "The note did say that he killed his father."

"But are you sure that he wrote the note?" Bridie asked. She was already asking the right questions. Growing up with me and Daniel had given her a feel for investigating already.

"No, we're not. It was typed. Cornelius was in his father's study so he could easily have typed it. But another person could have typed it as well." I had a sudden fear that she would mention this in front of Blanche and Junior. "I know you and Blanche are detecting,"

I warned her, "but let's not discuss any of this with Blanche when she is here."

"Because her family are the main suspects?" Once again Bridie went to the heart of the matter.

"Yes, and because it is distressing. I'm not sure how much her mother has told her. She might have just told her Cornelius is ill, trying to spare her the details."

"I bet that's what she did," Bridie said thoughtfully. "Blanche worshipped her father and she loves Corny. I won't mention it at all, Mama. We'll just try to cheer her up." She rose from the table and I stood as well to give her a hug.

"You're growing up so fast. I'm so proud of you. Two weeks ago this girl was your enemy and now you are acting as a true friend to her." I kissed the top of her head.

"I'm going to go and find some books that she would like to read before she comes over," she said, cheerful again. "And see if I can find any more of those books with 'Billy' in them and put them on a low shelf so Junior can reach them."

"That's thoughtful," I said. "Perhaps you should call him Mr. Mc-Cormick, Bridie. He is not a relation, and it sounds rude to call a man by a pet name like that."

"He did tell me to call him Junior," she said. "He's peachy now. Blanche said he used to be horrible to her sometimes but now he treats her like a real brother."

"Yes, but you are not his sister," I insisted. Bridie seemed to feel like one of Blanche's family. Normally that would make me happy, but in the current circumstances it worried me. If Cornelius was the killer then I could relax. But if he had written that note to cover up for someone else, then a killer was still on the loose; what's more, a killer who could come and go without notice from the McCormick home.

Finn's face came into my mind. Big Bill and Cornelius had both trusted him without question. What if Cornelius had wanted to tell

Daniel something he had found out about Finn and Finn had overheard? How hard would it have been for Finn to offer Cornelius a drink? Perhaps Finn knew where Cornelius stashed the morphine he had stolen from Junior. A few drops might be enough to kill. Finn walking around with a whiskey glass would not have been remarked on in the least. And didn't morphine make you sleepy? Cornelius would feel tired and lie down to rest before the party. Then my blood froze. That was exactly what had happened to Big Bill, only, being the man he was, he would never have gone to his bed during a party. He set his head down on his desk to rest and he never woke up.

I couldn't shake a feeling of unease as I left the house for the shops with Aileen and Liam. Jack was following as always. It was an absolutely beautiful day. The rain had washed the smoke out of the air, which now smelled fresh. The leaves were turning red and yellow and danced off the trees as a breeze sprung up. We walked through the park and Liam amused himself scooping a big pile of them together and jumping into it.

At the bakery I bought fresh bread and little tea cakes. I enjoyed dropping into my regular shops getting jam and loose tea at one shop and some smoked salmon at the Jewish deli. If I forgot about the fact that Jack was hovering outside I could almost imagine that I was back living my normal life. Students walked by and other mothers, out with their babies in prams, smiled at me. It was hard to put this normal fall day together with my recent brushes with murder. It was easier to believe that the most pressing problem I had was what to serve for tea.

I called Bridie downstairs when I got home to help me make some Irish soda bread. No matter how tasty the store-bought pastries were, I missed having something fresh and warm on the table and the delicious smell it gave the house. Since Constanza had already left we had the kitchen to ourselves. Mary came down, saw what we were doing, and gave a sniff of disapproval. I suppose she was not used to seeing the mistress of the house down in the kitchen covered with flour. I tried to summon up Sid's careless air of command and said, "Constanza is out and Miss Blanche and Mr. William McCormick are expected for tea. I will expect you to make the sandwiches and carry them up. I know that neither of us are cooks but we don't want to let down the McCormicks, do we?"

"Oh, no, Mrs. Sullivan." To my surprise her demeanor changed immediately. "Not after what that poor family has been through. I can't believe Constanza has gone off and left you to cook on an important occasion like this."

I didn't want to tell her where Constanza had gone so I said nothing. I was glad I had at least earned her cooperation. It felt so normal to be cooking with Bridie at my side that it raised my spirits. I had just put the soda bread in the oven when the bell rang.

"They're here!" Bridie was ready to sprint up the stairs.

"Hold your horses," I said. "Let's go to the parlor. Mary will bring them in." But Bridie was already pulling off her apron and heading for the front door. By the time we got upstairs into the foyer Mary had opened the door. Junior's footman, Charlie, was standing there. Blanche was right behind him, just as anxious to see Bridie.

"I'll help Mr. McCormick in," Charlie said, touching his cap to me and walking back to the automobile sitting out in front of the house. Blanche rushed in and she and Bridie hugged each other as if they had been apart for months.

"I found some books you don't have at your library," Bridie said happily. "There's a new Sherlock Holmes."

"Really!" Blanche's face lit up, but she remembered her manners. "Thank you for having me, Mrs. Sullivan." Mary helped her off with her coat. I could see through the door Charlie lifting Junior out of the automobile. I saw no sign of his chair and wondered how we would manage. As I had the thought, a horse-drawn cart pulled up, and two men lifted out a chair and brought it through to the parlor with Charlie following behind, Junior in his arms. It took some minutes to get the chair into the house and Junior into the chair. Bridie and Blanche slipped away to the library while Junior was getting situated.

The two men who had come with the chair disappeared as soon as they carried it through to the parlor, but Charlie stayed to make sure that Junior had a blanket on his lap and was comfortable before he left as well.

"Now you see why it is so difficult for me to visit," Junior said, when we were finally seated opposite each other in the parlor.

"Mercy me, what a lot you have to go through," I said, sympathetically. "I wondered why you hadn't come by to see your old house before and now I know."

"It's quite a lot of trouble and I'm afraid a bit embarrassing," Junior said, quietly. "So I only leave the house if it is to visit someone kind and sympathetic like you."

"I don't have anything very exciting planned. Tea will be in an hour. I don't know if we can pull Bridie and Blanche out of the library."

"Actually, I would love to join them if you don't mind," Junior said, eagerly.

"Yes, of course," I said, thanking heaven that the doors were wide enough for his chair and there were no lintels between the rooms. I wheeled him into the library. The girls were sitting side by side reading out of a book together.

"Look, Junior, it's *The Return of Sherlock Holmes*. I didn't know there was another one. Was this here when you lived here?" Blanche asked.

"You dunderhead, that's just come out," Junior laughed. "It must have been newly purchased by that man who was running for sheriff before Captain Sullivan."

"This one is yours, isn't it?" Bridie opened one of the books to the title page where "Billy" was written in childish handwriting.

"Yes, that was mine." Junior's face lit up. "I loved *The Frog Prince*. My mother used to read it to me."

"You should take it with you it, then," I said. "And any other books that belonged to you. I'll see what I can find." I started pulling off the shelves the books that looked as if they might have belonged to a child and making a pile of the ones that had belonged to him. In some he had written his name in that childish scrawl and a few had "Billy McCormick" written in the flyleaf in a feminine hand. A gift from his mother or grandmother, I supposed.

"I can't believe you young ladies are interested in Sherlock Holmes," Junior said. "Isn't that a book for boys?"

"We want to be detectives like Sherlock Holmes," Blanche said, "and solve mysteries."

"And smoke a pipe!" Bridie put in.

"You will not be smoking a pipe," I said, shocked.

"Aunt Sid does sometimes," Bridie said with the air of someone playing a trump card.

"Who is Aunt Sid? Isn't Sid a boy's name?" Blanche turned a fascinated gaze on Bridie.

"She is . . ." Words failed Bridie as she tried to describe Sid. "She's hard to explain. Come upstairs and I'll show you the purple dress she gave me."

"She gave it to me," I protested. But Bridie and Blanche were already gone and I could hear their giggling as they ran up the stairs.

Mary walked in. "Excuse me, Mrs. Sullivan. Did you have something in the oven?"

"The soda bread!" I jumped up in alarm. I had completely forgotten it. "Is it done?"

"I don't really know, Mrs. Sullivan." Mary made a face. "I'm not much of a cook."

"I had better go down and see. Mary, why don't you stay in case Mr. McCormick needs anything."

Junior looked up. "Oh, please don't," he said. "Not on my account. I really want to sit and read a few minutes. I'll be just fine." He looked as if he really meant it and I knew I could use a hand with the sandwiches.

"If you really don't mind being left alone we will just be a minute," I said, and practically ran down the stairs. Luckily I got to the soda bread before it burned. I left it on a sideboard to cool and had Mary

277

find a nice tea tray for me to lay out the cakes while she made the sandwiches. It took a little longer than I thought. I walked upstairs and was heading toward the library when Bridie came up to me, her face a mask of confusion.

"Mama, I have to tell you something." She looked in the direction of the library. "Come in the parlor," she said softly, taking my hand and leading me in there.

Oh, no, I thought. I hoped the girls hadn't had a spat already. "Is Blanche all right?" I asked.

"She's fine. She's in my room. I just came down to the library to get my Sherlock Holmes book so we could read some more." She said this solemnly as if she were explaining something really important. "Did you put any books back on the shelf? The books that belonged to Junior?"

"No," I said. She nodded as if this confirmed a suspicion.

"Well, you know how Sherlock Holmes says you have to notice things?" she said earnestly.

"Yes." I was getting a bit impatient now. I remembered the days not too long ago when I would dread a sentence that began, "You know the lamp that is in the living room?" and I would jump up to see what manner of mischief had been done to my lamp. But her whole demeanor said she was trying to explain something important to me.

"I noticed that *Tom Sawyer* was on a high shelf." She looked at me as if I should understand what this meant.

"And what in the name of all the saints is wrong with that?" I asked.

"It was one of the ones you pulled down and put on the table. It had Junior's name in it." Now I thought I could see what was upsetting her. "How could it have gotten there if Junior is the only one in the room?"

"That is strange," I said. "Mary has been down here with me and as far as I know Charlie has left the house."

"And I realized something else from when Blanche and I were looking for mud on people's shoes." She looked at me solemnly. "We found our clue but didn't realize what it meant. There were scuff marks on the bottom of Junior's shoes."

✣ Thirty-Five ✣

I almost laughed at her serious face. "There could be a lot of reasons for that, Bridie," I said. "He could scuff them on the wheelchair when he gets in and out. They could even be shoes from a time when he could still walk."

"Yes, but the book!" she insisted. "*Tom Sawyer* is up on the top shelf and it wasn't before. I know it."

"Why would Junior McCormick come to our house to place a book on a shelf in our library?" I said. "Unless it is the door to a secret passage," I teased. She knew as well as I did that there was no space for a passage behind the library.

"Don't tease me, Mama," she insisted. "I know it is a clue. And if Junior can stand up and walk that would change everything. The game's afoot!"

"The what?" I looked at her uncomprehendingly.

"Sherlock Holmes says it," she explained. When I thought about it she did have a point. Whose word did we have that the door to the study had been locked? Junior's. Whose word did we have that he could not walk across his father's study? Again, Junior's. But that was ridiculous. No one would spend day and night in a wheelchair on the off chance that he had the opportunity to murder his father. He must be truly afflicted with the disease that killed his mother. I determined to find out for myself. After all, if I pulled a book off the shelf and he looked up at me in surprise I could just say, "Oh, there's that copy of *Tom Sawyer* I had been looking for."

"Please go up in your room and entertain Blanche," I said to Bridie.

"I want to investigate!" she insisted.

I patted her on the arm. "You've done a good job this far. Now I want to make sure you are safe."

"From Junior?" She gave me a look of disbelief.

"Don't leave Blanche alone upstairs," I admonished. "You have a guest."

"I know what you're doing, Mama," she said, and wrinkled her nose. "Blanche and I will be down to investigate in a minute." And she took off up the stairs. I looked after her thinking how much she was like me. And I reflected that many times I had gotten myself into trouble that I had only escaped from by good luck. I had better figure out what was going on before she found herself and Blanche in trouble.

I walked into the library. It was a tranquil scene. A fire was burning in the grate. Junior was sitting in his chair absorbed in a copy of *At the Back of the North Wind*. A beautifully illustrated version of *Alice in Wonderland* lay on his lap, and on the table next to him was a stack of the children's books I had pulled out. He looked up with a smile.

"This was one of my favorites," he said.

"I wonder if any more of your books are here," I said, scanning the shelves behind him. Bridie had said the book was *Tom Sawyer*.

Was it my imagination or did he suddenly look nervous? "I think I have all I remember." He patted the stack beside him. "It is so nice of you to let me keep them." He closed the book he was reading and slid it into a leather bag that was hanging on the inside of his chair. I had never spent any time thinking what it would be like to not be able to get up and walk across the room for something that I wanted. What would it be like to only have access to the things you could carry with you? But, supposing Junior could stand, supposing Bridie was correct, where could he place a book? I let my gaze move upward from his chair and there it was, *Tom Sawyer*.

Junior saw me looking at the book and his fists clenched. "I'm feeling a little hungry. Is there any chance that soda bread is ready?" He attempted a smile but it looked forced.

"Here is one we missed," I said with my own bright smile. I stepped forward quickly and grabbed the book from the shelf.

"Oh, please don't bother. I'm sure that's not mine." His voice cracked as he said it. As I pulled the book out a folded paper fluttered out. Bridie had been right. Junior had hidden a paper in a book in my library. I darted forward to grab the paper and retreated to the couch to read it.

"I'm really not feeling well. Could you call the house and have Charlie bring me home? Right away?" Junior said loudly. I ignored him and opened the paper. It was a letter, somewhat the worse for wear—as if it had gotten wet and torn at one edge. "Re: William McCormick Junior" was neatly typed on the top left and the address of the McCormick house below it. On the top right was "Shady Groves Rest Home" with an address in Mount Vernon. "Dear Sirs," the letter began.

I enclose the final payment for the care of my Tammany charity patient Elsie Myers, recently deceased, and thank you for your diligence in her care over many years. Please find also enclosed a deposit. My son has a similar condition and the care you gave Miss Myers has recommended Shady Groves to me. I plan to have you take care of Mr. William McCormick, Jr. He will be joining you as a patient before the year is out. Please be kind enough to reserve a private room. Tammany Hall has also recognized the goodness of your charitable efforts and has decided to fully fund the new wing of the rest home that we spoke about last month.

Cordially,
William McCormick Esq.

I read the letter three times trying to understand what it meant. I looked questioningly at Junior.

"What does this mean to you? A charity patient your father was supporting?"

His face was twisted with pain, or was it anger? "Elsie Myers was my mother's maiden name."

It took me a moment to process this. "Your mother was alive all this time?" I asked. "Did you know?"

"Of course not." His voice was bitter. "I had no idea until I received this letter. I went to her funeral as a little boy. I mourned her."

"You received it?" I queried. "Isn't it a letter to the rest home?"

"I think there was a mix-up with the mail," he said. "It must have been Divine Providence because otherwise I would never have known. This came to me in a postal envelope with a note saying that the original envelope had been damaged beyond recognition in a railway accident and they were returning it to me. My name is across the top, you see." The look on his face was now strangely calm. "I said Providence arranged it, but perhaps it was the other place. What a farce to learn that my mother had been alive all of these years just after it was too late. Think of all the years I could have had with her."

"But your father." I struggled to understand. "He told you she died?"

"He told everyone she died," Junior said bitterly. "Big extravagant funeral. I presume they buried an empty coffin. And then he married Lucy. Just in time for the next election, as it turns out. And then this year he decided he wanted to be mayor." He paused as if digesting the facts himself before he said, "He obviously decided I'd be a detriment to him, so he arranged to put me away too at the same nursing home."

I wasn't sure what question to ask next. I stared at the letter in my hand. "Is that why you wanted to come to this house? To hide the letter in an old book?"

He nodded. "It had already done too much damage, you see." He looked at me appraisingly as if deciding how much to tell me. "I have so few options to hide anything. I can't exactly go out for a walk or even move around the house without help," he said.

"But you can stand," I guessed. "Otherwise how did you put it on a high shelf?"

"I can pull myself to standing," he admitted. "And take a few steps. It is exhausting and embarrassing to do in front of people." I considered the implications of this statement. If Junior was able to stand and walk it changed everything. He must have guessed my train of thought because he went on hurriedly, "I tried to hide the letter in the house. I had moved it out of my room since I knew the police would search there and put it in a drawer downstairs full of old bills and receipts. Cornelius must have been tearing the house apart looking for the will, because he found it."

"That must have been what he called Daniel about."

Junior was staring away from me, into the fire. "I only know he came to me very upset. He understood what it meant, what his father had done. And he understood that it made him and his sister bastards." I flinched at the ugly word. I hadn't had time to process that implication yet. Of course, if Big Bill had a living wife then Lucy could not have married him. Her children were illegitimate. And that was definitely grounds for murder. Except, why would she kill him right before he signed a document that gave her son control of a fortune and assured that she would inherit the house? That brought up another thought.

"Wouldn't you want this letter to be made public?" I said to Junior. "You are the sole heir to Big Bill's fortune and this letter proves it. You obviously don't want it destroyed for good, because I am sure your room has a fire. You could have dropped it in there if you wanted it completely destroyed."

"I suppose you are right about that," he said. "And I did think of doing that. But I couldn't bring myself to destroy the only evidence I had of what was done to my mother. Perhaps I can use this letter to threaten the directors of Shady Groves. If they ever try to put me

in a home like that I will make public what they did to my mother."
A hard look came into his face. "Do you think she would have gone
willingly? Leaving her ten-year-old son?"

I had no answer to that. For a moment we were both silent, thinking of that ten-year-old boy. But I still didn't have the answers I
needed. "Why not go public with it?" I asked again. "Why try to
hide it away?"

"Because of the look I saw in Corny's eyes. And then he tried
to kill himself and confess to the murder of our father." His voice
choked up again. "He did that to protect me. He confessed because
he thought that I was a killer."

The words "And are you?" hovered on my lips but I didn't dare
ask them. Junior had access to morphine, I knew. I suddenly remembered him handing a glass of champagne to Big Bill, who tossed it
down and made a face at its taste. I pictured Junior spending hours
in his room sharpening a letter opener he had stolen from Lucy. I
pictured him rising from the chair and lurching across the study,
holding on to that big desk, to plunge that letter opener into the
back of his father's corpse.

My eyes met Junior's and I knew he had seen my train of thought.
"You see," he said. "You think it too. No one will believe that I am innocent. Please put the letter back, Mrs. Sullivan. No good can come
from it. My mother is dead. The letter can't bring her back. It will
only bring pain to Lucy and Blanche."

"And Cornelius?" I challenged. "If he lives, he will go on trial for
the murder of his father."

"I won't let that happen," Junior insisted. What did he mean by
that? That he would confess? Was he confessing to me that he was
the murderer?

Bridie and Blanche walked in at that moment. Bridie saw the letter in my hand and the book beside me.

"So you did put something in the book, Junior," she said. I
groaned. I had wanted to keep Bridie out of this.

"What were you hiding away, brother, is it a love letter?" Blanche teased. She walked over to look at the letter. I quickly folded it up and put it back in the book.

"Don't tease your brother," I said, thinking quickly. "I'm afraid it is some bad news about his condition that he didn't want to worry you about. He has shared the doctor's report with me."

"Why would he . . ." Bridie started and then stopped when she saw the look I gave her.

"Let's go through for tea," I said, eager to get everyone out of the room. I placed the book with the letter on the highest shelf I could reach and rang a little bell in the room. I was at a loss as to what to do. Should I call the police or treat Junior like a guest? If he was innocent I would be putting a wronged man through hell for nothing. If he was guilty what could he do to hurt me? He was in a wheelchair. He was weak and frail. I decided it was safe to wait, to act as if I suspected nothing and to ask for Daniel's advice as soon as he came home. He could turn it over to the police. Blanche had had enough trauma without seeing her half brother hauled away in front of her.

"Mary, we would like tea now," I said when she appeared. "Can you bring up the cakes? We will eat in the parlor."

Blanche pushed her brother as we walked through to the parlor. I had cleared space on some low tables and Mary put the tea things out, arranging the cakes prettily. She came in and out several times bringing in teacups and little plates.

"I'm sorry it's taking so long, Mrs. Sullivan," she said. "Normally Constanza would be here to help." She looked quite put out. "I'll just bring the teapot up. It's steeping." She turned to leave and the doorbell rang.

"I'll get that," I said. "You bring the tea up before it gets cold. Help yourself to cakes," I said to Junior and the girls. Bridie rose and put some on a plate to offer Junior. I went into the foyer hoping it was Charlie come to check on Junior. The sooner I could get him out of the house the better. I needed some time to think and decide what to do. I opened the door.

"Well, for heaven's sake, you shouldn't be opening your own door, Molly! After all, you do live on Fifth Avenue now," said Daniel's mother, Mrs. Sullivan. Behind her was her maid holding a hatbox and two large suitcases.

❧ Thirty-Six ❧

"M other Sullivan. What are you doing here?" I blurted out. I realized that sounded rude and amended my statement. "What a nice surprise."

"I was in the city for some shopping and thought I would see your new house," she said.

"And you brought your maid? And luggage?" I couldn't stop myself from asking.

"Well, it is not a short journey. I thought that my only son and his wife might like to see me while I was in town. If I'm not wanted I can always find a hotel." Her voice took on a complaining tone I knew well from the time she had lived with us. Oh, heavens! If only Daniel would come home. I needed to think about Junior and what to do. But I couldn't turn away my mother-in-law.

"Of course you are welcome. I was just surprised, that's all. Please come in." She walked into the foyer and looked around critically.

"Do you not have a maid to assist your guests? I suppose Martha had better help me, then." The maid carried the suitcases into the foyer and helped Mrs. Sullivan off with her coat.

"We do have a maid," I explained, "but she is currently making the tea. We have guests."

"And the maid is making the tea? I thought Daniel wrote that you have a cook." Her eyebrows shot up as if she had never heard of such a thing. "I know you're not used to the ways things are done in big houses, my dear, but now that Daniel is going to be the important man I always knew he could be you will have to change your standards." She came over to me and patted my arm. "That's really why I'm here. Daniel thought you might need some help to bring the standards of this house up to snuff."

"He said what?" My temper started to rise and my voice did as well. Bridie and Blanche came into the foyer.

"Mama, can I pour the tea? Everything is ready," Bridie said as she walked in. Then she saw Daniel's mother.

"Hello, Mrs. Sullivan! I didn't know you were coming," she said with a smile. By now the foyer was rapidly becoming too crowded and I felt as if I were going to explode. I took a deep breath to steady my nerves.

"Excuse me, Mrs. Sullivan." Mary came up the stairs and stopped in surprise seeing us all in the entryway.

"Yes," Daniel's mother and I both said at the same time, and Mary looked even more surprised.

I decided to take control of the situation. "Mary, will you go and fetch another plate and cup for my mother-in-law? Bridie, I will pour the tea. Would you go back in the parlor and offer the soda bread around? And Mary, when you have come back, please show Mrs. Sullivan's maid the guest bedroom so she can unpack her things." I walked into the parlor. Junior was in his wheelchair beside the couch looking miserable. I knew I had to think of what to do. In many ways his fate was in my hands, and here we were playing at tea parties. I introduced Junior and Blanche to Mrs. Sullivan. She took in the cut of Blanche's fashionable dress and Junior's suit and put on her most polite tones as she spoke to them.

"How do you know my son?" she asked as she settled herself on the sofa.

"Blanche is Bridie's best friend at school," I put in hastily. What a time for her to arrive!

"And Mr. McCormick Junior is the son of Daniel's former bene-factor," I said, adding to myself "whom he just murdered." I imagined my mother-in-law's face if she knew I was sitting around calmly intro-ducing her to a murderer. Had he done it? Was I going to turn him in? I had fled to New York to escape a murder charge myself. And although the man I thought I murdered turned out to be alive, I knew my actions had been justified to save myself. Were Junior's? I had to talk to Daniel. I had a suspicion that he would be more on the side of the law, which was normal for a policeman. But he had a heart as well. I couldn't help feeling he would know what to do.

Bridie put pieces of the soda bread onto a plate and served them to Blanche and Mrs. Sullivan while I poured the tea and added milk and sugar to each cup, setting one down beside Mrs. Sullivan and one on a table by Junior.

"Would you like soda bread or cakes as well, Junior?" Bridie asked.

"No, thank you. I'm not very hungry." His voice was low. I no-ticed he made no move to take his tea.

I handed Bridie her tea and she took it with a smile. I heard the front door open and voices in the hall.

"I think I hear Daniel," I said to my mother-in-law. "Won't he be surprised to see you."

Out of the corner of my eye I saw Junior start as I turned back to pour my tea. His eyes were fixed on the teapot. I had a strange feeling that something on the table wasn't right. On the white cloth by the teapot was a small dark brown stain. It was too dark to be tea. It looked like a drop of coffee had spilled on the cloth. But it was definitely tea and not coffee I had poured. A great realization came over me and I spun around.

"Stop!" I cried. "Don't drink the tea." I knocked Bridie's teacup across the room. Daniel was just coming through the door, an ex-pectant smile on his face. The teacup smashed into the door inches from his face and he jumped back with a look of shock.

"Molly, what on earth?" he began.

"Don't drink the tea." It came out as a shriek. Mrs. Sullivan stopped with her cup raised to her lips.

"Why not? It tastes all right," Blanche said, staring at me.

"You drank it?" I said, horrified.

"Just a tiny sip. It's very hot. What's wrong?" She sounded mystified.

"It's poison," I said. "It's laced with morphine."

Mrs. Sullivan let out a cry and put her tea down quickly. "What on earth do you mean, Molly?" she asked.

"Junior has put morphine in the teapot," I said evenly. Everyone turned and looked at him. His face was unreadable.

"Junior would never do that," Blanche protested. "Don't be ridiculous. Why would he hurt me? I'm his sister."

"Molly, what is going on?" Daniel said, more insistently this time, then seemed to notice his mother and looked utterly bewildered. "Mother, what are you doing here?" He looked back to me. "And you think Junior was trying to poison you?"

Instead of answering I strode over to Junior and reached into the little bag that he carried on the inside of his wheelchair. He tried to stop me, but I was much stronger than him and his withered hands couldn't push me away. My hands touched something glass and I drew it out. It was a morphine bottle just like the one we had seen at the house. And it was empty. Blanche's face crumpled.

"How could you?" She looked at Junior in disbelief. "You're my brother. I thought you loved me."

"You're not my sister." Junior's face changed into a mask of rage. "You're the daughter of a whore and I hope you die."

Blanche jumped up and backed away from him quickly.

"Bridie, go and telephone the police," I said softly to her, picking up Mrs. Sullivan's cup and putting it on the mantel. I wondered if I should call a doctor for Blanche, but surely one little sip couldn't poison her. "This will be evidence." Bridie ran from the room.

"I will go," Daniel said. "They might not take her seriously. If you are sure you are safe."

In answer I put myself between Junior and Blanche.

"Call Lucy McCormick as well," I called after Daniel as he left the room. I didn't think Junior could get up and attack us. I had felt how weak his hands were, but I realized that I had vastly underestimated him this whole time.

"But I drank some!" Blanche wailed. "Is it poison? Am I going to die?"

"If you just took a sip I suspect you will just feel a bit sleepy," I said, hoping I was right. "We'll get your mother here right away and she can take you to the hospital if you feel ill. But now, please go and help Bridie." I felt desperate to get her out of the room. I knew I had to try to make Junior confess and I didn't want her to hear it. She had gone through enough trauma already. "And can you tell her I asked you both to wait upstairs until I come and get you? If you feel sleepy, lie down until your mother gets here."

"Molly, what in heaven's name is going on?" Mrs. Sullivan said. "I've walked into a house of horror. Who is this man and what do you mean he tried to murder you?" She sounded hysterical. "Nobody goes around murdering people in houses on Fifth Avenue!"

"I wish that were true. But this man has already killed once and tried to kill again." I turned to Junior. "Cornelius didn't try to kill himself. And he didn't confess to protect you. You tried to murder him, your own brother."

"He's not my brother either!" Junior's voice rose in an unnerving shriek. "He's a bastard. And the son of a liar and a murderer."

"Heavens preserve us." Mrs. Sullivan put her hand to her heart in dramatic fashion. I wondered if there was any way I could get her to leave. But then I reasoned that Junior was confessing to the murder and the more witnesses I had the better. He was so upset that I thought if I pressed him he would tell me everything.

I rounded on him. "Cornelius is your brother. You have the same father," I pointed out. "The father you murdered."

Another "saints preserve us" from Mrs. Sullivan that I ignored.

"If I am a murderer then it was only to protect myself," Junior said hotly. "He was going to put me in an institution. He wasn't the great man everyone thought he was. I heard it all. I heard him cursing and ranting about Hearst and his reporter. I heard him ordering someone in his office to make the problem disappear. Next thing I know it is all over the papers that the reporter has disappeared. Until then I thought I could change his mind, I could talk him out of putting me away. Maybe my mother had been so sick she didn't know where she was or who she was and it was a mercy to send her away. He would see that I was smart and capable and keep me in the family. But then I saw him looking at me with pity and I knew. I was a problem and he was going to make me disappear. Just like my mother. Just like that reporter. You would have done the same thing." He turned to me. The rage was gone and a pleading look was back in his eyes.

"I wouldn't have tried to kill my brother," I said hotly. Maybe I should have tried to placate him, but I just wanted to keep him talking until the police arrived. "I don't understand how you did that or why."

"He found the letter, just like I said," he said. "He was going to show it to Lucy."

"But wouldn't that have been a good thing?" I asked. "Everyone would know what Big Bill was and what happened to your mother. And it would mean you would inherit everything. Surely you wanted it found."

"He found it in my room," he yelled, hysteria rising in him again. "I had it hidden away. You should have seen the way he looked at me. He knew I could stand. He knew I could take enough steps to walk across Father's office holding on to the desk. I could see it in his eyes. He knew. I tried to explain what our father was going to do to me. Cornelius was sympathetic, but I could see the doubt in his eyes. I offered him a whiskey and when he wasn't looking I poured morphine in it. I thought he would go to sleep and never wake up again." His face twisted. "That was a kindness. He didn't want to face what I knew. That our father was a murderer and he was a bastard."

"Well, really! Such language," Mrs. Sullivan exclaimed in shocked tones.

"And now you were going to kill your sister." I looked at him coldly.

"I didn't want to kill her." His face crumpled. "I do care for her, really. Only I didn't know who would take which cup so I had to put the morphine in the pot. I couldn't let you tell the whole world what you knew."

"I was still deciding if I was going to," I said. "I do feel sorry for you, Junior. Your disease isn't your fault. And what your father did was monstrous. I might have just kept quiet. After all, you don't have long to live anyway. God is going to judge you."

Junior began to cry in earnest now, sobbing like a child. Even now, after all he had done, I did feel sorry for him. There was a good brain and a good heart in him, I believed, but it had been so twisted by the loss of his mother, by the suffering of his disease, and the lack of care from his father. I supposed they would hang him if he lived through the trial, and he and his father would meet each other in hell.

Daniel came in. "The police are on their way."

"Daniel, he's just confessed," I said quickly. "He killed his father and he tried to kill Cornelius. He can walk."

"Molly." His face was shocked and he moved quickly between me and Junior protectively just as I had done for Blanche. "I would never have left the room if I thought he might hurt you."

"I don't think he could hurt me physically," I said reassuringly. "I don't think he's that strong. I just don't think he is as weak as everyone believes. I know he can stand because he put this book up on a high shelf."

Daniel looked at me as if I were crazy. "What does that have to do with anything?"

"I'll explain later," I said.

"The police will be here any moment," Daniel said. "And I called the McCormicks. Lucy is on her way."

"Daniel, I think perhaps Molly is a little overwrought," Mrs. Sullivan began. "Almost hysterical. I've seen that look before. Is she in the family way? I can't believe you didn't let me know at once so I could come and help take care of her. Let me take her upstairs to lie down." She turned to me. "This is men's business, dear. Let's get you upstairs. How far along are you?"

"I'm not . . ." I began.

Just then the doorbell rang. Daniel jumped up.

"Molly, will you let them in? I don't want to leave you alone with him."

Mrs. Sullivan made a noise that sounded like "hmmf." "I'm here, son, in case you hadn't noticed. You haven't even said hello."

"Hello, Mother, lovely to see you. I'm afraid we have a bit of an emergency," Daniel said easily. "Molly, the doorbell?"

I went to the door. Lucy was standing outside. Finn and Jack were behind her.

"Molly, the hospital is not far from here and Roberts called and said there was a problem with Junior. Is he ill?"

"No." I hesitated, not sure what to say. "You had better come in." They all three stepped into the foyer.

"Is Cornelius any better?" I asked. I didn't imagine she would have left his bedside if he wasn't.

"He woke up this morning for a few minutes," she said. "He's gone back to sleep, but they think he will make it. They think all of the morphine is out of his system."

Mary hovered near the stairs, clearly confused to see me answering the door.

"It's all right, Mary," I said. "Please go upstairs and tell Miss Blanche her mother is here and will be up shortly."

"Is something wrong with Blanche?" Lucy sounded concerned. "Roberts said it was Junior."

"Lucy, I'm very sorry to tell you . . ." I wasn't sure how to begin. "But the police are about to arrive to arrest him for the murder of your husband."

"Junior, a murderer? I don't believe it!" Finn said as the color drained from Lucy's face.

"He has confessed to me," I said, reluctant to tell Lucy all that I knew. "His father was going to put him in a home." I put a hand on her shoulder to steady her. She looked as if she were going to faint. I wondered if I should bring her into the parlor. I decided I needed to tell her what I knew before she saw Junior.

"I'm afraid there is more," I went on. "He overheard his father giving an order to make the Hearst reporter disappear."

"I knew it!" I was startled by a man's voice from the direction of the stairs to the kitchen. I looked over and saw Gianni standing there with Constanza right behind him. They must have just come up. "I knew he was behind this." Then his tone turned from triumph to accusation. "And it was you that I saw. You dragged that reporter away."

At first I thought he was pointing at Finn, but Finn looked confused, not guilty.

"I saw you!" Gianni repeated. "I will swear to it."

Then I saw that he was pointing at Jack. Jack's face twisted in a sneer. "I don't know what you're talking about. Who is going to believe you, a dirty immigrant?"

"Actually, the police commissioner believed him this morning," Daniel said, coming out of the parlor. "All that was left was identifying the man and now we have done that." He put a restraining arm on Jack's shoulder.

"I told him he should have taken care of you when we did your old man," Jack bellowed at Gianni as he wrenched himself free of Daniel and ran for the front door. He threw the door open and bounded down the steps. Right into the arms of a startled Lieutenant Doyle.

❧ Thirty-Seven ❧

old him!" Daniel shouted. Doyle made no move to do so, but Corelli was right behind him and grabbed Jack in a firm hold. Jack struggled and tried to get away.

"Get off of me!" he grunted. "I didn't do nothing."

"Arrest this man, Doyle." Daniel came forward to help Corelli. "He helped to kill the missing reporter."

"Now don't you start giving me orders, Sullivan. Who do you think you are?" Doyle snapped.

"As of this morning, I'm your captain," Daniel said sternly. "The police commissioner reinstated me. And I think you need more time on the beat before you are ready for this job. Lieutenant Corelli, would you please take the suspect into custody while Sergeant Doyle goes inside to help me question Mr. McCormick." He emphasized the two men's new titles.

"You can't do that!" Doyle said defiantly. "I'm a lieutenant. You can't demote me."

"No, but the police commissioner can and has as of this morning. I had a chat with him about all of the evidence you missed in this case and how Corelli worked behind the scenes to help solve it. He was going to talk to you two about it when he gave you the news of my reinstatement. Now you have two choices, Doyle." Daniel turned to face him. "You can keep being an ignorant bully and you'll end up off the force within the month. Or you can shut up and learn something, and I'll make sure you have a career. What is it going to be?"

Doyle stared at him in disbelief. "I'll take this up with the commissioner myself," he said, and pushed past Corelli and a still-struggling Jack.

"I don't think he has a very long career ahead of him," Daniel said to Corelli. "Let me help you get the handcuffs on." Daniel and Finn held Jack's arms behind his back while Corelli slipped the big metal handcuffs on him and closed them tightly.

"Jack O'Doherty, you are under arrest for the murder of Ronald Walker," Daniel said, and then turned to Corelli. "You hold on to him. We have another investigation and I had better get to it." Just then there was a scream from the parlor.

"Mother!" Daniel's face went white. "I shouldn't have left her alone with him." We raced up the stairs, across the foyer. Mrs. Sullivan was running out of the parlor.

"He's coming at me. He's trying to attack me!" she shrieked. Just then we heard a crash and raced into the room. Junior had fallen, overturning the tea table as he fell. Daniel bent to turn him over.

"I wasn't attacking her," Junior protested, "I just tried to stand up." Daniel picked him off the floor and set him back in his wheelchair. Lucy and Finn came into the room and looked around in disbelief. Mrs. Sullivan followed them, still looking terrified.

"Don't touch anything!" Daniel said quickly. "This is a crime scene."

"I can't believe that Junior would hurt anyone," Lucy said. "It is not in his nature."

"That's what Cornelius thought right before he was poisoned. And just what your daughter said," I said, "right before she almost drank a cup of tea filled with morphine." Lucy clearly couldn't take both of these statements in.

"Poisoned? Morphine? Is she all right?" Lucy looked frightened.

"She only drank a tiny sip, thankfully," I said. "I realized what he was doing just at the last minute. He would have poisoned all of us."

"But why?" She turned to him. "Why would you do that, Junior?"

He remained silent.

"Junior found out some things that will be important for you to know," I began. Daniel looked at me curiously. "But it will be hard for you to hear. Junior's mother . . ."

"No, please don't tell her." Junior's voice was strained. "I don't want her to know."

"To know what?" Lucy looked between Junior and me, a bemused look on her face.

"It will come out at the trial," I said to him. "There's no holding it back now."

"I don't think there will be a trial," Junior said quietly. I wondered if he thought he would get away with it even now.

"Can you arrest him?" I asked softly, pulling Daniel to one side. "He confessed to me that he murdered Big Bill. And he tried to kill all of us."

"I need an arrest warrant," Daniel said. "This will be a high-profile case. We need to do it by the book. I'll take him to the police station as a person of interest."

"His prints will be on the teapot," I reasoned. "And you will find morphine in the pot and the teacups." As I said that, I looked at the tea table. It was tipped over and the teapot had cracked and spilled all over the carpet. So that must be why he had stood up, to destroy the evidence. Then I remembered the cup I had set on the mantel. I walked over to it and picked it up. It was empty.

I looked at Junior. He gave a little smile as he saw me realize what he had done. "It's better this way," he said. "I couldn't stop killing to protect myself. I guess I am my father's son. But if I go this way no one will have to know the truth."

300

"What truth?" Lucy was insistent now. I noticed that Junior's lips were blue.

"I'm sorry, Lucy," he said. His voice was losing its strength. "I killed my father and your husband and I'm sorry for it. He wasn't a good person, but you are. You tried to be a good mother to me so I am going to give you the only thing I can."

"What is that?" Lucy asked.

"A peaceful life." His eyelids closed.

"Daniel, we have to get him to a hospital," I said. "This cup was full of morphine." I held out the empty cup.

"Morphine doesn't work that fast," Daniel said, looking at Junior now sitting still, a peaceful look coming over his face. "Isn't it more likely he is trying to fool us again for some reason?"

"Who knows how quickly it works on someone with his condition?" I asked. "His heart might be weaker because of it."

"I'll help," Finn said. "We can take him to the hospital where Cornelius is. I have the automobile outside. That will be the fastest way." Together Daniel and Finn lifted him between them and carried him outside. I saw his eyelids flutter once. I followed back into the street. They put him into the automobile and Finn climbed into the driver's seat. I saw to my relief that Daniel was not going with him. I had been calm and strong and reasonable for the last few terrible hours and now it all came crashing down on me. Someone I thought was a sweet man and my friend was a murderer, and he was probably going to die. I felt I might cry at any moment. Then my stomach turned and to my great embarrassment I vomited right at the foot of the steps. I stood up still blinded by tears and now ashamed.

"This has been too much for you." Daniel was there instantly, his strong arms around me. "Molly, when I think of what could have happened. I still don't know how you worked out what was in that pot. It would have been all my fault." He kissed my forehead and then my eyes. "Molly, I'm so sorry for getting you into this. Can you ever forgive me?"

"Yes," I sobbed. "But can we please go home?"

It seemed like the day would never end, but at least Daniel stayed by my side until I calmed down. Mrs. Sullivan became uncharacteristically solicitous. She hovered over me insisting that I have something to eat, which actually did make me feel much better, and, after consultation with Constanza, found the ingredients for ginger tea. She wanted me to go up and lie down, but I was afraid my thoughts would keep me from any kind of rest, so I sat with her in the kitchen while the police came and went from the parlor and library. Finn telephoned to say that Junior had died on the way to the hospital, but that Cornelius was awake and ready to get out of bed. Lucy took Blanche home to get ready for Cornelius's homecoming and I let Bridie go with them. There could be no more danger now and I thought Blanche needed the support.

Hours later I was finally alone. Daniel had gone to the police station to file a report on Jack's confession. Mrs. Sullivan was out shopping for a late dinner with Constanza, having determined that they would make one of Daniel's favorite meals as a boy. I thought wryly that I should have invited her much sooner. She was a match for Constanza. I had to admit I had not been a great success at running a large household. I walked into the library and took the *Tom Sawyer* book from the shelf. Bridie had solved the case, I thought. She was going to make a good detective someday. I wasn't sure I should tell her that. It wasn't really a suitable job for a woman, especially a woman with high-powered friends.

I opened the book and stared at the letter Junior had hidden there. As far as I knew it was the only proof of a secret that, in the end, Junior had died to protect. I wondered if I would ever know the real man. He had screamed that Blanche and Cornelius were bastards, but he had died to protect the secret in this letter. This one letter could ruin the life of three innocent people. I walked over to the fire and dropped the letter into the flames. It twisted and blackened. I watched until it was nothing but ash. Then I put *Tom Sawyer* back onto the shelf and walked out into the foyer.

"Can I help you, Mrs. Sullivan? Do you want something?" Mary was coming up the stairs.

"No, thank you, Mary. I thought I might be hungry but I have just realized I am very tired," I said, suddenly feeling exactly that. "I think I'll go up for a nap." I climbed the stairs wearily and fell into my bed. I lay there going over the days since we had moved into this house. A reason for my tiredness and nausea had just occurred to me. I stopped to consider. Could it be true that I was finally pregnant again? I counted backward in my mind and realized it was possible. How annoying if Mrs. Sullivan was right! But how wonderful. I should stay up and tell Daniel, I thought. But I was too sleepy and I drifted off. I'm sure I had a big smile on my face. Hours later I was dimly aware of Daniel rousing me enough to take off my dress and slip on a nightdress. The next thing I knew it was morning.

"Good morning, sleepyhead," Daniel said, kissing me on the forehead. "Time to wake up, you slept all night. I started to worry you might have had some of that poisoned tea."

I shuddered. "Don't joke about that. I was just exhausted. But I'm starving now." I sat up, realizing how hungry I was since I had skipped dinner.

"My mother is showing Constanza how to make a decent breakfast. It should be ready in a few minutes."

"I don't know why we didn't invite her the minute we moved in," I said. "I am so used to being annoyed at her bossing me around it never occurred to me how good she would be at bossing the servants around."

"Yes, she is a force of nature." Daniel smiled. "It is almost a shame we won't be staying here now."

"Oh, no, it is not!" I retorted. "I can't wait to get back to Patchin Place. Do you really have your old job back?" I climbed out of bed and started to pull on my clothes.

"I really do." Daniel smiled again. "And with a nice bonus from Mr. Hearst. He came by last night while you were asleep. He would like to invite us to dinner this Saturday to thank us in person."

"That's wonderful." My mood was lightening as we spoke. "I'll go over to Patchin Place today and see when we can get our house back from Ryan's friend." And I realized that I would need to tell Sid and Gus that their friend's brother, the reporter who vanished, had definitely been murdered. How strange life was; it felt amazing to be bursting with new life and energy having just been in the presence of such death and sadness.

My hair was a tangled mess from sleeping with the pins in it. I took them out one by one, letting my hair cascade down as I spoke. "Daniel, I've been thinking. Aileen gets along so well with Liam. And we do have a room for her. Shall we take her with us to be his nanny?"

Daniel looked serious. "I was thinking that my mother would need that room to move back in with us." I looked at him in horror. He burst out laughing. "You should see your face. That's a grand idea, Molly."

"I'm not positive yet," I said. "But I think I might need the extra help. I think your mother might be right. I think I'm pregnant."

"Really? That's wonderful news!"

And Daniel gathered me into his arms and kissed me.

⚙ Thirty-Eight ⚙

Friday, November 1

M oving back into Patchin Place was harder than moving out had been. We no longer had a team of dockworkers to spirit our things away. Daniel and Finn borrowed a wagon and made several trips back and forth collecting our belongings.

I had worried that we would have to give Nikki time to move out, but it turned out he had already gone. He left the key in Sid and Gus's letter box. When I let myself in I found the floor littered with smashed vodka glasses and a life-sized portrait of Nikki in a very revealing satyr costume painted on my kitchen wall. I couldn't wait to get the story of how that painting came to be from Ryan, but I decided I was just as glad to be a steady police captain's wife and get only occasional glimpses into the artists' lifestyle! It took me a week to clean the house top to bottom with the help of Aileen and my mother-in-law. Finally, Daniel and Finn had collected all our belongings and we could move back home.

"This is the last of them," Finn said as he set down a heavy trunk on the parlor floor.

"Are you happy to be home?" Daniel asked me, coming into the room behind him with a case. "It's not many wives who would be happy to move out of a Fifth Avenue house and be back doing their own cooking and cleaning."

"Wouldn't Mrs. McCormick have let you keep living in the house now that she owns it?" Finn asked.

"She offered it to us, actually," I replied, "but we couldn't afford to keep up a big place like that even if I wanted to. Mary has gone to work for Lucy, and Aileen has come to work for us. That only leaves Constanza without a job. I feel bad about that. Her cooking was getting better, but I don't think she will be a sought-after cook."

"Tammany is giving her a pension," Finn said. "Since the papers are full of her husband's murder along with the reporter's. They want to make sure that only Jack is blamed and it doesn't go any higher. Typical Tammany."

"You've gone out of your way to help us," I thanked him. "It's no longer your job to take care of Daniel for Tammany, you know."

"I have another motivation." He smiled warmly at me. "Daniel has put in a good word for me with the police department. I think I might look forward to a change of career."

"That's wonderful!" I said, kneeling and opening the trunk. Finn deserved a life away from Tammany Hall. I pulled out the teapot I had carefully wrapped in newspaper and stood up. I had found enough of the pieces to glue it back together, though it still leaked slightly. We would need a new teapot, but it would do for now. "I'm glad you are done with politics." I smiled back at Finn. "I hope Daniel is, too. He needs a safer profession if he is going to support a family of four."

Daniel laughed, "And police work is safer than politics, I suppose." Then his face changed. "Did you say family of four? Are you certain?"

"Yes, the doctor confirmed it today. Liam is going to have a little brother or sister." I started for the kitchen. "Now who would like some tea?"

❦ Acknowledgments ❦

We'd like to thank Kelley Ragland and the wonderful team at Minotaur, who make working with them a joy; and of course the best agents in the universe, Meg Ruley and Christina Hogrebe; as well as our patient, long-suffering husbands, John and Tim.